Ce... ...rriage of Daisy
Huntingdon-Cross and Sebastian Beresford in

Expecting the Earl's Baby
by Jessica Gilmore

Save the date: on sale March 2015

Raise a glass to Rose Huntingdon-Cross and
Will Carter as they finally tie the knot
in

A Bride for the Runaway Groom
by Scarlet Wilson

Save the date: on sale April 2015

Join us in celebrating Violet Huntingdon-Cross
and Tom Buckley's star-studded wedding day
in

Falling for the Bridesmaid
by Sophie Pembroke

Save the date: on sale May 2015

Summer Weddings

A season of confetti and whirlwind romances!

You are cordially invited to attend the Huntingdon-Cross summer weddings.

Celebrate the shotgun marriage of Dan [illegible] Huntingdon-Cross and Sebastian Beresford in

Expecting the Earl's Baby
by Jessica Gilmore

Save the date: on sale March 2015

Celebrate as [illegible] Rose Huntingdon-Cross and Will [illegible] as they finally tie the knot in

A Bride for the Runaway Groom
by Scarlet Wilson

Save the date: on sale April 2015

Join the celebrations [illegible] Huntingdon-Cross and [illegible] wedding day in

[illegible]
by [illegible]

Save the date: on sale May 2015

FALLING FOR THE BRIDESMAID

BY
SOPHIE PEMBROKE

Published in Great Britain 2015
by Mills & Boon, an imprint of Harlequin (UK) Limited,
Eton House, 18-24 Paradise Road, Richmond, Surrey, TW9 1SR

ISBN: 978-0-263-25141-8

23-0615

Harlequin (UK) Limited's policy is to use papers that are natural, renewable and recyclable products and made from wood grown in sustainable forests. The logging and manufacturing processes conform to the legal environmental regulations of the country of origin.

Printed and bound in Spain
by CPI, Barcelona

Sophie Pembroke has been reading and writing romance ever since she read her first Mills & Boon® book at university, so getting to write them for a living is a dream come true!

Sophie lives in a little Hertfordshire market town in the UK with her scientist husband and her incredibly imaginative five-year-old daughter. She writes stories about friends, family and falling in love, usually while drinking too much tea and eating homemade cakes. She also keeps a blog at www.SophiePembroke.com.

For George and Karen, for making this book possible
through coffee, childcare and cheerleading!
Thank you both, so much.

CHAPTER ONE

THE SWEET SMELL of rose petals filled the evening air, giving the falling dusk a sultry warmth. Music sang out from the band on the patio, romantic with just an undertone of sexy. Fairy lights twinkled in the branches of the trees and inside the marquees, and around them leaves rustled in the still warm breeze.

The whole set-up was so perfectly loved-up Violet thought she might be physically ill if she had to suffer through it a moment longer.

Glaring down at her lavender bridesmaid's dress, she slunk to the edge of the celebrations where she could watch the live band play in peace. She needed to make more of an effort to enjoy the evening, and maybe the music would help. Her parents' vow renewal ceremony had been beautiful, and the party that followed a huge success. Later, she had no doubt, her dad and the boys from The Screaming Lemons would take to the stage and wow the remaining guests all over again, even though they'd finished their official set an hour ago. Knowing Dad, it would probably be a lower key, acoustic set the second time around.

Keeping Dad off the stage was always more trouble than getting him on there, and he always wanted one more encore. But for now the support act seemed to be doing well enough. The courtyard in front of the stage was filled with people dancing, or just holding each other, or kissing. Falling in love.

Violet scowled and looked away.

Of course, the situation wasn't helped by her family. There, leaning against her new husband—Lord Sebastian Beresford, Earl of Holgate, if you please—was her youngest sister, Daisy. No, the Lady Holgate now. Hard to believe that Daisy-Waisy was an honest-to-God countess, but somehow not quite as impossible to process as the slight swell of her baby bump under her carefully chosen emerald-green bridesmaid's dress.

Just a few more months and Violet would officially be the maiden aunt of the family. Hell, she was already doing the church flowers most weekends, and taking tea with her mother's 'ladies who lunch' crowd. Maybe she should just skip straight ahead to adopting a three-legged cat and taking up crochet.

Actually, she'd quite like to learn to crochet, but that wasn't the point.

Seb rested his hand against his wife's stomach, and Daisy's soft smile grew into a fully fledged grin as she tilted her face for a kiss. Violet turned away, suddenly embarrassed to be staring.

But unfortunately her gaze just landed on Rose and Will, looking equally wrapped up in each other. Her twin sister and her best friend. Violet had to admit she really hadn't seen that one coming either. An attraction, perhaps, or maybe even a fling. Not that Will would give up his runaway groom status for good and marry into her family. But there Rose stood in her own wedding dress, after sneaking away for their own secret marriage ceremony once their parents' vow renewal service was over.

Maybe she just had no sort of love radar at all. Or maybe it was broken. That would explain a hell of a lot, really.

Will glanced up at just the wrong moment and, this time, Violet couldn't look away quick enough. Even staring pointedly at the band, she couldn't miss the whispered conversation between Rose and *her* new husband. Probably trying to decide whose responsibility Violet's hurt feelings were now.

Violet sighed. It wasn't that she wasn't happy for her sisters—she really, truly was. And she knew that their happiness shouldn't make her own sorry situation feel so much worse. But it did.

Swallowing, she looked down at her feet, and the high heels pinching her toes. It would pass, she knew. Any day now she'd be able to look at all the happy and loved-up people around her and just smile, without the bitter tinge that threatened to colour her whole world.

That day just wasn't yet, that was all.

'She thinks you're cross with her, you know. Or me, possibly,' Will said, standing beside her with his hands in his pockets. Such a familiar sight at these events. Usually Will's presence was a comfort, a reliable soul to help her through the amused looks, the only half-whispered comments, and the occasional drunken suggestion from guys she barely knew but who clearly thought they knew all about her—and her sexual proclivities.

Today, though, he was just a reminder that things wouldn't ever be the same again.

'Cross with Rose?' Violet asked, mustering up a smile. 'Why on earth would I be cross with her? For stealing you away from me? Good riddance, I say.'

The startled look on Will's face told her she'd misjudged something very badly.

'Uh, no. She thinks you're mad because you got landed with picking up that reporter guy from the airport tonight, so you're missing out on the good champagne. That or the whole Benefit Concert thing.'

Ah, that. Yeah, that would make more sense. Especially since she hadn't been completely silent about her unhappiness that the reporter was coming at all.

'I hadn't really...you think she stole me away from you?'

Violet gave him a withering stare. 'Yes, Will. I've been lusting after you, pining away for you through every one of your ridiculous engagements and runaway groom stunts. And now you've finally married my sister, I don't think I will ever recover.'

Her deadpan delivery apparently sold it because Will laughed with obvious relief. 'Good. That's...okay, then. And you're not mad about the reporter either?'

'I'm mad about the champagne. Otherwise, I'll cope.'

'You're sure? I know you're a little...'

Violet tried to guess the word he was avoiding saying. Nervous? Worried? Paranoid?

Probably paranoid.

'Apprehensive about him coming,' Will finished.

Violet sighed. Apprehensive wasn't the half of it. But her dad had made up his mind that he wanted to tell his story, have that official biography on the shelves, and he'd picked this guy to do it. Rose had looked at her with worried eyes when he'd announced it, but even she admitted it made sense to do it now, ahead of the new tour and album. The reporter guy would have exclusive access, in-depth interviews and enough connections to get a real buzz going in the media.

'Rose says he's nice,' Will tried. 'They met in New York before she came home.'

'I'm sure he's a doll,' Violet replied. It didn't matter who he was. He was press, and only interested in them as a story, as something he could sell.

Violet had learned that lesson the hard way.

Will frowned. 'Maybe if you talk to your dad…'

Shaking her head, Violet gave him a gentle smile. 'It's fine. I promise.' Dad had made up his mind and that was it. As always. Nothing Will, Daisy, Rose or Violet could do to change it. And so there was no point dwelling on it. She'd just stay out of his way as much as possible and hope for the best.

What else could she do?

'And about the Benefit Concert—' he started, but Violet cut him off.

'Go on, Will.' She pushed against his arm. 'Go whisk Rose away on your honeymoon. I'll take care of things here, I promise. Since you've apparently already texted the reporter guy my phone number, he's my responsibility now, and I think I can manage one airport pick-up. You two go relax for a bit. Get used to being married for once, instead of just temporarily engaged.'

'Okay. See you soon, kid.' With a quick hug and a peck on the cheek, he headed back towards Rose, and Violet was alone again.

As usual.

She hadn't exactly *lied* to Will, she decided. She had never thought of Will as husband material—or even one-night stand material. He was worth far more to her as a friend, and she'd never felt that spark, that flash of something more that hinted that they could be anything else.

It was just kind of weird that he obviously felt that flash with *Rose* of all people. Her so-identical-it-was-actually-spooky twin sister.

Although, really, she should be used to people seeing something in Rose that they never saw in her. After all, hadn't their parents made Rose stay home instead of going back to the States after Daisy's wedding, just so she could organise their vow renewal ceremony and party? Even though Violet had been right there, with time on her hands, happy to help?

Not that she was bitter. She knew why they hadn't asked—because they'd been sure she wouldn't want to do it. Wouldn't want to have to deal with so many people, so many knowing eyes.

And they were probably right.

Will hadn't thought about that as he'd told her where to find Rose's black planner, though, and asked her to make sure everything kept ticking over for the annual Huntingdon Hall Benefit Concert while they were away on their honeymoon. Maybe he'd just been too caught up in the flush of true love to think about it. Or maybe he expected her to hand it over to some agency person, hired to cover Rose's job.

Maybe she should. After all, she knew absolutely nothing about how to organise a concert for thousands of people. Will had insisted that Rose had already done all the hard work, that there'd be practically nothing left for Violet to do.

Because obviously otherwise they'd have found someone more competent to put in charge.

Violet shook her head. She was being ridiculous. She hadn't wanted to organise the vow renewal anyway. Or the Benefit Concert, come to that. She had other obligations. But now that Rose had told their dad she'd be stepping down from her job managing the PR and events for The Screaming Lemons once she got back from her honeymoon...well, someone would have to do it. And Violet couldn't ignore the very small part of her brain that thought that person could be her.

No. She had no experience, and no desire to deal with people who laughed at her behind her back all day long.

She'd just stick to things she knew she was good at. Like arranging flowers, thank you very much.

The flower displays she'd designed for the vow renewal were, she decided, by far her best displays yet. Lots of exotic blooms in deep jewel colours. Striking and memorable, just like her parents. Her flowers rocked, everyone said so.

There you had it. Twenty-seven years on the planet, and that was all she could say about herself.

Violet Huntingdon-Cross—kick-ass flower arranger, wannabe crocheter. Potential cat lady in waiting.

No, that wasn't all. That was just all that other people saw—and she was happy to keep it that way. She made a difference in the lives of young people and teenagers every day, even if no one ever knew it was her. After all, if word got around that Violet Huntingdon-Cross was manning the phones at the troubled teen helpline, their calls would skyrocket with people wanting to ask her about her own past, or just talk to a minor celebrity—and the kids she really wanted to help wouldn't be able to get through at all. So she helped where she could. Even if she wished she could do more.

Her parents did the same, helping out charities anonymously when they could. The only difference was, they also did enough charity work—as well as music and the occasional modelling gig respectively—in public that everyone assumed they already knew everything there was to know about Rick and Sherry Cross.

But with Violet...well, Violet could only imagine what they were *still* saying about her. Probably the nicest was that she'd become a recluse.

Still, that was a hell of a lot better than what they'd been saying about her eight years ago.

Pulling her phone from her tiny clutch bag, she checked the time and then double-checked the email Will had sent her from Rose's account with the reporter guy's flight details. Thomas Buckley…that was his name. She must make an effort not to just call him reporter guy all the time. Although it never hurt to have a reminder that the press were press and always on the record, whatever they said. Not something she ever wanted to forget again.

Time to go. She'd get changed out of her bridesmaid's dress, grab the ridiculous name card Rose had left for her and be at Heathrow in plenty of time to grab a coffee before his flight landed. And, best of all, she wouldn't be stuck in romance central another minute.

Moving towards the side door to Huntingdon Hall, Violet paused as she caught sight of her parents, dancing in the light of the just risen moon. So wrapped up in each other that the couple of hundred people watching, who'd come all this way to celebrate with them, might not even be there at all. Sherry Huntingdon and Rick Cross were famously crazy about each other, but it wasn't until Violet caught them in moments like this that she really believed the media hype.

And that, she finally admitted to herself, was the real reason all this love stuff was getting to her. Deep down, she'd always believed that she'd just fall into a perfect relationship like her parents had, like both her sisters had now found too.

Instead, she'd got something else entirely. Like antilove. The sort of relationship that tore up your insides and made you someone else. After that, if she was honest, Violet wasn't sure she'd ever have the courage to try again.

Her phone rang in her hand and Violet answered it automatically, glad for the distraction. 'Hello?'

'I was under the impression that you, whoever you are, were supposed to be meeting me at the airport about twenty minutes ago.' The American drawl made Violet's eyes widen. The reporter guy. Except Rose's email had him landing in an hour and a half. Dammit!

'I'm so sorry, Mr...' Oh, God, what was his name?

'Buckley.' He bit the surname out. 'And I could care less about apologies. Just get here, will you? I'll be in the bar.'

And, with that, the line went dead.

Picking up her skirt, Violet dashed for the garage and prayed no one had blocked her car in. She'd have to borrow one of her dad's if they had. No time to change now, or even pick up that specially made name card of Rose's. If she ever wanted to be relied on for more than flowers, she needed to not screw this up. And since the bad impression she—and by extension her family—had made on the reporter guy was already done, she needed to find a way to fix it. Starting with getting to Heathrow as fast as humanly possible, *before* he started drafting his story. She knew journalists. The truth seldom got in the way of a good story, and once they thought they knew all about a person it was almost impossible to convince them otherwise.

And Violet had already earned the Huntingdon-Cross family enough bad press to last a lifetime.

CHAPTER TWO

TOM PUSHED HIS way to the counter, dragging his suitcase behind him like a weapon. A coffee shop. What the hell kind of use to him was that, especially at this time of night? He needed a drink—a proper one. But that was arrivals for you—never as good as the departures lounge. After so many years travelling the world, you'd think he'd remember that. Except he was usually being collected straight off a plane these days, and got whisked through arrivals to some hotel or another without even clocking his surroundings.

He'd just have to hope that whoever the ditsy woman Rose had assigned to pick him up was would check her phone and see his text telling her to meet him here instead.

Staring at the menu above the counter with bleary eyes, Tom tried to figure out his best option. He'd already consumed so much caffeine in the last two weeks that his muscles appeared to be permanently twitching. Add that to the distinct lack of sleep, and he wasn't sure another shot of the black stuff was quite what he needed. Of course, what he *needed* was a big bed with cool sheets, a blackout blind and about twenty-four hours' solid rest.

None of which was a remote possibility until his ride pitched up.

Ordering a decaf something-or-other, Tom tossed his

jacket and laptop into the nearest bucket chair and hovered impatiently between it and the counter while he waited for his drink. If he'd flown first class, or even business, he could have had as many free drinks as he liked on the plane. But old habits died hard and, since this job was entirely on spec and therefore on his own dime, he'd been paying for his own flight. Something inside him still baulked at shelling out that much cash just for a better seat, even though money wasn't really an object any more. Certainly not the way it had been growing up.

His music journalism career had taken off enough in the past few years that he could rely on his contacts for a good life and a better income. He'd come a long way from his first big, explosive story, almost ten years ago.

So yeah, he could have afforded the upgrade, easily, and without tapping those savings. And if he'd remembered about the free booze aspect of things, he probably would have done. As it was…

Snatching his coffee from the girl behind the counter, he settled at his table and prepared to hang around a while. God only knew how long it would take his ride to get there from wherever she was, but he might as well get some work done while he waited. Even if he felt as if his eyes might jump right out of his head if he didn't close them soon.

At least the work was worth travelling all the way from New York for. A story like this, a break this big…it could make him, permanently. He'd be the go-to person for anything to do with The Screaming Lemons, and that was serious currency in the industry. It would give him access, and opportunities with the newer bands coming through. He'd have the pick of jobs.

He'd already made a pretty good name for himself with the bigger music magazines, websites and even the colour supplements. But this trip, these interviews, this was something more—it was a book in the making. That was what Rick Cross had promised him. And Tom was going to make sure the old man made good on his word.

He was annoyed to have missed all the upheaval in the Huntingdon-Cross family over the past two months, but it couldn't be helped. He'd already been committed to another project at home in the States and, anyway, who could have predicted that one of Rick and Sherry's famously blonde and beautiful daughters would get married and knocked up all within the space of eight weeks? And who knew what was going on with Rose now? She'd been in the press recently herself, he remembered, pictured with the famous Runaway Groom—who he'd *thought* was famously her sister *Violet's* best friend. Maybe something had happened there—and he'd missed it, again. All *he'd* had was a text message when he turned his phone back on after the flight, with a contact number and the information that, due to unforeseen but brilliant circumstances, someone else would be collecting him.

Or not, as the case might be.

Tom sighed. He'd just have to make sure he got good interviews with them all when he could. And, wherever Rose might be, at least one daughter was still living at home—probably the most famous one, if you counted notorious Internet celebrity, which Tom did.

Opening his laptop, he pulled up his notes on the family. He was staying at the family home, Huntingdon Hall, so he needed to be prepared from the get-go. He'd spent weeks compiling old interviews, articles and photos of the whole family, and felt he had it pretty much down. And after speaking with Rose in New York and on the phone while planning the trip, he'd thought he had at least one ally there—until she'd decided to swan off and abandon him with no notice.

Presumably she'd got an offer too good to refuse, no matter how much it inconvenienced anyone else. Celebrity kids—always the centre of their own world, however nice and normal Rose had seemed when they met. He needed to remember that.

He'd only had one conversation with the man he was really there to see, though—Rick Cross himself. Rock star, family man, reformed wide boy. The interviews Tom had on file dated back almost thirty years, back to when The Screaming Lemons were the next big thing on the rock scene. Nowadays, they were the old standards—and they had to try harder to shock or surprise.

With his plans for a tell-all book about the band and his family's history, it looked as if Rick had plans to do both.

Tom had asked him, 'Why now?' It couldn't be money—the band still sold enough greatest hits records and got more than enough airplay that it didn't matter if their latest album tanked. But all Rick would say was that it was time.

Scrolling through his family crib sheet, Tom reminded himself of all the most pertinent facts.

Most people in Britain and the States could pick Rick Cross out of a line-up and tell you his story. Same for his wife, the beautiful and rich mostly ex-model and now English society stalwart, Sherry Huntingdon. With his fame and her family, they made quite the impact.

Then there were the girls. The youngest, Daisy, was the newest Lady Holgate, which seemed pretty much par for the course for celebrity kids, Tom decided. After all, if you already had money and fame, surely a title was the only thing left to go for? Especially in the UK.

The twins were a few years older at twenty-seven. Rose, he knew from personal meetings with her, had been living in New York for the last few years, although she had planned to be in England until the annual benefit concert at least.

And then there was Violet. Tom had enjoyed the hell out of researching her. The thought made him smile even as he rubbed at his gritty eyes.

A commotion at the counter made him look up, and he blinked at the sight of a tall blonde in a ridiculous dress and heels crashing past a table full of customers. Was that Rose? Or a sleep deprivation induced hallucination?

'Sorry!' the blonde yelped, and he decided that she was probably real. Hallucinations didn't usually yelp, in his experience.

Shaking his head to try and wake up, Tom packed up his laptop. It looked as if his ride had made it after all. Any time now he could fall into that nice, peaceful, quiet bed and sleep for a week. Or at least until Rick Cross summoned him for his first interview.

From all the reports he'd read, Tom was pretty sure Rick wasn't an early riser. That lie-in was practically in the bag.

'Rose,' he said, hoisting his bag onto his shoulder and reaching for the handle of his suitcase. 'I thought you were going away? You didn't have to come all the way out here just because the idiot you asked to pick me up forgot. I could have just caught a cab, you know.'

Rose looked up, eyes wide, her hands still gripping her skirt. 'Oh, um, no, it's fine. Thomas. It's fine, Thomas.'

Why did she keep repeating his name? And why was she calling him *Thomas* instead of Tom all of a sudden? They'd spoken plenty of times before, and even had lunch once. It wasn't as if she might have forgotten it all of a sudden.

Unless…

The smirk formed unbidden on his lips. 'I'm sorry, *Violet.* I thought you were your sister for a moment. And it's Tom.'

'That's okay. You're not the only one to get confused.' She pulled a frustrated face, and Thomas couldn't help but laugh. It was just so *familiar.* And not from Rose.

'What?' Violet asked, obviously startled by his outburst. Maybe he should have had caffeinated coffee. Obviously the sleep deprivation was starting to affect him.

'I'm sorry,' he managed, trying to keep his smirk in check. 'But for a moment you looked just like you did in the—' Self-preservation kicked in as her face turned stony and he cut himself off.

'No, really. Do continue.' Her cut glass accent was sharp enough to wound, and any humour Tom had found in the situation ebbed away. 'I believe you were about to finish that sentence with the words "leaked sex tape", right?'

'I'm sorry,' Tom started, realising he'd apologised to this woman more in the first three minutes of meeting her than he'd normally need to in even a month of *dating* some-one. But Violet interrupted before he could get to the part about sleep deprivation and inadequate impulse control.

'That's right,' she said, a little louder than Tom thought was strictly necessary. 'I'm the famous Huntingdon-Cross Sex Tape Twin. Not one of the two sisters who found true love and settled down. The one who men only want so they can film us together and put it on the Internet. Get your autographs here.'

The café was almost empty, but a couple of guys sitting at the table nearest the front definitely had their camera phones out. What kind of audacity did it take to stand up in public and admit to being the star of a ridiculously ex-plicit sex tape watched by half the world? The sort only the rich and famous had.

'And apparently, according to the frustrated and an-noyed look on my face, it can't even have been good sex. Personally, I don't remember, but Mr Buckley here has obviously watched it often enough to be considered an expert. Do feel free to ask him questions, if you like. I'm not in a hurry. I mean, I'm only missing my parents' marriage renewal ceremony to be here. Carry on.'

Waving an imperious hand towards him, Violet perched on the edge of a stool by the counter and waited. Feeling the heat of embarrassment in his cheeks, Tom grabbed the last of his things from the table and headed for the exit. Violet Huntingdon-Cross might be used to this sort of exposure, but he certainly wasn't.

'No questions? Oh, what a shame. I suppose we'd better be on our way, then.' Violet hopped down and followed him out into the arrivals hall.

'I suppose I deserved that,' he muttered as she held the door of the terminal open for him. He had laughed first. But she'd been over an hour and a half late to collect him. So the sleep deprivation was at least partly her fault, right?

'I suppose you did,' she replied. 'And I'm very sorry for being late to collect you. Rose gave me the wrong flight times.'

Damn. There went that argument.

'This is where you apologise to me for humiliating me in front of a crowd of people,' Violet prompted, and Tom raised his eyebrows.

'Me? Trust me, sweetheart, you did the humiliating all by yourself.' As if a performance of that sort was second nature to her. Which, judging by the sex tape, it might well be. He'd heard that Violet had calmed down in more recent years, but maybe the family had just got better at hiding her exploits from the media.

Her whole face flushed bright red at his words, and she pushed past him as they left the terminal. 'I'm parked in the short stay car park,' she called back over his shoulder.

He was pretty sure he wasn't supposed to hear her muttered words as she strode off towards the car, but he did. 'Hopefully not as short as your stay with us, though.'

Tom allowed himself a smile. Violet Huntingdon-Cross was definitely a worthy interview subject. And if he could get some new or hidden scandals on the eldest family wild child to help sell his book proposal, well, he'd be an idiot not to. Right?

CHAPTER THREE

VIOLET'S HANDS WERE still shaking as she tried to get the key into the ignition. At the back of the car, Tom was struggling to open the boot for his cases, but she had no intention of helping. Not least because the way her body was trembling meant she'd probably be even worse at it than him.

What on earth had possessed her? Eight years of best behaviour, of keeping her head down, of politely ignoring all the comments and jokes—all gone in one moment of frustration and humiliation in an airport coffee shop.

It had been his laugh, she decided, as the key finally slid home. It had made it so abundantly clear that she wasn't a real person to him, just a hilarious anecdote. One she had probably now ensured he would be dining out on for all time.

She was used to being seen as a public figure more than herself. She was always Rick and Sherry's daughter first, and often Rose or Daisy's sister before she was ever a person in her own right. Except when she was the Sex Tape Twin. And, quite honestly, she'd rather be nobody than *that*.

Except that was all she ever seemed to be to anyone outside her own family. And God, was she sick of it.

The car boot slammed shut; Tom must have managed to stow his cases away. Any moment now he'd slide into the passenger seat beside her and they'd have to make polite conversation all the way home. That, or sit in frosty silence. Violet wasn't sure which would be worse.

She sighed. Yes, she was. Silence would be worse. Because only her dad had any idea how long Thomas Buckley would be staying at their house, and she couldn't simply send him to Coventry indefinitely. This wasn't boarding school; it was real life. And somehow that had turned out to be even more confining and stifling than the strict Catholic school they'd all been sent to.

She was a grown-up now. The mistakes of her youth were *supposed* to be in the past. She was more than the stories people told about her. Which meant sucking it up and making nice with the offensive American music journalist who would be writing some sort of tell-all about her family and their life any time now. And hoping he'd forget what a disaster this whole night had been.

It was like her dad had said, back when That Tape had first hit the internet and suddenly her sex face was splashed all over magazines and newspapers everywhere. He'd left the rest of the band in some hotel somewhere, mid-tour, and come home to check on her. While she'd lain sobbing on her bed, he'd rubbed her back and told her, 'At least you know now, honey. Not everyone out there wants what's best for you. And only you can decide who to trust.'

Well. There was an easy answer to that one, Violet had found. Don't trust anyone—except family.

Will had been an exception to the rule, and a hard-won one at that. But it helped that he'd only ever been friend material. She wouldn't trust even her best friend with her whole heart. Not like Rose had done.

The passenger door opened and Violet sucked in a breath before plastering on a smile. 'All okay?'

Tom gave her a slightly wary look, as if uncertain

whether she might just drive off with him half in and half out of the car. She couldn't really blame him; she hadn't been exactly consistent since they'd met.

Time to start mending fences before he started writing articles.

'Fine.' Tom slid into the seat beside her. 'And, uh, you?'

She forced her smile to brighten further. 'Just dandy.'

'Right. And are you always prone to such extreme mood swings?'

Oh, God, he was probably thinking that she was on drugs, or bipolar, or something else that would make a good story. This was *not* going well.

Violet sighed. Time to try honesty. 'Okay, look. We got off to a rotten start here, I know. But Dad wants you staying with us, working with him, and Dad doesn't change his mind once it's made up. So I just have to suck it up and get on with things, right? And since I don't particularly want to spend the next however many weeks avoiding you or trading insults on sight, I figure the easiest thing is to pretend the last half an hour didn't happen. Okay?' Partial honesty, anyway. She didn't need to mention—

'Plus you don't want me to tell the story of this evening in any future articles or books?'

Damn. 'Well, do you blame me?'

Tom was quiet so long that she had to glance over to check that he hadn't fallen asleep. When she looked, he was holding out his hand.

Eyebrows raised, she took it, biting her lip at the slight tingle she felt at his skin against hers. For heaven's sake, it was a handshake! Had it really been so long since someone she wasn't related to by blood or marriage had touched her that her body had forgotten what it felt like?

'I'm Tom Buckley,' he said with a half smile. 'Nice to meet you. Thanks for coming to pick me up.'

'Violet Huntingdon-Cross. Sorry I was an hour and a half late.'

He chuckled. 'Let's just blame Rose for everything, yeah?'

'That's what I've been trying to do for the last twenty-seven years,' Violet said, and sighed. 'Sadly, it never seems to stick.'

At Tom's laugh, she slipped the car into gear and pulled out of the parking space. 'Come on. Let's get you home. I bet you're tired after your long journey.'

'Exhausted,' Tom admitted, and when she looked she could see the dark circles under his eyes, even in the poor lighting of the airport car park. 'That's kind of my excuse, actually. For, well, everything. Sleep deprivation. It's been a hell of a week.'

'I'm sure. Rose said you were working out in Miami?'

He nodded. 'For the last week. Then a flying visit home to New York to repack my bags, then straight here. I feel like I haven't slept in a month. I'm looking forward to some peace and quiet, actually. Your dad told me that Huntingdon Hall is out in the middle of nowhere, right?'

'Ye—es,' Violet said, biting her lip as she remembered the party she'd left just a couple of hours before. It was long gone midnight. Surely everyone would have gone home by the time they arrived, right? Oh, who was she kidding? Rick and Sherry's parties were legendary. They'd be lucky if they didn't find anyone passed out on the tennis court in the morning, this time.

'That sounds ominous,' Tom said. 'Do they have guests? Wait…' Glancing over, she saw him frown, the moment it clicked into place for him. 'Oh, hell. It's their vow renewal today, right? You said you were missing it… That's why you were so annoyed about having to come and fetch me?'

'And why I'm wearing this fetching yet inappropriate

dress,' Violet confirmed. No need for him to know that, actually, she'd been happy to get out of there. 'I'm afraid there's a very real chance the party might still be ongoing.' She glanced at the dashboard clock. 'In fact, I think Dad and the boys will probably be taking the stage for their encore session right about now.'

Tom groaned and let his head fall back against the headrest. 'So, no sleep tonight is what you're telling me.'

'Basically. Sorry! Maybe you can get some sleep in the car?' She should feel worse about this. The guy was obviously exhausted to the point of losing all social niceties. She should feel bad that her parents and their friends were going to keep him up for *another* night.

She really, really didn't, though.

It seemed to Tom that no sooner had he closed his eyes than a car door was slamming, then another opening, and cool night air flooded over his face. Followed swiftly by his ears being assaulted by one of The Screaming Lemons' classic hits being played as an acoustic number.

Normally, he'd be up at the front of the stage, soaking in the moment, tucking the memories away for future articles, trying to find the right words to describe the perfection of that three and a half minutes.

Tonight—or rather this morning—he just wanted it all to go away. Including Violet Huntingdon-Cross.

'Wake up, Sleeping Beauty,' she said, in a voice far too jolly for someone who had recently glared at him with such loathing. 'You're missing the party.'

He cracked open one eyelid and waited for the yellow blur of her hair, the pale fuzz of her face and the purple blotch that was her dress to come into focus. Then he blinked; she was closer than he'd thought, and suddenly the only things in focus at all were her bright blue eyes, peering down at him.

'Oh, good,' she said, straightening up. 'I thought for a moment I was going to have to leave you here for the night. That or get someone to come carry you to bed. That sort of thing never makes a terribly good first impression, you know.'

Unlike, for instance, pointing out a woman's sex tape history within five minutes of meeting her. God, when he woke up properly he was going to have to work at getting Violet back onside. As the only daughter living at home, he had a feeling she could make life difficult for him if she wanted.

And he rather suspected she might more than want to. It might actually be her burning life ambition at this point.

'I'm awake,' he half lied, forcing himself to straighten up. Another couple of moments and he might even make it out of the car.

Violet grabbed his hand and, even through his sleep fog, he couldn't help but be aware of the feel of her smooth, cool skin, or the way something indefinable crept up his arm at her touch. Something that seemed to crackle with possibilities.

Something that woke him up completely.

Blinking again, he twisted round to get his feet firmly on the ground and stood up, belatedly aware that he was still gripping onto Violet's hand, probably rather tighter than she'd like.

He dropped it fast, but her blue, blue eyes were still fixed on his and the puzzled crease between her eyebrows told him that whatever he'd felt, she'd felt it too.

At least he had the excuse of sleep deprivation. What justification was she using?

Violet shook her head and stepped back, nicely out of

his personal space. 'I know you're exhausted. But given that sleep is likely to be impossible for the next couple of hours at least, and since you *are* here to observe and interview and write about the band… Why don't you come and meet Dad?'

Dad. Even after an hour in the company of one of the most famous celebrity kids in the world, it still felt strange to hear her refer to the infamous Rick Cross as 'Dad'. How different a world must Violet live in to the real one he inhabited, to so casually be able to think of Huntingdon Hall as home, and one of the most recognisable couples ever as Mum and Dad?

Different, certainly, to the kid from New York who never even knew who his father was, only that he wouldn't have done him any good in life if he'd stuck around anyway. The kid whose mother had so disapproved of the method he'd used to get out of the gutter, she hadn't spoken to him for three years before her death.

Yeah, there were worlds between him and Violet. And however long he stayed at Huntingdon Hall, he had to remember that.

'Isn't he still playing?' Tom said, hoping it wasn't painfully obvious he was stalling. Rick had seemed sharp on the phone, the sort to see through people's masks. He wanted to be on top form when he sat down with Rick for the first time.

Violet tilted her head to the left, listening to the music, he presumed. 'This is usually his last number. He'll be off stage soon and still on that performance high. It's a good time to meet him if you want him to like you.'

'And do *you* want him to like me?' Tom asked. It seemed strange that she would, given everything.

A look of annoyance flashed across Violet's face, as if

she weren't used to being asked this many questions about her motives and feelings. Maybe she wasn't. 'Yes.'

Tom couldn't resist. 'Why?'

'Does it matter?' Violet tossed her hair back over her shoulder as the last chord rang out from the stage. 'We're going to miss him.'

'You haven't answered my question.' Tom folded his arms, leant back against the car and waited.

With an impatient huff, Violet grabbed his hand and started dragging him towards the stage. Tom didn't budge until she started talking.

'Because Dad makes up his mind about people and things in an instant, and that's it. You're here; you're going to be writing about him and us. If he likes you, he'll show you his best side, the stuff *I* want you to be writing about. If he takes a dislike to you…'

'Things could get messy?' Tom guessed.

Violet sighed as they reached the edge of the stage area. Even though the party was obviously filled with friends and family, the cheering as the band came off stage was still as loud as Tom had heard in any stadium.

'Let's just say this whole experience will be a lot less fun. For all of us.'

Suddenly, the familiar craggy face of Rick Cross appeared at the top of the stage steps, mouth open and laughing at something his band mate was saying behind him.

'Showtime,' Tom whispered, and Violet flashed him a quick grin—the first honest smile he'd seen from her.

Tom took a breath. Time to meet the parents.

CHAPTER FOUR

VIOLET HID A grin at the slightly shell-shocked look on Tom's face as Dad and the boys traipsed down the temporary stairs at the side of the stage set, all laughing, chatting and still clearly caught up in their own world—a world that consisted of music, noise and melodies.

She knew the kind of impact they could have, just off stage. When she was younger, just old enough to be allowed to stay up to watch the occasional gig from the wings, she and Rose had found it hard to understand this part—when Dad wasn't Dad, just for a moment. He was all Rick Cross, rock star, right now. And that was a sight to behold.

The adrenaline would wear off soon enough, Violet knew. He'd come down, hug his wife, ask for a drink, and before too long he'd be heading to bed to sleep it off. Well, maybe after a little more time with his closest friends—drinking and talking and probably singing.

Right now, in this moment, he was exactly who Tom Buckley had come here to interview. She hadn't lied when she said that this was the best time for Tom to make a good impression with her father. But it was also the best time to remind Tom that this wasn't just *anybody* he'd come here to write about.

The press could publish all the stories they liked about

her and her sisters—and heaven knew they would. But they couldn't touch her parents. Rick and Sherry were rock royalty, beyond reproach. There were no affairs, no addictions, no mistakes made—nothing to latch on to and use to make their lives hell. It might have been different back in the day, but not any more.

Now they were national treasures, and Violet was unbearably proud of them for it.

'Mr Cross.' Stepping forward, Tom stuck out his hand, smiling warmly. Violet had to give him credit—if he hadn't been slumped over in her passenger seat for the last forty-five minutes, she'd never have known he was utterly exhausted. He looked professional, ready to do a great job.

She just hoped that Dad's idea of a good job and Tom's meshed.

'Mr Buckley, I presume!' Rick's famous smile spread across his face. 'Great to have you here.' He shook Tom's hand with what looked like painful enthusiasm. 'Boys, this is the guy I've invited over to write our musical life story.'

'And your family's,' Tom put in. Violet rolled her eyes. As if any of them would forget that he was here to expose all their private lives as well as their public personas.

'Oh, he's here for the dirt, Rick.' Jez—Uncle Jez to the girls—the band's lead guitarist and Rick's best man, elbowed his friend in the ribs. 'Time to hide those skeletons in better closets!'

Rick laughed, his head tipped back in pure amusement and joy. Violet bit the inside of her cheek and just prayed there wasn't anything hidden there that she didn't know about. She couldn't imagine how there could be, given how closely she'd been involved in her parents' lives and work since she'd moved back home eight years ago.

But you could never be too careful when it came to the

press. And if Dad had any secrets, Uncle Jez would be the one to know them.

'Trust me, I'm just here to write the best, most honest story I can for your legion of fans. They're only interested in the truth.' Unlike Tom, presumably.

'And that's just what you'll get.' Rick clapped a hand on Tom's back, and Violet knew the reporter had passed some test that no one but her father would ever understand. 'The complete unvarnished truth, ready to be written down for posterity.'

Relief warred with apprehension inside her, and Violet clenched her fists so tightly her nails bit into the palms of her hands. On the one hand, the fact that her dad liked Tom would make the interviews go more smoothly, reducing the chances of a story about a recalcitrant, difficult star. On the other, it opened up the opportunity that Rick would get *too* close to Tom. As much as he talked about the unvarnished truth, surely her father realised there were some parts of their family lives, and history, that none of them wanted shared with the world. For the umpteenth time in some cases.

Well, there was nothing for it now but to see how things went. And try and keep tabs on both Tom and Rick, so she could try and head off any prospective trouble *before* it turned up in the papers this time.

'Darlings, you were brilliant as always.' Sherry floated up to them, kissing each of the band members on the cheek before planting a rather more thorough kiss on her husband. Tom, Violet noticed, was politely staring at the floor. Everyone else was too used to it to even bother.

'Mum, this is Tom Buckley,' Violet said once the public display of affection was over. Might as well get all the introductions over in one go. 'He's the writer Dad—'

'The writer who's going to tell our little story! Of

course.' Sherry held out a hand, although whether she intended it to be kissed or shaken Violet wasn't sure.

Tom went for the handshake. Not fully charmed yet, then. Mum might have her work cut out with this one. Obviously he wasn't taken in by her disingenuous description of his subject matter. Nobody in the world would describe the history of The Screaming Lemons and the Huntingdon-Cross family a 'little story'. Least of all anyone who had lived it.

'It's a pleasure to meet you, Mrs Huntingdon-Cross,' Tom said, releasing her hand.

'Oh, call me Sherry, please.' Mum flashed that legendary wide smile, the one that had been seen in magazines and on billboards for decades now. 'Anyone who stays here at Huntingdon Hall rather automatically becomes part of the family, I'm afraid. You might as well get used to it!'

Tom Buckley, part of the family? Not on Violet's watch.

But that was the problem with her parents. It wasn't that they were overly trusting or naïve, particularly. They knew the dangers of fame as well as anyone, and took care to live their lives circumspectly. But once they'd taken someone in and claimed them as a friend…it took a lot to shake their faith in them. And that could be dangerous.

'Where's Daisy?' Violet asked. She needed backup here and, with Rose and Will already gone on their honeymoon, Daisy-Waisy was going to have to be it.

'Oh, she and Seb have already turned in, I think,' Sherry said with a dismissive wave of her hand. 'Daisy was exhausted, poor thing—pregnancy is extraordinarily tiring, you know,' she added as an aside to Tom, who nodded, despite the puzzled crease between his eyebrows. 'And I think Seb wants to get off back to Hawkesley first thing.'

Curses. With Tom about to collapse from sleep deprivation, the chances weren't good that he'd be up in time to meet Daisy before she left. Which meant Violet was on her own trying to keep this whole project from blowing up in their faces. Lovely.

'And Rose has already left?' Tom asked politely. 'I met her in New York last month, and I know she'd planned to be here right through until the concert…' He left the sentence open. Not actually a question, so not really prying, but enough that politeness insisted that someone fill the gap. Tricky.

'Oh, yes,' Sherry said, beaming. 'She and Will left on their honeymoon a couple of hours ago.'

Tom's eyebrows inched up towards his hairline, and Violet winced. 'Honeymoon?' he asked. 'I didn't realise that she was planning a wedding.'

Or that she was even dating anyone, just like the rest of them. In fact, Violet was willing to bet that what Tom really meant was: *Two daughters married in a suspiciously short space of time, and one of them pregnant…there has to be a story here.* Especially if he'd seen the photos of Will and Rose in the papers.

Time to put a stop to that.

'Oh, yes,' she said, smiling cheerily. 'Will has practically been a part of the family for years now. We're delighted that they've made it official.' All true—Will *was* part of the family—certainly more than Tom Buckley ever would be. And why did he need to know that up until the last month or so, Will had only been there as Violet's best friend? And if he never realised that Will and Rose hadn't met until Daisy's wedding…well, that would be great. She just hoped that Tom Buckley didn't keep up with the UK celebrity gossip too closely.

Rick slung an arm around Tom's shoulders as the rest of the band wandered off in search of a drink or a bed. He had to reach up quite a bit to do it, Violet realised.

'That's the only downside of having daughters, you know,' Rick said, grinning at Violet. 'Having to give them away to unworthy men.'

'Oh, hush,' Sherry said. 'You know you adore Will. And Seb is going to be a wonderful son-in-law.'

'True. I have lucked out.' Rick turned his wicked grin onto Violet, and she felt her stomach clench at what he might come out with next. The inability to keep his inappropriate comments to himself was definitely a downside to the post-performance adrenaline. 'Makes me worry who Violet might decide to bring home. I can't possibly get that lucky three times in a row.'

Heat flooded Violet's cheeks. She'd spent more time blushing in front of Tom Buckley than actually talking to him at this point, she was sure.

'*Not* something you need to be worrying about, Dad.' Or be talking about in front of reporters.

Rick's face turned a little sad. 'No, I suppose not.'

'Anyway, Rose will be back soon enough, and you'll be able to catch up with her then,' Violet said with forced jollity. Tom gave her a look that left her in no doubt he knew exactly what she was doing—steering the conversation away from anything interesting. Violet made a mental note to warn Rose that it might look better if her whirlwind romance with Will hadn't been quite so…whirlwind-like. Rose would understand. Once she got home, everything would be so much easier.

'Actually, darling,' Sherry said, her smile just a little too wide, 'I spoke to Will as they were leaving. I understand they're going to be away for four weeks.'

Four weeks. Suddenly, with Tom Buckley standing there, it seemed longer than ever. Just when she really needed her twin at home with her. What had Will been thinking? Not about his best friend, stuck at home with the man who wanted to ferret out all her secrets. No, he'd been thinking about getting her twin sister naked for longer.

Damn men and their inability to think about more than one thing at once.

'That's right,' she said, forcing a smile. 'Although I couldn't get him to say where they were going.'

'Me neither,' Rick said. 'Will said he couldn't risk it. You know your mum would have texted Rose on the way to the airport and ruined the surprise.'

'Anyway. They won't be back until two days before the Benefit Concert, but Will said he'd left Rose's notes with you.' Mum had her 'tiptoeing' voice on. As if she was taking the long way round getting to the point.

'Yeah, it's all in Rose's study, apparently. Her black planner and all the files and contracts and stuff.'

'And...Will mentioned that you'd agreed to, well, keep an eye on things while they were away.' Ah, that was what Mum was working up to. Of course. Concern that Violet had agreed to something that, when it came down to it, she wouldn't be able to, or want to do.

Well, maybe it was time for her to prove her parents—and Tom Buckley—wrong. If Rose could organise a benefit concert, so could she.

'That's right.' And she'd do it too. But she really didn't want to get into this with Tom standing right there. Then again, there wasn't a chance of her getting any sleep tonight if they didn't agree a plan for the concert. The last thing they needed was the annual benefit being an utter disaster zone because Rose wasn't there, the one year they had a reporter on site recording all the behind the scenes activity for posterity.

Damn it! How could Will and Rose do this? Clearly, love had driven them crazy. It was the only explanation.

'You're looking worried, honey.' Her dad wrapped an

arm around her waist and hauled her close for a hug. 'But there's nothing to fret about. Rose has been running this thing like clockwork for years. The set-up's all done; everything's been booked for months.'

Violet turned her head to raise her eyebrows at her father. If everything was already sorted, then why was Rose always running around like a mad thing in the last few weeks before the concert every other year?

'Maybe your dad is being a little optimistic,' Sherry said. 'But really, darling, everything is in hand. All that's left is the fiddly last-minute stuff. And I'm sure we can find someone to handle that, if you don't want to. Rose and Will would understand. I'll call up an agency or something.'

Agency staff. Another stranger in their home all the time, taking responsibility for the biggest concert in The Screaming Lemons' calendar. Someone who had absolutely no reason to care if things went perfectly or just well enough to get paid.

Violet risked a glance at Tom. She could almost read the story writing itself behind his tired eyes. Thoughtless wild child celebrity daughter disappears on eve of major charity event after whirlwind romance, leaving benefit concert in chaos. Sex Tape Twin decides she'd rather pick flowers than take on the job.

Almost as bad a start as her scene in the coffee shop.

'No. I can do it. We don't need to call the agency. I'll take care of the concert. I've seen Rose do it, and I'm sure she's left really good notes. I can do it. I'd like to.'

A complete lie. The last thing she wanted to do, when she should be keeping an eye on Tom, was take on a high profile project that would put her in the public eye and require speaking to all the people she'd been happily avoiding for eight years. But sometimes proving a point—especially to someone like Tom Buckley—required sacrifice.

'Are you sure, darling?' Her mother's perfect face crinkled up into a frown. 'It doesn't really seem like…well, like your sort of thing.'

Of course it didn't. As much as she might have moaned about her parents calling Rose in to organise their wedding, she knew exactly why they'd done it. To spare Violet the misery of having to brave the public and the publicity again. It was bad enough doing so as a guest at endless charity functions, or just appearing at the benefit concert. Anywhere there were cameras, her nerves started to tremble. And this…this would mean liaising with pop stars, working with celebrities.

There were going to be a *lot* of cameras. Her fingers felt shaky just thinking about it.

'I'm sure,' she said as firmly as she could. 'The Benefit Concert is important. I want to make sure everything goes just as well as it would if Rose was here.'

Maybe she could just pretend to be Rose. Maybe no one would notice that she was actually the *other* twin. You know the one.

'Well, honey, if you're sure.' Rick's forehead had matching creases. Then he broke into a smile and clapped Tom on the back. 'Hey, maybe Tom here can give you a hand!'

CHAPTER FIVE

TOM COULDN'T BE sure if it was the sleep deprivation or if he really was missing something in the conversation going on around him. It felt as if there were actually two discussions taking place—one with words and one entirely conducted through concerned eyebrow gestures.

Still, he was pretty sure he didn't stand a chance of understanding the eyebrow conversation until he got some actual sleep. In fact, he was just plotting the best way to get shown to his room when Rick volunteered him.

'Me?' Tom wished that had come out slightly less squeakily. 'Help with the Benefit Concert?'

Sherry clapped her hands together. 'What a brilliant idea! I knew I married you for a reason.' She planted another kiss on her husband.

Violet, Tom noticed, hadn't responded at all. In fact, she looked as though she'd been sent into a state of severe shock and might need therapy to even deal with the idea.

God, he just had the best way with women, didn't he?

'Unless...Violet, darling, are you sure you really want to do this?' Sherry's eyebrows were doing the very concerned thing again, mirrored by Rick's. Yeah, Tom was definitely missing something here.

But Violet shook off the shock, smiled widely and said, 'Of course I do! And I'd appreciate any help that Tom is able to give me, in between the work he's *actually* here to do.' She even managed a sincere smile for him as she spoke, which Tom thought might be a first.

'Well, that's settled then.' Rick clapped his hands together, but his eyebrows suggested that nothing was settled at all. Tom suspected there'd be some private family conversations going on once he'd finally found a bed to fall into.

Well, so be it. Despite Sherry's enthusiastic welcome, he wasn't actually family. He didn't need to know all their tiny moments and their every word. He just wanted the stories. And, he'd admit it, the secrets. *They* were what would set his book apart from everything else ever written about Rick Cross and co.

And he was pretty sure he'd get them. Starting tomorrow.

'Guys, if I'm going to be ready to start interviews, write a book *and* organise the best concert in the history of benefit concerts, I'd better get some sleep.' Tom gave them all his friendliest all-in-this-together smile.

'Oh, of course!' Sherry immediately went into hostess mode, something Tom imagined she had honed and perfected over years of events, guests and parties. 'Violet, why don't you show Tom to his room, darling?'

Violet's smile was starting to look a little fixed, but no one except Tom seemed to notice. 'Of course. I might turn in myself.' She kissed her parents on their cheeks. 'It was a brilliant day. Here's to many more happy years of marriage.'

Tom followed Violet away from the stage, across the gardens. The party had obviously started to wind down after the Lemons had left the stage. The fairy lights in the trees shone down on abandoned glasses and plates and grass-stained marquee floors. A few stragglers still loitered by the temporary bar, where the last remaining barmaid yawned expansively, but most people had already headed home to bed.

Tom applauded their sensible natures. Of course, it was gone 4:00 a.m., so maybe they weren't that sensible.

Glancing over his shoulder, Tom saw Rick and Sherry making their way across to where the rest of the band sat with their partners or friends under the moonlight. Jez was strumming an acoustic guitar and laughter and conversation floated among the notes in the night air.

'I don't know how they're still going,' Violet said, following his gaze. 'I'm knackered. But they're always the last ones standing at a party. I think it's a point of pride these days. And they always finish the night together, just the gang of them who've been there from the start.'

He should be over there, soaking up the moment. Taking in the atmosphere that would make his book authentic. Except…it was a private moment and he was new on the scene. He couldn't force his way into that close-knit group. He had to earn his place, and that would take time and trust.

Violet was giving him an odd considering look. 'You still want to go to bed?' A slight flush of colour hit her cheeks in the pale lights, and he knew somehow that she was waiting for him to make a joke about whether that was an offer to join him. So he didn't.

'Alone, I mean. Not with me,' Violet babbled, as if he had. She must get that a lot, although he'd expected her to just brush it off or turn it back on the joker to embarrass *them.* After her display in the airport café, he knew she had the confidence and the fire.

Except…here, now, this seemed like a different Violet. One who'd known humiliation and pain. One he hadn't expected to meet when he'd sat in Miami and New York reading up about the wild child Sex Tape Twin without shame.

She'd never even put out a statement, he remembered. No apology for being a bad role model, for letting down her fans or those young girls who looked up to her. No regret for the shame and embarrassment she'd brought on her family.

Why was that? Suddenly, he desperately wanted to know. But those questions too required patience and trust to be earned. Maybe in a few weeks. After all, they were going to be working on the concert together. He had all the time he needed to learn everything there was to know about Violet Huntingdon-Cross, and her family.

'Honestly, Violet, I think I'd pass out on you tonight even if it was an offer.' He gave her a friendly smile to show it was a joke, that he didn't mean any offence. But, as her gaze met his, even his exhausted body had a moment where it wished that wasn't the case. That maybe, just maybe, this beautiful, confusing woman might actually make that offer to him.

Which was clearly ridiculous. They had nothing in common. She'd never understand him or his life, and he'd long since grown out of sleeping with any beautiful woman who offered. He liked his sexual encounters to mean something these days. Maybe not true love and forever, but a meaningful connection at least.

He couldn't really imagine any connection between him and the self-absorbed daughter of a celebrity. Still, he felt a little relief as the colour in her cheeks faded and she gave a quick nod.

'Come on then. Your bedroom's this way.' Violet started off towards the main staircase.

Tom bit his tongue to stop himself asking where hers was as he followed.

Violet woke up exhausted. Maybe it was all the excitement and chaos of the day and weeks before, but even once the big vow renewal was over and Rose was safely off on honeymoon she couldn't relax enough to sleep—despite the fact it had been gone four by the time she'd made it to bed. Eventually, after an hour of fitful tossing and turning, she'd given up and turned on her bedside light to read for a while.

She'd woken up four hours later, with the light still on and her face smooshed against her book. Not the perfect start to the day.

Scrubbing a hand across her face to try and persuade her eyes to stay open, she glanced at the clock. Nine thirty a.m. Chances were, the rest of the household would be sleeping in until well after lunch, but there was a nervous energy running through Violet's veins that she knew from experience wouldn't let her go back to sleep.

A shower, her most comfortable jeans and a T-shirt in her favourite shade of lavender-blue made her feel a little more human. She scraped her hair back into a clip to dry naturally, slathered on what claimed to be a rejuvenating moisturiser and headed downstairs in search of coffee.

'Coffee will make all things better,' she murmured as she switched on the espresso machine. The lie was a soothing one, at least. How could one poor drink be expected to deal with all the worries that had piled on in the last twenty-four hours?

'Think it can even help your poor old dad?' Rick leant against the door frame from the hall, his weathered face looking a little grey under his summer tan. 'I think I'm getting too old for the partying lark, honey.'

'Never.' Violet grabbed another espresso cup from the shelf. 'You'll still be rocking with a walking stick when the rest of us have grown old and boring.'

Except she didn't even need to age to grow old and boring; she was already there, wasn't she? Her entire existence already fitted within the grounds of Huntingdon Hall. Or it had. Maybe the Benefit Concert would be her chance to spread her wings.

'Only if I have my girls there to help hold me up,' Rick said, settling himself into one of the chairs at the kitchen table. 'Wouldn't be any fun without you all.'

'Mum sleeping in?' Violet handed her dad his coffee, then sat down to blow across the surface of her own cup.

'She says she needs her beauty sleep.' Rick laughed. 'Course, we all know she's plenty beautiful without it.'

'I didn't expect anyone else to be up for hours,' Violet said.

'I've got a shift down at the centre this morning,' Rick said. 'No one else could cover, so…' He shrugged.

Violet gave him a sympathetic smile. While everyone knew that Rick and Sherry supported all sorts of charities publicly, very few people were aware of all the private time they put in. Her dad did a lot of work for Alzheimer's charities, as well as helping out at a local drug rehabilitation centre, while her mum put in time on a children's helpline, amongst other things. Would they share that side of themselves with Tom? Violet had no idea.

'I'll be back to give Tom his first interview this afternoon, though,' Rick said, suggesting that he might. Violet was glad; more people should know about all the good they did. 'And what are you up to today?'

Violet sipped her coffee. 'I was planning on raiding Rose's files to get an idea of what I've let myself in for with this Benefit Concert.'

Rick's face turned serious. 'Now, honey, you know you don't have to take that on. It's not too late to change your mind.'

'Don't think I can do it, huh?' Violet said, eyebrows raised.

'Violet, I truly believe you could do anything in the world you dreamt of, if you decided to. It just comes down to if you really *want* to.'

Violet bit her lip. Dad thought she could do it. He had faith in her. And maybe, just maybe, he knew something she didn't. At the very least, she wanted the *chance* to prove him right.

'I want to do it,' she said, ignoring the way her whole body felt as if it might start trembling any second. This was her chance—her golden opportunity to do that *something more* she'd been wishing for. 'It's important to me, and I think it's time.' Time to stop hiding behind the walls of Huntingdon Hall at last. Time to start living in the real world again, even if it was still filled with monsters.

The smile that split Rick's craggy face was reward enough for her decision. 'I think you might be right, honey,' he said, and pressed a kiss to her hand across the table. 'I think it's time the whole world got used to seeing the *real* Violet Huntingdon-Cross for once.'

Violet smiled back through her nerves. *Wouldn't that be something?*

CHAPTER SIX

HUNTINGDON HALL WAS ridiculously large, Tom decided, after getting lost on the way to the kitchen for the third time. Tastefully redecorated, with none of the attempts to recreate the Regency or whatever that he'd half expected from the almost aristocracy. But then, this family were unusual in almost every other way, why not this one too?

There were so many contradictions for him to uncover, but that was half the fun.

Contradiction one. Sherry had inherited this hall from her blue blood family—but had obviously renovated it entirely using her husband's money—or her own, Tom supposed. She had enjoyed a very lucrative modelling career, after all. Anyway, the point was, while the outside of Huntingdon Hall still looked like something from a period novel, the inside was entirely modern.

As Tom made his way down a corridor that looked almost exactly like the one he'd just explored, Violet's directions from the night before seemed even more ridiculous. *Just follow the walls,* she'd said. *Eventually all of them lead back to the main staircase.* Follow the walls? What kind of advice was that? Especially since it appeared he'd been following the walls in the wrong direction for the last five minutes. Why wasn't there a helpful servant around here somewhere?

Of course that led him to contradiction two. In a house this size, with a family this rich, he'd have expected dozens of flunkies running around doing things for them. But he'd seen nobody. Oh, he was sure there was a housekeeper somewhere, and he highly doubted that Sherry did her own cleaning, but apart from that? Everything seemed to be kept in the family. Rose took care of the band's PR and everything else that needed organising, it seemed.

At least until she ran away on her honeymoon and Violet stepped in, rather than hire someone else.

Violet was, without a doubt, most definitely contradiction number three.

Tom turned another corner, dutifully following the wall and, finally, stumbled across the staircase. At last, his path towards coffee and maybe even breakfast was clear.

He hopped down the stairs in double time, smiling as he heard voices coming from what he hoped would prove to be the kitchen. Part of him was surprised not to be the first up—it had been a ridiculously late night, but even with his exhaustion level he'd found it impossible to sleep past ten. Too many years of risking missing the tour bus or a flight somewhere had left him a very light sleeper.

'Good morning.' Both Rick and Violet looked up at his words, and Tom got the unerring feeling that he'd interrupted something.

'Ah! Our guest awakes.' Rick moved towards the coffee pot. 'Strong and black? Or do you drink what can only be described as "warm milk with a coffee scent" like my daughter?'

'Strong and black, please,' Tom replied. Actually, he normally preferred it somewhere in between, but he wasn't taking the chance of failing the Rick Cross coffee test. Or any other tests he threw his way before Rick actually opened up to him and gave him the material he needed.

Rick nodded as he poured. 'Good choice. Now, about today.' He handed Tom a tiny steaming espresso cup with an apologetic smile that made Tom's heart sink. There were going to be no interviews today, he just knew it.

This was always the risk in coming here. Staying at Huntingdon Hall gave Tom unprecedented access, yes. But it also gave the subject the illusion of limitless time—and plenty of excuses to dodge sitting down and talking to him.

Tom did not have limitless time, and he needed this story.

'I was hoping we could make a start on some questions about what the Lemons are doing now,' Tom said, hoping the allure of potential publicity for the new album would draw him in. 'I've got a couple of possible slots in magazines and supplements coming up, and it would be good to let people know what's next for the band.'

'Rose would kick me if she heard me turning down the publicity, but I'm afraid I have some commitments today that I need to take care of before I can sit down with you.' Rick reached for his own coffee mug—which, Tom noticed, had milk in it, damn him. 'Sorry, Tom. I'll be back this afternoon, though. And I'll get Sherry to book some time with you too, as well as the boys from the band. I want us to get the bulk of the first few interviews down over the next week or two, so we've all got more time to focus on the Benefit Concert when it comes around. That sound okay to you?'

'That's…great, actually.' So much for the old man trying to avoid the interviews. Maybe Rick Cross was as serious about this book as Tom hoped after all. 'And I can probably find something to entertain me around here this morning.'

He hadn't meant to look at Violet, but somehow his gaze just sort of slid over in her direction. Her blonde hair looked darker—was it wet?—and strands were curling around her face. In jeans and a bright blue T-shirt, without make-up, she looked a lot younger than she had the night before. And, from the redness around her eyes, more vulnerable.

What had she been discussing with her father before he walked in? Suddenly, Tom wished he'd stopped outside to eavesdrop.

'You can help Violet go through all Rose's files!' Rick sounded immensely pleased with himself at the idea. 'Get up to speed on all the plans for the Benefit Concert. I just know my Violet is going to knock this one out of the park.'

He reached across and squeezed his daughter's shoulder, and she gave him a rather weak smile in return.

'Still, everyone needs a little help sometimes, right, honey?' Rick went on.

'Yeah, I guess.' With a deep breath, Violet straightened her shoulders visibly and looked him in the eye. 'So, Mr Buckley, how about it? You up for a challenge?'

'Absolutely.' Tom drained his espresso and smiled, unsure if the challenge was the concert or understanding the woman sitting in front of him.

'Okay. So…Will said that Rose left everything she had to do with the Benefit Concert in here.' Violet approached the door to the seldom used study on the first floor with more than a little trepidation. She hadn't been in this room since it was their homework room, years ago. Since she'd handed in her dissertation, she hadn't so much as opened the door.

It was Rose's room, not hers. As close as the twins were, Violet had to admit that they'd lived very separate lives over the last few years. With Rose in New York, that distance had only grown.

Oh, they still talked about pretty much everything. Violet still knew her sister's mind and heart, and she knew that if she needed anything Rose would be there in a heartbeat. But their lives were different. Rose jetted around the world, building her career working for The Screaming Lemons' PR, but also cultivating her passion making jewellery. The wedding rings she'd crafted for Seb and Daisy, and the bracelet she'd designed and made for their mother, were amongst the most beautiful things Violet had ever seen. Rose had real talent, and Violet knew that Will would encourage that—especially now Rose had made the decision to give up the PR side of things and follow her dreams.

Maybe it was time for Violet to do that too, she thought as she pushed open the door. Starting with the Benefit Concert.

'Huh.' Behind her, Tom stared over her shoulder. 'Did Will say where, exactly?'

It was a valid question. Violet's heart sank as she took in the piles of paperwork, the overflowing files and the stack of wedding magazines on the desk. Poor Rose had been swamped for the last month or more, with preparations for the band's latest tour, album promotion and not to mention planning their parents' vow renewal service and party. No wonder she hadn't had time to tidy up.

Well, that just made step one in the 'get-back-out-there-and-show-the-world-what-Violet-Huntingdon-Cross-is-really-made-of' plan all the more obvious.

'We need to start with a clean sweep,' she said, picking up Rose's battered, precious black planner from the middle of the piles covering the desk. 'We'll sort through everything in here, clear up and find all the relevant stuff, then set up my office in here. Will sent me the link to the Dropbox folder Rose was using for all the electronic stuff, and she's given me access to the email account she uses for the Benefit Concert each year. So I should have everything I need to get started…'

'Once you can find the desk,' Tom finished for her.

'Yeah.' She turned to look at him. 'Sorry. This probably isn't what you were hoping to do this morning.'

Tom shrugged. 'Not entirely. But this afternoon should make up for it. And it doesn't have to be a total waste. I can ask you some basic interview questions while we're working.' He pulled out his smartphone and scrolled through to an app with a microphone logo. 'You don't mind being taped, right?'

Violet's body froze, her back so stiff she thought it might snap. At least he was asking, she supposed. She hadn't been given that courtesy last time.

'I think maybe today we should just focus on getting this office sorted.' She knew her voice was stilted, but she couldn't seem to do anything about it. 'If I'm going to be on the record, I want to be sure I'm giving your questions my full attention.' That way, it would be harder for him to sneak in trick questions, or twist her words around later. She'd spent some time, after everything, researching the best way to deal with the media. Of course, when every question was about a sex tape, there was only so much you could do. But she knew more now than she had at nineteen and that knowledge gave her a little confidence, at least.

She could deal with Tom Buckley. As long as she kept her wits sharp.

'Okay. Fair enough.' Tom slipped the phone back into his pocket and Violet's shoulders dropped back to their usual level. If he had any idea why his request had her so rattled—and surely he must—Tom didn't show it. He was a professional, she supposed. 'So, where do we start?'

Violet surveyed the room. 'The desk? I mean, that's probably going to have her most recent stuff on it. And once we've cleared that, at least we have somewhere to work.'

'Sounds like a plan.' Shifting a pile of papers and a red polka dot cardigan from the leather chair on the visitor's side of the desk, Tom grabbed the first stack of files from the edge of the desk and took a seat.

Selecting her own pile, Violet settled into the desk chair and started to read.

'So, is your sister always this messy when she works?' Tom asked, and Violet's hackles instantly rose.

'She's been incredibly busy recently,' Violet said. 'I'm sure that, if she were here, she'd know exactly where everything was, though. She's very efficient.'

'I'm sure she is.' Tom dropped his first file onto the floor. 'That's my "wedding vow renewal" pile, by the way. I guess that must have taken up a lot of her time. You all helped, though?'

'Where we could,' Violet replied. Of course, with Daisy suffering from first trimester woes, and herself relegated to flower arranging, it had mostly been Rose. As usual. 'Mum was pretty burnt out from organising Daisy and Seb's wedding, so she left a lot of it to Rose. I took care of the flowers, though.'

Tom's gaze flicked up to meet hers, faint disbelief marring his expression. 'You arrange flowers?'

'I do.' Violet looked back down at the file in her hands. This, at least, had to be a safe topic. No one expected the Sex Tape Twin to spend her weekends fiddling with oasis and floristry wire in the church hall, right? 'I took over the local church flower committee a few years ago now.'

That, of course, had been a local scandal in its own way—she was too young, too inexperienced, or just had too much of a reputation. But, whatever anyone said, that scandal hadn't made the national press, at least.

'Huh. I always imagined church flower ladies were...' Tom trailed off and Violet raised her eyebrows at him as she waited for him to finish the sentence. 'Married?' he said finally, as if asking her to tell him what to say to get out of the conversation.

Violet huffed a laugh and reached for the next file. 'Married. That's the best you could do?'

'Well, okay, fine. I thought they were older, more boring, greyer and considerably less beautiful than you.'

Despite the warmth filling her cheeks, Violet resisted the urge to say, *You think I'm beautiful?*

He'd just think she was fishing for compliments, anyway.

'As it happens, I'll have you know that floristry is more popular than ever.' She had no idea if that were actually true, but it sounded good. 'Young women across the country are taking courses in flower arranging.' Probably.

'Did you?' Tom asked. 'Take a course, I mean?'

'Not...exactly.' Damn. There went the legitimacy of her words.

'So how on earth did you get to be head of the church flower committee? I've watched enough rural British murder mysteries to know that kind of job is usually enough to kill over.'

'We live in Buckinghamshire, not Midsomer,' Violet pointed out. 'We haven't had a murder in the village in almost seventy years.'

'Still, I bet there was a queue of blue-haired ladies waiting to take over. Weren't they a tad annoyed when you swanned in and stole it from right under their noses?'

Well, yes, of course they had been. But Tom made it sound as if she'd just rocked up and demanded she be given the job because of who her parents were, just like some people she'd known back in the day had demanded access to exclusive nightclubs. And usually been let in, too.

'I'd been trained up by the last head of the committee for five years,' Violet said, trying not to notice the lump that still formed in her throat when she thought about Kathleen. 'When she got sick, she insisted that I take over. She dictated arrangements to me over the phone, made me bring her photos to show her I was doing it right. When she died…I was voted in the day after the funeral.' Kathleen had actually tried to leave her the position in her will, but of course it hadn't been hers to give. So there had to be a ballot of the whole committee—which she'd won by just one vote.

Still, Violet hoped she'd won over the doubters over the last few years. God knew, she'd achieved very little else. Until now. It might be a bit of a jump from flower arranging to concert arranging but, come hell or high water, she'd prove herself here just like she had on the committee.

'But you obviously wanted it.' Tom tilted his head to one side as he studied her. It made Violet want to flinch, so she worked really hard at keeping her muscles still instead. He *wanted* her to flinch, she was sure of it. And she wasn't giving Tom Buckley *anything* he wanted.

'It meant a lot to Kathleen that I take it on,' she said evenly. 'And I get a lot of pleasure from working with flowers.'

He nodded absently, as if taking everything she said as accepted truth. But then he fixed her with his clear green eyes and said, 'So, tell me. How did the daughter of rock royalty go from starring in her very own porno to arranging the Easter flowers?'

CHAPTER SEVEN

VIOLET WENT VERY still for a moment, the fingers clutching her file almost white from tension. Tom sat back and waited. He knew this part. In any usual interview, this was the bit where the subject tried to recall all the advice from the PR guru on how to spin their misdeeds in the best possible light.

And Miss Violet Huntingdon-Cross had clearly had some ambitious PR advice, probably from her twin sister, actually. Keep your head down, take on some charity work, or work in the community. Rehabilitate your character until everyone forgets the part about how they saw you naked on the internet, mid pretty boring sex.

Was this why Rick had pushed for him to help her out with the Benefit Concert? Tom had no doubt that Rick's first concern was publicity for the band, but maybe the relaunch of his eldest daughter as an upstanding member of society was a nice side benefit. Hell, maybe that was why he was doing all this now. With two daughters married, he could happily portray them as settled down and mature—and Violet could ride in on their coat-tails.

Except Tom had seen her lose it in the middle of an airport café. He'd glimpsed the real passionate, wild Violet—and he really wasn't buying the Sunday school teacher act.

'I thought we agreed that this wasn't the time for an interview,' Violet said, her voice stiff and prim.

Tom shrugged. 'It's not. I'm not recording anything. Just asking an idle question.'

'Sure.' Violet's mouth twisted up into a bitter smile. 'I bet we're off the record and everything, right? No, thanks. I know how that works.'

'If I say something is off the record, I mean it.' Tom sat up straighter, bristling a little at the implication. 'Your dad brought me here because he knows my reputation as a fair, honest, accurate reporter. I'm not trying to trick you into anything here, Violet.'

He'd worked too hard at building up that reputation—after the story that made his name—to risk it now, over one blonde wild child. If his mother were still alive, even she'd have to admit that he'd turned it around. He was respectable now, dammit.

Violet met his gaze, her blue eyes wide and vulnerable. She'd probably practised that look in the mirror, too. 'Okay, then,' she said finally, giving him a small nod.

But she didn't answer his question. Instead, she turned back to the file in her hand, giving it her full attention as a little crease started to form between her eyebrows. Tom wanted to ask her what she was reading—until he realised there was a much more pressing question to be answered.

'What did you mean, when you said you "know how that works"?'

Violet shrugged, not looking up. 'You know. Off the record is only valid until someone says something worth breaking the rules for.'

'That's not true.' The defence of his profession was automatic—even as he admitted to himself that for some reporters it was entirely true. The sort of reporter who would hack voicemails or intercept emails didn't care very much about a verbal agreement about 'the record'. Hell, it was barely more than a social convention anyway, a nicety to make interview subjects feel more comfortable.

But he'd stuck by that convention for his entire career, bar one story. And he didn't intend to ever break it again.

'Really?' Violet raised her pale brows at him in disbelief. 'You really believe that all reporters honour the privacy of things said off the record?' She shook her head without waiting for an answer. 'The only way to be safe is to assume that you're on the record at all times. Whatever anyone says.' The way she said it, the conviction she gave the words…this wasn't just some advice from a media expert. This was the mantra Violet lived her life by—or at least it was now.

'When talking to reporters?' Tom asked, wanting her to admit to what he suspected. 'Or when talking to anybody?'

Her gaze slipped away from his. 'Depends on who you're talking to. And whether you trust them not to sell your story to the papers.'

'And who do you trust that much?' Tom had an inkling it would be a very short list.

'Who do you?' Violet threw his own question back at him, and he blinked in surprise.

'Trust me, no one is interested in any story about me.' Just the idea of it made him laugh. He was a reporter, always behind the scenes, shedding light on other people's lives. No one ever needed to examine his—and he really didn't want them to.

'Just suppose they were. Hypothetically.' Violet leant forward and, even with the desk between them, her piercing stare made her feel uncomfortably close. 'Imagine that something happened in your life—you won the lottery, or wrote the next Harry Potter, or married a celebrity, whatever. Suddenly everyone in the world wants to know your secrets. Who would you still tell the truth to?'

No one. The thought felt empty and hollow even as it echoed through his brain. There was no one he trusted with that much of him. No one he'd tell about his hopes and dreams—and no one he'd trust with his failures or regrets.

Oh, he had friends, plenty of them. Enough in every country that he always had someone he could meet for dinner, or go out for drinks with. And he'd had girlfriends, too—also plenty. The fact he didn't have one right now made absolutely no difference to the trusted person question. He hadn't told any of the previous ones any more than he thought they needed to know. His mother had probably been the last person he'd trusted that way, and she was a long time gone. Not to mention the fact that even telling *her* the truth hadn't ended so well.

He wasn't the story. He never was. That was kind of the point of being a reporter.

'Never happen,' he said as breezily as he could. 'My utter unremarkableness is one of the main reasons I've managed to build up a successful career as a music journalist. So, go on, your turn. Who do you trust that much? Rose, I imagine. And Daisy and your parents. Who else?'

'I think that's plenty, don't you?' Violet sat back and picked up her file again. 'After all, it's obviously still four more people than you have,' she added, not looking up.

Tom didn't have an answer to that one, either.

It was going to take them forever to wade through all of Rose's files. Violet bit back a sigh—Tom would only have a sigh-related question waiting for her. Maybe ask her if she was frustrated by her sister's departure or, worse, in love with her new brother-in-law. She had a feeling it was only a matter of time before someone noticed that Rose had married the man who'd been squiring her twin around for the last few years and jumped to the obvious—but erroneous—conclusion that there was a really juicy story there. She'd place money on it being Tom, and before the week was out.

Sneaking a glance at him across the desk, Violet considered the way he'd evaded his own question about who to trust in this world. On the one hand, she'd been surprised to find someone whose list was shorter than her own. But then, given his profession, perhaps that wasn't so surprising. He had to know that everyone had their price, when the story—or tape—was good enough.

Still, she'd have expected him to have *someone.* A trusty sidekick best friend, perhaps. Or a loyal, long-suffering girlfriend. Not everyone was lucky enough to have a built-in best friend from the day they were born, like she and Rose had been, but she'd have thought he'd have found at least one person to trust over the last few decades.

Strangest of all was the feeling she'd got, watching him dodge the question. The odd sensation that in that moment they'd both looked past a mask neither of them usually lifted, and seen something they never intended the other to see. Had he really seen her fear, her mistrust in a way that even her family couldn't quite grasp? Or had she imagined that strangely searching look?

And what about him? Had she truly recognised another person who understood that the truth was a private thing, that who a person was deep down didn't always need to be shared? At the least she knew he didn't trust people any more than she did.

Was he lonely? Or did he like being alone? Did it make it easier for him to do his job, not worrying about friends or family who might be disappointed in him, or disapprove of the stories he chose to tell?

Or had he had someone once and betrayed them for a story, like Nick had done to her?

Shaking her head, Violet looked back down at the file in her hand. She was projecting now. Whatever Tom's history was, and whomever he chose not to share it with, she was pretty sure it had nothing in common with hers.

Violet added the file in her hand to the 'album promo' pile and was just reaching for the next one when her phone buzzed in her back pocket. Standing to fish it out, she checked the name on the screen.

'It's Rose,' she said, her finger hovering over 'answer'. 'I'll go take it in the other room.'

'See if you can find out where she's hidden all the bands' contracts while you're at it,' Tom said. 'And the notes on the riders. They'd be really useful around now.'

Violet nodded and escaped into the sitting room next door to talk to her sister. She really didn't want an unreliable audience when she was talking to one of her four people.

'Hey, where are you?' Violet shut the door carefully behind her, just in case Tom got it into his head to eavesdrop. 'Is it glorious and sunny and beautiful?'

'All of the above,' Rose said with a laugh. 'I have to admit, Will has outdone himself. But you'll have to wait and see the photos when we get back. I want to see who guesses where we've been first.'

'Meanie.' Violet pouted but, since her sister couldn't see her, the effect was rather wasted. 'Are you happy, though?'

'Very,' Rose promised, her tone suddenly serious. 'Really, Vi...I'm so much happier than I thought I could be. Ever.'

Violet's heart ached at the truth in her sister's words. 'I'm so, so happy for you,' she said as sincerely as she could. But even as she spoke, she rubbed the space between her breasts, just over her heart, and wished that she could find such happiness.

'What about you?' Rose asked. 'How are things there?'

That, Violet knew, was her cue to tell her sister light-hearted stories about everything that had happened in the less than twenty-four hours since she'd left. Only problem was, she was struggling to think of any.

'Um, fine. Nothing much to report, really. Mum and Dad stayed up super-late with the guys, and Dad headed off for his shift at the centre today looking half dead, even after a couple of coffees. Mum still hadn't surfaced last time I checked.'

'So, the usual,' Rose summarised.

'Pretty much, yeah.'

'How about Tom? Did you find him okay at the airport?'

'Yeah, eventually.' Violet bit the inside of her cheek. She really, really wanted to point out that Rose had given her the wrong flight times. But if she did she'd have to explain what happened next. She was just trying to think of a way to fudge the subject when Rose spoke again.

'Hel—lo. What happened? Tell me immediately.'

'I don't know what you're talking about,' Violet lied.

'Yes, you do. That was your "I'm mad at you but don't know how to tell you" voice. Twin here, remember?'

'Okay, fine. You gave me the wrong flight times! He ended up calling and demanding to know where I was, so I rushed all the way over to Heathrow in my bridesmaid's dress and heels then humiliated myself in front of everyone in the coffee shop.' Violet finally took a breath and relaxed once the words were out. Not telling Rose stuff took far more energy than just telling her everything.

'Will just forwarded you his email with the flights on,' Rose said mildly. 'If they were wrong, it was his own stupid fault. Now, humiliated yourself how, exactly?'

Maybe it would have been worth holding back that part, though.

'His fault? Fantastic. So it was all over nothing in the end, anyway.' Violet sighed. 'I was so determined to make a good impression—to make him like us so he'd write nice things about us. But after his call and the traffic, I was kind of flustered. And it had been a really, really long day.' A long, loved-up, excruciating sort of day for the one single girl in a family of people madly in love with their spouses.

'Oh, God, what did you do?' Rose asked with the sort of dismayed expectation that came from having been witness to every single one of Violet's screw-ups for the past twenty-seven years.

'He thought I was you!' Violet said. Rose knew how much she hated that. And after the day she'd had…well, some sort of blow-up was inevitable.

'Tell me you didn't berate that poor man in public for not being able to tell apart identical twins he's barely met.'

'Of course not! In fact, I played along for a moment or two, but he figured it out pretty quickly.' Violet swallowed at the memory. She hated this bit, but Rose was going to hate it even more. 'He said he recognised my facial expression. From the video.' No need to say which one.

Silence on the other end. But only while Rose caught her breath, Violet imagined.

'I will fly home right now and beat him up if you want.' Rose swore, quite impressively. Violet recognised a few words they hadn't learnt at boarding school. 'I can't believe I thought he seemed like a good guy! I thought we could trust him with this interview, with Dad. But now… I'll call Dad. Get him to send him back to whichever rock he crawled out from under.'

Warmth filled Violet's chest at her sister's unqualified

support. But part of her couldn't help but feel a little responsible too.

'In fairness, he was severely sleep deprived and overcaffeinated at the time,' she said. 'And he didn't really say it in an offensive manner. Well, as far as you can remind someone of the biggest mistake of their life without meaning to offend them.'

'It wasn't your fault,' Rose said automatically, just as she had every time it had been mentioned for the last eight years. 'You trusted him. And you had no idea he was filming you—let alone that he'd put it out on the internet. Do not blame yourself for the actions of Nefarious Nick.'

'*Anyway,* I don't think Tom meant to cause offence. And I might have overreacted a little bit.'

'Overreacted?' Violet was pretty sure she could *hear* Rose wincing. 'What did you do?'

'Announced to the whole coffee shop that yes, I was the Huntingdon-Cross Sex Tape Twin and if they had any questions they should ask Tom, since he'd clearly watched it plenty of times.'

Rose let out a burst of laughter. '*Really?* Oh, that's brilliant. And the first time I've ever heard you joke about the whole thing.'

'I wasn't joking,' Violet muttered.

'So, did he make it to Huntingdon Hall alive? How are things going? I mean, after that kind of a start I'm assuming he's probably part of the family already.' Apparently, Rose's romantic happiness hadn't dulled her ability for sarcasm.

'Actually, we agreed to start over. He's helping me with the Benefit Concert.'

'You took it on?' Rose asked. 'I kind of hoped you might when Will said you'd agreed to take care of things. But I wasn't sure if you'd...well, feel comfortable doing it. You know, you can always get someone in from the agency we use if you're not happy.'

'It's fine. I said I'd do it and I will.' And hearing how everyone else expected her to pull out every five minutes was only making her more determined that it would be a raging success. 'Although we're having some fun trying to sort through all your papers.'

'Yeah, sorry about the mess. But there's a system, I promise.'

'Care to explain it to me?' Violet asked, settling back on the sofa to take detailed notes as Rose explained the meanings of different file colours, and how the left side of the desk was only ever used for pending stuff. She just hoped she and Tom hadn't already messed up whatever weird system Rose had developed…

CHAPTER EIGHT

TOM STARED AT the blank laptop screen in front of him, then rubbed his eyes. He'd been at Huntingdon Hall for almost a week, sat down for detailed, open interviews with both Rick and Sherry, plus most of the band members. He had hours of audiotape, plus a whole notebook full of scrawled notes. He'd even managed to put together a preliminary article for one of his favourite editors, talking about the exciting opportunity he had, staying at Huntingdon Hall. When it went to print in one of the supplements this weekend, it should build excitement for the Benefit Concert, help with the album promo and even start some buzz for the eventual band biography. It had been a productive, worthwhile week.

So why the hell was he still thinking about Violet Huntingdon-Cross, drowning in paperwork in her sister's study?

She was the only one he wasn't certain he could get to open up, that was all. He had appointments to talk with Daisy, and even her new husband, in a couple of weeks when they came for the benefit, and he felt sure he could collar Rose and the new Mr when they got back from their honeymoon. But Violet...she was right there in the house with him, and yet he couldn't get close. Even when they were in the same room, she made it very clear there was an exclusion zone around her—one he would never enter.

Maybe he'd got too close with their conversation about trust—even if he had come out the worst for it. But that only meant he needed to push a little further.

Tom closed his laptop. He could take a break from writing if it meant getting Violet to open up. After all, her parents were off doing the first of many promos for the Benefit Concert—radio today—her sisters were both busy being married and happy...it was just the two of them there now. They might as well get used to each other's company.

Another thing he had managed over the last week was learning his way around Huntingdon Hall. At least he no longer got lost looking for the kitchen.

Tom knocked on the study door, waiting for Violet to call for him to come in, but she didn't answer.

After a moment, Tom pushed the door open, just enough to peer through the crack.

'Yes, I understand that, Mr Collins. But—' Violet sat at the desk, phone clamped to her ear. Strands of hair were escaping from the clip she'd used to keep it back, and she rubbed her forehead with her free hand. 'And, as I've already told you—' A sigh, as she was presumably cut off again.

Slipping through the open door, Tom took the seat opposite the desk and she glanced up at the movement.

'Who is it?' he whispered.

'Olivia's manager,' she mouthed back. Damn it. Olivia was the hot new American act Rose had booked for the benefit. Tom had interviewed her once or twice before, and each time the star's list of demands had grown. Word in the industry was that no one could wait until her star burned out and she had to start begging *them* for the press. But while the kids were still downloading her music...

Reaching over, Tom stabbed the speakerphone button with his finger, and Mr Collins's diatribe became audible.

'All I'm saying is that I think I need to talk with someone with a little more authority over there. Olivia isn't just some local act, taking part for the exposure. She's the biggest thing in pop music right now, and I don't think that some girl who's only famous for who her parents are and for getting naked on the internet can really appreciate—'

'Mr Collins—' Tom struggled to keep his tone professional as inside him indignation and anger burned brighter '—this is Tom Buckley. We've spoken before, when I've been commissioned to write pieces about Olivia.'

'Tom. Right.' A little unease threaded through Mr Collins's words now he knew he was talking to the press. Tom didn't imagine for a moment that he had *much* power in the world, but the ability to make famous people look ungrateful, stupid or plain mean was always worth something. 'You're covering this concert?'

'I'm helping Miss Huntingdon-Cross organise it this year.' Maybe his words were a little sharp, but Mr Collins deserved a hell of a lot worse. 'All for charity, you know. I've got Olivia's rider right here.' He held out a hand and Violet passed it over. Tom scanned through the pop star's list of demands for her performance and backstage requirements, eyebrows raised. 'She does realise that all the profits from the day go to very worthwhile charities, yes?'

'Well, of course she does,' Mr Collins blustered. 'She's always keen to help those less fortunate than herself.'

'In which case, I'd imagine that she wouldn't want the sixty-seven requests she's made to result in us not being able to meet our giving targets for the year, right? I mean, I'm sure that nobody would ever say that Olivia places more importance on having the appropriately named Diva vodka available backstage than she does on starving children getting a hot meal, but...well, you have to admit, it doesn't look all that good.'

There was a pause on the other end of the line. Tom waited it out. The next move had to be the manager's.

'I'm sure Olivia would be satisfied with a more…easily available vodka,' Mr Collins said eventually.

Tom drew a gleeful line through the words reading 'Three bottles of Diva vodka' on the piece of paper in front of him. 'I'm sure she would too. In fact, why don't you go back to her and see which other items she might be willing to forgo? For the sake of the children.' And her publicity, of course. Tom was under no illusions about that.

'I'll see what I can do.' Mr Collins hung up.

Beaming, Tom handed the rider back to Violet. 'And that is how you deal with ungrateful, self-important, egotistical teenage stars.'

'By threatening to expose them in the press as terrible people?' Violet, for some reason, didn't look quite as pleased with his victory as Tom thought she should.

'By making them aware of the truth of their situation,' he replied. 'They're public figures, and their attitudes and behaviour are noted. Don't you think the world should know that she wanted a bottle of three-thousand-dollar vodka more than she wanted to help the charity she was supposed to be appearing for?'

'No. Yes.' Frustration crossed Violet's face. 'Look, the point is, I didn't need you to save me. I could have dealt with it myself.'

'I'm sure you could.' Something told him this might be the time to tread gently. 'But sometimes these guys react better to the press than to…' Hell, now he was stuck. How to describe her in a way that wouldn't make her fly off the handle?

'Some girl who's only famous for who her parents are and for getting naked on the internet?' Bitterness filled Violet's voice as she quoted Mr Collins.

'Okay, I definitely wasn't going to say *that.*'

'But it's what you were thinking, right?' Violet gave him a sad smile. 'I know how people see me.'

The disappointment on her face made her look more fragile than he'd imagined she could, especially after their explosive first meeting in the airport. This wasn't a woman who revelled in her notoriety, who defended her mistakes and delighted in the press coverage. This wasn't the woman he'd watched—very briefly, before embarrassment got the better of him—in that sex tape.

'Does that happen a lot?' he asked, suddenly furious at the idea that it wasn't just one stupid man belittling Violet, but a whole host of them.

'Mr Collins?' She shrugged. 'Sometimes. I don't... Mostly, I'm not around people like that, so it's fine. If we're at a charity event or something, usually people won't say it to my face. But I hear the snickers and see the smiles, you know? I guess it's the only thing I'm famous for, so it's all anyone wants to talk about.'

'But it's not all that you are.' It surprised him how strongly he believed that—and how ashamed he felt that, when he'd arrived, he'd probably thought the same. What had changed?

'Was this why you didn't want to be in charge of the Benefit Concert?' he asked.

'I do want to do it,' she snapped. 'But...it's why my parents were worried about me doing it, yeah.' Her hands were busy playing with some stress toy she'd found in Rose's drawer when they were sorting the study—a globe that she could stretch and squeeze. After less than a week, it already looked considerably more worn than when they'd discovered it. 'They know I don't enjoy dealing with people so much these days. That was always left to Rose, really.'

These days. Since the sex tape? Tom frowned. Since

then, she'd stopped trusting anyone outside her immediate family, and avoided other people as much as possible.

Huh. Perhaps the stories he'd read when researching Violet Huntingdon-Cross weren't all there was to know. And he was a reporter—he always wanted to get to the truth, the real story.

Standing up, Tom reached across the desk and rescued the poor battered globe from between her fingers. 'Come on.' He took her hand and pulled her to her feet.

'What? Where are we going?' That puzzled frown line between her eyebrows was actually kind of cute, Tom decided.

'Lunch,' he told her. 'Completely off the record. I promise.'

It quickly emerged that Tom had no idea where they could actually go for lunch. 'Hey, you live here,' he said. 'Where's good?'

Rolling her eyes, Violet grabbed her handbag and car keys. 'Come on.'

As she started the engine, and tried to ignore Tom fiddling with the radio, she weighed up her options. There was the Peacock in the village, but that was just across the road from the church and the vicar's favourite afternoon haunt. She could almost guarantee that having lunch there with Tom would mean that the whole flower committee would be talking about her again by Sunday. There was the Three Tuns in the next village over, but Mum and her ladies sometimes took lunch there mid-week, and Violet couldn't remember if it was one of those days. Even if Mum wasn't there, the ladies might be.

So that left the Fox and Hounds, three villages over and with hand-cut chips to die for. Violet felt she could live with that.

'Is there any reason we're crossing county lines to grab a sandwich?' Tom asked as they drove past the turning for the village.

'Hand-cut chips,' Violet replied. It was only a partial lie, at least.

'Fair enough.' Tom settled back into his seat, the radio playing something obscure and jazzy, and folded his hands behind his head.

'So, these questions you want to ask…' It made Violet a little nervous, how relaxed he was. As if he already knew the answers to the things he was going to ask.

'When we get to the pub.' Were his eyes closed? Violet snapped her gaze away from the road ahead just long enough to check. Yep, he was half asleep in her car. Again.

'Okay, but you know I don't believe in off the record, right? I distinctly remember having that conversation.' That too revealing, too intimate conversation. Since then, she'd taken care to keep their interactions to a minimum. When he'd stopped by to see if he could help with the Benefit Concert a few days ago, she'd handed him a call sheet and left him to it. And when he'd been helping her sort the study, it had been easy to just boss him around.

Until today. Violet was under no illusions who was in charge today, even if she was the one holding the steering wheel. And she really didn't like it.

Beside her, Tom sighed, brought his hands down to rest in his lap and opened his eyes. 'Okay, look. This is how this is going to work. We are going to have lunch. Over lunch, we will make friendly conversation. We will probably talk about our families, our friends, our lives. Because that's what people do when they go out for lunch.'

'Not always,' Violet interjected. 'When we have flower committee lunches we mostly talk about other people. In fact, most lunches I've ever been to have been filled with people talking about other people.' Seemed people were always more comfortable gossiping about people they barely knew than about themselves. In fact, they especially seemed to like talking about her, she'd found.

'Fair point,' Tom conceded. 'Okay, then, imagine we're at some sort of internet dating meet-up thing.'

Violet couldn't help but laugh. 'No way.'

'Why not?'

'Because no logical computer programme in the world would ever put us together!' The journalist and the woman who got screwed over—quite literally and in front of millions—by one. Not a natural match.

'You don't know that!' Tom twisted in his seat to grin at her. 'We're both relatively young, relatively attractive...'

Violet tossed her hair over her shoulder, the way her mum did when she was dealing with idiots who didn't know they were idiots. 'Relatively?'

'In your case, relative to the pop stars and supermodels of this world. In mine...relative to everyone else.' Tom shrugged, as if to admit he knew the argument was kind of weak.

Violet raised her eyebrows as she pulled into the car park of the Fox and Hounds.

'Regardless of our relative attractiveness levels, I can assure you that our personality profiles would be very, very different.' Violet switched off the engine.

'Oh, I think we could have stuff in common.'

'How would you know? You don't know the first thing about me, apart from what you've read on the internet.' And watched, of course, although she didn't feel the need to remind him of that.

'Exactly.' Tom flashed her a grin and opened the door. 'And you don't know anything about me.'

'Except that you're a reporter.'

‘That’s my job, not who I am.’ He got out of the car.

‘So who are you then?’ Violet called after him.

‘Come to lunch and find out.’ Tom leant down, rested him arms on the door frame and peered in at her. ‘I’ll do you a deal. For every question you answer of mine, I’ll answer one of yours. Off the record.’

‘I told you, I don’t believe in that.’

‘You might by the end of lunch. Now come on. I’m starving.’

CHAPTER NINE

VIOLET HAD BEEN RIGHT—the hand-cut chips were definitely worth the trip. The conversation, not so much. So far, over a pint of bitter for him and an orange juice for her, they'd discussed the menu, the merits of starters over puddings and the general preference for both, whether a table by the window might be nicer than one by the bar, and if the couple arguing in the car park were ever coming in.

But now, as the waitress retreated after leaving them their meals, he had his chance.

'So, do you want to go first, or shall I?' Tom popped another chip in his mouth while Violet considered her answer. Then, since it seemed to be taking her a while, he ate another. 'That wasn't meant to be such a brainteaser, you know.'

'It's a big decision!' Violet said. 'Like that bit in *The Princess Bride* with the iocane powder. You know… *Are you the sort of person who'd put poison in your glass or my glass?* That bit.' She looked down and selected her own chip, biting it in half.

'How, exactly, is lunch with me like deciding whether to drink poison or not?'

'Not lunch. The question thing,' Violet said. 'I mean, if you ask first, then I'll know the sort of level of questions we're asking, which makes it easier for me to come up with mine. But if I go first, then I can see how good your answers are before deciding how good *my* answers should be. See?'

'Sure.' Or, you know, not at all. 'So, you like movies?' Tom asked, oddly charmed by her uncertainty.

Violet's gaze flew up to meet his. 'Is that your first question? Because I hadn't decided…'

'Okay. Not an official question. Just an idle wondering.' Anything that got her talking was good with him.

'Then, yes. I like movies.' She took a breath. 'So, my turn.'

'You've decided, then?'

Violet nodded. 'I think so.'

'So was that me going first, or did that one not count and this next question is you going first?' He grinned at the frustration that crossed her face.

'Does it matter?'

'Not really, I suppose.' Tom settled back in his chair. 'Go on, then. Ask away.'

'Why did you agree to come and stay at Huntingdon Hall, and work on this book for Dad?'

Was that an easy one, to lull him into a false sense of security? Or did she just have no idea what to ask? Either way, he wasn't going to be so gentle.

'Because it's the chance of a lifetime,' he said with a shrug. Faint disappointment coloured Violet's face, and he realised suddenly that maybe this wasn't an easy question. Maybe she was asking more than he'd first thought. He paused, and considered the real answer. 'The Screaming Lemons were my mum's favourite band; they were the soundtrack to my childhood. So even if this wasn't a great opportunity to really make my name—and hopefully some money—I'd still have wanted to take the job. Your dad, his friends, your family—you're part of modern history. You matter to the collective memory of music lovers everywhere. I don't want that to be lost when we're all dead and gone.'

'The music would live on,' Violet said, her head tipped slightly to one side as she studied him. 'Isn't that enough?'

'In lots of ways, yes. But the Lemons were more than just the music. They're people too—people who mean a lot to their fans, like my mother. And I don't want the truth of who they are to be lost to the stories and anecdotes of people who barely knew them.' Had he even realised why this mattered to him until she'd asked? He didn't think so. Until this moment, he'd thought he was just there to do a job—a fun, fulfilling and hopefully lucrative job, but a job nonetheless. Now it felt more like a vocation.

'So is your mum pleased you're doing it?' Violet asked.

'That's a separate question,' Tom pointed out with a frown. Why had he even mentioned his mother? She was the last thing he wanted to talk about, and he had put the idea in her head. He was normally sharper than this. 'My turn first.'

Violet took a deep breath, as if steeling herself for something deeply unpleasant. 'Go on, then.'

What to ask? Or, rather, what to ask first? He had a lengthy list in his head of things he wanted to know, but where to start? If he went in with something too heavy, she might shy away. But if he started out gentle and they ran out of time, or she called a halt earlier than he'd like, he might never get to the important questions. Tricky.

In the end, he went for something in the middle.

'How do you feel about your twin sister marrying your best friend?'

Violet rolled her eyes and picked up her sandwich with both hands. 'I wondered how long it would take you to get to that.' She took a bite of her sandwich—a stalling tactic,

Tom decided. Something to make her look busy while she considered her answer.

'You promised me the truth,' he reminded her.

Violet swallowed her mouthful. 'I know, I know. Okay, it's a little bit weird, but I'm honestly really happy for them. I thought I was going to have to spend the rest of my life pretending to like Will's fiancées, then celebrating when he inevitably ran off and left them at the altar. This time, I was praying for him to go through with it. They're a good match.'

'So why is it weird?' Tom asked, hoping she wouldn't notice him slipping in the extra question.

Violet tilted her head to the side, considering. 'I guess just because it was never like that with us. Rose is practically my double, but there's a chemistry and a connection between them that just never existed between me and Will. And now it's my turn again.'

She smiled, her gaze catching his, and Tom found himself mesmerised by those bright blue eyes once more. He knew what she meant about the chemistry. He'd met Rose, had a very pleasant lunch and conversation with her. But he'd never found himself wanting to uncover all her secrets, or wanting to reach across and tuck a rogue strand of hair behind her ear. If Rose had told him that no dating agency in the world would set them up, he'd have laughed with her—not stubbornly set out to prove her wrong.

Which was ridiculous. Violet was right—they had nothing in common, no shared history or world. So why was he trying so hard to find a connection between them? Even he wasn't oblivious enough to pretend it was just for a story.

'Go on, then,' he said, breaking away from the look first. 'Ask.'

'I already have. Is your mum pleased you're doing this story?' Violet asked, and Tom's gaze flew away from hers.

'Sorry, only…you mentioned her before—that she was a big fan of Dad's. I just wondered if you were close, I guess.'

'She's dead,' Tom said, wincing at how blunt it came out. 'I mean, she died, about seven years ago now. So, uh, she doesn't know I'm here, but if she did…yeah, I think she'd be pleased. I think she'd have wanted to come too!'

'I'm sorry.' Violet's eyes were wide and sad. 'The way you talked about her, I just assumed… It must have been awful.'

Tom shrugged. 'It was. Still is, in lots of ways. I miss her, of course. And I think about her a lot. But…' Did he want to tell her this? One confidence in the hope of winning a lot more from her in return. 'When she died…we weren't on the best of terms. That's what I regret most. Not having the time to make things right with her before she died.'

He'd expected the sympathy in Violet's eyes, but not the sadness. 'I really am sorry, Tom. But I think she must have known how much you loved her—I can tell just from five minutes speaking with you, and she knew you your whole life.'

'I hope so.' Tom reached for his pint as a distraction. 'My turn. So…' This was it. This was his chance to ask the question he really wanted to know the answer to, while she was still feeling sorry for him. So why didn't he want to ask it, all of a sudden?

He pushed himself to, though. 'The sex tape. Why did you never issue a statement about it? An apology or an explanation?'

'Because it was nobody's damn business,' Violet snapped. 'If they want to watch it, fine, I can't stop them. But I don't have to acknowledge it.'

'Yeah, but a leaked sex tape… There's always talk that the subject might have put it out themselves. For the publicity or whatever. You didn't even deny that.' And *everybody* denied that. That was what made the whole Sex Tape Twin scandal so strange.

Violet looked him straight in the eye, her mouth hard and her jaw tight. 'Since I didn't even know I was being filmed at the time, it seems unlikely that I'd have been able to leak it to the media, doesn't it?'

'You didn't…you honestly didn't know you were being filmed?' Because that made it a whole different story. That…well, that explained a lot about why Violet was so touchy on the subject of trust.

'Of course I didn't! Do you really think I'd let someone film me doing…that?' She shook her head. 'Of course you do. Because you don't know me at all, just like I said. All you know about me is what you've read on the internet, the same as everyone else. Despite the fact you've spent the last week in my home—and apparently learnt nothing at all.'

'I didn't… I just assumed…' His arguments sounded stupid now. Of course Violet wouldn't—this was the woman who trusted no one outside her family. Why would she trust someone to film her being that vulnerable? Except, of course, something had to have happened to make her that wary. And it would make sense for this to be it. 'You looked straight into the camera, Violet. You had to know it was there.'

She blinked at him, shock in those blue eyes. 'I…I did? God, how many times did you watch it, Tom?'

'Not even once all the way through,' he promised. 'But there are stills…'

'Oh, I know. Someone sent a whole pack of them to my parents, along with a note that read "Your daughter is a whore" in bright red lipstick.'

'That's…wow. That's awful.'

'Yeah.' Reaching over, Violet stole his pint and took a sip. Then she sighed. 'Okay, look. I will tell you the story of the sex tape saga. But then that's it for today, yeah? And if you use *any* of it in this damn book of yours—'

'I should. You should want me to,' Tom interrupted. 'The world thinks that you filmed that tape on purpose. Half of them probably think you leaked it yourself. That's all the world knows of you. Don't you want them to know the truth?'

'I just want them all to forget,' Violet whispered, and something in Tom's chest clenched tight at the misery in her voice.

'Tell me what happened,' he said, reaching across the table to take her hand.

Violet looked up, her eyes wide and sad, and said, 'Okay.'

Oh, God, she didn't want to talk about this. Didn't want to admit all over again how stupid she'd been. Stupid, naïve and blind. Or, as Rose put it, nineteen.

'So, after I left boarding school, I took a gap year. I did some work experience at a newspaper because I thought I wanted to study journalism.'

'*You* wanted to become a reporter? You?'

Violet rolled her eyes at the mocking disbelief on Tom's face.

'Yes. I was eighteen then, and a totally different person. And this will go a lot quicker if you don't question everything.' If he interrupted her too much, Violet wasn't sure she could get through to the end of the story at all.

'Sorry. Carry on.' Tom took a big bite of his burger to show he wasn't going to talk any more.

'Okay, so I was working on this paper where no one cared who my parents were—or if they did, it was mostly only to complain about it. I wasn't getting paid, and mostly I fetched coffee, made photocopies and—eventually, once they realised I wasn't an idiot—checked copy and wrote filler pieces from press releases that got emailed in.'

'Sounds familiar,' Tom said through a mouthful of lunch.

'While I was there, I met a guy.'

'Less familiar.'

Violet tried to smile, to acknowledge his attempt to lighten the mood. But just thinking back to those days made her chest hurt. She'd been so young, so carefree. She'd really believed she could do anything she wanted, could be anyone if she just worked at it hard enough.

Finding out she was wrong had almost broken her.

'He was called Nick. He was one of the paper's senior reporters and he kind of took me under his wing. At first I thought it might be because of who my parents were—even then, I was used to people trying to get close to me just so they could get closer to *them.* But Nick didn't seem interested in them. Only me.' He'd made her feel so special—as if her family were the least interesting thing about her. No one had ever managed that before.

Of course, it was all a lie, which might have made it easier.

'What happened?' Tom's expression was already grim, knowing how the story ended. Violet didn't blame him. It wasn't pretty.

'We dated for a bit. He took me places I'd never even thought of going before. I thought…' So, so naïve. 'I thought it was something real. That he loved me as much as I believed I loved him.'

'But he didn't?' There was no pity in Tom's eyes, which she appreciated. The pity was almost worse than the laughter.

'He filmed us in bed together without my knowledge, then put it out on the internet. I believe he also sold some of the photos to the highest bidder first.'

'Bastard.' Violet had never heard quite so much vehemence put into two syllables before.

'The worst thing was…it took me a while to realise what he'd done. I thought it was a fake, or that someone had filmed us without our knowledge…' She swallowed, not wanting to relive the next part. But she'd promised him the truth. 'I went to see him, talking about lawyers and what we could do to get it taken down…and he laughed at me. As did the woman who was in his bed at the time.'

Tom winced at that. 'Jesus. That's…what a piece of work. No wonder you've been hiding out at Huntingdon Hall for the last eight years.'

Violet shrugged. 'It's safe there. I don't have to deal with the press, or the public, or what everyone thinks they know about me, most of the time.'

'So…that's when you stopped trusting people?'

'Do you blame me?' Violet asked.

Tom shook his head. 'No. But one thing I don't understand. Why didn't you let people know the truth? Put out a statement, or sue the scumbag?'

Rose had wanted her to, Violet remembered. Had wanted her to fight back, to fight as dirty as Nick had. She'd wanted to use every connection their parents had to ruin Nick's life the way he'd wrecked hers.

But Violet had said no.

'I didn't want to be that person,' she said, wondering if Tom would understand. Rose had, eventually, but it had taken years. 'I didn't want to drag things out in the papers and on the news. I didn't want to make things all about me. I just wanted it to go away. For people to forget.'

'Except they never did,' Tom said.

Violet stared down at her plate. 'No. They didn't. And it's too late now to change anyone's ideas about me.'

'Maybe not.' Tom leant back in his chair, studying her so intently that it made Violet's skin itch.

'What do you mean?'

Tom shrugged. 'I just wondered if maybe your dad's determination to have me write this book, now, might have something to do with telling the truth about your story, too. Letting the world know what really happened at last.'

Violet shook her head. It wasn't enough. 'Why would they believe it? It's too late now, anyway. It's much harder to change entrenched beliefs than just telling the truth.'

Tom's smile was slow and full of promise. 'Then you clearly haven't read much of my writing. Just wait and see what I can do.'

CHAPTER TEN

'So, WHERE DO you want to start today?' Rick Cross lounged back in his chair in the little sitting room off his studio, looking utterly relaxed. A complete contrast to how his daughter had looked when Tom had asked *her* a few innocent questions over lunch at the start of the week.

Focus, Tom. He had *the* Rick Cross here ready to interview, and he did not have time to be distracted by thoughts of Violet.

'Well, we've covered the basic history of the band—although there are lots of areas I want to dig deeper into later, when we have more time. But since I know you need to head out again in an hour...maybe we should use the time to talk about where The Screaming Lemons are today, and where they're headed next?'

'And the family. Don't forget that,' Rick said. 'I want the story of my family to be told, as much as the band. And it's exciting times around here at the moment.'

'Of course.' Including, presumably, Violet's story. How did she feel about that? he wondered. On the one hand, it would mean everyone knowing the truth—and hadn't he promised her he'd change the minds of the Great British—and American—public with his words? But even if the new press attention was more positive than it had ever been before, it would still put her front and centre again. And leave people talking about her sex life more than ever.

From what he'd learned of Violet, that wasn't going to go down well.

'But let's start with the band,' Tom said. He wanted to talk to Violet some more himself before he started discussing her with her father.

Rick gave him a knowing look. 'Okay. What do you want to know?'

Tom already had every detail of the upcoming tour and album launch, what singles they were planning to release when, who'd written most of which song, and who'd done the cover art—and nothing that he couldn't have got from an informative press release.

He needed to go deeper.

'What issues did you run into writing and recording this album that you maybe haven't had to worry about before?' he asked.

Rick smirked. 'You mean broken hips and playing the guitar with a walking frame now we're all so old?'

'Not necessarily.' Tom gave him an apologetic smile. 'But your last album was five years ago now, and life has to have changed for you all. Two of your daughters have got married, your first grandchild is on the way… Jez got divorced a couple of years ago, right?' Rick nodded. 'And the world—the music scene particularly—has changed too. How did that affect things?'

Leaning back in his chair, Rick brought one ankle up to rest on his opposite knee, obviously belying the need for hip replacements. He was only sixty, if that, Tom thought. There was a lot more music to come from the Lemons yet.

'I think…the music scene changes by the minute. You can't write songs to that. I let the marketing people worry about it, and we just get on with writing the best tunes we can. As for the family stuff… Every year we become more settled, happier in the place we're in. We're fortunate. We're all healthy, living the lives we want to live.' An uncomfortable look crossed his face and Tom knew he couldn't *not* ask any more.

'Except Violet,' he said softly.

'Except my Violet,' Rick confirmed.

Tom put down his notepad on the low table between them, dropping his pen on top of it. His phone was still recording, of course, but he knew he wouldn't use whatever Rick said next. Not officially, anyway.

'Is that one of the reasons you asked me here?'

Rick raised an eyebrow. 'You think you can make Violet happy? Get her to follow her dreams at last?'

'Not that.' Tom shook his head, hoping he wasn't actually blushing in front of a rock legend. As if he'd be so presumptuous as to think he could fix Violet's life. 'I meant…the world never got to hear the true story. Their image of Violet, their beliefs about her—that's a large part of what keeps her hiding away here. It did cross my mind that you might want this book to change that. To let people see the real Violet.'

Rick studied him for a long moment before answering, and Tom fought his impulse to look away. He had a feeling that this moment in time, this answer, would set the tone for every interview that followed. That Rick was judging him and his abilities right now, making a decision about how much to tell him—for this question and every one that came after.

And Tom really, really wanted to be found worthy.

'I think, in the end, that Violet will be the one to show the world what she's really made of. She'll be the one to stand up and say, *You were wrong about me.*' Rick flashed a quick smile. 'But anything you can do to help that along would be appreciated.'

Violet glared at the piece of paper in front of her as the phone in her hand clicked over to voicemail again.

'You've reached Jake Collins, music agent. You know what to do at the beep.'

She hung up. If Olivia's manager hadn't responded to any of the other messages she'd left him in the days since their last phone call, not to mention the emails, then why would this message be any different?

Maybe she should threaten him, like Tom had. Except she was very afraid that Mr Collins would just laugh at her and go right back to ignoring her. Not ideal.

Placing her phone back on the desk, she read through Olivia's contract to appear in the concert again. That, at least, was signed. But since she'd somehow got a clause included that meant it was only valid with the accompanying agreed and signed rider, it wasn't worth the paper it was printed on. The rider was not only unsigned, but nowhere near agreed.

Violet had emailed over a revised version after their last conversation, deleting the request for ridiculously overpriced vodka amongst other things, and leaving in the more reasonable stuff. Since then, she'd heard nothing from Olivia's camp.

A knock on the door roused her from her thoughts and she looked up to see Tom loitering in the doorway. She scowled at him by reflex.

'What did I do to put such a look on your face today?' he asked good-naturedly, dropping to sit in what Violet had somehow come to think of as his chair. 'Since you haven't actually seen me since breakfast, when I think I was mostly inoffensive.'

'Jake Collins isn't answering my calls. Or my emails.'

'Olivia's manager?' Tom shook his head. 'He likes his games, that one.'

'I'd rather figured that out for myself, actually,' Violet snapped. 'And this particular game is down to you, I think.'

'You think he's ignoring you because of what I said to him the other day?' Tom shrugged. 'He still deserved it.'

Which was true, but not particularly helpful. 'I think he's stringing me along, making me fret until the very last moment when he'll show up with both the signed rider and my big name act for the concert.'

'Then why are you worrying?' Tom asked. 'Just ignore his little mind games and get on with everything else.'

He made it sound so easy. 'Because there's always the possibility that he's playing a different game. Olivia's contract is pretty much meaningless without the signed rider and if they pull out at the last minute, once all the concert publicity is done and the programmes printed…'

Tom winced at the implication. 'So what are you going to do?'

And wasn't that the three thousand dollar bottle of vodka question? What did she do? Keep phoning and emailing like a desperate person? The ballsy thing to do would be to cancel Olivia altogether, unless the rider was signed by the end of the day—Violet was sure that was what Rose would do. But Violet didn't have Rose's connections to help her find a suitably starry replacement at the last moment.

Which only left door number three.

'I'm going to go and find Jake Collins and his teenage pop idol and get a signature on this bloody rider, that's what I'm going to do.' Violet wished she felt as confident as she sounded. Turning her laptop so Tom could see, she elaborated. 'Olivia's in the middle of a UK arena tour at the moment. Today's Friday, so she's in…' she ran a finger down the list of tour dates on the screen '…Brighton. So that's where I'm going.'

Tom blinked at her, then a slow smile spread across his face. 'Road trip. Cool. When do we leave?'

'We?' That wasn't the plan at all. 'No we. Just me. I need to do this myself.'

'Hey, I'm not planning on interfering,' Tom said, holding his hands up in a surrender pose. 'I just want to see you take Jake Collins down yourself this time. Off the record, of course.'

'Of course,' Violet echoed with disbelief. As much as, oddly, she found she wouldn't mind Tom's company on the trip, she wasn't sure this was an episode she wanted finding its way into his book.

'Besides, I know the PR staff at the venue. I can probably get us press credentials to get us into the gig in the first place.'

Okay, now that would be useful. She hadn't even thought beyond getting to Brighton to how she'd actually get past security to see the star and her manager.

Decision made, Violet closed the lid of her laptop. 'Better grab your stuff then. If I want to get there before the gig, I need to leave in…' she checked her watch '…twenty minutes.'

Tom grinned and jumped to his feet. 'I'll be ready in fifteen.'

Which was all very well for him. Violet wasn't sure she'd ever be ready for a road trip with Tom Buckley.

CHAPTER ELEVEN

TOM WAS ALREADY leaning against the car when Violet emerged from Huntingdon Hall eighteen minutes later, overnight bag in hand. He hadn't wanted to risk her disappearing without him.

Inviting himself along on her little road trip had been a spur of the moment decision, but he'd decided while packing that it was a good one. From a purely professional standpoint, watching Violet take on Jake Collins could be pure gold for the book—not to mention the fact that a couple of hours trapped in a car together would give him plenty of time to interview her on the way to Brighton. For once, she wouldn't be able to escape his questions.

He was less comfortable with his other reasons for wanting to accompany her. Because he had to admit the truth—to himself, if not to Violet—that when he'd made the decision to join her he hadn't been thinking professionally at all. He'd been thinking about the look on her face when Jake Collins had spoken to her as if she were nothing. He'd been thinking about her plucking up the courage to face him and demand a signature.

He'd been thinking that he didn't want her to have to do it alone. And he wasn't sure he wanted to know why it mattered so much to him that he would be there to protect her.

Shaking his head to clear his rebellious thoughts, Tom grinned at Violet as she drew close. 'Ready?'

'As I'll ever be.' She gave him a less certain smile. 'You know, you really don't have to come. I'll be fine.'

Tom shrugged. 'I know. But I've been in the country for over a week now, and still haven't seen anything but the airport and Huntingdon Hall. I'm ready for a road trip.'

Violet opened the trunk and they both stashed their bags. 'You've been to Britain before, though, right?' she asked as she slid into the driver's seat.

'Loads of times,' Tom admitted. 'But I've never seen any of it with you.'

She opened her mouth as if about to answer, then closed it again, frowning at the steering wheel. 'We should get going, then.'

Tom settled back into the passenger seat as Violet started the engine, turned on the radio and pulled out onto the long driveway. At least he wasn't the only one a little unsettled by their connection.

They travelled mostly in silence, content to listen to the radio, until they reached the motorway—and stationary traffic. Tom's only attempts at conversation—gentle precursors to the questions he actually wanted to ask—had been rebuffed by a sharp, 'I'm trying to concentrate on the road right now,' from Violet. Not that he believed her. He knew a stalling tactic when he heard one.

But as the motionless cars spread out ahead of them as they crested the slip road, he straightened up in his seat and prepared to try again.

'Looks like we might have to catch Olivia after her performance,' he said, as casually as he could.

Violet swore in response, and he hid a grin. Where had a nice girl like her learnt words like that?

'That was off the record, by the way,' she added.

'Of course,' Tom said, as seriously as he could manage.

'Dammit.' Violet thumped a hand against the steering wheel. 'Can you check the traffic reports? See how bad this is likely to be?'

Tom nodded and reached for his phone but, before he could find it, a shrill ringing filled the car.

'That's mine.' Violet nodded towards where her phone sat in a little space below the dashboard. Cars up ahead jerked forward, just enough for her to try and edge the car onto the main motorway. 'Is it Mr Collins?'

Tom fished out the phone and looked. 'It's your mother.'

'Of course.' Violet sighed. 'I'll call her back when we get there.'

'Or I could just…' Tom swiped the screen to answer, and gave Violet an innocent smile in response to her glare. 'Hello, Sherry. Violet's just driving at the moment. Can I help?'

'Tom, great—yes, please. Can you tell her that I just had Frances Littlewood on the phone, asking who Violet is bringing as her plus one for Henry's wedding next weekend? She says one of Henry's ushers is single if she's stuck…'

Sherry sounded harried, which was very unlike her. But then, Henry Littlewood's wedding was the theatre dynasty event of the summer. In fact, he had a feeling that Rick and Sherry were godparents to Henry himself. The Littlewoods had the same sort of money, prestige and power in the acting world as Rick and Sherry had in the music one. It was bound to be quite the event. Quite the *public* event. Just the sort of thing Violet usually avoided, as far as Tom could tell.

He covered the phone with his hand. 'She wants to know who you're taking to Henry Littlewood's wedding next weekend. Otherwise, Frances Littlewood is setting you up with an usher.'

Violet swore again and Tom grinned, glad Sherry couldn't hear.

'Not looking forward to it?' he asked, already pretty sure of the answer.

'Henry's a family friend, and his mother made his fiancée make me one of her bridesmaids too, which she probably hates me for.' Violet sighed. 'I want to go for him, and Mum and Dad will be there, probably Daisy and Seb too… It's just…'

'You don't want to face all the people. And the cameras.'

'Yeah.'

Tom considered. There was a chance Violet might never forgive him for what he was about to do. On the other hand, if he could convince her of the truth—that it was the act of a friend, that he honestly had no ulterior motive for this… maybe it could bring them closer.

Maybe, one day, Violet would learn to trust him.

He lifted the phone to his ear again.

'Sherry, if it's okay with you and Rick, I'm going to accompany Violet. As her date, not a reporter on this occasion!'

'Well,' Sherry said, sounding taken aback, 'that sounds lovely. I'm sure we'll all have a delightful day.'

'Me too.' Although, judging by the shocked glare on Violet's face, only if he lived that long. 'See you later, Sherry.'

Silence reined in the motionless car for a long, long moment.

Then Violet said, 'You are never answering my phone again.'

What was he thinking? Well, actually, Violet was pretty sure she knew exactly what he was thinking—what a perfect way to further his career by sneaking into a society wedding under the guise of being her date. It wasn't as if she hadn't got used to being used for her name and family over the years, but this one really did take the biscuit.

'I meant what I said,' Tom told her, his expression deceptively earnest. 'I'm not going to the wedding as a journalist.'

'No, you said you were going as my date. Aren't you supposed to *ask* a girl before declaring something a date?' Because if he'd asked she could have said no. And she almost certainly would have. Probably.

'Well, it was kind of a spur of the moment decision. Much like this road trip.' He shot her a sideways glance she pretended not to see. 'Is it such a bad idea?'

'Yes!'

'Why?'

'Because...oh, so many reasons. Because you're not my boyfriend; you're the guy who's here to research and write about me and my family. Because you're always, always a reporter, no matter how much you pretend you're taking a day off. Journalists don't do off-duty.'

'Okay, answer me this one question honestly.' Violet stared out of the windscreen at the road as he talked. Because she needed to concentrate on driving, not because she was ignoring him. Really. Even if the car wasn't moving. 'Will the wedding be more or less fun with me there to keep you company?'

Damn him. Violet bit the inside of her cheek to keep from answering. Even with Daisy and her parents there, it would be better with Tom. Because Daisy and Seb would be all loved-up again, and so would Mum and Dad probably, and everyone would start telling stories about their own weddings or engagements or romantic moments... and, for once, she wouldn't have to sit there as sorry single Violet whose heart had been betrayed and broken by the only man she'd ever loved.

'Violet? More or less fun?' Tom pressed.

'More.' The word came out begrudgingly.

'Great! Then it's all settled.' Tom beamed at her and Violet almost missed her chance to move forward two metres.

Settled wasn't the word she'd use at all. In fact, things felt more unsettled than ever to Violet.

'So, how many times will you have been a bridesmaid this year, after this one?' Tom asked.

Violet tried to pretend her cheeks weren't getting warm. 'Three, including Mum and Dad's renewal. And you know what they say…'

'No idea, actually,' Tom said cheerfully.

'Three times the bridesmaid, never the bride,' Violet quoted. 'Of course, this is actually the sixteenth time I've been a bridesmaid, so I think we're long past worrying about that.' Not that that would stop everyone there thinking it, or whispering it behind her back, she was sure.

Tom let out a low whistle. 'Sixteen. That's, wow. A lot.'

'Yeah. Most of them were as kids—you know, family friends or people who just wanted cute, famous twin girls to walk down the aisle with them or to make sure Rick and Sherry were photographed at their wedding. You know how it goes.'

'Yeah, I guess.'

'I've only done it five or six times since I left university. Mostly for friends.' Why was she still talking about this? He couldn't possibly care.

'Still, it's a good job you look so great in bridesmaid dresses,' Tom said with a grin.

No pretending she wasn't blushing this time. But thinking about bridesmaid dresses just made her remember the one she was wearing when she'd met him, and what had followed next.

Still not her finest moment.

'Did you check that traffic report?' she asked, eager for a change of subject.

Tom pulled out his own phone and jabbed at the screen for a while. 'Okay, it looks like this carries on for the next couple of junctions. Then we should be clear.'

Violet sighed. 'So, after the gig it is. There's no way we'll make it before at this rate.' They'd been cutting it close as it was. And by the time the gig was over she was going to be exhausted, even if things went well.

'Want me to see if I can find us rooms at a hotel somewhere near the arena?' Tom asked, as if he'd read her mind. It was kind of disconcerting.

She bit her lip. Did she? It would mean a whole night away with Tom Buckley, plus the drive home tomorrow. He was bound to use that to his advantage, even if she was slightly reassured by his use of the plural 'rooms'. But was that more dangerous than driving home exhausted? No. Of course it wasn't.

She sighed. 'Yeah, I guess so.'

They inched forward another few metres as Tom frowned at his phone screen. Eventually he gave a little cheer of triumph, and tucked his phone away again.

'Got something?'

'Nothing near the arena,' Tom said, 'but I got us two rooms right on the front, in some hotel with an old-fashioned name. I'm not sure I've ever seen the ocean in Britain.'

'It's the sea here,' Violet corrected him. 'And the British seaside is an institution, I suppose. You should see it.'

A broad smile split Tom's face. 'Great! Only thing I

can't figure out is why one of the rooms was half the price of the other.'

Violet could guess. Not all of those old seaside hotels were in the best of repair these days. 'Well, tell you what, you can take that room and find out. Okay?'

Tom's smile didn't even fade an iota. 'Whatever you say, boss.'

Violet turned her attention back to the traffic ahead of her. She had a feeling it was going to be a very long night.

CHAPTER TWELVE

THE CONCERT HAD to be well underway by the time Violet swung her little car into the car park nearest to the arena. Tom had exercised discretion as the better part of valour and avoided asking too many questions for the latter part of the journey, as Violet's expression grew stony and set as the traffic worsened.

He almost pitied Jake Collins, the mood she was in. But only almost.

'You can definitely get us in there, yes?' Violet asked, switching off the engine and lights. At high summer, the sun was still going down but it still felt late.

'It's done.' Tom stretched his legs out of the door, feeling his back pop as he arched it. 'There should be passes waiting for us at the door.' He didn't mention exactly how much favour currency he'd exchanged for that privilege.

Violet stalked off in what he presumed was the direction of the arena and he hurried to catch her up, pausing only briefly to admire the look of her determined walk and her behind in tight blue jeans.

As he'd promised, they were waved through backstage without any noticeable delays. From the amused look one of the security guards gave Violet, Tom had a feeling that she could probably have talked her way in there without him anyway. She had a very famous face, after all. Not to mention the rest of her.

Violet paused for a moment in the empty corridor backstage as they approached the star dressing room. The sound of Olivia's latest hit echoed around the hallways. Tom stood beside her as she leant against the cool painted wall.

'You ready for this?' he asked, his voice low, relying on his close proximity to ensure he was heard.

'No.' She gave him a wobbly smile. 'But I'm going to do it anyway.'

God, you had to admire that kind of spirit. That kind of grit. The woman he'd thought she was when they met wouldn't have been afraid, and the one he'd come to know in his first days at Huntingdon Hall wouldn't have dared. But this Violet—the woman he was beginning to think of as his Violet, without any justification—she was braver than either of those other women he'd thought he knew.

She was magnificent.

'I'll be right here,' Tom promised. 'But you won't need me.'

Her smile firmed up a little at that, and something in his chest grew warmer. Was it his heart? It had been so long he could hardly tell.

Slowly, Tom leant forward to press a kiss against her forehead, but she tilted her head up to look at him and then...well, it was only natural for him to place that kiss on her lips, right?

'Yeah? Well, you tell them not to call me again until we're talking about top billing, okay? My girl headlines or nothing at all.'

The terse voice cut through what Tom thought was pretty much a perfect moment. Violet jerked back, putting unwelcome inches between them, and Tom bit back a growl of frustration.

'Mr Collins,' Violet said, in what Tom recognised as a dangerously sweet voice. Shaking off the kiss fog that had filled his brain, he tried to focus on what was happening in front of him. How much had the agent seen?

Jake Collins blinked, then jabbed at the screen of his smartphone and slipped it into his pocket. 'Miss Huntingdon-Cross. What a…surprise. And Mr Buckley, correct? Now, what can I do for you two lovebirds?'

Damn. That answered the question of whether Jake had noticed them kissing. Violet's cheeks grew a little pink and Tom cursed his lack of impulse control. Couldn't he have waited to kiss the girl *after* she'd taken care of business?

'I won't take more than a moment of your time, Mr Collins,' Violet continued smoothly, ignoring Jake's amused look and raised eyebrows. Tom stayed a few steps away to the side, close enough to see everything, but not so close that Jake Collins would be able to turn things round and try to deal with him instead. This was Violet's rodeo.

'We're actually in the middle of a pretty big gig here right now, in case you haven't noticed.' Jake's gaze flicked over to Tom. 'I realise you may have had other distractions to deal with.'

Again, Violet ignored the innuendo, so Tom resisted the urge to land a punch on the manager's face. Just.

'Trust me, Mr Collins, I'm here on business,' Violet said crisply. 'Olivia hasn't signed the revised rider yet. You may not be aware but the contract for her to appear at the Benefit Concert is void without the signed rider.' Jake's mouth twitched up at that. Of course he was aware. But Violet kept talking. 'Since I couldn't get hold of you by phone or email, I thought the simplest thing would be to come down here in person with the rider.' She pulled a folder out of her bag and handed it over.

Jake didn't even open it. 'Obviously you realise that

Olivia needs to sign this? And she's a little busy right now.' As if to punctuate his statement, Olivia hit the high note of her latest single and the walls around them vibrated with the sound.

'We can wait.' Violet smiled patiently and Tom brought his hand to his mouth to hide his own grin.

With a sigh, Jake flipped open the cover of the folder and glared at the paper inside. 'This isn't what I agreed with your sister.'

'That is the standard rider that every other act appearing in the concert has signed, plus a couple of the more reasonable requests from Olivia's original list,' Violet said. 'If it isn't acceptable to you, or to Olivia, I need you to tell me now. We have just over a week until the concert and if I need to find a replacement I need to do it immediately. I'm sure you understand.'

Tom glanced down at Violet's hands, resting at her sides, and noticed they were trembling, just slightly. Jake wouldn't have noticed, he was sure. No one who wasn't looking, or who didn't know Violet, would. She sounded completely in control of the moment, of the man even.

Only Tom knew she was terrified.

Had she been scared that night at the airport? He hadn't known to look for the signs, then. Had just assumed that she was the cocky, self-assured celebrity kid he was expecting.

Now he knew her better. And cared for her all the more for it.

'You really think you could find an act of the same calibre as Olivia in a week?' Jake shook his head and laughed.

'It's not the calibre I'd be worried about,' Violet shot back. 'The same level of fame may be a problem, but I could call a dozen better acts and have them on the stage in moments.' Tom winced at the sting in her words.

'Of course, the real problem would be the fans,' Jake threw back. 'Because, whatever you think of her talent, Olivia is the one they want to see. I'd like to see you fill that concert without her.'

Violet nodded, her face solemn. 'And I'm sure Olivia would hate to let down her fans. Which is why, if she's not planning to appear, it would be best to know now. So I can put out an official statement apologising to her fans on Olivia's behalf. I'm sure they'll understand when I explain that we were unable to divert enough money from the charity account to satisfy her. Especially when that information comes in a paragraph after a detailed description of all the good causes that money is used to support.' She looked thoughtful for a moment. 'Maybe I'll get Dad to put out the statement. After all, it's his concert, and his charities. We could include a list of all the acts who waived their fee for the concert altogether for comparison. What do you think?'

It was more or less the same threat Jake had made himself, but with more teeth. If Olivia pulled out now, Violet would eviscerate her reputation. Jake didn't want a diva on his books—even if that was what he had. He needed Olivia to appear wholesome and loving and giving, so the kids' mums would let their pre-teens buy her music.

Jake Collins glared at Violet for a long moment before flicking his gaze over to Tom. With a 'What can you do?' smile, Tom shrugged.

'Fine.' Jake snapped the word out as he flicked the folder closed again. 'I'll get her to sign it tonight and courier it to you tomorrow.'

'Perfect.' Violet's smile was sharp, with a hint of teeth. 'And if it's not with me by Monday, I'll issue that press release.' She held out a hand, which Jake took, obviously reluctantly. 'I'm so glad we were able to clear this up. I hope the rest of the tour goes well.'

Jake Collins turned on his heel and stalked away down the corridor without so much as a goodbye. Tom watched him go, aware Violet was doing the same. Then, once he'd disappeared around the corner, Tom let out a long breath.

'You did it,' he said.

'I really, really did.' Violet's eyes were wide, her expression stunned. 'I did it, all by myself.'

Tom grinned. 'So what now?'

The shock faded from Violet's face, replaced by elation. 'Now we celebrate!'

CHAPTER THIRTEEN

THE HOTEL BAR was mostly deserted, but Violet managed to scare up a barman to fetch them some drinks, while Tom carried their bags in from the car and got them checked in. She was glad of the few minutes alone; it gave her a chance to process everything that had happened since they'd arrived in Brighton. And somehow the confrontation with Jake Collins was fading in her memory, compared to the brief, soft, mesmerising kiss she'd shared with Tom beforehand.

But all too soon Tom was back and Violet found herself trying very hard not to stare at his mouth. Why had he kissed her? And was he planning on doing it again?

And if he wasn't, would she?

'Here's to beating that scumbag at his own game.' Tom raised his pint to Violet's glass of wine, and she dutifully chinked them together.

'You don't think I went too far?' Violet asked. After all, it was one thing to stop Jake Collins from trying to ruin her concert, another to behave just as badly to get her own way.

Tom shook his head. 'Trust me, I've seen too far. That was just far enough. Your sister would be proud.'

'Except we're not going to tell her about this, right?' Violet said. 'And it's definitely not going in your book.'

'But it's such a great story!' Tom protested.

'About me,' Violet replied. 'A story about me. And the book is supposed to be about the band, in case you've forgotten.'

'And your family. Your dad has been very specific about that.'

Violet rolled her eyes. 'I have no idea why. Him and Mum, yeah, I get. People want to read about their epic romance. And okay, maybe a tiny section on Daisy marrying into the aristocracy, or looking at all the work Rose has done with the band. But what is there to write about me except a sex scandal I'd much rather no one ever mentioned again?'

'I don't know,' Tom said. 'That's what I've been trying to find out.'

'By asking a thousand questions.'

'That you don't answer.' Tom raised his eyebrows. 'Why is that?'

God, he was unstoppable. 'I answered every question you asked me at lunch the other day. I told you everything you could possibly want to know.'

'About one bad experience with a guy eight years ago, yeah,' Tom said. 'But what about who you are now? What's happened in your life since? Your entire existence can't revolve around one bad sex tape, Violet.'

Except it did, however much it hurt to admit. 'Why does it matter so much to you that you know everything about my life?'

'Because I want to understand you!' Violet glanced around her to make sure no one else had come into the bar and started listening, but Tom obviously didn't care if they had. He was on a roll. 'Violet, you are a mystery to me. And uncovering mysteries is kind of my job.'

'But why do you care?' Violet whispered, knowing she

was really asking *Why did you kiss me?* and wishing she didn't need to know the answer so much. How had he got so cleanly under her skin? She'd only known the man a couple of weeks, but suddenly all she wanted in the world was to hear him say that she mattered to him.

'Because...because you're more than your past. You're...God, Violet, you could be anything you wanted, and you're hiding away at Huntingdon Hall. I want to understand you, to know the truth of you. I want...I want you to trust me.'

Didn't it always come down to that? Violet took a breath. 'I came here today, didn't I?'

'You did,' Tom admitted. 'And why was that? I mean, why did you take on the concert at all if you're not desperate to get back to doing *something* with your life?'

Why had she? It seemed so long ago already that she'd agreed to it. 'I think it was partly to prove a point to you,' she admitted. 'After we met at the airport... It felt like you thought I was nothing more than my parents' name and my own infamous internet appearance. I wanted to prove I was something more, I guess.'

'Good! Because you are. And I'm so damn glad you're starting to see it.' He took a long sip of his pint, then frowned. 'If that was only part of the reason, what was the rest?'

He was sitting too close to her to let her think straight. Violet wished she'd picked one of the other tables, one with two chairs on opposing sides, rather than this booth table with one long semi-circular seat. Here, he could keep sliding round until their legs were nearly touching and she couldn't concentrate on anything else...

A question. He'd asked her a question.

'I guess...I didn't want to let Rose down. Or my parents. And...'

'Yeah?' Another inch closer, and she could feel the length of his thigh against hers, warm and comforting. His arm was almost around her shoulders, resting on the back of the booth behind her, cocooning her, keeping her close and safe. Letting her know she could tell him her secrets.

'I wanted to do…more, I guess. I know you think I've just been hanging around at home, arranging the odd bouquet or something. And maybe that's what I wanted people to think, because then they wouldn't expect too much. I don't know.' She took a breath. This wasn't like her past, this was her life, and she wasn't ashamed of it—actually, she was pretty proud of it.

'I do a lot in our community, besides just the flowers, you know. I help out with pensioners' lunches at the church, I run a counselling group and…Mum and I, we set up a helpline. It's national, and it doesn't have our name on it anywhere. But we take calls from kids and teenagers who just need someone to talk to, or need help escaping from dangerous situations. I do a shift on the phones most days, and I take a lot of calls from teenage girls in their first relationships. Girls who've got in too far too fast and don't know how to get out again. I help them.'

She stopped, aware that Tom's hand was on her shoulder now and he was staring down at her, his eyes full of intensity and feeling she couldn't quite decipher.

'So, anyway. Not just sitting around arranging flowers,' she said. 'But I wanted to do more, and the concert… well, it wasn't about me, so it seemed like a safe way to try and do it.'

Tom shook his head. 'Every time I think I've got you sussed out, you go and surprise the hell out of me again and prove you're more than I could have even imagined.'

Violet stared up at him. 'Yeah?'

'Yeah.' Their gazes locked, and she knew before he dipped his head that he was going to kiss her again. And she wanted it so much…but something made her pull back.

'Wait,' she said, and hoped she wouldn't regret it for the rest of her life.

The woman was trying to kill him. That was all there was to it.

Swallowing hard, Tom backed up. Not too far—not far enough to let her forget that gorgeous chemistry that sizzled between them. Just enough for her to know that he wouldn't push anything until she was ready.

'What's the matter?' he asked, trying to find some rationality. But all he could think about was kissing her again, even when she'd made it very clear she didn't want that.

God, he was an idiot. What was he doing? Hell, what was he thinking? She was a subject. Not even that, the daughter of his subject. A secondary interest, worth about twenty pages in the book.

Not someone he should be falling for.

'I don't know.' Violet stared down at her hands, and Tom wished he could read her mind. 'I just…I'm not sure this is a good idea.'

Tom was. At least his body was damn certain it was the best idea he'd had in years.

'Why not?' he asked, disappointment clenching his chest even as he tried to fight it off. She was wary, he knew that. He just needed to win her over. Talk her round. It was all just words—and he was good at words. It was kind of his job, right?

'Because you're a reporter. Because I don't really do relationships. Because you're working for Dad. A million reasons.'

'None of which sound like you don't feel the same things I do when we're together.' She had to feel it too, right? No way that kind of connection only worked one way. It wasn't possible.

Violet sighed. 'Look, I'm not saying I'm not…that there isn't… Okay, fine. Yes, I'm attracted to you, even when I don't want to be. But that doesn't mean we need to…do anything about it. You're staying with my family, working with my parents… We can't risk screwing all that up.'

'It would be worth it.' He was damn sure of that. Even if she was only making the same arguments that had been buzzing round his head for days.

'Come on, Tom.' Violet's lips twisted up in a half smile. 'This is your big break. Don't tell me you'd be willing to risk that just for a quick tawdry fling with the Sex Tape Twin.'

'Don't say that,' Tom snapped. How could she still say that, after everything she'd just told him? 'That's not who you are. Not any more. And never to me.'

'I was, though. That was the first thing you knew about me. And the first thing I knew about you was that you'd watched that damn video.'

'It was work. I didn't…' God, there was no excuse here that would work, was there? 'You weren't…you to me then. You weren't Violet.'

Violet's smile was sad. 'But that's the point, isn't it? I'm not me to anyone. I'm just that stupid, naïve girl in a sexy video. I'm never just Violet.'

'You are to me now,' Tom promised.

'I hope so.' She looked up at him at last, blue eyes wide. 'But in lots of ways you're still just The Reporter to me. I don't…it's weird to think that I've opened up to you more than anyone since Will, but I still barely know anything about you.'

Well, that he could fix, surely? 'What do you want to know?'

'Everything,' Violet replied. 'But not tonight, I don't think. I need a little time to…process everything. I mean, I did something huge today, facing down Jake Collins. I couldn't have done that before, not even a month ago—I just froze up in front of people like that, knowing they were laughing at me inside. I'm changing, and I like it, and I think…I think a lot of it has to do with you being here. But it's all happening so fast, and I still have so much left to do for the concert, and…'

'You need time. I get that.' Disappointment warred with relief inside Tom. She wanted to know everything—and that meant she wasn't the only one who needed time. He needed to think about this too. To figure out how much he could tell her, how far he could let her in before she reached the stuff that would just make her kick him out completely. 'This wouldn't…this isn't a fling, Violet, not for me. And I don't think it is for you either. So we can take our time.' Even if the restraint it required was physically painful.

He managed a small smile for her, and shifted just a little further back. 'We'll talk soon, yeah? I need to go figure out all my cutest childhood tales and stories of selfless behaviour to win you over with.'

Violet paused with one hand on her handbag and threw him a serious look. 'Those aren't the ones I want to hear, Tom. I want the truth, same as you. It's the only way I can learn to trust you.' She leant over and pressed a kiss to the side of his mouth before grabbing her room key from the table and heading for the lobby.

The truth. Tom stared after her as she disappeared into the elevator, her golden hair flowing behind her.

The truth was the one thing he definitely *couldn't* tell her.

Draining the rest of his drink, Tom grabbed his own room key and prepared to head up. He had a lot of thinking—and writing—to do.

CHAPTER FOURTEEN

VIOLET HAD A horrible feeling that Tom was avoiding her.

They hadn't talked much on the way home from Brighton, mostly because Tom had been passed out in the passenger seat after muttering something about the mini bar, a spring sticking in his back, a broken window and a dripping shower keeping him awake. Violet hadn't slept much better, but since her room had been perfectly comfortable the only excuse she had was her own thoughts.

She did think, as she got back onto the motorway, that if he'd been that uncomfortable he could have always come and slept in her room…

Except she'd made it very clear that was off the cards, at least until she got to know him a little better. She'd been in a relationship before where the guy knew all her innermost thoughts and dreams and it turned out she didn't know him at all, and look how that ended. But while she knew that was a perfectly sensible decision in principle, that hadn't made it any easier to dismiss the thoughts of what might have happened if she'd just let him kiss her again.

In the days since then, he'd been nowhere to be seen. He hadn't even joined them for dinner last night. 'Working hard', her dad had said with a wink. And Violet might have believed it if it wasn't now *Friday* and she'd seen neither hide nor hair of him all week.

Oh, he'd been around, she knew that much. Locked away in the studio with her dad conducting more of the interviews he had, in fairness, travelled thousands of miles to do. She'd even overheard him talking with her mother once or twice—more interviews, she supposed—before she'd stopped listening at doors and got back to what she was supposed to be doing.

At least getting on with the planning for the Benefit Concert had mostly distracted her. With only a week left to go, she was reaching the hectic last few pages of Rose's carefully made lists. Jake Collins had even sent in the signed rider, so she didn't have to follow through on her publicity threats.

Things were good, and dealing with Jake had given her added confidence to get on with her job. She was on top of everything, had spoken with almost everyone involved, or at least their representatives, personally—without a single mention of the words 'sex' and 'tape' in the same sentence. She was making progress.

But, she had to admit, she missed Tom.

'Miss him how, exactly?' Daisy asked when she came over to try on potential wedding outfits the day before Henry Littlewood's wedding. 'I mean, he's right here.'

Violet sighed, and tried not to think that Rose would have understood. Even her twin would probably have struggled with this one, especially since Violet wasn't sure even *she* understood it.

'I guess I'd just got used to having him around.' She grabbed another dress from the pile of maternity eveningwear Daisy had brought with her. 'How about this one?'

Daisy shook her head. 'Lily Taylor wore that one to a gala last month. It's already been photographed, and I don't want to be in any of those "which mum-to-be wore it best?" comparison pieces.'

So why did you bring it? Violet wanted to ask, but didn't. Pregnancy had made Daisy a little touchy.

'And he's still around.' Daisy shifted on the bed, her hand cupped around her growing baby bump. 'He's just a bit busy interviewing Dad and Mum, I suppose. And me.'

'He's interviewed you?' Violet stopped looking through outfits and stared at her sister.

Daisy blinked back blankly. 'Well, yes. He's interviewing all of us, isn't he?'

'Of course. Yeah.' She'd just imagined that he might start with her.

Daisy shifted again to tug on Violet's hand and make her sit on the bed. 'Okay, seriously. What's going on with the two of you? He's coming as your date tomorrow, Mum said the two of you disappeared to Brighton, of all places, last weekend, and now you tell me you haven't seen him all week. I know you'd probably rather tell Rose, but she's not here. So, fess up—what's going on?'

Violet bit her lip. In some ways, it was probably for the best that Rose wasn't there. She'd have sussed out there was something going on by the time Violet and Tom went for that first lunch. As much as she loved her twin, maybe it was better that she didn't have her über-protective identical sister around right now.

And Daisy…Daisy had always been a good listener, when they'd given her something to listen to.

'To be honest, I have no idea.' Violet fell back to lie on the bed, feeling lighter just for saying it. 'He indicated that he has…feelings, I guess. For me.' By kissing her and making her whole world spin.

'And you said?'

'That it was a bad idea.' Which, now, a week later, felt like a fairly epic mistake in its own right.

'Why?' Daisy asked, eyebrows raised in astonishment.

'He's gorgeous, seems nice, Dad adores him, which is always a good sign, and you're obviously a little bit besotted. So what's the problem? He's…oh. He's a reporter.'

Rose would have got there half an hour ago, but in some ways it was more useful to hear the reasons why Violet *should* say yes. Or maybe that was just wishful thinking.

'Actually, for a reporter, he's kind of…un-slimelike.' The admission didn't come easy.

'You really do like him, don't you?'

Violet sighed. Did she? She thought back over the last couple of weeks. Even after their awful first meeting, when really what she'd most wanted to do was strangle him, there'd still been a weird connection when she'd taken his hand. And he truly had been a help with the Benefit Concert. The way he'd spoken to Olivia's manager… He'd stood up for her, been offended on her behalf. And then he'd taken her out for lunch to cheer her up—and interrogate her, of course. Then he'd come all the way to Brighton and stood back and watched her deal with things herself, and knowing he thought she could had given her the confidence she needed to do it.

He understood about not trusting people. And she hoped he'd understood when she'd told him that she needed to know him better to trust *him*. Hoped he realised that just thinking she might eventually be able to trust him was a huge step for her.

Hoped he wasn't actually avoiding her.

'I do,' she admitted. 'I do like him. I just…he's asking all these questions about my life and my family. By the end of this book, he'll be an authority on all things Screaming Lemons and Huntingdon-Cross. I just want to know him as well. Does that make sense?'

'Of course it does!' Daisy stroked a hand down Violet's arm. 'Oh, Vi, I hope he opens up to you. And if he does…

if he gives you what you've asked for…you'll give him a chance, right? I know it's risky—relationships always are—but we all want to see you happy, and if Tom can make you that way…you have to let him try. Okay?'

Violet nodded. Eight years was too long to hide away, anyway. She'd dealt with pop stars, managers, suppliers and even the press covering the concert over the past week. She could deal with one date with a reporter who made her skin tingle. Right?

Saturday morning came almost too fast for Tom. He'd had a plan, a way to convince Violet that he was worth a chance. She wanted to know all about him? Fine. He'd tell her, up to a point. Nobody really needed to know everything about another person, right? She just needed to feel as if she understood where he came from, and that much he could give her.

Except, he realised quickly, he was always better with the written word than the spoken one. So he'd decided to find the time to write it all down, starting in a freezing, leaking hotel room in Brighton and continuing in between interviews and typing up his notes and a rush job on a short article for an editor who'd called and offered him a last minute slot.

Somehow, it wasn't until Saturday morning that he realised that what he'd written was his own obituary.

Tom stared at the words printed in front of him. Perhaps not the most auspicious start to a relationship, but it did give her all the pertinent information. At least all the information he felt able to share. And it was a start, right? A sign that he could give her what she wanted.

And besides, it was too late to change it now.

A quick shower and Tom dressed in his best suit, ran some gunky stuff through his hair to try and make it behave, and hoped he'd be good enough for the Littlewoods. And Violet.

Rick was already in the kitchen pouring the coffee when Tom made it downstairs, and Daisy's husband, Seb, sat at the counter sipping his own mug as he read the paper.

'Ah, our third compatriot,' Rick said, grabbing another mug and filling it to the brim with hot, strong black coffee. Tom took a sip the moment Violet's father handed it over. Somehow, in the last three weeks, he'd actually converted to *liking* his coffee black. 'This, gentlemen, is the part where we wait.'

Tom checked his watch. 'Aren't we supposed to be leaving soon?'

'Theoretically? Yes. But in reality?' Rick shook his head.

'We told them we needed to leave an hour before we actually do,' Seb explained. 'That way, we might actually get out of here on time.'

Taking a seat, Tom tried to imagine Violet taking hours to get ready. For someone who mostly lived in neat jeans and blouses, with her hair clipped back, it seemed unlikely. But, then again, once Sherry got involved...yeah, he could see things taking a while.

Violet, as a bridesmaid, should, by rights, have stayed at the hotel the night before with the rest of the wedding party. But, as she'd pointed out to everyone at dinner earlier in the week, she was only a bridesmaid on the bride's sufferance, so she wouldn't inflict her presence too early. 'There are, like, ten others anyway. No one is going to miss me.' So, instead. she'd arranged to have her hair and make-up done to match everyone else's at the house and would travel down early with the rest of them.

If she ever finished getting ready.

Two cups of coffee later, Violet appeared, dressed in a

pale blue bridesmaid's dress that left her shoulders bare. Her hair had been pinned back from her face and fell in curls at the back, and her wide dark-lashed eyes looked bluer than ever.

'They are coming, honest. Daisy's just changed her mind about which dress to wear. Again.' Violet swished across the room, her skirt floating around her legs, to fetch herself a coffee. Her shoes were silver, Tom realised. And sparkly.

And he was totally staring.

Blinking, he tore his gaze away, just in time to see Rick hide his smirk behind a coffee cup. Fantastic.

'I'll, uh, go see if the cars are here, shall I?' Tom said, heading out to the front of the house before anyone had time to reply. Maybe the fresh air would help clear his head.

Since they weren't expected for another thirty minutes, of course there were no cars. Stepping to one side of the front door, Tom leant against the brick wall.

'Hey.' He opened his eyes and found Violet standing beside him, cup of coffee in hand. 'You okay?'

'I'm fine,' Tom lied. 'No, actually, I'm not. I have something to give to you, and I'm not sure if I should, if it'll help or if it will scare you off for life…'

Violet raised her eyebrows. 'Well, now you have to give it to me. Because the things I'm imagining just *have* to be worse than whatever the reality is.'

Reaching inside his suit pocket, he pulled out the carefully folded sheet of paper.

'Okay, so you said you wanted to know about me. About my life. And so I thought I'd write it down—that's what I've been doing this week, when I wasn't interviewing your family. So…here it is.' He held out the piece of paper and waited for her to take it, half wishing that she wouldn't.

But she did, her wary eyes huge as they met his. Then she unfolded it, looked down and her eyebrows drew down as her brow furrowed.

'This is… Is this your obituary?'

'Kind of.' Tom hunted for a way to explain. 'When I used to work on a local newspaper, one of the things I was in charge of was keeping the obituaries up to date for local celebrities. So that if anything happened, we were ready to run. I have a few on hand for musicians I've written about or interviewed a lot, too, ready for when the time comes. So when I sat down to write about my life…it just kind of came out that way.'

Violet stared at him. 'You really are a journalist all the way to your core, aren't you?'

'Apparently so.' He just wished that wasn't the one thing she didn't want him to be.

'Is the car here yet, darling?' Sherry's voice floated down the stairs and out of the front door. 'We don't want to be late.'

Violet folded the paper again and slipped it into the tiny silver bag she carried. 'I'll read this later,' she promised. 'And then…maybe we can, uh, talk again?'

'I'd like that a lot,' Tom replied. Of course, first they had to get through the Littlewood wedding. Suddenly, he'd never been so unexcited at the prospect of spending a day with the rich and famous.

CHAPTER FIFTEEN

'So, WHAT DO we think?' Daisy asked as they finished up their puddings later that evening. 'Better or worse than my wedding?'

'Our wedding,' Seb put in, around a mouthful of chocolate and pistachio torte. Daisy waved a hand dismissively at him.

'Not a patch on yours, Daze,' Violet assured her sister. 'Was it, Tom? Wait, you weren't there, were you?' Maybe that third glass of champagne had been a bad idea. Bubbles always did go straight to her head.

But there'd been so many people, so many knowing glances. And even with Tom on her arm, she'd needed something else between her and all of them.

'I was not, unfortunately.' Tom smiled across the table at Daisy. 'But, delightful as today has been, I can't imagine it being a patch on a wedding organised by Sherry Huntingdon.'

'A safe bet,' Seb murmured.

Leaning back in her chair, Violet tried to spot the waiters coming round with coffee. Maybe that would help her focus on the special day going on around her.

Because all she'd been able to think about so far was the piece of paper folded up in her clutch bag.

She'd tried to concentrate on smiling as she and the

other bridesmaids walked in front of the beautiful bride down the aisle, and on Henry looking handsomely nervous at the front of the church. And she'd tried to listen to the vicar talking about the importance of love and forgiveness and understanding in a marriage. But really her mind had been buzzing with the knowledge that in her lap she held the history of Tom Buckley. His life and times. His secrets.

And she really, really wanted to know them.

But she wanted the time to savour them, too. To absorb and understand them. And she couldn't exactly sit there and read it at the dining table surrounded by her sister and brother-in-law, and three of Henry's cousins and their wives.

The cousins, fortunately, had wandered off towards the free bar before Daisy had started comparing weddings. But that didn't mean she could just get reading. Did it?

Violet glanced up. Daisy, Seb and Tom were deep in conversation and she didn't seem to be required. Mum and Dad were sitting three tables over, chatting with some old friends. It was entirely possible that no one would notice if she disappeared for ten minutes.

'I'm just going to…' She waved a hand vaguely in the direction of the bathrooms as she stood, but no one seemed bothered.

Pausing in the doorway to the main ballroom, where the wedding breakfast had been served, Violet checked to ensure no one was watching her, then headed in the opposite direction from the bathrooms—towards the gardens.

It was easy enough to find a secluded bench, hidden away behind the walls of the rose garden. If anyone stumbled across her, she could just say she needed a little air. After all, the weather was warm and the five hundred guests had made the ballroom a little stifling. No reason for anybody to suspect anything.

Especially not that she was hiding away to read the obituary of a man still very much alive.

She unfolded the piece of paper, wondering if the fact he'd written it told her more about him than even the words contained could. Only a journalist would think of doing such a thing, which was a permanent worry. But, on the other hand, he'd wanted her to have all the facts, the truth, laid out in a way they were only ever told after death.

This was who he was, how he thought he'd be remembered, everything he felt was important to say about his life. All in two pages—which Violet figured was probably a good page longer than hers would have been. Or a page and a half longer if you omitted the sex tape thing in the interests of good taste.

Yeah. No one was ever going to omit that.

With a deep breath, Violet focused on the words. Even with the dispassionate tone an obituary demanded, she could still hear Tom talking to her with every line.

She lived Tom's childhood in New York, his early career, his estrangement from his mother and his pain at her death, his tours with bands and his relationship history, all in his own words. And by the time she reached the end she almost, almost felt as if he was sitting there beside her.

'So, do you have questions?'

Violet jerked her head up at the sound of Tom's voice, blushing when she found him leaning against the garden wall watching her, one eyebrow raised.

'I probably will have, later.' After all, the plain facts weren't the same as actually *knowing* a person, were they? But after the last few weeks, it was really only the facts that she'd been missing. Swallowing hard, Violet got to her feet. 'But there's something else I want to do first.'

He didn't move as she stepped towards him, and she

understood that this was all on her now. This was her decision. And he would wait and let her make it.

She just hoped it wasn't a mistake.

She stopped, close enough that she could almost feel his breath on her face, but still not touching. Violet looked up into his eyes and saw the control there. He was holding back. So she wouldn't.

Bringing one hand up to rest against his chest, she felt the thump of his heart through his shirt and knew she wanted to be close to that beat for as long as he'd let her. Slowly, she rose up onto her tiptoes, enjoying the fact that he was tall enough that she needed to. And then, without breaking eye contact for a moment, Violet kissed him.

It only took a moment before he responded, and Violet let herself relax into the kiss as his arms came up to hold her close. The celebrity wedding melted away, and all she knew was the feel of his body against hers and the taste of him on her lips. This. This was what she needed. Why had she denied herself this for so long?

And how could it be that kissing Tom somehow tasted like trust?

Eventually, though, she had to pull away. Tom's arms kept her pressed against him, even as she dropped down to her normal height, looking up into his moss-green eyes.

'You liked my obituary, then?' he murmured.

Violet shook her head. 'Not one bit. I'd like it to never be written, please. But…I liked knowing you.'

'Is this where I give you some kind of line about getting to know me even better?' Tom asked, one eyebrow raised.

Violet's laugh bubbled up inside her, as if kissing Tom had released all the joy she'd kept buried deep down. 'I think it probably is, yes.'

'In that case, how long do you think we need to stay at this hootenanny?'

'There's five hundred people here,' Violet pointed out. 'What are the chances of them missing just two?'

'Good point.' And with a warm smile spreading across his face, Tom grabbed Violet's hand and they ran for the waiting car.

'Are you asleep?'

It was many hours later, and Violet's voice was barely more than a whisper. He felt it against his bare skin more than heard it.

'Not quite.' He shifted, pulling her closer against his side. Now he finally had her where he'd dreamt of her being, he wasn't willing to put up with even a centimetre between them. 'You okay?'

'Mmm, fine. More than fine. Kind of awesome, actually.' She smiled sleepily up at him, and he felt a puff of pride at the relaxation and satisfaction he saw in her face. She rubbed her cheek against his chest like a contented kitten.

'Told you this was a good idea,' he murmured into her hair.

Violet laughed, low and warm. 'You did. And you were right.'

Too damn right. This was more than a good idea. This was more than he'd dreamt it could be. He'd known from the first that he was attracted to Violet, but had never really expected to do anything about it. Never imagined he'd want to, not this badly.

But then he'd got to know her. Understand her. Even let her in a bit to understand him. And now look at them.

And she thought it was a good idea, at last.

'I'm glad you think so.'

'Plus, with the…last-minute nature of everything, I'm pretty sure you wouldn't have even had time to set up a video camera.'

It was a joke, he knew, but there was still something brittle behind the words. Something not quite healed. It made him want to wrap her up and keep her safe—not an emotion he was used to feeling about the women he dated. And in this case…he had a feeling that Violet had been kept safe for too long already. She'd had enough of being protected—and she was ready to take care of herself for a change.

Tom sank down a little lower in the bed, turning on his side until they were face to face. 'You know I wouldn't do that, don't you? You have to know that.' She might not need him to protect her, but she did need to trust him. To know he would never, never hurt her.

He wasn't that man any more.

'I do. I do.' Violet inched closer and placed another kiss on his lips. 'I'm just still…adjusting to the idea.'

'I can understand that.' Wrapping his arm around her waist, he pulled her against him. 'I just hope you can learn to trust me.'

'I think I already do.' The hope in Violet's eyes meant he just had to kiss her again.

But when they separated, the hope had faded away and left a question there. 'What is it?' he asked.

'I just wondered…in your obituary, you talked about your mum, how you fell out. And I know you said you hadn't made up when she died. But you never said what you argued about. I guess I just don't understand…what could have been that important that you didn't try to reconcile with her?'

Despite the warmth of the bed and Violet's body, a shiver ran through him and his muscles froze.

'Pride,' he whispered. 'What else? Stupid, pointless pride.'

Violet pressed a kiss against his collarbone. 'Tell me.'

Except he couldn't, could he? Because that one fact, that one omission from his obituary, was the one thing she'd never forgive. Still, he had to tell her something, and the trust in her eyes made him want it to be as close to the truth as he could manage.

'When I was just starting out as a reporter, I worked for a…less reputable paper. The sort that my mom felt was beneath me. It was run by a guy who believed that the ends—a good story—justified any means. And he expected his staff to do whatever they needed to, in order to get the copy.' And slowly, the longer he'd stayed there, the more desensitised he'd become to those methods.

'Mom said I was wasting my talents, that selling my soul for a job wasn't worth it.' He swallowed at the memory of his mother's face, full of righteous fury. 'She told me she'd brought me up better than that, that she didn't want to know a son who could sink to such depths.'

Tom risked a glance at Violet, where she lay silent, her cheek resting against his shoulder. Her eyes were damp and he fought back against the instinct to tell her how much he didn't deserve her pity or her tears.

'What happened next?' she murmured, her hand caressing his arm, a comforting, caring touch.

'I told her she didn't understand journalism, that she'd never get it. That this was what I had to do to build my career. She kicked me out of the house and told me to come back when I'd found my honour again.' He squeezed his eyes shut. 'It didn't take me too long to figure out she was right. But my pride made me stay away too long. I didn't know she was sick, and by the time I found out…it was too late.'

He'd quit the paper long before then, of course, the moment that terrible story broke and he realised what he'd done. But when he'd lost his mother's respect, he'd lost any respect he had for himself too. How could he go back until he'd regained that? And it turned out respect took far longer to earn than to lose.

Violet wrapped her arms tightly around his middle, shifting until she was almost lying on top of him, protecting him from the world. 'I'm so sorry.'

'It was a long time ago.' As if that made a difference to the pain.

'Still. I wish I could make it better.'

Tom curled his body around hers until they were touching skin at as many points as possible. 'Trust me, you are. Just being with you…watching you move past your own history, it helps.'

'Is that all that helps?' Violet raised her head slightly to look at him, and he felt himself warming at the heat in her blue eyes.

'I can think of one or two other things,' he said, and kissed her again.

CHAPTER SIXTEEN

VIOLET STRETCHED OUT against the sheets, listening to Tom's steady breathing beside her. The sun was almost fully up outside; it had to be around six. She'd heard her parents, Daisy and Seb returning hours ago, listened to their giggles and their good-nights. She'd texted Daisy from the car to say that she and Tom were heading home early—she figured she didn't really need to elaborate. Daisy might not be her twin, but she was still her sister. She knew her well enough for this.

What would they all think? Would they be pleased that she was moving on at last, or scared for her because of whom she'd chosen to move on with? Would they understand? And how would it affect the job that Tom was there to do?

'You're thinking too loudly,' Tom murmured, shifting beside her. 'Go back to sleep.'

'I will,' Violet lied. Running her hand down his arm, she listened until Tom's breathing evened out again. He probably wouldn't even remember his strange comment when he woke up.

But he'd remember the rest of the night, she was sure. That, at least, was impossible to forget. She might not be the most experienced of women, but the chemistry between them, the connection she felt when they were skin against skin…Violet had never felt anything like that before.

She stifled a laugh as she remembered Tom's first words to her—about how the frustrated look on her face reminded him of that hideous tape. Maybe Rose had been right when she'd recounted the incident to her. Maybe she really was finally able to laugh about the whole thing.

That had to mean she was moving on. And it was past time.

She glanced across at Tom, one arm thrown above his head as he slept, his dark hair rumpled and his bare chest so tempting. She could just curl back up beside him right now, rest her head on that chest and drift back to sleep until he woke up again for a repeat performance of last night.

The plan had many, many merits.

With one last look and a quiet sigh, Violet slipped out from between the sheets, slowly enough not to wake him. She needed to think, and that was practically impossible while in bed with Tom. The man was just too distracting—even asleep.

Grabbing a pair of leggings and a long T-shirt from a drawer, and, giving silent thanks that they'd made it back to her room, not Tom's, the night before, Violet dressed silently, then crept out of the room. She'd use the bathroom down the hall to freshen up, rather than her own en suite bathroom, then grab some coffee and head to Rose's study. No one was likely to interrupt her there, at least not for a while. After the late night at the wedding, everyone was likely to sleep in, and Tom…well, he was probably a little worn out too.

She couldn't help the smile that spread across her face as she thought about it. One thing she had no doubt about—last night had *definitely* been a good idea.

Now she just had to figure out what happened next.

The study was blissfully cool, quiet and private. Resting her cup of coffee on the corner of the desk, Violet curled up in her desk chair and stared out of the window. There was probably work for the Benefit that she should be doing, but she knew she'd be good for nothing if she didn't sort out last night in her head first.

He'd talked about his mother, and about the dark side of reporting—as if she didn't know it well enough already. But he'd got out, and the guilt he carried from his mother not knowing that before she'd died…Violet knew that was strong enough to keep him honest for ever. Tom would never be the sort of reporter Nick was. He'd told her the truth about everything.

This could have been history repeating itself all over again—but it wasn't. Because Tom wasn't Nick. And, for the first time in a long time, she honestly found herself hopeful and trusting in her future.

The phone on her desk rang, and Violet frowned at it. Who on earth would be calling so early on a Sunday?

'Violet Huntingdon-Cross,' she said, answering it.

'Miss Cross. It's Jake Collins here.' Ah, of course. Only the most offensive manager on her list of acts—who else? Probably looking for a way to get back at her for the rider thing. 'We're in Dublin airport right now, about to fly back across to your own fair green isle for the Benefit Concert.'

Well, that explained the early morning wake-up call. But not why he was actually calling. And wasn't Ireland the fair green isle, anyway? At least he was sounding civil. Almost friendly, in fact. It was enough to make her suspicious.

'Mr Collins,' she said as brightly as she could, 'how can I help you today?'

'It's rather more a case of how we can help you, I think. I appreciate that the news isn't official just yet, but you know how the industry is. There were enough people at that party last night that it really wasn't a surprise.'

What party? The Littlewood wedding? But the only thing that had happened there… Violet bit back a groan. She'd place money on some camera somewhere catching a shot of her and Tom in the garden. But did anyone really care about that? And what on earth did it have to do with Jake Collins, anyway?

'I'm sorry… I don't understand.' And she wasn't sure she wanted him to explain it, either.

'Of course, of course. I totally get that you need to await the official announcement. And, of course, there will need to be the appropriate period of mourning, especially for your family. But no one would want to see the Benefit Concert cancelled, I'm sure. So all I wanted to say was… if your father feels it inappropriate for the Lemons to perform, Olivia would, of course, be more than happy to help out by taking over the headline slot.'

Mourning? Why would they…and what would make them think of cancelling the concert?

'Mr Collins, really—'

'Oh, I know, too soon. Too soon. But it's out there now. I'll call again at a better time and we can talk. So sorry for your loss. Please, pass my condolences on to your parents.'

The line went dead, and Violet stared at it in her hand for a long moment before a truly dreadful thought hit.

Rose and Will.

Violet's heart beat treble time in her chest. She had no idea where they were, what the time was there and she didn't care. Grabbing her mobile with shaking hands, she pressed the speed dial and prayed for Rose to pick up.

'Vi?' Rose's sleepy voice came over the line and Violet's breath burst out of her in relief.

'Oh, thank God. I just had the strangest phone call and

I thought…never mind. You're okay. Everything's okay. Go back to sleep.'

''Kay. Call you later.'

Violet hung up. Whatever Jake Collins's deal was, he was obviously mistaken. Everything was fine. Violet's heart rate started to return to normal and she reached for her coffee cup.

She only managed one sip before the police banged on the door.

'What's going on?' Tom asked as he stumbled into the kitchen, wishing he'd taken the time to go back to his own room and find something other than yesterday's suit to wear. But when he'd woken alone in Violet's bed, heard voices downstairs then spotted the police cars on the driveway…he hadn't really been thinking about his own sartorial elegance.

Violet looked across from the coffee maker, her expression tense. There were lines around her eyes he didn't remember from the night before and they looked puffy and red, as if she was trying really hard not to cry.

Sherry wasn't even trying. How she managed to still look beautiful with tears streaming down her face, Tom had no idea. Rick had one arm around her, his other hand covering his face. Seb held Daisy in the corner, her face hidden against his chest.

And next to the kitchen table stood two police officers and a man in a suit—utterly incongruous in the Huntingdon-Cross kitchen.

'I'm sorry, sir,' the suit said, not sounding at all apologetic. 'I'm Detective Inspector Trivet. And you are?'

'Tom Buckley. I'm here interviewing the family.' Except he'd never felt more like an outsider than at this moment.

'You're press.' The detective's mouth hardened. 'I'm

sorry, but the family has requested no reporters be allowed in at this time.'

Tom's heart sank, a dead weight in his chest. Of course not. Whatever was happening, this was for family only. 'Right. I'll just—'

'No!' Violet said, too loud in the subdued kitchen. 'Tom's a…family friend. Right, Dad?'

Rick looked up just long enough to nod. His craggy face looked ten years older, Tom realised.

'In that case, I'll tell you just what I've told the others,' Trivet said. 'I'm afraid that in the early hours of this morning one of Mr Cross's cars was discovered along the riverbank, halfway between here and London. The man behind the wheel was Jez Whittle.'

The Screaming Lemons' lead guitarist. But, more importantly this morning, Rick's best friend.

'Is he…?' Tom hardly dared ask. The answer was already written on the face of everyone else in the room.

'It appears that he died in the early hours of this morning.'

'From the car crash?' Tom asked, but Violet shook her head.

'Mr Whittle died from a fatal overdose of heroin.' Trivet's expression was solemn as he spoke. 'People at the party he'd attended in London confirmed that he had seemed unstable before he left and had talked about needing "something more" to take the edge off.'

'He'd been clean for years!' Rick's head shot up, his distress clear on his face. 'I mean, twenty years. You don't just fall off the wagon after two decades. Not without talking to someone first. Without talking to *me*.'

Oh, God, he shouldn't be here. This wasn't meant for Tom to witness. He shouldn't be watching Violet go to her parents and wrap her arms around them both, tears on her cheeks. Because if he was here…he had to write about this moment. Had to tell this story.

And how could he, now?

'What happens next?' Seb asked, his voice low and even. He was family now, even if he'd only married in. He could take charge and ask questions and take care of people. While Tom had to just fade into the background and pretend he wasn't intruding on this incredibly private grief.

Except he wanted to. He wanted to take Violet in his arms the way Seb had held Daisy, wanted to make this easier for her, any way he could.

'There'll be an official inquest, of course,' the detective said. 'And we'll need to ask Mr Cross a few questions about the car and such. But mostly, I imagine, you can expect an influx of paparazzi, and soon. I can leave a couple of uniforms here to watch the door, if you want. Might dissuade most of them from trying anything extreme.'

Like climbing in through windows, harassing the family every time they even looked outside. Oh, God, this was going to be hell for Violet.

Seb nodded. 'Thank you. And if that's all…' The Earl had the aristocracy's way with dismissal hints, Tom realised, and almost smiled.

'For now.' Detective Inspector Trivet motioned towards the door with his head and the policemen all filed out, leaving the family alone. With Tom.

'I should…' Leave, he wanted to say. But how could he when Violet's head jerked up, her blue eyes huge and wide in her pale face and her gaze pleading. 'Make more coffee,' he finished. 'Or food. If anyone wants something to… Or something else. Anything you need.'

'Thank you,' Violet whispered. But no one else was listening.

'I don't *understand* it.' Rick crashed his fist down onto

the table, rattling the coffee cups. 'Why didn't he talk to me? Of all the people...he knew! He knew I could help.'

'I set up a drug rehab and addiction counselling centre years ago.' Rick's words from one of many interviews floated through Tom's mind. *'I always felt it was important to pay back, for all the narrow escapes friends have had. I wanted to help.'*

And was this why? Had Rick been thinking about Jez when he'd started that project? That it would have made his friend's life easier—or even that it would be there, ready for him, if he ever needed it again?

Stories of Jez's addictions had appeared in the papers regularly, back in the day. But the band had always closed ranks around him, Tom remembered from his research. And in those days they hadn't had the internet or camera phones to contend with. By the time they'd been invented, Jez had sobered up and flown right.

Until last night.

'He was probably on his way here, Rick.' Sherry sounded exhausted, even though they'd all only been up for an hour or so, Tom guessed. 'He always, always came here when he was in trouble, you know that. He came to us and we fixed it.'

'Except this time he left it too late.' Rick's melancholy tone tore another sob from Daisy, and Violet looked paler than ever. Her hands were shaking, Tom realised. He wanted to go to her. Wanted to know what to say, how to help.

But then the phone rang and Tom realised there was, at least, one thing he could do.

'That'll be the papers,' Sherry said softly.

'Vultures.' Rick glanced up. 'No offence, Tom.'

'None taken,' Tom assured him.

'Do we answer it?' Daisy asked. 'Or just leave it.'

'They won't stop calling,' Seb said.

Tom took a breath. It wasn't his place. He wasn't part of the family.

But he would do this for Violet.

'I'll deal with them,' he said. 'All of them. You just… look after each other, and don't worry about the press, or the photographers, any of it. I'll take care of it all.'

He wasn't quite sure if Violet's expression was grateful or concerned, but it didn't matter. If she didn't trust him completely after this, she never would.

CHAPTER SEVENTEEN

Nothing was ever going to be the same again.

It wasn't the first time Violet had experienced that sort of revelation in her life, but this time it felt impossible to see how her family would ever find their way back to being whole again. The grief they were all experiencing permeated the house, a silence that crept through the hallways and clung to the curtains.

That silence had sent her running for Rose's study, the place she'd spent the most time over the last few weeks. The place she'd hoped would help her take control of her life again, to grow up and start living instead of just hiding.

But hiding was all she wanted to do now.

Uncle Jez. She'd known him since before she was born, had grown up with him always there for birthdays and parties and jam sessions and just when he was craving ice cream. He had free run of the house—especially the kitchen if he felt like making pancakes. He'd treated Dad's collection of cars as his own, had famously said he could never marry because Rick had stolen the only woman worth settling down for, then gone on and married—and divorced—four times. He was wild and free and enormous fun and she would miss him, always, in a corner of her heart that would never heal.

But most of her grief was for her parents. For their loss.

And for the horrible, unexpected proof that everything they'd told her, her whole life, was wrong.

Everything wouldn't be okay if they just stuck together. As long as they had each other, terrible things could still happen. There were some things in this world that family just couldn't fix.

And the worst thing was that she'd known that, really, of course she had. But she'd never actually believed it until this morning.

'Hey.' Tom stuck his head around the door at the same time as he rapped his knuckles lightly across the wood. 'Do you need anything?'

He hadn't asked if she was okay, which she appreciated. In fact, he'd been great at avoiding the stupid, unnecessary comments and questions and just getting on with what needed to be done. He'd gone out and faced the pack of press hyenas outside the house and asked that they respect the family's privacy and grief at this terrible time—not that any of them imagined that they would. Still, it had made it clear that no one intended to make a fool of themselves in front of them, or give them a new sound bite or photo to focus on.

Violet had watched him on the telly, too scared to even risk appearing at a window hiding behind a curtain to see it live. He'd looked in control, but also as if he cared.

As if he was part of the family.

Violet took a breath. 'To be honest, I could do with a hug.'

'That, I can do.' Tom smiled and shut the door behind him. Stepping forward, he opened up his arms and she practically jumped into them. How had it only been a matter of hours since she'd been curled up naked in his arms? And how could so much have changed since then?

'Rose is on her way back,' she murmured after a long

moment of just being held. 'At least she hopes so. She and Will were heading to the airport to see if they could get an earlier flight home when I spoke to them last. Although, since I still have no idea where they are, God only knows how long it will take them. I said I'd go pick them up if they let me know when their flight gets in.'

'I'll come with you,' Tom said. 'Just let me know when.'

'I'd like that.' Violet wondered if he could sense the relief in her voice. She could have sent a car, but it was important to her that Rose saw family when she arrived. But that didn't mean she wouldn't appreciate some backup when the inevitable comments and photos and looks started at the airport.

Strange to think that this time they'd be because of Uncle Jez rather than her own mistakes.

'How's your dad doing?' Tom asked and Violet pulled back from his arms with a sigh. Back to the real world.

'He's…devastated, basically. Mum's with him, though, so that will help. Daisy and Seb are going to stay on for the next week, too. Seb's popped home to get their stuff, and Daisy has gone for a lie down.'

'And you? How are you doing?' That question at last. She supposed even Tom couldn't hold off asking it for ever.

'I'm…angry. At Uncle Jez, at those vultures outside our door—no offence—at the world.' But Violet had learned that just being angry didn't get you anywhere. You had to do something with it or it was just wasted.

She'd spent the last eight years being pointlessly angry, and look where it had got her.

'I realised I'm angry because it's so meaningless,' she said, looking straight into Tom's eyes. 'So I decided to make it mean something.'

Tom blinked. 'Mean something. How, exactly?'

Taking a deep breath, Violet held up the new poster

mock-up she'd spent the morning working on. 'I know the concert's only five days away, and I know this would mean a ridiculous amount of work to pull it off—especially since we don't even know if Dad and the rest of the boys will even want to get on stage. But what do you think? Will you help me?' Violet glanced down at her newly appropriated poster, now proclaiming the Benefit Concert to be wholly in support of addiction support centres across the country. It would be a lot to do. But it would definitely mean something. It would be worth it.

A smile spread across Tom's face, and she knew she had him.

'Just tell me what you need me to do,' he said.

Violet had spent two days working like a woman possessed. Tom watched her in awe, taking every task she gave him and completing it as efficiently as possible, mostly because he wanted to get back to watching her work. If he'd ever thought of her as a spoilt celebrity kid who only wanted the spotlight without having to do anything beyond getting naked to earn it—and, okay, he had—she was proving him wrong by the second.

She amazed him. All day long she made the calls he knew would have terrified her a few weeks ago, speaking to not just people in the business but the media too. She fended off questions about her family and her dad's reaction to Jez's death like a pro, as though they didn't touch her at all. Tom knew they did—knew that when she clung to him in their bed at night she was thinking of all those people out there, desperate to know every detail of her life and use it against her.

He did his best to distract her at those moments.

And she amazed him there, too. When she wasn't being professional Violet, organising the Benefit almost from the ground up again, or family Violet, taking care of her distraught parents and pregnant sister, or even community Violet, fending off well-meaning locals who came with flowers or food. When she could just be his Violet, alone in the dark, letting him see the heart of her. As if Jez's death had torn down the last of her barriers and given him a clear path in to the real Violet.

They'd never really had The Talk—the one about their future and what they both expected out of this relationship, if it even was a relationship. But somehow, Tom felt, they didn't need to. They'd instinctively moved past that, to an understanding that this was what it was—and it was what they both needed right now. They mattered to each other, and the world was easier with each other in it. That was all Tom cared about.

'Okay, so what's left?' Violet asked, tapping her pen against her notepad as she frowned down at her list.

Tom refrained from pointing out that she was the one with the checklist in front of her. Instead, he moved behind her, rubbing her shoulders firmly as he looked down at the lines after lines of her handwriting, all with tiny check boxes beside them.

'Well, most of the stuff that needed printing—the new signs and programmes and stuff—that's all taken care of,' he said, assessing the ticks in the check boxes. 'And we've spoken to every act and sponsor and media partner between us, so they all know the score.'

'And they're all on board,' Violet added, a hint of amazement in her voice. As if she couldn't believe that *she'd* actually talked them all into it.

'With your incredible persuasive sell? Of course they are.' Tom dug his fingers into a particularly tight knot in her back. 'The riders for all the acts are sorted—even Olivia's. And all the technical stuff is more or less unchanged.

The new wristbands and such are en route, ready to hand out to the vendors when they arrive, to sell alongside everything else. What else is there?'

Violet's shoulders stiffened, beyond the power of his fingers to relax them. 'The headline act.'

'Apart from that.' Tom let out a long breath and moved his hands to just rest against Violet's skin, a reminder that he was there, that he wanted to help. 'Have you spoken to your dad yet?'

'Not about this,' Violet said. 'About the funeral arrangements, about the good old days, about the clinic, about what he'd have done to help if Jez had just come to him… But not a word on if The Screaming Lemons are planning to perform at the Benefit Concert.'

'He hasn't spoken to any of the rest of the band either,' Tom confirmed. 'Jonny actually asked *me* yesterday if I knew what was going on.'

'I need to ask him.' Violet put down her pen, obviously not willing to add this action to the list. 'If he wants to play…we need to get in another guitarist. They've worked with some great session musicians over the years…'

'Actually,' Tom said, the word out before he'd even completed the thought, let alone decided if it was a good idea, 'I might know someone. Someone I think your dad would approve of.'

Violet turned in her seat, twisting under his hands until she was almost in his arms. 'Really? Who?'

Tom shook his head. He didn't want to get her hopes up if it didn't work out. 'Look, you talk to your dad first. If he says he wants to go on…I'll make some calls.'

'Okay.' She gave him the sad half smile he'd grown too used to seeing over the past few days. 'Thank you, Tom. For everything you've done this week. I know this wasn't exactly what you came to Huntingdon Hall for.'

'Neither was this.' He dipped his head to press a kiss against her lips. 'And I wouldn't give us up for the world.'

A faint pink blush spread across her cheeks. Was that a step too far? Too close to the 'talking about things' line they weren't crossing? Because if there was one thing Tom had realised over the last couple of days, it was that he *wanted* to talk about things between them. He wanted to put a name on their relationship.

He wanted to tell her he had fallen in love with her.

But now wasn't the time. After the Benefit, once things had calmed down, and once Rose was back and her family was a little more stable again. They had time. He just had to pick the right one.

Love, it turned out, was worth waiting for.

'I mean it, Tom.' Violet's expression turned serious. 'You came here for a tell-all book, the exclusive stories that would make your name. And here you are, in the middle of the biggest story to hit the Lemons in thirty years, and you're spending all your time telling other reporters "no comment". I know it can't be easy for you—you're a born journalist; we both know that. But you haven't chased this story, haven't exposed Dad's grief. And I really, really appreciate that.'

Tom's smile felt fake and forced. A born journalist. Was that what he'd always be to her? And, worse, was it true? 'Of course I wouldn't. I'm here for you right now—and not as a reporter. When your dad is ready to resume our interviews, fine. But for now…let's just focus on the Benefit, yeah?'

Violet nodded. 'Are you still coming with me to the airport to fetch Rose and Will this afternoon?' The honeymooning pair had ended up having to take three separate flights over thirty-six hours to get home just one day earlier than planned, but Rose had insisted on doing it anyway.

'I'll be there,' Tom promised. 'I'll meet you at the front door at two, yeah?'

'Okay.' Violet leant up and pressed a kiss to his mouth. 'And, in the meantime, I need to go talk to Dad.'

'You do.' Neither of them were admitting it, but if the Lemons didn't play at the concert, the Benefit would lose a lot of impact. Yes, people might understand Rick's reluctance to get back on stage so soon after Jez's death, might even respect it. But without Rick Cross on stage, the Huntingdon Hall Benefit would just be another concert. And Violet, Tom knew, wanted this year's Benefit to be much, much more than that. She wanted to use it to change attitudes, to promote the availability of aid—for addicts and their friends and family.

She wanted to make a difference, and Tom honestly believed she might.

Plus, if there was anyone who could talk Rick Cross into anything, it had to be Violet.

'Wish me luck,' Violet said.

'You don't need it,' Tom told her, but he kissed her again for luck anyway. Just in case.

CHAPTER EIGHTEEN

VIOLET JANGLED THE car keys in her hand, barely resisting the urge to tap her foot. Where was he? It was quarter past two and still no sign of Tom. She really had to leave to fetch Rose and Will—unless she wanted them grumpy and fed up after a thirty-six hour flight with no one there to meet them.

'Any sign?' Sherry appeared through the kitchen door.

Violet shook her head. 'You haven't seen him either?'

'Afraid not. I checked the study again, and his room.'

'Did you ask Dad?' Violet asked, then regretted it when Sherry's face turned a little grey. Rick hadn't been in the best mood after Violet's conversation with him that afternoon.

'He's shut himself away in the studio,' Sherry said. 'I thought it best to leave him for now.'

'Yeah, I can understand that.' Guilt knotted in her gut. She shouldn't have pushed him, certainly not so soon. It was just that she was so desperate to make this year's Benefit Concert more of a success than ever. For Uncle Jez.

'Violet…' Her mother paused, and Violet felt the knot in her stomach twist tighter.

'I know what you're going to say, Mum. Don't worry. I'm not going to pester him again.'

But Sherry shook her head. 'It's not that. Sweetheart…

we're so proud of how you've stepped up these past few weeks. Taking over the Benefit, dealing with everything—even Tom being here.' She gave Violet a sly smile. 'Although I suspect that one wasn't quite the hardship you imagined, right?'

'Mum, I—'

'Darling, I think it's marvellous. He's a great guy, and it was past time for you to find something worth coming out of hiding for. No, all I wanted to say was…I'm so proud of what you're doing, turning this Benefit into a fitting memorial for your Uncle Jez, and a way to help others who might not know where to turn. It's important work, and I know how much it took for you to do it.'

Violet's eyes burned. 'Thanks, Mum.'

'So, so proud, darling.' Sherry wrapped her arms around her daughter and squeezed her lightly in a hug. 'And I do think the Lemons should play. I know your father isn't quite there yet, but I think he will be, once some of the fog clears. So…I'll talk to the boys, get them all on board. So we're ready when your dad bursts out of that studio ready to take to the stage, yes?'

'That would be great. Thanks, Mum.' Violet hugged her back, thinking, not for the first time, that the whole family would have been doomed years ago if Sherry hadn't been there to take them in hand.

'Now, you get off and fetch that twin of yours and her husband. We need all the family here right now.' She made a shooing motion with her hands. 'Go on. I'll tell Tom you couldn't wait for him when he shows up. He's probably on a call or something.'

Sherry was probably right, Violet decided as she pulled out of the garage and prepared to drive past the reporters still camped out on their doorstep. Tom wouldn't have left her to do this alone unless something important had come up. And since he'd taken on the job of distracting and dealing with the media and their many, many questions about Uncle Jez and the family, the chances were he was probably yelling 'no comment' down the phone at someone he'd previously considered a friend and colleague right now.

'Violet! Violet!' The calls started the moment her car pulled around to the front of the house and headed for the driveway out to the main road. She checked her windows were completely shut, but it didn't seem to do much for keeping the shouts out.

'How's your dad?' someone called.

'Any news on the car? How did Jez get hold of it?' yelled a less concerned reporter.

'Are Rose and Will coming home?'

'Is it true that Daisy went into premature labour and is now on bed rest?'

Violet had to smile at that one. Daisy was only five months pregnant and, if she was in bed, Violet was pretty sure she was 'seeking solace' in the arms of her rather attractive husband. Really, did they not think if something had happened to the baby they'd have seen the ambulances and medical experts lined up by the dozen? Sherry Huntingdon was taking absolutely no chances with her first grandchild.

The questions followed her as she sped down the driveway and faded away as she hit the open road. It was strange to think that the last time she'd driven this way had been when she'd headed to the airport to collect Tom. So much had changed since then, she barely recognised the frustrated, lonely woman who'd let loose on him in the coffee shop.

In the end, it turned out that Rose and Will's last leg flight had been delayed. Sighing as she checked the arrivals board for updates, Violet spotted a familiar-looking coffee shop and decided that was as good a place as any to try and avoid attention. Picking up a paper on her way, she grabbed a coffee, settled herself into a corner where she could still see the screens with flight information and prepared to wait.

She heard a few murmurs as people spotted her, probably exacerbated by the fact that the front page of the newspaper had a splashy sidebar about Jez's autopsy, but no one approached her directly, which Violet appreciated. In fact, it was possibly the most peace and quiet she'd had in days.

She should have known it wouldn't last.

Violet was halfway through reading an editorial piece about the price of fame, idly making her own comments in the margins with a pencil, when her phone rang. She didn't recognise the number, but that wasn't exactly unusual these days. She had all the main contacts for the Benefit Concert programmed in, but every time someone rang from a different office line or their home phone instead of their mobile, it threw her off.

'Violet Huntingdon-Cross,' she answered, trying to sound both welcoming—in case it was someone from the Benefit—and dismissive—in case it was another reporter who'd got hold of her number—at the same time.

'Hello, sweetpea.' The voice on the other end made her muscles freeze up, her whole body tense. For eight years she'd avoided that voice, and the man it belonged to. Eight years she'd spent trying to pretend he didn't exist—which was almost true. The man she'd thought she loved didn't exist at all. Only this man, who could betray her in a moment for a good story.

'Nick.' She should hang up, switch her phone off and pretend this never happened. Go back to hiding away from him and everything he represented.

Except she wasn't that Violet any more, was she?

'What do you want?' she asked, her tone clipped. She was so far past him now. One little conversation wouldn't kill her.

'The same thing everything wants from you right now,' Nick said. 'An official comment on the recent untimely death of your father's lead guitarist.'

Violet laughed, loud enough to draw attention from the people sitting at the next table. 'Why on earth would you imagine I'd give you that?' Or anything else he wanted, for that matter.

'Maybe for old times' sake?' Nick said. 'But I suppose I should have known better.'

'Too right you should.'

'I mean, you've got another journo on the line these days, haven't you? Stringing you along, just waiting for the story of a lifetime. I bet old Tom couldn't believe his luck.'

'You know Tom?' It wasn't really a question; Nick had always known everyone. Tom might be from the other side of the pond, but that wouldn't mean much. They ran in the same circles. But Nick was wrong if he thought Tom was anything like him.

'Doesn't everybody?' Nick said lightly. 'But I suppose the real question is how well *you* know Tom. I mean, have you ever read through his stories? Not the recent ones, but the early stories. The story that gave him his first big break, for example.'

'I don't know what you're talking about, and I don't want to.' Violet swallowed down the fear that rose up her throat as she remembered Tom talking about the first paper he'd worked for. The one that had caused such a rift between him and his mother. He'd never talked about the stories he wrote for that paper…a fact she'd wilfully ignored in the face of their romance. 'Tom's not like you. And what the hell does it matter to you anyway?'

'Maybe I just couldn't bear to see you taken in so completely all over again.' There was a pause, then Nick laughed. 'Okay, take this call as your reminder. When you figure out what he's really like and you realise that we're all the same, us journos, perhaps you might think *better the devil you know*, yeah? You've got to talk some time. Might as well talk to me as the next man.'

'It will never be you,' Violet bit out. How could he even think that? And what did he think he knew about Tom that would make *Nick* seem like the better option? She couldn't even think about it. 'Goodbye, Nick.'

She ended the call, her heart still racing. He was probably just winding her up. Taking a chance on having an in on the story of the century, or whatever. His editor had probably put him up to it. He couldn't have ever imagined she'd actually talk to him, right?

Which meant he was probably making it up about Tom, too. What the hell did Nick know, anyway? All Tom's stories were music based—even his early ones for that cursed paper were probably album reviews. What could possibly be contentious in that? Maybe he gave the Lemons two stars once or something, but that wasn't enough to drive a wedge between them. The past was the past; it didn't matter now.

Except...Nick had said they were all the same. And Violet knew some of the stories Nick had written. Had starred in a few.

Tom wouldn't write anything like that. Would he?

Violet glanced up at the arrivals screen. Still no word. So she had time to kill. It didn't mean anything.

At least that was what she told herself as she pulled her tablet out of her bag and began a search on Tom's name.

It took less time than she'd imagined. She wasn't exactly an internet geek, but even she could find basic information on a person—and the articles they'd written. And it wasn't exactly hard to figure out which one Nick had been referring to.

There, in amongst all the album reviews, band interviews and concert coverage, dated ten years earlier, was the story that had started Tom Buckley's career. And it made Violet's stomach turn just to read it.

Teenage starlet in nude photo scandal.

The photos had clearly been taken up close and in person, rather than by telephoto lens. Whoever had taken them had got close. Very close. And had been invited there.

Violet remembered the story breaking, remembered how these very photos had been splashed across the news, the papers and the internet within a matter of hours. And the text, the background info...he'd gone out looking for this, Violet could tell. Maybe he'd had a tip-off, maybe he'd played a hunch—whatever. Tom had deliberately and wilfully pursued and exposed this story. And maybe even seduced the actress to do it.

Kristy Callahan had been barely eighteen at the time, Violet remembered. She'd been famous for starring in a wholesome family sitcom. And Tom's story had destroyed her career.

Violet didn't want to know this. But now that she did... she couldn't pretend the story didn't exist. That she didn't know what Tom had done. He hadn't fallen out with his mother over the paper he worked for—it was because of this story. It had to be. He'd been lying to her after all, just at the moment she'd thought she had the truth. That she could trust him.

She glanced up at the screen; Rose and Will's plane had landed at last. She needed to find her sister and her best friend.

And then she needed to go home and find Tom.

CHAPTER NINETEEN

GOD, WHAT A DAY. Tom had been surprised when Rick had called him into his studio, and stunned when he'd insisted on doing an interview right now.

But the material he'd got was golden.

'I think, whenever you lose someone close to you, you always wonder if there was something more you could have done. Some small thing that would have kept them with you.' Rick shook his head, staring down at his hands. 'With Jez…knowing that I really *could* have done more—that I could have saved him if he'd let me, if he'd just called. That's going to be hard to live with. As is the guilt. Wondering if I should have seen the signs sooner, should have taken more precautions.'

Tom swallowed before asking his next question, reminding himself that today Rick was a subject, not a friend, not the father of the woman he was in love with. That he was here to do a job—one Rick had hired him for. That meant not shying away from the hard questions.

'Do you think…were there signs? Ones that you missed?'

Rick sighed. 'Probably. But, then again, maybe not. When an addiction takes hold…sometimes it can be a slow build towards cracking again, but more often it can just be one moment, one instant that flips you from recovering to addict again. There's such a thin line…and sometimes Jez liked to walk it. To put himself in the way of temptation.' He shook his head again. 'I don't know. If he wanted to hide it from me, he knew how. And with everything that's been going on here the last few months…maybe I wasn't paying the attention that I should have been.'

Guilt was etched in Rick's craggy face, whatever his words. Tom knew that guilt. That was the sort that never went away, the type you could never make up for once that moment had passed, the opportunity had been missed.

Rick Cross would blame himself for his best friend's death for the rest of his life, whether there was anything he could have done to prevent it or not. Facts didn't matter here, only love.

'Dad?' The door to the studio creaked open and Violet appeared through it. 'Rose and Will are here. And…have you seen…?' She trailed off as she caught sight of him. Tom gave her an apologetic smile, hoping she wasn't too mad about him missing the airport run. He'd planned to talk to her about it, but Rick had been very insistent that the interview was happening now or not at all.

'They're here?' Rick wiped his cheeks with the back of his hands and jumped to his feet. 'Sorry, Tom. We'll do this later, yeah?'

But Violet wasn't looking at her dad. She was still staring at Tom. And he had a horrible feeling that this might just have been his last interview with Rick Cross.

'I'm sorry I couldn't come to the airport with you,' Tom said as Rick shut the door behind him. 'Was it okay?'

'What were you talking to Dad about just then?' Violet's tone was clipped and her gaze sharp. 'Never mind; I'd rather hear it anyway.' She held out a hand for his phone and, with a sense of foreboding, Tom handed it over.

'He asked me to come in here,' he said as she fiddled

with the settings. 'He wanted to talk about some things with me now, while they were still fresh. He said you'd asked him about going on stage for the concert and he wasn't sure. He still needed to work some things out. He thought doing the interview might help.'

He sounded as if he was making excuses, Tom knew, when he had nothing to excuse. He'd been doing his job—and trying to help Rick at the same time. And Violet, for that matter, if it helped him get back on stage for the Benefit.

She had absolutely no reason to be mad at him, and yet he was pretty damn sure she was.

Violet pressed play and Rick's voice filled the room, cracked and broken and distraught.

'I think, whenever you lose someone close to you, you always wonder if there was something more you could have done. Some small thing that would have kept them with you. With Jez...knowing that I really could have done more—that I could have saved him, if he'd let me, if he'd just called. That's going to be hard to live with. As is the guilt. Wondering if I should have seen the signs sooner, should have taken more precautions.'

Violet jabbed a finger at the phone and the voice stopped.

'This is why you came, isn't it?' she said, her voice too even, too calm. 'I think I forgot that, with...everything that happened between us. But you were only ever here to do a job, weren't you? To find out all the dirty little secrets in the closets of my family and friends and put them on display for the world to see. Uncle Jez said—' She broke off, and Tom could see her hands trembling as she held his phone. He wanted to go to her so much it burned. 'He told my dad to find a better closet to hide those skeletons in. But in the end, he was the biggest story you could have hoped for, wasn't he? You must have been so frustrated to miss all the drama of Daisy's wedding, and then Rose's too. But at least there was still one sister here for you to get close to and seduce. And then Uncle Jez overdosed in Dad's car and you realised you had the story of the century right here. An interview with a grief-stricken Rick Cross. All you had to do was make sure none of the other journalists got to him first.' She gulped back a sob, and the sound broke his heart. 'And to think I thought you were doing *us* a favour, turning them all away.'

'Violet, no. You're wrong.' She had to be wrong. None of this had been planned—least of all the part where he fell for her. 'I told you. I'm not that kind of journalist.' He just had to reason with her. She was upset, and that was understandable, but she'd come round once she calmed down and saw the truth. That was all. He just had to be patient and not lose his temper and everything would be fine. 'Your dad asked me to come here; you know that. And he asked for the interview today.' He stepped closer, reaching out for her, but she flinched away. 'And I know you've had bad experiences before so I understand why you might be a bit sensitive—'

'A bit *sensitive?'*

Tom winced. 'Bad choice of words. I mean, I can see why you might worry about these things. But you don't need to. I'm not like your ex. I'm one of the good guys.'

'Yeah?' Violet's expression tightened. 'And is that what you told Kristy Callahan?'

The bottom dropped out of Tom's lungs, leaving him fighting to suck in the air he needed to respond. Just the sound of her name sent the guilt crashing in waves over his shoulders and, in that moment, he knew just how Rick felt. Worse, because Rick hadn't actually done anything wrong. Whereas he had known exactly what he was doing and had done it anyway.

God, Violet was right. He was every bit as bad as her ex; he just hid it better.

'How did you…? Never mind.' It didn't matter now, anyway. She knew, and that was enough. 'I can explain. Will you listen to me?'

Violet barked a laugh, harsh and uncompromising. 'Listen to you? I don't even need to, Tom. I know exactly what you're going to say. That she knew what she was doing. She was a celebrity; she knew the score, and the risks. That it was different then—that she meant nothing to you. That *I'm* different…we're different. If you're really desperate, you'll probably trot out the love line. How being with me has changed you, that now you love me you could never do something like that again.'

The vitriol and bitterness in her words was sharp enough to cut, and the worst part was that she was right. He'd tell her anything to win her back right now. And she'd never believe it was because he truly did love her.

She'd never believe anything he ever said again.

But he still had to try.

'It was a mistake. I was just starting out and the paper I worked for… I didn't take those photos; you have to believe that much. I wouldn't do that.'

'No, you'd just syndicate them in papers and news outlets around the world.' Her mouth tightened again. 'This was the real reason you fell out with your mother, isn't it? This was what she couldn't forgive.'

'Yes. It was. But…it wasn't like you think.' He had to find some way to make her understand. She might never trust him again, and his chances of getting her to fall in love with him were non-existent now. He'd thought he had time, and now he was scrambling just to make her believe he wasn't the biggest scumbag on the planet.

Which, given some of his past actions, was a lot harder than he'd like.

'Really, Tom? You're going to try and tell me what it was like?' She gave him a mocking half smile. 'Trust me, I know. I lived it, after all.'

No. He wouldn't let her think that he was just like her ex. He'd made a mistake, sure, but he hadn't planned it. Hadn't deliberately set out to destroy that girl. And she had to know that.

'It's not the same. Violet, you have to listen to me—'

'No! I don't! Not any more. I listened to you, right from that first night. And I should have known better. I *knew* what you were, and I *knew* how this would end. I should never have let you in, never let you close.' She shook her head sadly. 'You said it the night we met. I was never anything more than the Sex Tape Twin to you. Someone you could use to get what you wanted because I didn't matter at all. I'm just a punchline, right? Just a grainy video on the internet for late night comedians to use to get a cheap laugh, even all these years later.'

How could she think that? After everything they'd shared, after the way they'd been together?

'You know the worst part?' Violet asked. 'I actually trusted you. All that talk about never trusting anyone outside my family and I just let you in. Because you were nice to me.' She laughed, low and bitter. 'How desperate must I have been? God, you must have thought you had it made.'

Anger rolled through his body, working its way up through his chest and finding its way out of his mouth before he could even think to censor his words.

'You talk about trust? If you trusted me one iota you'd listen to me. You'd let me explain. You'd trust me enough not to jump to the worst conclusion at the first sign of trouble.' Violet stepped back at the force of his words, and he wanted to feel bad about that but he couldn't find it in himself. 'How did you even find out about that story? Did you go hunting for a reason to put between us? Or did someone tip you off?' The faint splash of pink that coloured her cheeks told him that he'd hit the mark. 'Who was it? Rose? Or another reporter?' The obvious truth slammed into him and he almost laughed at the ridiculousness of it. 'It was him, wasn't it? After everything he did to you, you still trust his word over mine.'

'I trust facts!' Violet shot back. 'How I found out doesn't matter—except that it wasn't from you. If you want my trust, you have to give me the truth.'

'How could I tell you this?' Tom asked. 'Violet, you've been hiding away here so long, so scared of what people might think or say, you don't even know what trust looks like any more. You wouldn't even talk to me about whether we were in a relationship! I was falling madly in love with you and I couldn't even say the words in case I spooked you. In case you jumped to exactly the conclusions you ran to today.'

'The *right* conclusions,' Violet countered, conveniently ignoring all his other points.

'No.' The anger faded, as fast as it had come, and all Tom was left with was that cold, hard certainty. 'You're wrong about me. I made a mistake ten years ago. But since I've come here the only mistake I've made was believing that you could move past *your* mistakes, your history, and find a future with me.'

Violet stared at him, her eyes wide, and for just a moment he thought she might actually listen to his side of the story. Then she held out his phone and her thumb grazed the play button again.

'Do you think...were there signs? Ones that you missed?'

His own voice, pressing Rick for more answers, a deeper admission of guilt.

Violet's face turned stony at the sound.

Rick's heavy sigh echoed around the studio.

'Probably. But then again, maybe not. When an addiction takes hold...sometimes it can be a slow build towards cracking again, but more often it can just be one moment, one instant that flips you from recovery to addict again. There's such a thin line...and sometimes Jez liked to walk it. To put himself in the way of temptation.'

She pressed 'stop' again and dropped the phone to the table as if it were poisoned.

'I'm not ignoring the signs,' she said, each word like a bullet. 'And I'm not staying anywhere near temptation. I want you to leave. Today.'

'Your father—' He couldn't go. Never mind the story of a lifetime; if he left her now Tom knew Violet would never let him back in, no matter how fast he talked.

'Will understand when I explain exactly what you've done.' Her eyes were cold, her arms folded across her chest like a shield. 'You're just a reporter. I'm family. Trust me on this. I know which one he's going to choose.'

So did Tom. And he knew when he was beaten.

He gave a slight nod and reached for his phone. 'I'll pack now and be gone within the hour.'

He'd gambled everything on this being more than a story. Time to admit he'd lost.

'Goodbye, Violet.'

CHAPTER TWENTY

VIOLET STOOD SHAKING in the middle of the studio for long minutes after Tom left. She needed to move, needed to talk to Rose, needed to explain to her father what she'd done. But how could she when she felt as if her heart, along with some other essential internal organs, had been ripped out?

She'd known, from the moment she saw that story with his name on it, exactly how the day would go. Had known she'd be standing here alone again at the end of it. Seeing Tom abuse her father's trust and exploit his grief for a story had only made it easier.

She'd made the right decision. She'd got out before Tom could tear her life apart again.

So why did she feel so broken all the same?

'Violet, honey?' When had her dad come in? How had she missed that? 'Where's Tom? Your mum said she just saw him walking out the front with a suitcase.'

'I told him to leave.' The words came out as barely more than a whisper. Would Dad be mad? He'd invited Tom here, after all. He was his guest—his employee, really. It hadn't been her place to send him away.

But what else could she do?

His expression cautious, Rick put his arm around her and led her over to the sofa, away from the chairs he and Tom had been sitting in when she'd entered the room. How long ago was that now, anyway? Time seemed strange. Confused.

'What happened, honey?' he asked, sitting beside her. 'Tell your old dad.'

Violet frowned, trying to find the right words to explain. In the end, what came out was, 'Did you really ask him to interview you about Jez today?'

'Why, yeah. I did.' Rick's eyebrows lifted with surprise. 'Is that what all this is about? Vi, honey, it was my choice. When you asked me earlier about going on stage this weekend…I wasn't sure what I wanted to do. I figured talking it out some might help. And Tom, well, he's a good guy, right? And since all this will probably end up in the book eventually anyway, I wanted to get it down—how raw it feels right now. In case it helps anyone else going through the same thing.'

In case it helped someone else. Sometimes Violet wondered if her parents thought too much about that and not enough about themselves. But that was who they were and she loved them for it, all the same.

'Are you sure it was a good idea?' she asked. 'I mean, everyone wants that interview, and you don't know what Tom is going to do with it now he's—' She broke off with a sob before she could reach the word *gone*.

Rick tugged her closer and she buried her face in his shoulder. 'Do you want me to get your mum? Or your sisters?'

Violet shook her head against his top. 'No. I just…I just need a few minutes.' A few minutes to let the misery out. To let go of all the hope she'd clung to over the last week or so. The chance that her future might be different to her past.

Uncle Jez had probably had that hope too, and look where it had got him.

That thought set off another wave of tears, and Violet didn't try to fight them. She might be all grown up these days, but sometimes a girl still needed her daddy's shoulder to cry on.

Eventually, though, the sobs faded and her tears dried and she knew her dad was going to want some answers.

'You sent him away,' Rick said. Not a question, not even a judgement. Just an opening, to show he was listening if she wanted to explain.

'I found something out about him,' Violet replied, unsure how much she really wanted him to know. Except this was her dad. He'd been there through everything. He'd understand, right? He'd want his little girl safe and happy. 'I know you thought he was a trustworthy journalist, I know that's why you picked him to write your book. But Dad, he wrote a story once. A story that destroyed a girl's life—just like Nick destroyed mine.'

Rick stilled, his arms securely tucked around her. 'You're sure?'

'Very. He admitted it.' Well, sort of. 'He claimed it wasn't the same but then he would, wouldn't he?'

Rick sighed, deep and heartfelt. 'Then I understand why you did what you did. But Violet, I need you to remember something very important, okay?' He pulled back to stare into her eyes, and Violet gave a small nod. 'Your life wasn't destroyed. Remember that.'

Shame filled Violet's chest. Here she was complaining when Uncle Jez's life was gone for ever. And she'd give anything for him to be caught up in a sex scandal right now, even if it meant the papers dragging up her own sordid story all over again.

'I know. Compared to Uncle Jez—'

'That's not what I mean,' Rick said with a sharp shake of the head. 'Think about it, Violet. You still have your home, your family. They took your confidence, and I'll never forgive them for that. But you're still you. You're still my daughter. And you are still loved.'

Warmth filled her, from the heart outwards. 'I know. And I'm so lucky to have you all. But it felt like…they made me someone I wasn't. So they took away who I really am.'

'But they can't.' Rick tapped her on the forehead with one finger. 'She's still in there. And it looked to me like Tom was helping you remember who she is.'

'I thought so too.' Until she'd found out the truth.

There was a pause, and when Violet looked up she saw her dad had on his thoughtful face. The one that always made her mother nervous.

'How did you find out about it? The story he wrote, I mean?'

Violet grimaced. 'Nick called. Told me I should look into his earlier stories.'

'Nick?' Rick's eyebrows launched upwards. '*The* Nick? And you *listened* to him?'

'I hung up on him,' Violet said. 'But…I was curious.'

'As ever.' Rick sighed. 'Did you talk to Tom about it before you threw him out?'

'A bit. I think he wanted to say more,' she admitted.

'Maybe you should listen.' Rick threw up his hands in pre-emptive defence. 'I'm not standing up for the guy—you get to make your own choices about him, and if you tell me he's not someone we should trust then I'll can the whole book idea altogether. He can publish what he has in interviews, but there's not even enough for a novella there. But Vi, if he matters to you—and I think he does—then you have to hear him out. Don't let someone else's version of who he is make your mind up for you.'

Violet nodded, and Rick bent over to kiss her on the

top of the head before moving towards the door. 'Listen to your old dad, yeah? He's been around awhile and sometimes, just sometimes, he knows what he's talking about.'

'I will,' Violet promised. But she couldn't help but be afraid this might not be one of those times.

'Hey, did you see this?'

Violet looked up from the file in front of her to see Rose in the doorway to the study, holding up a newspaper.

'It's less than twenty-four hours until the Benefit, Rose,' Violet said. 'I don't have time to read the paper.'

'You need to read this one.' Rose slipped into the room, revealing Daisy behind her. Daisy took the visitor's chair, rubbing her baby bump, while Rose perched on the edge of the desk, holding out the paper.

Violet sighed. Apparently she wasn't getting out of this without reading something. 'What is it?' she asked, reluctantly reaching out for the paper.

'Tom's first article from his interviews with Dad,' Daisy said, and Violet froze, her fingers brushing the edge of the newsprint.

'You really do need to read it,' Rose added.

God, but she didn't want to. One way or another, this would settle it. If he'd written the sort of story she expected him to, then there'd be no point listening to his side of the story about anything. It really would be over.

And if he hadn't...if by any chance he'd written the sort of story she'd want to read...what would she do then? Risk giving him a second chance?

She wasn't sure she could.

Swallowing, Violet took the newspaper from her sister's hand and skimmed over the section she'd folded it over to. Then, letting out a breath, she read it over again, slower this time.

'It's good, isn't it,' Daisy said after a moment. 'I mean, the guy can really write.'

'Sensitive, too,' Rose added. 'He really got Dad. I've never read an interview with him that made me feel like I was actually there talking with him before.'

'Vi, are you sure…?' Daisy trailed off as Violet shot a glare at her.

She really didn't want to talk about this. On the one hand, she should have known better than to get involved with a reporter in the first place. And if he really, truly did turn out to be a different breed, the lesser spotted good guy journalist…what did it matter now anyway? He was gone. She'd sent him away, and for good reason.

'Did you hear who he got to stand in for Uncle Jez tonight, by the way?' Rose asked. 'God only knows how. I tried to get the band to play second billing to the Lemons when we first put together the programme, but their schedule was crammed. Tom must have really pulled some strings.'

'I'm organising the concert, Rose. Of course I heard,' Violet snapped, then sighed. 'Sorry. I know. He's been great. Right from the start.'

'And yet…' Daisy prompted.

Violet dropped the paper to the desk. If there was anyone she could talk to, anyone who could tell her what she should do next, surely it would be her sisters. Especially since *they* at least seemed to have love all sussed out.

'Have Will or Seb ever done anything, like, in their past? Something you're not sure you could ever understand? Or forgive?'

Rose laughed. 'Vi, honey, Will left four women at the altar, remember? You're his best friend; you know he's not perfect. And was I damn afraid he might do the same thing to me? Of course I was.'

'But you married him anyway,' Violet said.

Rose shrugged. 'It's like Mum and Dad always say. When you know, you know. Will is the one for me. Once I accepted that…everything got a hell of a lot easier.'

Violet turned to Daisy. 'What about you?'

'I thought my marriage could only ever be a show, a business deal,' Daisy reminded her. 'But Rose is right—when you know, you know. So, the question is—do you know?'

Did she? Violet wasn't even sure. 'All I know is that it hurts, not having him here,' she admitted.

Rose and Daisy exchanged a look. Violet wasn't used to being on the outside of those looks. She didn't like it.

'Hurts like a dull ache, like something's missing but you can still feel it?' Rose asked. 'Like a phantom limb?'

'Or hurts like a sharp, blinding pain. The sort that consumes you until you can't think about anything else?' Daisy added.

'Both,' Violet admitted. 'And all the time.'

Rose and Daisy grinned across at each other.

'Honey, you totally know,' Rose said as she hopped off the desk.

'Where are you going?' Violet asked, standing when Daisy stood to follow.

Daisy flashed a smile back over her shoulder. 'To look at maternity bridesmaid dresses, of course. In lavender.'

Violet sank back down into her chair. She wished she could be so confident. Maybe she would have been, before Nick and everything that followed.

She took a deep breath. Maybe she would just have to be again; maybe she could find that lost confidence—if it meant winning Tom back.

He shouldn't be here. Tom was almost one hundred per cent certain he shouldn't be here. But Rick had called and said he was playing after all, and did Tom have any suggestions for a one-off stand-in guitarist for the night...and Tom couldn't not help. Not when he knew what a difference it could make to the night he and Violet had worked so hard to put together.

Even if she didn't want him there.

'Thanks again for doing this,' he said to Owain as a wide-eyed volunteer let them through the artists' gate.

'Are you kidding? Playing with the Lemons? It's an honour, man.' Owain's smile was wide, genuine—and world-famous. Tom had met the guitarist when his band was just starting out, and he'd rapidly become one of those friends he could call on for a night out whenever they were in the same city. These days, Owain's band played sold-out arena tours and, while the frontman might be the most famous member, any true music lover knew it was Owain's guitar playing that made their songs so memorable.

It didn't hurt that he had legions of female fans either, Tom thought. That had to be a bonus for tonight.

'I guess this is where I leave you,' he said as Owain headed through to the bands area. Normally, Tom would have been in there too, mingling, chatting, lining up interviews and soaking in the atmosphere. Tonight, he couldn't take the chance of bumping into Violet.

She had to be around here somewhere, he thought, as he waved goodbye to Owain. Probably racing around, double-checking everything, keeping everything under control in a way he couldn't have imagined her doing when they'd first met.

Strange to remember how he'd thought she was a spoilt rich kid, incapable of doing anything except trade on her parents' names and her own notoriety. He was happy to admit he'd been totally wrong about her.

He just wished she'd believe she was wrong about him, too.

'Tom! You made it.' Rick Cross clapped a hand on his shoulder and Tom tried not to jump.

'Hey. Things going well?' Tom asked, since he couldn't exactly ask, *How's Violet? Where is she? Will she ever forgive me?*

'Best Benefit Concert ever,' Rick announced, then lowered his voice. 'Don't tell Rose I said that, though, yeah?'

'Wouldn't dream of it.'

'Speaking of my girls, have you seen any of them yet?' Rick asked, his tone far too nonchalant. 'Say, Violet, for instance?'

'Ah, no. I thought it was probably best if I stayed out of the way a bit tonight,' Tom said. 'I really just came to bring Owain as a favour to a mate.'

'I see.' Rick subjected him to a long assessing look. 'And here I was thinking that you were here to set things right between the two of you. Never figured you for someone who'd quit at the first hurdle.'

'I'm not...I never said I'd quit.' Tom *wasn't* a quitter. But he also knew when he wasn't wanted. 'Maybe I'm just giving Violet a little space before I make my move.'

'Or maybe you're too scared she'll never trust you.'

How did the old man do that? See right to the heart of his every worry? Tom could understand it working with his daughters, but he'd only known the man a month.

Rick flashed him a quick grin and gripped his shoulder again. 'Don't worry, son. I'm not a mind-reader. But I've been where you are. Sherry and I always say "when you know, you know" and it's true. But we got married in a hurry, and knowing it's the real thing doesn't always make it any easier when times are hard. It just means you know it's worth fighting through.'

'And fighting for,' Tom murmured, almost to himself.

'Always that,' Rick agreed. 'Go on. Go find her. I think she's backstage.'

He shouldn't. This was her big night. She'd worked damn hard for it, and he didn't want to get in her way now. But on the other hand…how could he let this awful feeling in his chest that had started the moment he'd left Huntingdon Hall grow any bigger?

'Backstage, you say.' Tom squared his shoulders, wishing this didn't feel so much like heading into battle. 'Then I guess that's where I'm going.'

CHAPTER TWENTY-ONE

THE ATMOSPHERE BACKSTAGE was incredible. How had she never experienced this before? Normally at the Benefit it would be Rose rushing about behind the scenes, while Violet, Daisy and their mum would watch from a carefully sectioned off area of the crowd.

But now Violet knew—backstage was the place to be.

The act on stage finished their last song with a resounding chord that echoed off the trees surrounding the concert area, and the audience exploded into wild applause. Violet grinned and clapped along as the band traipsed off, high-fiving each other as they came.

'Great job, guys,' she told them, and got wide smiles in return. This was what all the work had been for. To put together a spectacular night that would help raise money and awareness for a cause that really counted.

It almost didn't matter that the person she wanted to share it with wasn't there.

Almost.

'Violet?'

Her breath caught in her throat at the sound of Tom's voice behind her. Of course he was here. How could a music journo miss a night like tonight?

She turned slowly, barely registering the next act as they took to the stage, even as the singer, Sammy, called back to her, something about a shout-out. There was cheering and music and noise all around her, and all she could see or hear was Tom, standing there, solemn-faced, watching her, waiting for her to speak.

And suddenly she had to figure out what she wanted to say.

She'd thought she would have more time. That she could tackle this at her own leisurely pace. But, instead, here he was and she needed to fix things. Somehow.

This could be her last chance.

'Tom.' His name was a start, right? A very small one, but still.

He stepped closer, just one pace. 'Things seem to be going great tonight.'

'They really are.' She bit her lip. 'I wasn't sure if you'd come.'

'Neither was I. But Owain asked me to come with him.'

'That's the only reason?' She almost didn't want to ask. Just in case.

'No.' How could one word send such a flood of relief through her system?

'I'm glad you came,' Violet admitted. 'I wanted to…I never gave you a chance to explain, last time. And I think…I'll listen now. If you still want to talk.'

'I do,' Tom said, but the hesitation in his voice made Violet nervous.

'But?'

Tom shook his head. 'You have a lot going on here today. It can wait.'

'I'm not sure it can.' Violet frowned. There was something more here. Something she wasn't getting. 'What is it?'

Tom leant back against the side of the stage with a sigh, and Violet had to step closer to even hear him over the noise of the band starting up. 'I can explain everything, and I think I can probably do it well enough to make you forgive me. This time.'

'Well, good?'

'But the thing is, Violet, that's only good for this time. What happens the next time I do something you don't agree with, or the next time something reminds you that I'm a hated journalist. You kick me out without listening again?'

'So…you're saying it's not worth trying?' Her stomach dropped lower and lower as every second passed without Tom's answer.

'I'm saying it's something I want you to think about. I want to know that you can trust me because I'm *me.* Not because I can tell you that my editor got a tip from an anonymous source and those photos in a brown envelope, and gave me the story to write as a test. To prove I could. To earn my stripes. And I thought it was just a practice run, that it wouldn't go to print. I don't want you to trust me just because I swear to you I asked him not to print it, and he laughed at me and I realised Mom was right all along.' He sighed, running a hand through his hair. 'I can explain as much as you want, Vi, and I will, probably often if we decide to make a go of things. But I need to know you trust me enough to not *need* the explanation to keep loving me. Does that make sense?'

It did. It was just an awfully big ask.

She opened her mouth to respond, to promise him whatever he wanted if he'd just *stay* long enough for them to sort things out. But then she heard her name blaring out of the speakers on stage, via Sammy, the lead singer's, microphone.

'And a huge shout-out to Violet Huntingdon Cross for putting together such an epic party! Come on out here, Violet!'

'You should go,' Tom said, stepping back from her. 'I don't think she's used to being kept waiting.'

'But we need to—'

'I'll find you later,' Tom said. 'We'll talk then.'

But later would be too late; Violet knew it in her bones. Which meant it would have to be this way, instead. 'Go find Mum and Daisy and Rose. They're out front.'

Tom nodded, and was gone before Violet even stepped out onto the stage.

The lights flashed and burned her eyes and the cheers made her head pound, but nothing could dim her determination. She knew what she needed to do now. She just needed the courage to go through with it.

'Thanks, Sammy,' she said, stepping up to the microphone. She couldn't make out anything beyond the blurs of light in the crowd; she just had to trust that Tom was out there, listening. 'And thank you all for coming tonight.' She paused while the crowd cheered, and tried to ignore the way her knees were shaking. 'The Huntingdon Hall Benefit Concert is always a highlight of the year, but this is the first time I've been able to be so involved in it. You might have noticed that I've been keeping a bit of a low profile over the past few years. But that's…' she stumbled over her words for a moment and bit the inside of her cheek hard, determined to keep it together '…that's going to change.'

There were murmurs running through the crowd now, questions and speculations and probably a few off-colour jokes, too. Violet ignored all of them, looked up into the lights and said what she needed to say.

'I wanted tonight to be a memorial for my Uncle Jez, for his life, and a way of raising both money and awareness for people who find themselves in the same position and need our help.' She took a breath, drawing in courage.

'Whenever we suffer a loss—from a loss of a job, or our reputation, all the way up to a beloved family member—we have to grieve. We have to heal and we have to move on. And sometimes that can be the hardest part—letting go of the past and opening ourselves up to the possibilities of the future. It's taken me a while, but I'm finally able to do that. I am moving on. And you're going to be seeing more of me because of it. I'm going to be out there, raising awareness everywhere I can. I want to let people know that if they need help, it is out there for them. And I want to make sure they get it—because if I can spare one other family a loss like we've suffered this week, it will be worth every minute.'

The roar of the crowd's applause rumbled in her ears and the heat in her cheeks started to fade. She'd done it. She'd taken that step forward and moved on—she just hoped that Tom had seen it.

Because now she needed to find him for the next part.

Handing the microphone back to Sammy, she rushed off stage as the band started up their next song. Weaving her way through the business backstage, smiling vaguely at every clap on the back or supportive comment, she headed for where she hoped Tom would be—with her family.

The pride in his chest felt too big for his body, as if it might burst out of him at any moment. Never mind talking to the press on the phone or holding meetings with managers. Violet had put herself back out there—completely. She'd stood up in front of the crowd, the press and everyone watching on TV and declared herself part of the world again. A woman with a mission.

She wasn't ashamed any more, and it was beautiful.

'Did you *see* that?' Rose bounced up next to him, pure delight shining from her face.

'She was magnificent!' Daisy agreed.

'She most certainly was,' Sherry said, smiling with pride.

'Where is she?' Rose asked. 'I need to hug her.'

'Not until I do,' Tom murmured, and the three women turned to look at him.

Which was, of course, when Violet bounded in.

'Vi! You were brilliant!' Rose and Daisy reached for their sister, and Violet grinned—but her gaze was fixed on Tom's face. He could feel it, even as he stared back.

'Sorry, guys, but I need to talk to Tom,' Violet said.

They both ignored the knowing looks her family exchanged as they headed out of the private area, past the edge of the crowd and around through some of the smaller stalls set up on the outskirts of the concert. Tom vaguely recognised some of the women from the village manning one of the charity support stalls. As they passed them, Violet waved, then reached out to hold Tom's hand. Another sign she was done worrying about what others thought? He hoped so.

Of course, right now he was more interested in finding out exactly what *she* thought about their potential future together.

Eventually, they reached the security barriers out of the concert site, and Violet slipped them through with her pass. 'Where are we going?' Tom asked.

Violet shrugged. 'It doesn't really matter. I just...some things are still private, right?' She flashed him a quick smile and tugged him further along, until they were surrounded by trees at the edge of the wood. 'This will do.'

Tom wanted to ask what, exactly, it would do for. But Violet seemed nervous enough. For once, he'd have to curb his natural impulse to ask questions, lots of them, and let her talk in her own time.

Sometimes, he'd learnt, you got the best interviews that way.

Violet sucked in a deep breath, then let it out again. Tom stamped down on the impatience rising inside him. He had to let her take her time.

'Okay, so…I learnt something while you were gone. Or realised something, I guess. That…maybe people have never been able to move past my past, so to speak, because I've never done anything else. I need to replace those memories—those stories and those jokes—with new and better ones.'

'And that's what you were doing up there on the stage,' Tom guessed.

Violet nodded. 'Starting to, anyway. And it means moving on. Not just from that stupid sex tape, but from the last eight years of hiding, too. Of not trusting anyone and always expecting the worst.'

'Well…good.' Because that sounded positive. But he still needed to hear her say the words.

Violet looked up and met his gaze, her eyes wide and blue and totally open for the first time since he'd met her. 'My mum and dad, they always say that when you know, you know. And I think they're right.' The side of her mouth twisted up into a half smile. 'And I *did* know, deep down. It was just hard to see, behind all that doubt and fear and mistrust.'

'And now?' Tom asked, his heart thumping too hard, too loud in his chest.

'And being without you…it swept all that away. It hurt so much to be apart from you that none of the rest of it mattered any more. All that mattered was telling you that I love you. And I trust you. I do.'

'Really?' God, why couldn't he just take her words at face value?

Violet took his hand between hers. 'Enough to trust you with the rest of my life. If you'll have me.'

Tom blinked. 'You want to get married?'

Violet smiled, slow and warm. 'Why not? It seems to be all the rage this year. Besides, when you know, you know.' She reached up and kissed him once on the lips. 'And I know that whatever happens, whatever you've done or whatever you will do, I trust you to do it for us, not just for a quick story. I'm not the same person I was when that sex tape was made, and I know you're not the same person who let his editor use that story. And I'm not interested in who we were. Only who we can be together.'

And that was all he needed to know. Wrapping his arms tight around her waist, he pulled Violet close, kissing her long and deep until the sounds of the concert, the lights, even the breeze through the trees ceased to register. All that mattered was him and Violet, and their future together.

Finally, he pulled back, just enough to rest his forehead against hers. 'You did the same for me, you know,' he whispered fiercely. 'I spent so many years carrying around the guilt from that story, from my mom never knowing that I realised she was right, even if it was a little late. Meeting you…it made me face that guilt, and all my preconceptions about who you were. If you hadn't shown me that it was possible to move beyond our own pasts…I never could have come back here today. I never could have told you I love you too.'

Violet kissed him again, swift and sharp and full of feeling. But Tom wasn't done talking.

'I should get down on one knee, I know, but I don't want to move that far away from you,' he said, and Violet laughed. 'Violet Huntingdon-Cross. Will you do me the honour of becoming my wife?'

'Only if you'll do me the honour of being my husband,' Violet said, and kissed him again.

'Then it's settled. Your mum gets to plan another wedding.' He squeezed her tighter. 'What do you think? Next summer? Big celebrity bash?'

Violet laughed. 'Haven't you heard? The Huntingdon-Cross sisters don't wait that long for their happy ever afters.'

'True.' Tom smiled. 'Next month, then?'

'Sounds perfect,' Violet said. 'I'm ready to start our new lives. Together.'

EPILOGUE

THE SUMMER SUN shone down on Huntingdon Hall as crowds gathered for the fourth, and final, Huntingdon-Cross wedding celebration of the year. Violet peeked through the curtains of her bedroom, careful not to be seen, and watched the cars pulling up on the long driveway.

Somewhere out there, probably pacing with his soon-to-be brothers-in-law at his side, was her fiancé. She wondered what Tom was making of being the centre of attention for once, instead of just writing about other people's fame.

'Are you ready?' At the sound of her twin's voice, Violet let the curtain fall back into place and turned to smile at Rose.

'More ready than I thought I could ever be,' Violet said.

Stepping forward, the lavender silk of her bridesmaid's dress rustling around her, Rose hugged her sister, a feeling so warm and familiar that Violet felt love in every squeeze.

'Mum is downstairs, waiting to give final approval on the three of us before she heads out to the ceremony area,' Daisy said, her seven-months-pregnant bump appearing a moment before the rest of her came through the door. 'And Dad's just putting the finishing touches to his speech. Again.'

'"Final approval"?' Violet asked with a smile. 'Is she

worried Daisy might get jam on her dress, like she did when she was bridesmaid at Uncle Jez's second wedding?' The pang of pain at the thought of Jez was still there, but already it felt more like a loving memory than a searing loss. The hole he'd left would always be there, but they'd learn to live with it, Violet knew, to move on and make his death meaningful, at least.

'I was five!' Daisy pointed out indignantly.

'Just think, soon it will be your little bump trailing down the aisle in jam-smeared taffeta, leaving rose petals in her wake,' Rose said.

'Well, as long as it's not me, for once,' Violet said, checking her reflection one last time before they headed downstairs. 'I'm done being a bridesmaid, I think.'

'And today you're the bride.' Daisy's words came out a little watery, and Rose handed her a tissue for the inevitable tears.

'Don't start yet,' Rose said. 'We've got the whole ceremony to get through!'

'Not to mention Dad's speech,' Violet added. She wasn't sure if she was dreading or looking forward to hearing which tales of her life Rick Cross thought appropriate to share with the assembled company.

'Can't help it,' Daisy sniffed. 'Hormones.'

'Yeah, yeah,' Rose replied. 'A convenient excuse. They don't seem to be slowing you down any, though, do they? Seb was telling me all about your plans for Hawkesley Castle and his new TV series at dinner last night. It would be nauseating how much that man dotes on you if it wasn't so well deserved.'

Daisy elbowed Rose in the ribs. 'Don't tell me you didn't shed a tear or two when you were making those gorgeous rings for Violet and Tom.'

'Maybe just one,' Rose admitted. 'And they are very pretty, aren't they?'

'They're perfect,' Violet said. 'Just like everything else about today. Now, come on, let's go present ourselves for inspection.'

Violet followed her sisters out of the room, pausing to shut the door behind her. Strange to think she was leaving this place as herself, but would be returning as a married woman. Almost as impossible to believe as the thought of her getting married at all.

But here she was, with her sisters at her side, preparing to say *I do* to the last man she'd ever imagined marrying. And she couldn't be happier.

Sherry Huntingdon-Cross clapped her hands together with delight at the sight of them. 'Oh, don't you all look perfect,' she gushed before wedding planner mode took over again. 'Right, I'm going to head down and take my seat—that's the sign for the ushers to get everyone else seated. Rose, Daisy, you follow just behind me. Then Rick—where is your father, anyway?'

'Here, honey.' Rick Cross came rushing out of his studio, shoving pieces of paper into his pocket. 'Just a couple of last-minute edits. Don't worry,' he added with a wink at Violet. 'I kept the story about that time you fell in the pond at that hotel roof garden when we were on tour in Europe.'

'Oh, good,' Violet said unconvincingly.

'Right,' Sherry said again, commanding everyone's attention. 'I'm leaving. Daisy, Rose, prepare to follow.'

The wedding procession had been timed to perfection. As her father took her arm and led her out of the front door of her childhood home behind her sisters, Violet took a deep breath and followed her family down to the shady clearing, just behind the trees, where they'd set up the chairs and ceremony area. It wasn't a huge wedding—

despite Sherry's attempts—but neither was it the tiny one Violet would have insisted on even a few months ago.

She wasn't scared to share her new happiness, to let others see her moving on with her life in exciting new directions. She wasn't hiding any more.

At the front of the aisle, Tom turned, as if sensing her presence, and Violet couldn't hold back her smile at the sight of him in his perfect suit, waiting for her to join him.

'You ready for this, honey?' Rick asked as the string quartet struck up the canon.

'How could I not be?' Violet whispered back. 'After all, when you know, you know.'

* * * * *

MEET THE FORTUNES!

Fortune of the Month: Galen Fortune Jones

Age: 34

Vital Statistics: Tall, dark and muscley, he's a fine, upstanding rancher—and stubbornly single.

Claim to Fame: The oldest of Jeanne Marie Fortune's seven children and possibly the sexiest boy of the bunch.

Romantic Prospects: He is currently getting married to Aurora McElroy four times a day in the Wild West Wedding stage show. You tell me!

"I keep telling you, it's all for pretend. I can't help it if people think that 'Rusty' and 'Lila' look like a real couple. I'm just doing this to help out a friend. Aurora is like my little sister. A little sister with long red hair, big blue eyes, a little bitty waist... uh... The other part? Agreeing to be her fake husband for a week? I'll admit, it's complicated. But it's only until her college roommate leaves town. And we are *not* playing house. What do you mean I'm protesting too much? We've known each other forever. We are *just friends*. I. Am. Not. Getting. Married."

The Fortunes Of Texas: Cowboy Country
Lassoing hearts from across the pond!

FORTUNE'S JUNE BRIDE

BY
ALLISON LEIGH

Published in Great Britain 2015
by Mills & Boon, an imprint of Harlequin (UK) Limited,
Eton House, 18-24 Paradise Road, Richmond, Surrey, TW9 1SR

Special thanks and acknowledgement to Allison Leigh for her contribution to the Fortunes of Texas: Cowboy Country continuity.

ISBN: 978-0-263-25141-8

23-0615

Harlequin (UK) Limited's policy is to use papers that are natural, renewable and recyclable products and made from wood grown in sustainable forests. The logging and manufacturing processes conform to the legal environmental regulations of the country of origin.

Printed and bound in Spain
by CPI, Barcelona

A frequent name on bestseller lists, **Allison Leigh**'s high point as a writer is hearing from readers that they laughed, cried or lost sleep while reading her books. She's blessed with an immensely patient family who doesn't mind (much) her time spent at her computer and who gives her the kind of love she wants her readers to share in every page. Stay in touch at www.allisonleigh.com and on Twitter, @allisonleighbks.

For my daughters—as beautiful on the inside
as they are on the outside.

Chapter One

"I need you to marry me."

The words came out of left field.

Literally.

Galen Fortune Jones stared down at Aurora McElroy. He was pretty sure the last time he'd seen his neighbor had been a few months ago. They'd run into each other at the Horseback Hollow feed store. There had been no romance involved, considering that at the time he'd paid more attention to helping her daddy, Walt, load up his truck, before tending to his own business there.

Now he looked from her hand, clutching his left arm, back to her dark blue eyes. "Beg your pardon?"

She huffed, pushing a shining red ringlet out of her face. "It's an emergency, Galen. I need a groom. Right now!"

You will marry a woman in white and be married within the month.

The words echoed inside his head and he wanted to shake it hard, just to see if something had come loose inside.

Instead, he glanced around where they were standing on a side street of Cowboy Country, USA, the Western-style theme park where just last week—in a moment of apparent insanity—he had agreed to be an "authenticity consultant." And where, just a few weeks prior to that, one of the "Wild West" fortune-tellers had told him he would soon be hitched.

He'd laughed it off then as nonsense for two simple reasons. One, he didn't believe in fortune-tellers, and two, he'd reached the age of thirty-four without *once* entertaining the idea of marrying someone.

So he looked back at Aurora and adjusted his hat. "You're dressed for the part," he allowed. "I'll give you that."

In fact, she looked downright pretty. All dolled up in an old-fashioned-looking dress with beads and lace hanging off her slender shoulders and her eyes made up to look even bigger than they already were.

She gave him a look that ought to have scorched his toes. "Of course I'm dressed for the part." Her hands spread a little wider. *"Wild West Wedding!"* She raised her eyebrows, clearly waiting for some response. "The… noon…show," she elaborated at his blank look.

She twitched her skirt, drawing his attention. It was some sort of filmy, lacy thing about the same color as the doily his mom had had forever sitting underneath a vase in the front parlor of the house he and his four brothers and two sisters had grown up in. Sorta white. Sorta beige.

"Oh, for heaven's sake, Galen." Aurora sounded exasperated. "The noon show! I'm playing Lila, the Wild West bride. But I just found out my groom, Rusty, was hauled off a little while ago to see Doc Shoemaker, because he went and fell off his horse." She shook her head. "Lord save me from city boys who think they know everything about a horse just because they've watched *Butch Cassidy and the Sundance Kid*."

Comprehension finally dawned. Maybe it would have more quickly if Galen hadn't gotten distracted thinking about that fool fortune-teller business.

"Wild West Wedding," he repeated. "That's the show you put on at the center of the park."

"Yes." Looking relieved that he'd finally gotten a clue, she lifted her other hand and shoved a dog-eared script at him. "It'll take ten minutes of your time, Galen. Please."

"I'm no good at playacting."

"How do you know? Have you ever tried?" She stepped closer and her shoulder brushed against his ribs as she flipped open the pages, seeming to take his compliance as a foregone conclusion. "It's not complicated. I'm Lila. You'll be Rusty." Her slender finger jabbed at the words on the page. "There's not really much time for you to memorize before we need to start, but the premise is simple. Lila and Rusty are in love. Frank, the villain, is determined to have Lila for himself, but what he really wants even more is the deed to her daddy's ranch so his railroad can go through."

"Original," Galen drawled.

"It's a ten-minute attraction at a Western theme park," she countered. "Be glad it's not Shakespeare or we really would be in trouble. Are you willing to do this or not? After all the problems we've had since Cowboy Country opened last month, the last thing this place needs is another canceled show. It's bad publicity when we're finally having a week where nothing seems to go wrong."

The "bad" was one of the reasons for Galen's presence. But agreeing to answer a bunch of questions about tending cattle and horses and walking around the park taking note of anything that belittled the ranching community didn't involve filling in for somebody who probably shouldn't have been on a horse in the first place.

"Weren't you always in the school plays when you and Toby were kids?" His younger brother had gone to school with her. When Galen had been that age, he'd have been one of the kids sitting in the auditorium, hooting over every flubbed line. Though when he thought about it, he couldn't recall Aurora ever flubbing hers. Even as a kid, she'd been memorable with her flaming red hair.

"If you want to walk down memory lane, we can do that later." She grabbed his arm again and was dragging him toward the rough-hewn gate at the end of the make-believe street. "Right now, you need to get into costume."

He grimaced, eyeing the mass of sausage curls streaming down the middle of her back. Her waist below that seemed cinched down even smaller than usual. "Just what all does *that* mean?"

She pulled open the gate and shot him a grin. "You're not going to have to fit into a corset, if that's what you're worried about. They save that torture for the girls." She tugged him through the gate, pushed it closed, and headed toward a trailer that was a century more modern than anything visible within the guests' portion of Cowboy Country. Even the thrill rides were couched in Old West touches.

Aurora lifted her skirts and darted up the two metal steps, disappearing inside the trailer. "Come on. We've only got a half hour before we're on."

He went up into the trailer and found himself standing inside a miniature warehouse, crowded on all sides by racks loaded with costumes and props. He pulled a bull whip off a hook. “Ohhh-kay.”

“That’s for *Outlaw Shootout*,” she said. “The show’s shelved temporarily until they work out some kinks with the stunts. Here.” She whisked his black cowboy hat off his head and plopped a creamy white one in its place. “Rusty wears a white hat. Naturally.”

“Naturally,” he repeated drily, even though he was wondering what the hell had gotten into him. He hung the whip back in place.

“You need to change your shirt, too.” She shoved a hanger at him that held a rough cotton button-down. “At least Joey—he’s the guy who plays Rusty—hadn’t changed into his costume before he fell off a darn horse.” She tsked as she pulled open one drawer after another. “Being the big-budget show that we are, we’ve only got one.”

She glanced at him. “What’re you waiting for?” She waved her hand at the hanger he was still holding and turned back to the drawers she was pawing through. “You can get by with wearing your own Levi’s and boots, but that shirt’s gotta go.”

Stifling a passel of misgivings, since he’d yet to actually *agree*, he dumped the script on a pile of folded Mexican blankets, set the white hat on top and pulled his NASCAR T-shirt over his head.

“Ah. Success.” Aurora pushed the drawer closed and turned to him, a black string tie in her hand.

Her eyes seemed to widen a bit at the sight of his bare chest, and she dropped the tie on top of the white Stetson, then quickly turned back around to yank open another drawer while he pulled on the shirt. “It’s a little Wyatt Earp–ish, à la *Tombstone*,” she chattered, “but what it might lack in historic accuracy is at least recognizable for the customers. So I hope it passes muster on your *authenticity* scale."

She pushed the drawer closed again without removing anything and turned back to face him. Her cheeks looked excessively pink to him. Like she wasn't all that used to seeing a guy shirtless. "Anyway, about the, uh, the show." She pulled the script out and muttered under her breath when the cowboy hat fell on the floor, quickly followed by a cascade of colorful woven blankets.

He crouched down to help her right the mess. "Relax, Aurora. The show's still gonna go on. Though I seriously think you'd do better with just about anyone besides me."

"You fit the shirt," she said with a shrug.

He let out a wry laugh. "Well, hell, then. Guess that makes me feel real good."

She smiled. "And soon as I saw you, I knew you wouldn't let me—the park, I mean—down. If you weren't already on staff, we could never get away with this, though. I'm sure there'd be insurance issues and all of that."

They reached for the same blanket at the same time, knuckles knocking, and she snatched her hands back, straightening quickly to swipe her hands down the sides of her dress.

"Thanks." She sounded breathless. "I'll, uh, just wait for you outside." She shoved open the trailer door and brushed past the guy who was coming up the steps. "Hey there, Frank," he heard her say. "I found us a Rusty, so we're still on."

"Cool."

Blankets stacked once more, Galen straightened and stuck his hand out toward the newcomer as he came into the trailer. "Galen Jones," he offered, and sent a silent apology to his mom for omitting the "Fortune" part that they'd all been adding to the "Jones" ever since his mom's birth family had found her. He was trying to get used to the addition. But it still didn't come all that naturally. Not because he was opposed to acknowledging the Fortune connection. But to him, it just all sounded sorta…fancy. Which he wasn't.

The other man shook his hand briefly before grabbing a black hat—a whole lot cleaner and dandier-looking than Galen's usual one—and setting it on his gleaming blond head. "Frank Richter," he said, studying his reflection in the mirror over the drawers. "I play Frank, the dastardly villain. Nice to have the right name already for a part." He adjusted the hat so it sat at an angle, dipping low over his right eye. "Haven't seen you around here before. You been with Moore Entertainment for long?"

"Not all that sure I'm technically 'with' Moore Entertainment." Galen didn't need to adjust his hat. He dropped Rusty's Stetson on his head the same way he did with his own cowboy hat every single day. Didn't matter if it was black or white or straw. For him, the covering wasn't a matter of costume, but nature. Same as his leather Castleton boots that he got resoled every few years. "I'm the authenticity consultant." He felt more than a little stupid just saying the words, same way he felt using Fortune Jones as his last name when all his life, "Jones" had been plenty, and he flipped up the collar of Rusty's shirt and started on the tie. He didn't need a mirror for that, either. He'd worn a similar one to the Valentine's Day wedding when three of his brothers and one of his sisters all got hitched on the same day.

The powers that be for Moore Entertainment considered *him* a cowboy. So he guessed that made the tie authentic enough for the theme park.

"Heard they'd hired something like that." Frank was running some dinky comb covered with clear goop through his eyebrows, and Galen nearly stared. "You're supposed to make sure Cowboy Country rings *true*." Frank air-quoted the word and looked over his shoulder at him. They were about the same height, though Galen damn sure never once combed his eyebrows, with goop or without.

"That's about it." Galen finished tying the tie and flipped down the collar.

"Well, make sure your punch during today's show doesn't ring entirely true," Frank said, looking back at his reflection. "I don't need to end up with any real bruises. I'm getting new head shots done tomorrow. I'm trying to get into the Moore Dinner Theatre in Branson. Lot more exposure there than in Hicksville Horseback Hollow." He made a face in the mirror, then pulled another, and another, stretching his face into comic proportions before he fixed on a dark handlebar mustache over his top lip. "Most any one of Moore's other Coaster World locations would be better than here. Not surprised they're having a hard time getting Cowboy Country off the ground in a little Texas backwater like this." He glanced over his shoulder again. "Know what I mean?"

"Wouldn't know," Galen said with irony. He, for one, was glad that the company had chosen not to follow the Coaster World model like the rest of its theme parks. Horseback Hollow was special.

Any park that was going to be there needed to be special, too.

He grabbed the script and reached for the trailer door. "Seein' how I'm one of the hicks."

He stepped outside and spotted Aurora leaning over her old-fashioned buttoned boot that she'd propped on a picnic bench. The curls of her hair hung over her shoulder, leaving the crisscross laces on the back of her dress visible. They cinched together down the center of the lacy fabric hugging her torso, seeming to make a point of showing off the way her waist nipped in all small and female, and swelled out again over her hips.

He frowned, yanking his eyes away.

He'd always lumped Aurora in the same category as his little sisters. She'd been the kid sister of one of his best friends. Noticing anything about her waist or hips, or anything else for that matter, wasn't something he was altogether comfortable with.

He settled his hat more squarely on his head and made some noise thumping down the metal steps, and as he'd hoped, she lowered her foot and straightened as he approached.

Her blue eyes ran over him. "I *knew* Rusty's costume would fit you." She gave a quick smile. "You don't know how much I appreciate you doing this."

"Don't y'all put on this wedding show more than once a day?" The other shows he'd noticed in his week working here had repeated themselves several times a day. There was a bank robbery thing that happened out on Main Street as Aurora's show did, a stunt show that was held at the far end of the park in the corral set in the shadows of a wooden roller coaster complete with two loop-the-loops, a saloon girl dancing show held almost hourly inside the Texas Rose restaurant, and a few others that seemed to alternate, all designed to keep the guests entertained.

Aurora was nodding. "You and I…well, *Rusty* and *Lila* get to pledge their troth four times daily." She pulled on the thin gold chain hanging around her neck and a locket emerged from the front of her dress. He realized it was a watch when she flipped it open. "Which we've got to do in ten minutes." She slid the locket back into her cleavage.

Somehow he'd missed the fact that Aurora McElroy

even possessed cleavage. That time at the feed store he was certain she'd been wearing a plaid work shirt that had been big enough to fit her daddy.

He dragged his mind away from cleavages. They were fine in their place. He was even a man who enjoyed his fair share of 'em.

But not when their existence seemed to come out of the same left field as Aurora's "I need you to marry me" had.

"Seems to me missing one show wouldn't be the end of Cowboy Country," he said, keeping his eyes well above her neckline.

"We get paid by the show," Aurora said. "Maybe it *wouldn't* be the end of Cowboy Country. But it cuts into the performers' paychecks, believe me." She gestured at the script. "Did you look through it?"

He grimaced and dutifully opened the script. Fortunately, it was easy to read. Only a few words per line, running down the center of the page. The action took up more space than the dialogue and attested to what he already knew—that the show involved stagecoaches, racing horses, and a lot of melodrama. "I guess I can manage," he muttered.

Even a hick rancher could read a few lines of dialogue.

He scanned through the pages, easily grasping the gist. He was to escape Frank's goons who were holding him captive and race to Aurora's rescue with the deed to her daddy's ranch in Rusty's name, narrowly preventing Frank from forcing her to say "I do" in front of the preacher.

Like Aurora had said. It wasn't Shakespeare.

It was just a ten-minute show that took place in the middle of the whole dang park since someone, in their brilliance, had recently decided the *Wild West Wedding* stage needed to be relocated there.

People could be eating hot dogs in the Main Street Grill, watching a demonstration over in the smithy or buying hand-dipped candles in Gus's General Store; they'd catch the wedding.

"It'll be fun," Aurora promised.

He snorted softly. "Getting my teeth drilled appeals more than making an ass out of myself in front of Cowboy Country's paying customers."

"You're not going to make an ass of yourself," she assured dismissively. She reached up and adjusted his tie, then stepped back, her hands tucked behind her back. "You actually look perfect for the part." She smiled, but her eyes didn't quite meet his. "Better than Joey, even, but don't tell him I said so." She smiled a little impishly. "His ego is a tad delicate."

"Well, it's probably dented pretty good now he's fallen off a horse. Where'd it happen? Here at the park?"

"No, thank goodness." She rolled her eyes. "Can you imagine the publicity we'd get about it after already having a horse stampede during the soft opening? But from what I heard, he might have sprained his ankle. And I can't see him resuming Rusty's role if he's sporting a modern splint. Don't worry," she added quickly, seeming to recognize Galen's alarm, "the casting department will be able to find someone to replace him. Right now, I'm concerned with getting us through today."

"Hold on." He closed the script and tossed it on the picnic table. "I remember something about this taking ten minutes of my time." The authenticity-consultant business was temporary and only took up part of his day. He might not have been a real fan when the park first opened, but even a man like him could recognize that the park's success meant success for Horseback Hollow as well.

He hated change, but he loved his hometown more. So he was willing to do his part. And the fact that Moore Entertainment was willing to pump some serious money into the town contributed to that willingness.

Nevertheless, he still had his own ranch to run, and even at the best of times, that was a 24/7 job.

"That's all I agreed to," he said. "Once I embarrass myself in the noon show, your—" what had she called it? "—*casting* department better be finding someone else in the two hours before the next show."

"I'm sure they will," she soothed. She slipped a tube out of some mysterious pocket hidden in the side of her skirt and ran it quickly over her lower lip, leaving it pinker than it ordinarily was and intriguingly shiny. "In the meantime, we've got a crowd to entertain. Okay?"

He dragged his eyes away.

What the hell was wrong with him? A corner of the McElroys' spread had butted up next to his folks' property his whole life. He wasn't all that sure that his little brother Jude hadn't dated Aurora once upon a time. Before Jude fell for Gabriella Mendoza last year, he'd changed girlfriends more often than Galen changed shirts.

"Yo, yo, yo," Frank hailed, joining them. He dropped a proprietary arm around Aurora's shoulders and squeezed. With his free hand, he twirled one side of his fake mustache and leered at her. "Ready to become my wifey, my dear?"

Aurora's smile thinned a little. She unhooked Frank's arm from her shoulders and stepped away from him. "Save it for the crowd, Frank." She sent Galen a smile and marched ahead of them to climb into a buckboard that would carry them down the center of Main Street while the guests were safely held back from the action with ropes carried by security guards dressed as old-time railroad workers.

As he watched, she worked a small headset into her riotous curls and he felt a fresh wave of misgivings. That headset was a microphone. She followed up the headset with a lacy veil held onto her head by a band of white roses.

"Rory likes playing hard to get," Frank was telling Galen in a man-to-man tone that set Galen's teeth on edge. "Makes the gettin' all that much more fun."

Galen eyed Frank, realizing he wore a tiny microphone, as well. "Am I gonna have to wear one of those?"

"Nah. Your important lines are picked up by the stage mics. Just remember they don't kill the audio until right before you kiss Lila." He clapped Galen on the shoulder. "Break a leg," he said before sauntering ahead to climb up beside Aurora. She had her head tilted back, seeming to be looking up at the sky.

Another young man whom Galen didn't know handed Frank the reins for the horse's harness, then moved up to the front to lead the horse around toward a wide gate that he swung open.

Over the loudspeaker, a deep-voiced announcer was telling all comers to hold on to their chaps 'cause they were in for a hog-tying good time down on Main Street.

On cue, Aurora looked back at Galen and gave him an encouraging thumbs-up. Then Frank flicked the reins and the buckboard rattled out of the gate just as adventurous music blasted over the loudspeakers. A moment later, Galen could hear Aurora's and Frank's voices as the show began in earnest.

"Good grief," he muttered, feeling a strong urge to sit

on the picnic bench and stick his head between his knees. What the hell had he agreed to do?

But there was no time for second thoughts. Over the speakers, he could hear "Lila" proclaiming her faith in her beloved "Rusty."

"You're the new Rusty?" A vaguely familiar-looking skinny guy wearing a ten-gallon hat and a bright, shining sheriff's star on the chest of his blue shirt got his attention.

"Only for this show," Galen allowed.

"Come on, then. I'm Sal the Sheriff." He shoved a bedraggled-looking scroll into Galen's hand. "That's the deed you need to wave in Frank's face before you knock him out and kiss Lila. Try not to drop it like Joey keeps doing when we're riding down Main Street."

Galen started, but Sal was already hurrying him to another gate farther along than the one the buckboard had gone through. There were ten horses waiting, eight of them already mounted with riders. Some were dressed like Frank. Some like Sal.

He tucked the deed inside his shirt and swung easily up into the saddle.

But his thoughts were nowhere near so calm.

He should have paid more attention to the end of the script. He'd gotten to the punching Frank part. But he'd clean missed seeing that he got to kiss the fair Lila at the end.

Galen had never gone to school to study acting the way Aurora had. As far as he was concerned, kissing Lila would be as good as kissing *her*.

And even though he was rapidly realizing that wasn't an entirely unappealing notion, it wasn't something he necessarily wanted to do in front of an audience!

Chapter Two

Aurora didn't have to work too hard to look dismayed as she fended off Frank's advances when he pulled her unwillingly toward the wooden stage at the end of Main Street, where a preacher paced back and forth in front of the old west building facade of a bank, a boardinghouse and a feed store. Frank had been making advances toward her for the past two weeks—ever since he'd joined the cast—and didn't seem to take the hint that she wasn't interested.

"I don't *want* to marry you," she cried out loudly for the crowd who'd been following them along Main Street as her trials and tribulations were extolled. "I love Rusty. He'd *never* desert me like you claim!"

Frank pulled her close, his leer exaggerated for the audience. "He's gone off to Dodge City, my dear." He twirled his mustache for added effect. "He's never going to come back. Your only hope to save your departed daddy's land from the *railroad*—"

The crowd booed on cue.

"—is to marry me!" He swept her off her feet, carrying her, kicking and struggling, up the steps and onto the stage. "That's it, Preacher Man," he boomed and set her on her feet. "Get us wedded and hurry up about it."

Behind them, the onlookers sent up a cheer as horse hooves pounded audibly down Main Street, accompanied by the triumphant music swelling over the loudspeakers.

Lila tried to pull away from Frank, but he held her arm fast.

"Dearly beloved," Preacher Man started off in a quaking voice. "We are gathered—"

"Get on to the vows," Frank demanded, looking nervously over his shoulder.

Preacher Man gulped. "Do you, sir, take this, ah—"

"Lila," Frank growled loudly. He pulled out his pistol and waved it, and a sharp *crack!* rent the air. Down the facade in front of the feed store, a bag of seed exploded. "Hurry it along, Preacher Man, or the next one goes in you."

Preacher Man's eyes widened. "Take *Lila*, to be your wife—" His fast words practically fell on top of each other.

"I do," Frank yelled, "and she does—"

"Not!" Rusty had vaulted from his horse and stormed up onto the stage, sweeping Lila away from Frank. "She'll never be your wife, Frank. No more than that land'll ever be yours." He pulled the deed from inside his shirt and waved it in the air. "They're both mine, and I'll never let either one go!"

"Oh, *Rusty*." Lila nearly swooned as the audience hooted. Aurora caught the faint grin on Galen's face before he turned to take on the villain of the piece, and felt a little bit swoonish inside for real.

She'd gotten over her schoolgirl crush on him ages ago, but Galen Fortune Jones was still the kind of man that could make a girl's heart stutter.

She clasped her hands together over her breast, crying out as Frank aimed his pistol at Rusty's chest.

But Lila's white-hatted hero fought off the hand holding the gun and swung his fist into Frank's chin, knocking him comically right off the stage where he fell ignominiously on his butt in a pile of fake horse poop.

Sal the Sheriff and his men stood over Frank and his goons, whom he and Rusty had already dispatched, looking satisfied at the turn of events.

She waited until the cheers died down slightly. "I *knew* you'd save me, Rusty!"

"I'll always save you, Lila." Galen's voice was deep and loud and definitely heroic as he tossed the "deed" to the sheriff, who caught it handily. "Will you finally be my wife?"

She fanned herself, simpering. "You know I will, Rusty."

They turned to Preacher Man, who stopped gaping comically at Frank and flipped open his oversize Bible again. "Dearly beloved," he began again.

"I do," Lila burst out. "And he does, too!"

The audience laughed and Preacher Man held out his hands as if to say, what could he do? "Then I now pronounce you husband and—"

Galen swept off his hat with one hand and grabbed her around the waist with his other. "Wife," he finished loudly, then bent her deep over his arm, while she buried her face against his chest.

"Am I s'posed to kiss you for real?" Galen whispered in her ear as the crowd cheered and the music crescendoed from the loudspeakers to its triumphant conclusion.

Something inside Aurora's tummy fluttered. The way Galen held her, nobody beyond the stage would be able to see that Rusty and Lila weren't actually locking lips. She shook her cheek against his, though she wished he hadn't asked. That he would have just gone ahead and done it.

It was as close as she'd ever get to actually kissing the man for real, that was for certain.

Sal the Sheriff and his men pulled Frank from the horse manure and clapped him in chains before leading him and his goons off at rubber gunpoint through the audience.

As they did after every show, the onlookers dispersed quickly, anxious to get to the next attraction. The next cotton candy. The next roller coaster.

She didn't mind the quick loss of attention.

She was just happy to be part of a show again. Playing Lila in *Wild West Wedding* was a far cry from the acting career she'd once dreamed of having, but for a rancher's daughter who spent day in and day out helping her father, it was more than she'd thought she'd ever have.

And being held in a close embrace against a seriously handsome cowboy wasn't anything to sneeze at, either.

Feeling breathless inside, Aurora patted Galen's shoulders. "You can let me go now," she whispered. It was safe to break character, because the mics were cued to be killed at Rusty's last word, "wife."

"Yeah. Right." Galen straightened, letting her loose. All around them, people were streaming away from the stage, calling out smart remarks and still clapping.

She beamed at them and tucked her arm through Rusty's, clinging to him as they and Preacher Man left the stage and strolled in the opposite direction from where Frank had been taken by the sheriff to the jail across the street. As long as any of the cast members were in costume out in the public areas of the park, they remained in character.

Over the loudspeaker, the music had softened to a background melody of "Yellow Rose of Texas."

When they passed through a gate once more to the backstage area, though, she forced herself to let go of Galen's arm. "You did a good job," she said, slipping past him. "Didn't he make a good Rusty, Harlan?"

"Hell," Galen said, stopping short. He peered at Preacher Man's face. "I didn't even notice that was you, Mayor."

Harlan Osgood grinned, pulling off his bottle-glass round spectacles and the fake gold caps on his front teeth. "Got myself a helper at the barbershop these days," he said. "Been having some fun doing this a few times a day."

"Harlan switches off with Buddy Jepps playing Preacher Man," Aurora provided. She pulled off the veil and microphone, then the hairpiece she wore over her own pinned-up hair, and saw Galen's look.

She laughed a little awkwardly, holding up the thick fall of ringlets that perfectly matched her own dark red hair. "My hair is straight as a stick. It would take hours to curl like this. And pretty as this is," she held out one side of her skirt and gave a quick curtsy, "it's about as comfortable as a straitjacket. So I'm going to change." She headed toward the costume trailer, leaving the two men still talking.

The corseted wedding dress wasn't quite as uncomfortable as she'd made out.

But she had no intention of admitting that she was finding it a tad difficult to breathe normally after being clasped up against Galen.

Being held by Frank was a requirement of the role she was playing.

Being held by Galen Fortune Jones was something entirely different...

She left her veil and microphone out so the production crew could reset them in the buckboard for the next show, then stepped behind the changing screen to peel down the hidden zipper in the side of the old-fashioned-looking dress. She hung it on the hanger and tucked it, as well as her boots, away in the corner of the wardrobe trailer she'd purloined for her own use. Then, changed once more into her own knee-length sundress and cowboy boots so she'd be free to move throughout the park until the next show, she left the trailer again.

Galen was still talking to Harlan, and his dark brown eyes crinkled a little as she approached them.

Her gauzy white tiered dress wasn't at all confining, but she still felt a constriction in her chest when he looked her way.

It was a little annoying, actually. And embarrassing.

Because if Galen had been at all interested in her *ever*, he'd have had ample opportunity to do something about it. It wasn't as if they lived on opposite ends of the planet, after all. A corner of her daddy's ranch bordered his daddy's, and she'd spent nearly all thirty years of her wholly single life living there.

Which was vaguely depressing, when she really thought about it.

Thirty years old.

She wouldn't say she'd never been kissed, because she had. She'd even been in love until he'd been stolen away from her. But that time with Anthony Tyson had been years and years ago, back during the days when she'd still had dreams in her eyes about a life that held something more than cows, cows, and more cows.

And certainly more than little ol' Horseback Hollow.

But life, at least Aurora's, was about more than dreams. It was about loving her family and hard work and trying to replace a brother who was never coming back.

She added some briskness to her pace. "I'm going to head over to casting and see how they're coming along on replacing Joey," she said when she reached the two men. All around them, the performers for the next show, *The Great Main Street Bank Heist*, were beginning to arrive and the backstage area was becoming increasingly noisy.

"I should probably get back into my own stuff first," Galen said, plucking the shirt.

She nodded. "Thanks again for pinch-hitting on such short notice."

She still could hardly believe that he had. But then, she still had a hard time believing that he was helping out at Cowboy Country at all, considering that—like a good number of Horseback Hollow residents—at first he hadn't even been a proponent of the theme park opening.

Tall, dark and swoonworthy he might be. But Galen Fortune Jones had ranching in his roots and ranching in his blood. And he'd never made any secret that he liked their little town just fine the way it was. He didn't want to see outsiders and fat wallets coming in and gentrifying things.

She, however, had been practically champing at the bit to get her name added to the list of supporters. And as soon as she'd discovered that Moore Entertainment wanted to hire as many local performers as it could for the live entertainment at Cowboy Country, she'd hustled her tush right into line.

Yes, *Wild West Wedding* was as campy as it got. But in

the two weeks since they'd opened, the guests had been enjoying it, and so was she.

"If you hold up a sec, I'll walk with you," Galen offered, surprising the heck out of her.

She realized she was twisting one toe of her prized Castleton boots into the dirt and made herself stop. "Sure."

He smiled and strode away toward the trailer, all long legs and brawny shoulders.

"How's your mama and daddy doing, Aurora? Haven't seen Walt and Pru in months, it seems."

Glad for the distraction, she smiled back at Harlan. "Real fine, Harlan. They're going on a cruise, actually. To Alaska. They leave week after next."

The mayor-slash-barber beamed at her. "That's good news. I can't remember a time when your folks ever went off on a real vacation. Not since—" He broke off and his smile turned a little awkward. "Not in a long time," he amended. He patted her shoulder like a benevolent old uncle. "Be sure and give 'em my best, will you?"

"I will." If her daddy hadn't been bald as a cue ball and her mama hadn't always cut her own hair, they'd have spent a little time in the Cuttery, the barbershop/salon where Harlan usually spent most of his time when he wasn't acting as mayor, or playacting as Preacher Man.

Harlan headed off and Galen returned, wearing his own shirt and usual hat. On him, the black hat wasn't the least bit villainous. It was just authentic.

"You even wore a cowboy hat back in high school, didn't you?" she said aloud.

"Huh?" His fingertips lightly touched her back as they set off for the closest gate.

Her cheeks felt warm, but it was nothing compared to the shiver spiraling down her spine. "Nothing. Just thinking that Cowboy Country did a good job choosing you to make sure all things cowboy around here are actually believable."

He grimaced, looking self-conscious. "It's extra money in the bank," he muttered. They'd reached the gate and he pulled it open for her, waiting for her to walk through first. "Every smart rancher knows it's good to set some aside for leaner times."

She watched him from the corner of her eye. "Your spread's doing okay, though, isn't it?"

"Yeah." He stopped outside Gus's General Store where a selection of leather goods was on display. "My mom would like this," he said, lifting a leather purse. But when he looked at the price tag, his eyebrows shot up. "Holy Chr—" He bit off the rest. "Even with all the Fortune money she refused to take from her newfound brother, that's a ridiculous price." Shaking his head, he dropped the purse back in place and continued down the boardwalk fronting the stores, the heels of his boots ringing out.

"I've heard a little about that," Aurora said, skipping a few times to keep up with his long-legged pace. "Mostly that Jeanne Marie found out she's twin sisters to British royalty?"

"She's one of triplets," he corrected. "Lady Josephine Chesterfield and James Marshall Fortune. Separated when they were babies. Josephine grew up in England. James in Atlanta. Mom here. Their birth mother only gave up the girls."

She made a face. "I'm sure there's a reason, but that sounds terrible."

"She's dead. It was only 'cause James started looking that they know anything about each other at all."

"What's it feel like finding out that you have scads

of family across the world that you never even knew existed?"

"Pretty much the same way it felt not knowing they existed. I know it's been important to my mom finding out about her birth family. The fact that both Josephine and James and their other brother, John, are all loaded is beside the point. But to me, it just means more cousins around the dinner table." He gave her a sideways look. "You're not one of those folks who got all het up about the royalty thing, are you?"

She shrugged and shook her head, even though it was a lie. She'd been just as fascinated as every other person in Horseback Hollow when their one-horse town first brushed up against royalty. "I ran into Quinn and Amelia Drummond the other day outside of the Hollows Cantina. They had little Clementine Rose with them. She's a doll."

"I guess so. Haven't given the baby much thought."

She tsked. "Just like a man."

"What?" He frowned. "I know my new cousin had her in January. And I know things sure got interesting around these parts last year when the media found out *Lady Amelia* was pregnant."

That was certainly true. A person hadn't been able to get through town without running into one of the reporters camping out everywhere trying to get a shot of Lady Amelia and her rancher lover.

"Besides that," he continued, "it's like I said. Another person around the dinner table." He shot her a grin. "Only the little munchkin is sitting in a high chair with strained peas all over her face."

She smiled. "Still, I'd think it would feel pretty strange," she said.

"Ending up with a passel of cousins?"

"Finding out I have more family than just Mama and Daddy."

Galen shot her another glance. His grin died. "I still think about your brother," he said quietly. "About Mark."

"Me, too." She was glad they'd reached the end of the block and gestured. "Casting is back this way." She turned the corner and walked even more quickly down the street. She didn't want to talk about Mark. Didn't want to think about him, actually.

Maybe that made her the worst sister in the history of the world, but she wasn't sure she'd ever be able to forgive her big brother for dying the way he had. For leaving her parents so broken it had taken them a decade before they were managing to find a little joy in life again.

In silence, she passed the Olde Tyme Photography studio, where guests could dress up in vintage clothing to have their portraits done, and went through another wooden gate, this one manned by a uniformed security guard.

"Afternoon, Tom," she greeted as they passed from the nineteenth-century cowboy town back into the very modern present of steel and glass and asphalt.

Thanks to the park's clever designers, neither the stark building housing Cowboy Country's business offices nor the large employee parking lot were visible to Cowboy Country guests.

Excruciatingly aware of Galen following close on her heels, she went inside the office building and made her way back to the casting office.

"Hi, Diane," she greeted the sleek, black-haired young woman sitting at the main desk in front of a half dozen hard chairs, most of which were occupied by people clutching comp cards in one hand and job applications in the other. "Have you gotten any word yet on how Joey Newsome is doing?"

Diane shook her head, barely looking at Aurora because she was too busy visually devouring Galen. "Who are *you*?" she asked in her throaty voice.

"Cowboy Country's authenticity consultant. Galen Fortune Jones," Aurora said abruptly. In her dealings with the casting department so far, she knew that Diane used to work at a modeling agency located in Chicago, where Moore Entertainment's corporate headquarters was located.

Undoubtedly, the woman was stripping Galen down in her mind to chaps and nothing else.

Then Aurora wished she'd left off the "Fortune" part, because Diane's eyes seemed to grow even more interested, if such a feat were possible.

"Galen *Fortune* Jones," she purred, rising slowly from her desk, putting Aurora in mind of a cobra rising from her nest. "I've been learning *lots* about the Fortunes." She actually put her slender hand on Galen's shoulder and circled around him, giving every inch of him a closer look.

And while it made Aurora's nerves itch as though they'd been dipped into fire ants, *he* didn't seem to be bothered one little bit.

"I'm more Jones than Fortune," he drawled. He'd removed his cowboy hat the second they'd entered the building, and he gave Diane the same crooked smile that used to have cheerleaders and bookworms alike swooning back when Aurora was a high school freshman and he and her brother were the senior football stars. "Haven't seen you around Horseback Hollow. I'd have remembered if I had."

Diane laughed, low in her throat. "I drive over from

Vicker's Corners," she said, as if doing anything else was insane. "Offers a little more civilization for my tastes."

Aurora hid a sudden smile, for there was *nothing* more certain to turn off Galen Jones than to compare Horseback Hollow unfavorably against its nearest neighbor, Vicker's Corners.

"Well," Galen settled his hat back in place, even though they were indoors. "Always have said there is no accountin' for taste." His easy tone took the insult out of the words, even though Aurora was certain he meant each one. Then he looked at Aurora. "I'd better head back out there. I've only got a few more hours before I need to get back to my place. I've got chores piling up by the minute and I don't have anyone to help me around the place right now like your daddy has you."

"Okay." She rubbed her hands down the sides of her dress, wishing she had even a tenth of Diane's confidence. "Thanks again for helping out today." She glanced at the other woman. "He filled in for Joey so we didn't have to cancel the show."

Diane's red lips curved. "The hero rides to the rescue in more ways than one."

Galen looked uncomfortable. "Yeah, well." He glanced at the applicants sitting in the chairs who'd been following their exchange like viewers at a tennis match. "See you around, Aurora." He pulled open the office door. "Might grab a root beer at the Foaming Barrel later if you're interested."

She had to struggle not to look surprised, much less too interested. "Sure."

But the door was already swinging shut after his departure.

"*That* was a fine specimen of cowboy," Diane breathed.

Aurora couldn't get overly annoyed with the other woman for that, since she happened to agree.

But oohing and ahhing over Galen Jones hadn't gotten her anywhere when she'd been fourteen to his eighteen, and it wasn't going to get her anywhere now.

"So," she addressed Diane once more, "about Joey's part. Any chance you can find a temporary replacement for the rest of the shows today?"

The one guy sitting in the chairs perked up visibly.

Aurora could have told him not to bother. "Rusty" was written for a specific physical type and the hopeful applicant was about half the size he needed to be.

Diane returned to her desk and flipped open a folder. "I've been through all the performers on file." With Galen out of the room, she was all business. "We've got two who fit the type, but neither can ride a horse." She shook her head a little. "Casting shows for Coaster World's other locations is a lot easier than casting here," she murmured, tapping the end of her pen against the desk. She glanced at Aurora. "You can dance, right? Tap, ballet, that sort of thing?"

The question seemed to come out of nowhere. "Yes." She'd listed all of her skills on her application months earlier, well before Cowboy Country had opened to the public, even though they'd been learned as a little girl taking lessons over in Vicker's Corners. She'd also listed the few college parts she'd been able to play before she'd had to leave school after Mark died. "So, about Rusty's part?"

Diane lifted her shoulders and tossed down the pen. "If Joey's not back in the saddle tomorrow or the next day, it's possible we can bring in someone from another location," she said. "But that'll take some time."

"Which means, what?"

"Without a Rusty, there's no *Wild West Wedding*,"

Diane said with another shrug. "No worries, though." She picked up her phone and punched a few numbers. "Yeah, this is Diane in casting. Let me talk to Phillip."

Aurora winced, knowing she was calling Phillip Dubois, the production head.

Diane tucked the receiver in her shoulder and looked back at Aurora again. "I hear *Outlaw Shootout* will be set to go by the end of this week. It'll replace *Wedding*, and in the meantime we'll fill in—"

"—replace *Wedding*!"

Diane lifted her hand, speaking into the phone again. "Hi, Phil. We're going to need to pull *Wild West Wedding* from the sched—" Her jaw dropped when Aurora's fingers slammed down on the phone hook. "*Excuse* me?"

Aurora retracted her hand, flushing. "You can't just cancel the show."

Diane gave her a pitying look. "Stuff happens, hon."

"But Joey might well be back in the saddle, as you say, tomorrow."

"That doesn't solve the problem for three more shows today." Diane started dialing again.

"Please don't," Aurora begged.

Diane sighed loudly and looked up through her lashes at her. "Why?"

"The show means so much to, uh, to so many people," she said weakly. "We've got one of the largest casts in all of Cowboy Country's productions." The only shows with more parts were the *Sunday Go to Meeting House* with their choir show and the *How the West Was Won Saloon Show*, both of which were musicals.

Diane made a face. She replaced the receiver and folded her hands together, leaning across the desk toward Aurora. "You found yourself a Rusty for the noon show," she advised. "Get him to finish out the day. After that, we'll see."

Aurora nodded quickly. "Thanks, Diane."

The other woman shooed her away with a flick of her fingers before looking at the applicants waiting in her chairs. "You," she barked at the middle-aged woman sitting closest to her. "Can you yodel?"

Aurora quickly ducked out of the office while the applicant was still stammering.

Being cast as Lila was one of the brightest spots in Aurora's life right now. If that meant somehow talking Galen into repeating his part in the role of Rusty three more times that day, she was going to do it.

Even if it meant offering to take care of his ranch chores herself!

Chapter Three

"No way."

It had taken her a solid hour, but Aurora had finally found Galen out by the Twin Rattlers.

The roller coaster was the premier attraction at Cowboy Country, and after a start plagued with mechanical difficulties, it was now running perfectly. The line that wound like a serpentine around the base of the behemoth attested to its popularity.

"No way," he said again. "I agreed to play Rusty once, and that was enough for me."

"Galen, *please*. If you don't, they're going to cancel the rest of today's shows."

"And what happens if Joey's not back tomorrow? Or the next day?"

"Diane says they can probably bring in a performer from another one of their locations."

"Probably." He gave her a steady look. "That's not a certainty."

"No," she agreed unwillingly. She absolutely didn't want to share with him just how easily the management could supplant one production with another. "It's not a certainty." Her hands latched onto his forearm. "But you did a *really* good job as Rusty," she said quickly. "And it wasn't as awful as you thought it would be, was it?"

His gaze flickered over her hands. "I've got other responsibilities, too, kiddo," he said almost gently.

"I'll help," she promised even more quickly, letting go of him. She hadn't even realized she'd grabbed him like that. But now her palms felt all warm and tingly. "You know I'm a good ranch hand. One of me is equal or better to two of someone else," she added. "Daddy's always telling people that. You know he is."

"Why is it up to you to find a replacement for this Joey fella?"

"It isn't," she admitted. There was an entire production team, headed up by Phillip Dubois. And he wouldn't care any more than Diane did *which* show ran in *Wedding*'s time slots, as long as something did. She chewed the inside of her cheek for a moment. "I'm helping to pay for Mama and Daddy's cruise with the money I'm earning here," she finally admitted.

It was true. But it wasn't the only reason why keeping *Wild West Wedding* going was so important to her.

Somehow, she just couldn't bring herself to admit to him that being in those four performances every day was about the only thing she looked forward to these days. It would make her sound about as piddlin' pathetic as she'd been feeling until the role of Lila came along.

He exhaled and pinched the bridge of his nose. "Well, hell, Aurora."

Relief swept through her. She very nearly grabbed him again, but managed not to. "You'll do it, then?"

He nodded, though he didn't look any too happy about it. "I'll do it for *today*," he cautioned.

"Today will do," she said quickly. "Today will do just fine. And, uh, I meant it. About helping you out at your place. Whatever you need, I'm your girl. I can get Daddy to drop me by, or once they go on their trip, I'll be able to use the ranch truck."

His eyes sharpened a little. "You don't have your own transportation?"

She cursed her nervous blathering. "Until I started working here, I didn't really need my own vehicle, did I? I mean, it's not like I do much of anything besides helping out at home."

Galen eyed her. Her long red hair was pinned into a knot at the back of her head. She wore a pretty white dress that left her knees bare, and a pair of brown, blue-stitched boots that reached halfway up her calves. And even though he *had* heard Walt McElroy extoll the prowess of his only remaining offspring when it came to ranch work, right now the only thing Galen could imagine Aurora doing was clutching a bunch of daisies in her hands, dancing through some field.

He shook off the wholly ridiculous—and unwelcome—fancifulness.

"You've got enough work over at your place," he said gruffly. "Just consider today my contribution to your folks' vacation. It's been too long since they had some fun. And, you know, if you ever need a ride or something, just give a shout." He had to come to Cowboy Country anyway, at least until Caitlyn Moore, who'd been the one to hire him, decided his job was no longer needed.

"Thanks, Galen." She brushed her hands down the sides of her dress in the way he was beginning to recognize as nervousness. "They'll probably add some to your paycheck, too," she added brightly. "Every little bit helps for that rainy day, right?"

"Right," he said wryly.

He glanced around the area. There were at least fifty people lined up for the Twin Rattlers. He'd only jotted down two items for his daily report for Caitlyn. It was a huge improvement over the pages-long reports he'd started out with only a week earlier.

Caitlyn had wanted to make the park everything that her father, Alden Moore—a huge John Wayne fan—had ever dreamed of creating, and Galen was beginning to think Caitlyn might just pull it off. Considering she'd been summarily handed the job to get the place up and running when her daddy had some health troubles, Galen had to give her a lot of credit. She'd also lassoed one of Galen's new cousins, Brodie Fortune Hayes, along the way.

"Everything seems to be turning up roses these days, doesn't it?"

Aurora's words seemed to echo his own thoughts and before he knew it, "Want to grab that root beer?" came out of his mouth.

She smiled. And he realized that when she did, it seemed to show all over her entire person. From her eyes that seemed even brighter a blue, to her toes, which she went up on a little. "That sounds great."

"You always were a good kid." He wasn't sure what made him say the words. Except that, maybe, he was noticing the way the sunlight was shining through her dress, outlining the slender figure underneath. "Even Mark used to say so."

Her smile dimmed a little. Not on her lips.

But in her eyes.

"That's me," she said in a tone he couldn't quite read.

"The good kid." She gestured at the line of people waiting for the roller coaster as they left it behind. "Have you ridden it yet?"

"Nah."

"You like roller coasters, though, don't you?" She gave him a sideways look. "Every time the fair came through when we were kids, you and my brother were all over the thrill rides."

He took her arm briefly as they stepped up onto the boardwalk, continuing down Main Street. Unlike other redheads Galen knew, the only freckles on Aurora that he could see were a few spots across her nose. The rest of her seemed to be a smooth, creamy gold.

What he could see, anyway.

He shoved his hand into his pocket, reminding himself not to ponder too long or too well about what he *couldn't* see.

He'd never had trouble with the opposite sex, but since he had no intention of joining the passel of folks in his family taking the marriage bit between their teeth, he didn't tend to get involved with women who were right there under their noses.

In a small town, things got complicated in a hurry when a person did that. Wondering too hard what all delights Aurora McElroy hid beneath that pretty dress was a sure way to invite those kinds of complications.

And he liked things just fine the way they were.

"I don't think I'm much of one for loop-the-loops anymore," he said. "I'm a whole lot older than I used to be."

She snorted softly. "Please. You're thirty-four. Same age—"

"As Mark would have been," he finished when she broke off.

Her lips twisted. "Yes." She fell silent for a moment,

watching a little girl nearby purchase a huge yellow helium balloon from one of the street vendors. "It's strange," she finally said, once the girl dashed off with the balloon bobbing in the air after her, "the more I don't want to think about him, the more I seem to dwell on him."

He couldn't help himself. He slid his hand against the back of her slender neck. "I've got six brothers and sisters. I can't imagine losing one of them." Particularly in such a senseless way as getting behind the wheel of a big-ass pickup truck when he was three sheets to the wind drunk. "Maybe talking more about him will help the dwelling."

She exhaled loudly and shook her head as though she was shaking off a bothersome fly. "He died a long time ago." She pointed. "Looks like the lunch rush has hit the Foaming Barrel."

Sure enough, a line extended from the popular concession stand and Aurora had tugged her locket watch out from inside her sundress. "I don't think we've got time to wait before we need to get set for the next show. Rain check?"

"Sure."

She gave him that winning, whole-body smile again and started walking back the way they'd come.

Galen settled his hat down harder on his head and shoved his hands back into his pockets and away from… complications. Then he followed Aurora as she made her way from Main Street to the backstage area once again.

The space around the costume trailer was considerably busier now than it had been earlier. A half dozen leggy women were sitting on top of the picnic table, looking like a rainbow, dressed as they were in their colorful ruffled saloon-girl getups. Frank—handlebar mustache already in place—was hanging over one buxom girl in particular. She looked a lot more receptive to him than Aurora had earlier.

Galen followed Aurora into the trailer. It was now crowded not only with the racks of clothes and props he'd already seen, but bodies in various stages of undress, as well.

Maybe it was the hick in him, but he couldn't help doing a double take at one young woman, only realizing belatedly that she wasn't quite naked. The nude-colored bodysuit she wore just made her look like it as she stepped into a flaming red ruffled dress. She obviously had no problem not stepping behind the changing screen that was situated at one end of the trailer.

He realized he was sweating a little as he reached for Rusty's shirt and tie where he'd left them hanging, until he saw Aurora step safely behind the screen and he breathed a little easier.

Until a moment later when her white sundress was flung up to drape over the top of the changing screen and his temperature seemed to shoot up several notches.

He grabbed Rusty's white hat and brushed past several bodies, clomping down the trailer steps. Out in the open, he pulled in a long breath and exchanged his T-shirt for Rusty's button-down once again.

"Galen Jones, I *thought* that was you." One of the saloon girls had left the picnic table and was sashaying toward him in frilly peacock blue. Her hair was a pile of blond curls down the back of her head. "Serena Morris!" She patted her hand against her tightly fitted bodice, smiling widely. "Don't tell me you don't remember me. I'll be crushed forever."

"Serena?" He squinted at her face. Then couldn't help but laugh. "Last I saw you, you were—"

"—nine years old and mad as hops that my folks were

moving us to Missouri." She propped her hand on her shapely hip and grinned. "You look just the same."

He spread his hands wryly. "And here I thought the last two and a half decades might've made some difference."

She laughed. "What can I say? A girl never forgets her first kiss. You'll always be nine years old in my eyes." Her humorous gaze looked past him and Galen realized Aurora had come up behind him. "You're the new Lila," she greeted, sticking out her hand. "I've been hearing what a great job you've been doing."

Aurora warily took the other woman's hand, returning the greeting. "Aurora McElroy," she offered, watching Galen from the corner of her eye.

He was watching the other woman with nothing but pleasure on his face.

"And you," she hurriedly focused elsewhere, "are obviously in the saloon show."

"Serena," the other woman offered, moving her hip up and down. "This is how the West was won," she added, smiling mischievously. She glanced back at Galen. "Galen and I were quite the item once upon a time."

"Yeah. Fourth-grade time," he drawled. His hand slipped up Aurora's spine in a seemingly absentminded way. "Serena used to live in Horseback Hollow," he provided. "They moved away a long time ago."

"Don't remind me just how long." Serena ran her hands down her hourglass sides. "Getting harder every year to fit into these costumes."

"You look spectacular," Aurora said truthfully. The woman had enviable curves to spare.

"Well, after two kids, I guess I can be glad I am even competing with the likes of them." She tossed her feathered headdress in the direction of the other saloon girls.

"They're still so young they're wet behind the ears." She focused again on Aurora. "You're from right here in Horseback Hollow, aren't you?"

Aurora nodded. She was finding it hard to think of much of anything other than the feel of Galen's hand still resting lightly against the small of her back. "Born and raised," she managed. "Did you move back here just to work at Cowboy Country?"

"Transferred here from the Coaster World in St. Louis," Serena said. "I was with the dance corps there for years. But after my divorce last year, I figured it'd be easier raising my two boys in small-town USA." She looked back at Galen again. "We should get together. Catch up on old times."

Aurora could feel her jaw tightening, which was beyond ridiculous. It was none of her business who or what Galen went out with. But she also didn't want to stand there, with *his* hand on her back, while he made the plans. It was too eerily reminiscent of her brief college career when she'd been with Anthony.

So she pulled out the locket watch that had once belonged to her maternal grandmother and glanced blindly at the time before snapping the locket shut. "I'll leave you two to catch up," she said brightly, edging away from them. "I need to, ah, grab Frank for a minute before the show starts. Nice meeting you, Serena."

She barely stayed long enough to hear Serena's "you, too" before she hurried over toward Frank Richter where he was holding court among the other saloon girls. She wanted to talk to *him* about as much as she wanted a spike puncturing a hole in her head, but his was the only name that had come to her mind, so she was stuck.

She stopped next to him. "We should get moving."

He sent her a careless smile. "We've got a few minutes yet. And Cammie here was telling me all about herself."

Cammie giggled, looking naively thrilled by Frank's notice.

Aurora wanted to warn the girl—whose face looked like she still belonged in grade school despite her eye-popping bosom—not to get too excited, since she'd already had plenty of time to witness his alley-cat tendencies. But she said nothing. When she'd been as young as Cammie, she hadn't been interested in hearing what anyone had to say about the object of *her* affection, either.

From the corner of her eye, she could see Galen and Serena still conversing, so she made her way over to the buckboard and fit her microphone into place where it was mostly hidden in her hair. She wasn't donning the veil until she absolutely had to.

She patted her hand over the black horse already in harness. "Hey, pal. Ready for another show?" The horse, imaginatively named Blackie, jerked his head a few times before shaking his mane and turning his attention back to the few weeds sprouting up in the dirt underfoot. "I know. You've got a tough job," she murmured. "Running down Main Street a few times a day." The rest of the time, the show horses for Cowboy Country spent their days in pampered comfort in air-conditioned barns located behind the lushly landscaped public picnic grounds.

She gave him a final pat before hiking her wedding dress above her knees to work her toe onto the edge of the front wheel so she could pull herself awkwardly up onto the high wooden seat. She didn't mind portraying a nineteenth-century Western bride, but she sure was glad she hadn't been one for real.

But then again, she wasn't exactly a twenty-first-century bride, either.

She propped the thin sole of her old-fashioned boot on the edge of the wood footrest at the front of the wagon, pulled her heavy skirt above her knees, then lifted the curls of her hairpiece off her damp neck. It was early June in Texas, and the sun was high and hot overhead. And buckboards didn't come equipped with air-conditioning any more than they came with upholstered, padded seats and running boards to make climbing in easier.

Eventually, she saw her cast mates start assembling and Galen finally tore himself away from Serena the chatterbox to walk with Sal the Sheriff toward their own gate.

"You're getting grumpy in your old age, Aurora," she muttered under her breath, and sat up straighter, letting her dress fall back down where it belonged while she fit the brain-squeezing band of her veil around her head. The springs beneath the wood seat squeaked loudly as Frank climbed up beside her and fixed his mic into place.

"What's wrong with you?"

"Just hot." She looked over her shoulder. Serena had returned to the rest of her dance line and the women were all standing around, adjusting the straps of their vibrant dresses and tugging at the seams running down the back of their fishnet stockings.

She faced forward again. "You should leave Cammie alone," she told Frank. "She looks too young for you."

His shoulder leaned against hers. "Then stop saying no to me every time I ask."

She shifted as far to the right as she could without falling off the seat altogether. "I don't date people I work with." The statement was almost laughable, since she didn't date, period.

Over the loudspeaker, they heard their cue, which

meant whatever Frank might have said in response had to go unsaid since their microphones had gone live.

She swallowed, tilting her head back and closing her eyes as she willed away the surge of stage fright that made her feel nauseated before every single performance.

Frank took up the reins, lightly tapping them against the wood as he clucked softly to Blackie. The horse immediately lifted his head and shook his mane again as he started forward toward their gate.

And the next show began.

"And here, straight from his Academy Award–worthy stretch playing the ooh-la-la hero, Rusty, is our very own Galen—"

Galen shoved Liam's shoulder hard enough to push his brother—a year younger and four inches taller—right off the arm of the couch where he was propped. "Give me a break," he growled.

Liam laughed silently and moved around to sit properly next to his new wife, Julia, on the couch in their mama's front parlor.

It was Sunday afternoon, and Jeanne Marie Fortune Jones had called all her children home for a proper family meal. As if they didn't have one damn near every weekend to begin with. If *Wild West Wedding* didn't take a reprieve on Sunday afternoons so that the *Sunday Go to Meeting House* choir could use its stage, Galen would've missed out entirely on the only home-cooked meal he'd had in days.

Julia was smiling at Galen. "I still can't believe you've been playing a part at all at Cowboy Country."

"It's temporary." He pushed Christopher. "Get outta my spot, man."

At twenty-seven, Chris was the baby of the boys. But

his days of letting Galen order him around were apparently over, judging by the dry look Galen got in return. Chris, like Liam, Jude and their little sister Stacey, had gotten hitched just that Valentine's Day in the same big wedding. And marriage to the gorgeous Kinsley had definitely helped settle him, same as finding his footing in business with the Fortune Foundation. "Pretty sure your name's not stitched in the upholstery now any more than it ever was." To prove that he was staying put, Christopher propped his boot heels on the coffee table in front of his chair. "Get your own chair, brother."

Typically, when the whole family was around, seating was at a premium. Particularly now that his siblings had started adding spouses—and in the case of his brother Toby and his wife of a year, Angie, the three foster kids they'd adopted. Which meant every seat cushion in the parlor was wholly occupied by the backside of a Fortune Jones. Even the floor was taken up by Toby's two youngest, Justin and Kylie, where they were working a big old puzzle.

"I don't know how temporary," Julia was saying on a laugh. "Haven't you been playing Rusty all last week?"

Galen almost tugged at his collar, but managed to restrain himself. "'Bout that. Where's Stace?"

"Piper's got a summer cold," Angie said, speaking of Stacey's toddler. "She didn't want to expose anyone."

"Thought you told 'em you were only going to play Rusty for that one day." That came from Jude, entering the room with more brains than Galen had, since he was carrying a chair from the dining room table with him. He set it in the corner and promptly pulled his petite wife, Gabriella, down on his knee. "That's what you said last time I talked to you. What was it?" He and his bride shared a look that spoke of intimacies Galen didn't even want to contemplate. "Last Wednesday?"

"They were in a pinch," he muttered grumpily. "The original guy, Joey somebody-or-other, broke his leg. He's out for the next six weeks, at least." And Galen still couldn't explain his reasons for giving in when Diane in the casting department still hadn't produced a permanent replacement for the guy. It damn sure hadn't been because Diane was outright propositioning him.

But attributing it to keeping Aurora's whole-body smile going wasn't something he wanted to admit to, either.

Not to himself and definitely not to his pack of siblings and siblings-in-law.

He tried changing the subject again. "What about Delaney?"

"In Red Rock with the new fiancé." That came from Christopher. "Cisco's still getting some training with the Fortune Foundation there. We sent Rachel, also. Matteo flew 'em over." Matteo was Cisco's brother and a pilot at the Redmond Flight School and Charter Service. And Rachel Robinson was Matteo's fiancée and an intern with Christopher.

"You're going to be playacting the besotted groom for the next six weeks?" Jude wasn't swayed by their baby sister's whereabouts and was looking at Galen as if he'd announced he'd started building castles on the moon.

"Hell no," Galen assured emphatically. "Cowboy Country's got a whole department of people hiring folks. They'll get a replacement in a few days, I'm sure." And he was anxious to get off the subject. "I'm getting a beer."

"You are *not*," Jeanne Marie said, sailing into the room. She was taller than average and wearing her usual cowboy boots, which added a good inch and a half, bringing her silver head to merely a few inches below Galen's. "We're just about ready to sit down and eat and I'm not having beer at my Sunday dinner table." She propped her hands on the hips of blue jeans that were mostly hidden behind her old-fashioned apron. "Christopher, get your boots off the furniture. Just because I'm pleased as punch you've moved back home to Horseback Hollow doesn't mean you're getting away with that nonsense."

Chris grinned and dutifully put his feet down on the floor again. "Yes, ma'am."

Jeanne Marie turned her eyes back on Galen. "Where's your father?"

"Out back working on the truck."

"As usual." But the amusement in her eyes belied any annoyance her tart words carried. "Go and get him, would you please?"

Glad for an excuse to escape a room that was uncomfortably brimming over from matrimonial bliss, his "Yes, ma'am" was likely a mite enthusiastic.

Plus, he was able to grab a beer along the way, though he winced like a guilty teenager when he twisted off the bottle cap and the sound seemed to echo around the kitchen.

His mom didn't come after him with a wooden spoon, though, so he hustled out the back door and across the green expanse of lawn that was his mom's pride and joy every summer, over to his pop, who was leaning over the opened hood of his ancient pickup truck. Galen took up a spot on the other side. "What's the problem now?"

Deke Jones pulled off his sweat-stained ball cap, rubbed his fingers through his thick iron-gray hair and replaced the cap once again. "Running like a top for once," he drawled and lifted the beer bottle hidden in the depths of the engine. "Just didn't feel much like cleaning fresh green beans with your mama in that hot kitchen."

Galen chuckled. He and his father had done two things together while Galen had been growing up. Work on this same truck. And work the cattle. Now he was an adult, neither thing had really changed. "It is hot. Not even the middle of summer yet." He turned around and closed his eyes to the sunlight. But that only made him think about seeing Aurora do pretty much the same thing every time she climbed up in the buckboard, ready for another show to begin.

She'd tilt her head back, eyes closed, for a good minute or two right before she, Frank and the buckboard blasted beyond the gate while the *Wild West Wedding* theme song roared over the loudspeakers.

"How many years you and Ma been married now?"

His dad gave him a strange look. "Forty-one years."

"It's a long time."

"You'd think." Deke took another pull on his beer, glancing over his shoulder to the house some distance behind them. A bed of white and yellow flowers lined the whole back side of the house. "The longer we go, the shorter the time seems to be. Like there's not enough years left to spend together." Then he made a face at his beer. "Listen to me. Must be still a hangover from the *big* wedding." He eyed Galen. "You got girl trouble or something?"

Galen snorted softly. "You think I'd come to you if I did?"

Deke grinned slightly. As a father, he'd been a pretty silent authority figure. A hardworking rancher who'd passed on his work ethic and much of his stoic personality to Galen. Sometimes, Galen was grateful for that.

Other times, he sometimes wished he had the gift of gab like Jude, or the slick smarts like Christopher.

"Not exactly an answer, son," Deke drawled.

"No, I don't have girl trouble," he assured, swiping mentally at the image of Aurora in a white dress and cowboy boots, dancing in some damn daisy field. "Ma wants you in for supper."

"I know." Deke swirled the base of his bottle in the air a few times. "Crowded as heck in the house these days."

"That a complaint?"

"Nope. Just stating a fact." His father squinted slightly and looked back at the house again. "When your mama and I got hitched, it took a while before you came along. Then, *whoosh*. The floodgates opened and next thing I knew, we had seven of you." The corner of his lips lifted. "Now it's like that all over again, what with all of you getting married." He gave Galen a look. "'Cept you, of course. Now that Delaney's planning on getting hitched to that young Mendoza, you're the last holdout."

"Never met anyone who put me in the mind to marry."

Deke chuckled. "Now I hear you're doing it a bunch a times a day out at Cowboy Country."

Galen tugged his ear, hating that he felt a little foolish about it in front of his dad. "Playing Rusty pays even more than the 'authenticity consultant' business."

"You're still doing that, though, aren't you?"

He nodded. "For now. More money I sock away in the bank, the more I can think about buying that bull of Quinn Drummond's that he knows I want." Another bull would mean covering more cows to produce calves. More calves, more money. Better to focus on the financial aspect than on making Aurora happy.

"Seems like you must be spending a lot of your day

at Cowboy Country, then. How you managing to spare all the time?"

Badly, Galen thought. His sink was full of dirty dishes, his laundry hadn't been done in a solid week, and his cupboard was bare. The only thing he hadn't neglected entirely was his small cow-calf operation. He couldn't afford to neglect them, or he'd end up coming back home to live with his folks, his tail tucked between his legs. No number of prizewinning bulls would help then, and becoming a failure at thirty-four wasn't one of his aspirations in life.

"I'm managing," he said shortly. Then honesty got the better of him. "Only because we've got a few more weeks before I've gotta start working 'em and sorting. Just glad that Ma doesn't drop by my place too often these days. She'd have a conniption fit and fall right in it over the mess it's in."

Deke let out a bark of rare laughter. "'Spect she would, son. I expect she would." He jerked his chin. "Finish that up so we can go in and eat."

Galen took another pull on his beer, and set the still half-full bottle on the green, green grass beside his father's. Just as he straightened, the back screen door of the house slapped open and Jeanne Marie hung out. "Deke Jones, you get your hind end in here right now, or this roast is going to be shoe leather! Should've known better than to send Galen after you. Two peas in a pod, you are."

"Keep your apron on, Jeanne Marie," Deke returned without heat. "We're getting there."

Even across the spacious yard, they could hear her harrumph before she let the screen door slap shut again.

In accord, Galen and Deke began walking back across the lawn toward the two-story house that seemed way too small to have housed the large family they'd had. Not even learning she had a wealthy brother and even wealthier sister had changed anything about Jeanne Marie—namely, her love for her relatively simple life with Deke and their offspring.

"How'd you know Ma was the one?"

Deke squinted at him again. "Who is she? This girl you don't got troubles with?"

"Nobody." He yanked at his shirt collar. He was wearing one of his dress shirts—the ones he sent to the laundry to get cleaned and ironed—because he hadn't had anything else in his closet that didn't smell of sweat or dirt or cow manure. "Can't a man be curious?"

Deke smiled briefly and clapped Galen hard on the back. "I knew your ma was the one when I couldn't look at her without imagining her wearing a white wedding dress. Lot of men imagine a woman wearing nothing at all. Second nature, I guess." He nodded sagely. "But when he starts imagining her wearing a wedding dress? That's when you know you're dealing with a whole different kettle of fish. That what you want to know?"

Galen smiled weakly. "I don't want to think about you imagining *anyone* nekkid," he drawled with feeling, and reached out for the screen door when they reached it. "'Specially my mama."

His father's low laughter followed him.

Chapter Four

"Yo, Galen." Frank Richter stepped out of the trailer after their final show for the day. "Everyone's heading over to the Two Moon to grab a beer. Interested?"

Galen shook his head. After doing nine days of shows—thirty-six episodes of rescuing Lila from the villain's clutches—he was more interested in heading to the welcome silence his own house offered. "Burning the candle at both ends has a price," he excused. "Got chores waiting."

"At eight-thirty?" Frank was rolling up the sleeves of his black shirt until they were just so. "That's a crying shame. Friday nights ought to be for things a lot more fun." A movement from the trailer behind them drew his attention. "Like her," he said, nodding toward Aurora as she came down the steps wearing cutoff denims and a sleeveless plaid shirt. Her red hair streamed down from the ponytail at the back of her head.

"Thought you were seeing that little gal from the saloon show."

"And your point?" Frank's white teeth flashed. "Only thing better than one good-looking woman in your arms is two of them. They'd be fine bookends, wouldn't they? Sweet, curvy little Cammie on one side and lean, mean Rory on the other?" He rubbed his hands together. "Talk about anticipation."

"She doesn't like being called Rory," Galen said evenly. Since he'd found his boots sinking into Cowboy Country like quicksand, he'd learned it was easier to ignore Frank than get riled over every stupid thing that came out of his mouth. Far as Galen was concerned, there weren't enough hours in the day to spend 'em being annoyed by an idiot. "But you're right about one thing," he added abruptly. "A cold one at the Two Moon sounds good."

Suiting his words to action, he pulled his truck keys from his front pocket and let his path intercept Aurora's. "You heading over to the Two Moon Saloon?"

She jumped a little, like he'd startled her. "Um...yes." She pushed her fingertips into the front pockets of her cutoffs. They weren't all that short; his little sisters wore cutoffs that bared a whole lot more leg, but he'd never found himself getting distracted by the amount of thigh they'd exposed as he was finding himself now. "You?"

"Thought I might." He dragged his attention upward. Aurora might be lean, as Frank said, but she was built with the deceptive delicacy of a Thoroughbred racehorse. And Galen had always appreciated good lines. In a horse or a woman. "Need a ride?"

Her lips parted slightly. "Ah...sure. I usually hitch a ride with the mayor."

"Better Harlan than Frank," Galen muttered.

Aurora chuckled at that. "Just because I'm a small-town girl doesn't mean I'm a dolt. One dose of Frank's octopus arms was enough for me."

Galen shot her a look. "What's that supposed to mean? He's made a pass at you?"

She gave him an odd look. "Frank makes a pass at every female walking." She knelt down quickly to retie the shoelace on her plain white tennis shoes, and the back of her shirt rode up slightly, revealing an inch of smooth skin above the low waist of her shorts.

Galen ran his hand around the back of his neck, looking belatedly away.

Then she rose again as if she'd never stopped. "I think it's in his DNA or something," she continued. "A nuisance, but hard to take anything about him too seriously." She tugged out her locket watch and angled it toward the light shining down from the overhead poles. "If we hurry, we'll still be able to get hot wings on the happy hour menu. They're half price."

Nothing at the Two Moon Saloon was all that pricy. It would've never stayed in business otherwise. The place was attached to the Horseback Hollow Grill, and what it served up was long on cheap burgers and a helluva grilled cheese, and way short on ambiance. If a person wanted that, they went to the Hollows Cantina that had opened only last year.

"Half-price wings it is." He jangled his truck key. "I'm in the employee lot." They followed in the path of other cast members making their way through the circuitous backstage area circling Cowboy Country's perimeter. "Your parents left yet on their cruise?"

"Sunday morning," she told him with a quick smile. "They leave out of San Francisco, so I'll drop them at the airport in Lubbock tomorrow morning and be back in time for the noon show. They're pretty excited. Mama especially. She's always wanted to see Alaska."

The walkway narrowed between the back of a building on one side and the high hedges blocking off the fence on the other, separating the park from what was supposed to have been a hotel project before it'd been shelved because of construction and design issues, and he waited so she could walk ahead of him. "I'll bet."

"They'll be cruising part of the time, and land-touring part of the time," she said over her shoulder. "Daddy figures it's the best of both worlds, because he's not all that sure he'll like being cooped up on a boat for nearly two weeks." Her grin was impish in the dwindling light. "The cruise ship is like a floating city. Probably bigger than Horseback Hollow. Cooped up." She laughed a little, shaking her head. "What about you? Anywhere you dream of going?"

"To see a Super Bowl?"

She laughed. "Come on. Seriously."

The path widened out again and he came abreast of her. "I am serious. Where else would I rather be than here in Texas?"

"Football and cows being your ultimate fantasy, I guess."

"Well, shoot, honey. Didn't know we were talking *fantasy*," he drawled before he thought better of it. They were passing beneath another light pole and her cheeks looked as if they'd turned red. Which left him feeling like a jackass and awkward as hell. He cleared his throat. "What about you?" That wasn't any better. "About Alaska, I mean. Didn't you want to go?"

"With my parents on a cruise? I love 'em, but no thank you. Bad enough I'm still single and living at home with them."

"What's wrong with that?"

"At my age?" She made a tsking sound. "Please. How old were you when you moved out on your own?"

"That's different."

They'd reached the security gate leading out to the parking lot and she gave him a look as they passed through. "Why on earth is it different?"

He lifted a shoulder, wishing to hell all over again that he'd kept his mouth shut. It'd been easy for him to go out on his own. He was the eldest of seven kids. When he'd left the nest, his mama had still had a half dozen chicks left to fuss over.

Thanks to Mark's death, Aurora's parents had only her.

"So where *is* your dream vacation?" he asked instead of answering.

She spread her arms. "Anywhere other than here."

She'd smiled as she said it, but he could see the truth beneath it. And he remembered good and well Mark laughing way back when about his kid sister's "big city" dreams. "I remember you went off to college for a few years." He gestured toward his pickup truck parked at the far corner of the lot. "Where was it?"

"UCLA."

"Guess you probably got a good taste of city life in Los Angeles."

She waited while a car passed them. Galen recognized Frank behind the wheel with a few of the saloon dancers in his passenger seats.

"Two years was a pretty short taste, in the span of the rest of my life spent here," she said.

He studied her profile. The gentle point of her chin. The fine line of her narrow nose that was just a shade too long, making it all the more interesting. And the pale pink lips that he'd pretended to kiss thirty-damn-six times now. "Would you go back to California if you had the chance?"

She gave him a rueful look. "Maybe I'll go on a vacation there someday."

He didn't know why her answer sat so wrong, but it did. "If you hate it here, why don't you go? There is such a thing as hiring ranch hands, you know."

Her eyebrows rose. "I never said I hated it here." Her hands spread again. "I'm a Texas girl. Horseback Hollow is my home. I love my folks. Maybe if Mark hadn't died, I would have ended up somewhere else. But he did. My parents needed me more than I needed to follow some pipe dream that would probably have never gotten me any further than—" she thought for a moment "—than teaching high school drama classes." She started across the parking lot again. "Being away at college wasn't all that perfect, either. Don't expect it ever is for anyone."

"Texas A&M was pretty perfect in my eyes."

She grinned. "What a good Texas son you are. Bet you have Aggie pennants pinned on your bedroom walls."

He snorted. "Basement."

She laughed outright, and just like her smile, it seemed to show in her entire body.

He much preferred her in smiles and laughter over that solemn, vaguely fatalistic acceptance of her life's path.

In silence, they crossed the rest of the parking lot to his truck. He started to open the passenger door for her, but she beat him to it, climbing up handily inside.

So he rounded the front of the vehicle and got behind the wheel.

"This is nice." She was running her hand over her leather seat.

"It does the job." He started the ignition and worked his way through the parking lot. Even though their show was done for the day, the rest of the attractions would still be going strong until the park closed for the day. Which meant there were a passel of employees still at work and the lot was more full than not.

"My mother tried talking Daddy into buying a new truck instead of going on their trip." She crossed one leg over the other, and the toe of her tennis shoe bounced in time to the George Strait tune coming from the radio. "I'm glad he stuck to his guns even if it means driving that old Ford for a few more years."

He didn't have to work hard at recalling she was contributing to the cost of her folks' trip. It was one of the reasons he'd caved when it came to playing Rusty. That, and not being a cause of Aurora's disappointment. "If you need any help at your place while they're gone, just let me know."

She gave him an arch look. "And why would I let you help me, when you wouldn't let me help you?" Her eyebrows rose a little higher. "Don't confuse me with Lila, Galen Fortune Jones. I'm not sitting around waiting to get rescued. I may not be as strong physically as you are, but I can work just as hard."

"Whoa there, Nelly." He waved his hand in surrender. "I'm not saying you can't. It's just a—" he thought for a moment "—a neighborly offer. One I'd make to anyone."

She pressed her lips together and nodded once. "That's better," she muttered.

He bit back a smile that even he knew wouldn't be well received and turned the truck toward the Two Moon. "You guys get together a lot at the Moon?"

"The cast and crew, you mean? Maybe once a week, if that." Her toe tapped a few times. "Haven't seen Serena there, if that's what you're wondering."

"Wh— Oh. Serena. I wasn't." He ran his tongue

against the edge of his molars and wondered why *she* was wondering.

"Wasn't she the first girl you kissed?"

He couldn't stop the bark of laughter. "Well, yeah. But I was *nine*. At the time, I think I was more curious about whether or not our braces would get stuck together."

She muffled her laughter with her hand. "You were not."

He tried thinking back, and nodded. "Nope. No, yeah. I think I was. Your brother was the one who was more interested in copping a feel from a girl, even if she didn't have anything yet to feel."

"Sounds like Mark." She tugged her ponytail over her shoulder and started working it into a loose braid. "Ever since I could remember, excess was his thing."

And excess had been the end of him.

Galen caught her hand in his and squeezed. "What about *your* first kiss?" A few seconds too late, he remembered to let go of her hand again. "And don't tell me it was with one of my brothers. I'm already privy to more of their romantic lives than I like."

She folded her hands in her lap and seemed to be studying them. But at least she was smiling again, as he'd hoped. "No. It wasn't." She waited a beat. "Quinn Drummond, actually. He was only a year ahead of me."

"That's almost as bad as one of my brothers."

She smiled a little. "We were in junior high. Under the bleachers after a school dance."

"Please don't feel the need to share any more gory details. I see Quinn all the time."

"'Specially now he's married to your cousin, *Lady* Amelia?"

"She doesn't much like getting called Lady Amelia anymore'n you like getting called Rory." Which was the name that her brother had always called her, just because he'd known it always got her goat. It was enough to make Galen feel guilty for the way he used to tease his own little sisters. For that matter, the way he sometimes still did.

When he reached the Two Moon Saloon, the small parking lot was already crowded, so he parked in a dirt lot nearby. Inside the bar, it wasn't any better. But the Cowboy Country crowd had still managed to scope out a few long tables, and Galen followed Aurora through the crush of bodies.

He pulled off his hat and leaned over her. "I remember a time not too long ago when this place didn't have this much business in a month of Sundays combined."

"Right?" She looked up at him, and stumbled a bit.

He quickly moved the chair she'd bumped into out of their path and tried not to notice the way her hair smelled like flowers even at the end of a long day. A pointless exercise, since he noticed, anyway. "Crowded in here." Their heads were so close, he could have kissed her.

And maybe she realized it, because she gave a weak smile and stepped back, adding a good foot to the two inches separating their mouths.

He wanted to kick himself.

She was Mark's kid sister. She probably figured Galen was no better than Frank.

He jerked his chin toward the bar. "I'm going to get an order in, kiddo. You go on ahead."

Aurora swallowed the protest that rose too quickly to her lips. She still felt shaky from finding herself that close to Galen.

Which was silly, since she ought to be used to it by now after nine whole days of playing Lila to his Rusty. Instead of becoming accustomed to him sweeping her against him four times a day, though, it was turning into a slow sort of torture.

Foreplay with no chance of making it to "play." Not when she was just the kid sister of an old friend he used to have.

"Extra hot," she called after him a little too loudly, but thankfully, her words merely blended into the overall noise of the bar.

He heard, though, and gave a wave of his black cowboy hat as he shuffled back through the herd. Sighing a little, she continued onward and managed to secure two bar stools at one of the high-tops where Cabot Oakley, who played Sal the Sheriff, was sitting with his girlfriend, Sue.

"Crazy busy in here, isn't it?" Sue leaned toward her and raised her voice just to be heard. She was a comfortably plump woman in comparison to Cabot's extreme thinness, and worked as a teacher's aide at the elementary school. Until Caitlyn Moore had realized that the success of Cowboy Country relied on inclusiveness where Horseback Hollow residents were concerned, Sal's part had been played by a slick performer from Florida whose main interest was his next role. Preferably a bigger one.

He'd been even more self-involved than Frank, and Aurora hadn't been sorry to see him go. As far as she was concerned, Cabot did a much better job in the role of Sal. He wasn't aiming to gain anything personal but to give a good show and earn enough income to buy a ring so he could finally propose to Sue.

"I don't think I've ever seen it this crowded," Aurora agreed. "Maybe it's proof that Cowboy Country is doing what they promised to do. Bringing more revenue in general into Horseback Hollow."

Sue was nodding. "Cabot's been telling me how hard

a time they're having filling Joey's spot in the show. Says he figures they've already tapped out all the locals. Good thing you were able to talk Galen into helping out." She grinned and patted Cabot's arm. "Cab can't carry a tune in a bucket and he darn sure can't wear a saloon girl outfit. He'd be back to pumping gas part-time at his cousin's filling station in Vicker's Corners if it weren't for the wedding show."

Aurora smiled ruefully. "I don't think I, personally, had anything to do with Galen's decision. Maybe he wishes he'd played in more high school drama productions than football games."

Sue propped her chin on her hand and smiled reminiscently. "He *was* fun to watch wearing those tight football pants, wasn't he? Talk about a fine hiney. Him and your brother both, Aurora. Heartthrob material."

"Sue, honey," Cabot complained. "I'm right here."

"I know, sweetie." She patted his arm again. "Wouldn't want you anywhere else, but a girl still has her memories. Don't we, Aurora?"

Aurora smiled. "I'm not touching that one with a ten-foot pole," she assured. Galen might not wear football gear anymore, but as far as she was concerned, he looked even better nowadays in his typical blue jeans.

Sue chuckled and sat up again when Galen arrived bearing a pitcher of beer and several mugs. "Hero rides to the rescue yet again," she said brightly, reaching out to help untangle the mug handles from his long fingers.

He smiled crookedly. "Sue. Cab." His gaze fell on Cab's hand, circling Sue's shoulder. "Didn't realize you two were an item."

"Then you must be living under a rock," Sue accused good-naturedly. She looked at Cabot. "How long we been together now?"

"Three years."

The two were giving each other besotted smiles, and Aurora looked away, her gaze colliding with Galen's.

"Wings shouldn't take too long," he said, tucking the bar stool under him. The table was so small and the space around them so crowded that his thigh—warm even through his denim jeans—rested alongside Aurora's.

No amount of shifting was going to create space where there was none, but Aurora tried anyway as she pulled some folded cash out of her front pocket and handed it to him.

He didn't take it. "What's that for?"

"The hot wings. My share of the beer." She dropped the folded bills on the table in front of him and started filling the mugs.

"Keep your money." He nudged it back toward her.

She stopped the progress with her fingers. "Everybody splits, Galen." And she definitely didn't want him thinking *she* was thinking they were on a date, when they most definitely were not. "Frankly, we all should be buying your beer tonight. Right, Cabot?"

The skinny man nodded and lifted his soda, which was all Aurora had ever seen him drink. "Amen to that. To Galen!"

Frank, several chairs away at the next table, heard that, and picked up his squat glass. "To Galen!"

"Oh, Christ," Galen muttered, looking pained. "Shoot me now."

She held up her mug, too. "To Galen," she said firmly. "Without whom *Wild West Wedding* would have been put in mothballs this past week." She bumped her shoulder against his. "Smile, neighbor, and let us be grateful."

He gave her a sidelong look she couldn't read, and

exhaled. Then he lifted his mug in salute, too. "To *Wild West Wedding*!"

All around them, glasses clanked together and people cheered.

Aurora did, too.

But mostly she was thinking about the feel of his thigh against hers underneath the table, and wishing he wouldn't just see her as "kiddo."

Chapter Five

"You want me to walk you up?" Galen was peering at Aurora's house situated up the hill from where he'd pulled into the gravel drive. "It's pretty dark."

"I'm not ten," she protested grumpily.

"Yeah, I know. Ten-year-olds don't drink as much beer as you."

"I had three," she said, carefully distinct. And they'd been at the Two Moon nearly three hours.

"I know," Galen said in a soothing, indulgent tone that only added to her general sense of irritation. "And you were tipsy after just one." He handed her the foil container with the hot wings she hadn't been able to finish.

"Fortunately, I knew I didn't have to drive." She stared at him in the faintly blue light coming from his truck dashboard. "I'm not planning on following in my brother's footsteps."

He patted her shoulder. "I know."

All night, he'd sat next to her, his body heat searing down her whole left side.

And now he was reaching a long arm across her, pushing open the door for her.

"I'm not a kid, either."

He drew back more slowly and pulled off his cowboy hat, pushing it up onto the dash. "Trust me, Aurora. I know that, too."

The air had finally cooled off and now it was almost chilly. But she couldn't blame the shivers skipping up and down her spine on the temperature. Those were owed strictly to him.

Her mouth felt dry and she swallowed, unable to look away from him, still leaning half across her, so close. "Galen—"

Suddenly, the porch light up at the house went on and her mother was hanging out of the front door. "That you, Aurora, baby?" Her voice was loud enough to carry two counties over. "Getting kind of late, isn't it?"

Aurora wanted to sink through the floorboard of Galen's truck. "Not really," she muttered.

"It's midnight," Galen murmured, sitting back fully in his own seat. "Time for Cinderella to get inside."

"Only because she has to get up in the morning to drive her parents to the airport," she said. "Not because she believes in fairy tales anymore." She unclipped her seat belt. "Thanks for the ride."

"Guess you won't need anyone picking you up tomorrow to get to Cowboy Country. You'll have the ranch truck?"

"Right." She pushed the door open a little wider with the toe of her tennis shoe, but some devil made her lean across the console and press a quick kiss to his lean cheek.

He reared back as if he were stung, though. "What's that for?"

Trying not to gulp like some inexperienced ninny, she lifted the foil container between them. "Keep your shirt on," she said tartly. "Giving me your share of wings, of course." Then before she could make a bigger fool out of herself than she already had, she scrambled out of the truck and slammed the door.

"Hold the door, Mama," she called out, heading blindly up the familiar dark hill dotted with sweet gum trees to the bright light shining from the porch.

When she reached it, her mother tucked her arm around her. "Have fun, baby?"

Aurora looked over her shoulder, watching Galen's taillights as he drove back down the sloping gravel driveway. "Not as much fun as you and Daddy will be having starting tomorrow."

Pru McElroy's eyes were as excited as Aurora could ever remember seeing. "I still haven't finished packing," she said. "Your daddy's been snoring asleep for the past two hours, and I still can't decide what all I need to take!"

Aurora gave her a quick hug. "Well, let's go figure it out, then," she said. "So we can both get some sleep, too!"

Her mother squeezed her back. Then laughed again, and clutching Aurora's hand, pulled her into the house.

It was only later, after the two suitcases were fastened tight and waiting by the back door to be loaded into the truck in the morning, that Aurora stood staring out the dark window in her bedroom.

Sleep was the furthest thing from her mind. Because she couldn't stop thinking about what might have happened in Galen's truck if her mother hadn't chosen that particular moment to open the front door and yell down at her.

* * *

"Oh, my stars and body!"

Aurora flinched a little at the expression she hadn't heard in years and warily looked over the hot dog she was just lifting toward her mouth.

"Is that you, Aurora McElroy?"

She lost her appetite for the hot dog altogether and carefully set it in the paper basket sitting on the round umbrella-covered table in front of her.

"It is!" The woman who'd been speaking was waving madly as she pushed a giant baby stroller across Cowboy Country's Main Street toward Aurora. Her black hair was a glossy sheen under the brilliant sunlight, and even before she reached Aurora's side and pulled off the überstylish sunglasses she wore, Aurora knew the eyes behind would be equally dark and shining.

She swung her legs around the bench and stood. "Roselyn," she greeted before her old college roommate yanked her close for the same quick kiss-kiss-hug-hug embrace she'd favored even a decade earlier. "This is a surprise."

"Isn't it?" Roselyn tucked her glasses on the top of her head, her eyes widening for emphasis. "Here I bring little Toni and Tiffani to the park for a speck of entertainment with some furry creatures, and look who I find? Never in a million years would I have expected to see *you* here. What are you even doing in Texas?"

"I come from here," Aurora said drily. "I guess you don't remember. And I could say the same about seeing *you* here." Anthony had hailed from Red Rock, Texas. A town that was nowhere near as small as Horseback Hollow, but still one that didn't have the cachet that he desired. It was their common Texas background that had drawn them together at the beginning.

"Oh." Roselyn was waving her hand around. "Anthony's always teasing me about my memory. You haven't changed a bit!" She smiled brilliantly and her white teeth were so straight and bright that Aurora felt like squinting. "Mind if I sit?" She ran her hand—perfectly manicured as always and wearing a gloriously oversize wedding set on her ring finger—over the front of her scarlet blouse and Aurora realized the other woman was pregnant.

There was certainly no other reason Roselyn St. James—ever successful, and ever *perfect*—would have a bump the size of a basketball beneath her undoubtedly silk shirt.

Aurora automatically gestured to the other bench. In contrast to Roselyn's hands, hers bore calluses on the palm and her nails were perpetually short and unvarnished. "You're pregnant."

Roselyn smiled beatifically as she sat. She was wearing a short white skirt with her scarlet blouse that not even *un*pregnant women would be able to carry off so well, and her long legs were as shapely as ever. "Seven months." She practically purred with contentment. She rested a languid hand on her belly and her diamonds glinted in the sunlight. "Anthony and I are both thrilled, of course. We didn't think we'd have any more children after the twins, but—" She lifted her shoulder and gave a throaty little laugh. "They're nearly three now. And you know how these things happen. Wait until he hears about you."

Aurora felt a nervous start. She hadn't seen Anthony since he'd broken the news to her that he needed his diamond ring back, because he'd just eloped with her college roommate. "He's here?"

"Didn't I say?" Roselyn rolled the expressive eyes that had helped land her a successful run on a daytime soap opera before she'd even finished her second year of college.

A run that had ended only a few years ago when she'd chosen to give it all up to focus on her family, a decision that Roselyn had somehow managed to turn into a minor media event.

"He has a big meeting with Moore Entertainment," she was continuing. "They brought him here for a few days to see what he thinks of Cowboy Country. We're staying in Vicker's Corners, of course. They've put us up in a charming little B&B there." She pulled the stroller closer to her and peeked beneath the awning at the two cherubic children sitting inside.

Naturally, they had to be perfect, too.

Then Aurora chided herself mentally for being uncharitable. Little Toni and Tiffani couldn't help it that their mother was unquestionably Aurora's least favorite person on the planet.

So she leaned closer and smiled at the toddlers. They really *were* cute. A perfect combination of Roselyn's olive-skinned exoticness and their father's brilliant blue eyes. "How *is* your husband?" she asked casually.

"Fabulous," Roselyn said immediately. She squeezed Aurora's forearm. "We have *got* to get together. It's been such a long time. There is so much to catch up on!"

Like what? Aurora wanted to ask, but figured the irony would be lost on Roselyn. Besides, her onetime friend surely didn't mean it. Since she'd left UCLA with a soap opera contract in one hand and Aurora's fiancé in the other, Aurora hadn't heard from her once.

Not even when Mark had died two months later and Aurora had left school for good, too.

She nearly jumped out of her skin when Galen appeared next to the table, his cowboy hat pulled low over his brow. "Surprised to see you out here, wife of mine," he drawled humorously. "Better get moving, don't you think?" He tugged lightly on her ponytail as he strode past, seeming not to give Roselyn even a second glance.

Aurora pulled out her watch locket, checking the time. It had taken her longer to get back from the airport in Lubbock than she'd planned, so she'd come straight to the park, thinking she'd have just enough time for a dog and a root beer before getting ready for the noon show.

"I'm sorry, Roselyn." Though she wasn't. "I've got to go." She gathered up her hot dog basket. "Hope your kids have fun here today. If you want furry entertainment, try the petting zoo. There are three baby piglets there right now that I hear are supercute." And the petting zoo was on the opposite side of the park, as far away from *Wild West Wedding* as it was possible to get.

Roselyn was staring at her with a shocked expression. "You're actually *married*?" She said it with such astonishment that Aurora's teeth immediately set on edge. "To that hunk of cowboy?"

"What's so surprising?" Aurora managed with false cheer. "That I could find a man who'd stick, or that he'd look like Galen?"

Roselyn's mouth was open.

"Like you said," Aurora continued, saccharine sweet. "It's been a long time." She dropped her hot dog in the trash and leaned over Roselyn, airbrushing her cheek with a kiss-kiss. "Take care now."

Then she straightened and walked away, following Galen's route. A part of her felt silly for not correcting Roselyn.

The other part felt more than a little gleeful over rendering the woman speechless.

Even a decade after their time at college, being able to do *that* felt pretty darn good.

She quickened her step and turned up one of the side streets that would take her backstage. By the time she reached the wardrobe trailer, she was actually whistling.

Though that stuck between her teeth when she entered and found Galen in the process of pulling on his Rusty shirt, giving her an eyeful of very, *very* bare abs.

"Hey," she greeted a little breathlessly, and quickly squeezed past him, grabbing her wedding dress from the rack.

"Get your folks off okay?"

"Yup. The plane was late, so my mother was all worried they'd miss the cruise departure. Which is *tomorrow.* Needless to say, she's really excited." She stole a glance at his suntanned chest, intriguingly dusted with a swirl of dark hair, before stepping behind the changing screen. Would that chest hair be soft under her palms, or crisp?

She shook her head sharply and hurriedly kicked off her discount-store tennis shoes, which Roselyn would've never been caught dead in. Then she was annoyed for still allowing the other woman to even intrude on her thoughts. She yanked down her khaki Bermuda shorts and bumped her head loudly against the wall when she leaned over to pick them up.

"You okay back there?"

She straightened, rubbing her head. "Yes. Just clumsy. You ever had anyone in your life who gets on your nerves no matter what?" She draped her shorts over the top of the screen, which was much too tall for anyone to see over. "Probably not," she answered her own question. She tugged her T-shirt over her head and flipped it, too, on the top of the screen, then unclipped her bra since she couldn't wear it without the straps showing with the costume.

"Why probably not?"

She could hear him rummaging through the drawers. "If you're looking for your string tie, try the bottom drawer on the left." She unzipped the wedding gown and stepped into it, wiggling the boned corset up over her hips until she could slip her arms through the lace band that served as the top of the dress, stretching from one shoulder to the other. "The director for the *Sunday Go to Meeting* choir uses it and that's where he always sticks it." She heard him slide open another drawer. "Because you're so even-tempered I can't see anyone ever getting on your nerves."

"Good call. On the tie, that is."

She pushed aside the long strands of glass beads that hung from the lace band and began working up the hidden zipper beneath her arm.

"But I don't know about being all that even-tempered," he added.

She twisted her torso until she could see what she was doing in the narrow excuse for a mirror that someone had tacked against the sliver of wall in the confined space. "Seriously? Even when you went to the town meetings about Cowboy Country and were adamantly against it being opened here, you didn't lose your cool." The zipper stuck partway up as it often did, and she carefully worked it back downward again to start fresh. "Daddy, now. He was another story. When I told him I was coming to work here, I thought he'd split a vein."

"Didn't want to lose his best ranch hand?"

"I s'pose." The zipper caught a second time and she exhaled. Began again.

"So who is it that's getting on your nerves?"

She twisted a little more and realized the zipper was catching on a thread where the satin stitching was becoming frayed. "It was more rhetorical," she muttered. Her neck was starting to hurt from craning her head around the way she was and she lowered her arms, shaking it loose again. "Cowboy Country brings people from far and wide. That woman I was with at the Foaming Barrel was my old college roommate."

"What woman?"

She caught her reflection in the cheap mirror and made a face at herself to stop the sudden silly smile. "Doesn't matter."

Feeling immeasurably cheered, she went to work on the zipper again and this time, made it all the way to the top. She fluffed the tulle skirt that extended to her ankles below the edges of the scalloped lace overskirt and stepped out from behind the screen. "Almost ready. Where's Frank?"

"Saw him out by the buckboard already."

Which was a good reminder how far behind she was running. She always beat Frank to the buckboard. "I am not going to be late because of Roselyn St. James," she vowed and shoved her feet—white crew socks and all—into the old-fashioned boots in record time.

Galen retrieved the ringlet-curled hairpiece that was hanging from a display of them while she quickly twisted her ponytail into a knot. "That's her name?" He handed her the hairpiece. "The college roommate who gets on your nerves?"

"I didn't say—" She made a face and clipped the hairpiece into place, instantly adding a half ton of spiraling red hair to the back of her head. "Yes. That's her." She slid her watch locket down the front of her dress and spread her hands. "There. All set. Ready to ride to my rescue?"

He held his white hat to his abdomen and grinned slightly. “Be my pleasure, ma’am.”

Something inside her belly did a little jig and she quickly pushed open the trailer door, hurrying down the steps. “See you at the altar,” she managed blithely and picked up her skirts to jog toward the buckboard, since the theme music had just started to play.

She was breathless when she clambered up alongside Frank, who gave her a pointed look as he tapped his wristwatch-free wrist.

“Sorry,” she mouthed soundlessly and quickly pulled on her headset and veil. Then the gate opened, and Blackie burst through.

For once, Aurora didn’t even have time to feel her usual surge of nausea. She looked over her shoulder toward Galen and Cabot where they and the rest of the cast were mounting up.

Galen tipped his hat toward her and she grinned before the buckboard turned nearly on two wheels as Blackie raced right on cue toward Main Street. “My daddy will roll over in his grave if the railroad comes through our land,” she cried into her microphone. “I’d do anything to keep that from happening, Frank. But I can’t marry you! I love another!”

Galen realized he was grinning as he listened to Aurora over the loudspeaker.

“Looks to me like you’re having some fun at this,” Cabot observed.

Galen tucked the “deed” into his shirt and nudged along his horse, Blaze, with a squeeze of his knees. “Maybe,” he allowed. But only because he was having fun watching Aurora have fun. He set his white hat more firmly on his head so it wouldn’t go blowing off when they made their mad dash down Main. “But I’m definitely not looking for a career change. Ranching's in my blood. Only thing I ever wanted to do. Amusing as this might be for now, I'll be happy as hell to hand over Rusty's hat to whoever they get to replace Joey." He took in the other riders as well as Cabot and gathered his reins. "Y'all ready?"

They nodded, and as one, they set off in a thunder of horse hooves.

Eleven minutes later, on the dot, he was pulling Aurora into his arms after "knocking" Frank off his feet, saying "I do" to Harlan's Preacher Man, and bending Aurora low over his arm while the audience—always larger on a Saturday—clapped and hooted.

Unfortunately for Galen, the longer he'd gone without Rusty actually kissing Lila, the more he couldn't stop thinking about it as he pressed his cheek against Aurora's, her head tucked down in his chest.

"Big crowd," he whispered. The mics were dead and he held her a little longer than usual. Because of the lengthy applause they were getting, of course.

"Too big," she whispered back. "You going to let me up anytime soon?"

He immediately straightened, and she smiled broadly at the crowd, waving her hand as she tucked her hand through his arm and they strolled offstage.

But he could see through the smile to the frustration brewing in her blue eyes.

He waited until they were well away from the stage. "Sorry about that."

"About what?" She impatiently pushed her veil behind her back and kept looking over her shoulder as they strode through the side street. She was damn near jogging, and the beads hanging from her dress were bouncing.

"Holding the…uh…the…uh," he yanked his string tie loose, feeling like an idiot. "You know. The embrace."

She gave him a distracted look. "What about it?"

"Holding it so long."

Her smooth brows pulled together. "Don't be silly. You were showing great timing." She glanced over her shoulder again. "Oh, crud on a cracker," she muttered. "Why couldn't she just take her perfect two-point-five children to the freaking petting zoo?"

Galen looked back, too, to see what had her so agitated. All he saw was the usual line of people waiting outside Olde Tyme and several families moseying around shop windows. "Who are you talking about?"

"Roselyn," she said through her teeth. Her cheeks looked flushed. "The moment I saw her in the audience, I wanted to bolt. I swear, she's like a dog with a bone. Acting all sweet and nice when she has to know I'm not buying it for one second."

Genuinely curious, he glanced back again.

"Oh, sheesh. Don't *look*." Aurora's fingers dug into his arm.

"Aurora, Aurora McElroy!" One voice in particular separated itself from the general noise and Galen finally saw the dark-haired pregnant woman shoving a stroller ahead of her as she approached. "How could you not see me waving at you back there?"

"So close to escape. Yet so far away." Aurora finally sighed and let go of Galen's arm.

She obviously meant the backstage gate that was only a few paces away.

"This is humiliating," she said under her breath. "Whatever she says, just go with it, okay? I'll make it up to you somehow."

He frowned, but she was already turning to face the

oncoming woman with a wooden smile. "Sorry, Roselyn. You know how an audience disappears when you're onstage."

Roselyn finally reached them and she pressed the flat of her hand against her chest. "Mercy, I am out of breath chasing after you. Why didn't you mention you were performing in a little show here?"

Galen could feel Aurora stiffening beside him. "I didn't really have—"

Roselyn didn't let her finish, though. She'd pulled off her glasses and was giving Galen a head-to-toe look that made him feel sort of like a side of beef being examined by the butcher. "And playing opposite your own real-life husband," she went on. "How *sweet* is that?"

Galen stared. Real-life husband?

"I'm just dying to know how closely life imitates art, of course." The other woman extended her hand, almost as if she expected Galen to kiss it or something. "I'm Roselyn St. James," she introduced. "I'm sure Aurora has told you all about our time together in college. But I'm afraid I don't know even the teeniest thing about you." She smiled flirtatiously. "Which is simply a crying shame, don't you think?"

Galen wasn't ill-mannered enough to ignore the extended hand, so he shook it briskly.

And briefly.

"Galen Fortune Jones." For some reason, claiming the Fortune name just then seemed in keeping with her highfalutin' attitude toward Aurora. "But I'm afraid Aurora doesn't share much about her college years."

"Really?" Roselyn arched her dark eyebrows. "I can't imagine why. We had so much fun together, didn't we, Aurora?"

"A blast." Aurora's voice was beyond dry. "I'm sorry

to cut this short, Roselyn, but we've got to get set for the next show." She waved toward the wooden gate with the small cast-only sign on it.

Galen didn't react to Aurora's huge exaggeration.

"Well, let's get together later, then. For dinner?" One of the tots in the stroller started squawking and Roselyn jiggled the stroller. "Hush, baby. Mommy's talking." She didn't take her gaze off of Aurora. "I'm sure Anthony will be done with his interview—"

"Interview!"

Roselyn's wide eyes widened a little more at Aurora's exclamation. "With Moore Entertainment," she said as if that explained everything. "I told you—"

"You said he was having a meeting." Aurora's voice was increasingly tight.

"You're not bothered by the idea that you might be working for my husband, are you?" Roselyn laughed gaily. "I'm just kidding, of course. You wouldn't be working for him. But he is on the short list for a really good position with Moore. Not here in Texas. Anthony would never want to come back here for good." She jiggled the stroller more and gave Galen a confiding look. "Once he left the state, he dusted anything to do with Texas off his hands. He's a lawyer, specializing in real estate and the entertainment industries."

"Whoops." Aurora had pulled out her watch locket. "Look at the time. Really late now." She grabbed Galen's arm and pulled. "Tell your husband good luck."

Roselyn had a surprised look on her face that Galen didn't quite buy. Mostly because there was a sense of calculation emanating from her pores that he *did.*

"I'll be in touch," Roselyn said quickly. "I'm such a romantic. I can't wait to hear all about everything!

When you got engaged, what the wedding was like and everything!"

"Perfect," Aurora grabbed her skirt up with her free hand.

Galen tipped his hat briefly, and let her pull him through the gate, which she closed so hard after them that it vibrated on its iron hinges.

Galen crossed his arms and peered at her from beneath his hat. "So. What *was* the wedding like?"

Chapter Six

Aurora wearily pulled off her veil and microphone. She could hardly bear to look Galen in the eye, but she made herself do it. “I’m sorry. She always gets my goat.”

He let out a disbelieving chuckle. “So you told her we were married for real?”

“I didn’t think it would matter! I figured, *hoped,* I’d never run into her again.” She yanked off the hairpiece. “I know I shouldn’t have lied. And of course, the one time that I do, it jumps up and bites me on the tush.” She shook her ringlets at him. “You’re laughing. Why are you laughing? It’s not funny!”

He cupped his hand over his mouth but his wide shoulders still shook and his eyes were filled with amusement. “Sorry.”

She tossed up her hands, wedding veil and red curls and all, and turned around. Obviously they didn’t have to get ready for the next show immediately, but there was no point taking up space in the narrow backstage walkway when saloon girls were beginning to file through, trying to get where they needed to go, too.

"Hold on." He caught up to her. "Don't get mad at me when the honeymoon's not even over."

She glared at him. "Good to know I can count on you to help the situation."

He managed to stop chuckling, but he still looked as if he'd start again any second. "Why did you tell her that?"

She was squeezing her veil so hard, the band of flowers was in danger of being permanently bent out of shape. "Hold that." She shoved it at him so abruptly he had no choice but to take the veil.

"I'll hold it," he allowed drily, "but I draw the line at wearing it."

"Ha-ha." She pressed her fingertips to the pain that had formed behind her eyebrows the second she'd spotted Roselyn's scarlet shirt and glorious black hair in the second row near the stage when Frank had dragged her up the steps. "I told you she gets on my nerves."

"Which, after two minutes of her, I can understand."

She shot him a quick look. "You're joking, right?"

He tossed her long veil over his shoulder where it looked almost comical, dangling down his back like some sort of lacy white cape. "What's to joke about? She looks like a nosebleed to me."

She walked ahead of him through the narrowing walkway. "Yeah, well, you're probably the only male around who thinks so. Roselyn St. James collects admirers like my grandma used to collect string."

"She's pregnant, sports a rock the size of a golf ball on her finger and has two kids. Trust me, honey. She's not collecting anything from this old boy."

She rounded the corner, waiting until he came abreast of her again. “She’s beautiful.”

“Thought you didn’t like her.”

“I don’t. But that doesn’t mean I’m a fool, either.” She propped her hands on her hips. “She’s beautiful. Stop-you-in-your-tracks, make-you-take-a-second-look beautiful. She was ten years ago, and she’s even more so now. Pregnant or not. And for nearly two years, I roomed with her. I had ample opportunity to witness the effect she had on anyone who pees standing up. Including my own boyfriend.”

“Ah.” He nodded sagely. “Now I get it.”

“I am *not* jealous,” she said through her teeth.

“Are you sure?”

She exhaled abruptly, feeling like a balloon suddenly stuck with a big, sharp pin. “It doesn’t matter. I don’t plan to ever see her again.”

“Didn’t sound like she’s on that same page.”

“She didn’t even remember that I came from Horseback Hollow, and she doesn’t have my phone number,” Aurora dismissed. “It wouldn’t even occur to her that I don’t own a cell phone. They’ll finish up their business here and go on their merry way, never to darken Horseback Hollow again. Because there was at least one piece of truth in her supposed desire to catch up, and that is that her husband would never voluntarily return to Texas to live. He always hated having to say he came from Red Rock whenever somebody asked.”

He caught her arm, stopping her progress. “You’re not saying that her husband is—”

“—my old boyfriend?” She made a face. “Not that I want to broadcast the fact that I was thrown over for Roselyn St. James, but yes. She never had to work hard for anything in her life. Not grades. Not money for college. She even parlayed a bit part on *Tomorrow's Loves* into a main character. Whatever she wanted, she just lifted her pretty fingers, and it was hers. Including him." She rubbed her forehead again. "I know. I shouldn't have let that get to me, though. But you walked by the Foaming Barrel with that 'wife of mine' crack, and I didn't correct her stunned astonishment that her small-town roommate hadn't turned out to be an old maid after all. What can I say? Sue me."

"You're not an old maid."

"I'm not exactly the belle of the ball, am I?" She squeezed the back of her neck. "And that's exactly what she'd want to hear. The truth. That every male I know considers me just one of the guys. That I haven't had a real date in two years. That I'm still living at home in my childhood bedroom with my parents! Roselyn's personal enjoyment of life is directly related to the level of superiority she maintains over any female in her vicinity."

"Well, hell, honey." The corner of his lips tilted up. "Why don't you say how you really feel?"

She glared. But then her annoyance fizzled, like yet another spent balloon. "Don't make me smile."

"But you have such a good one."

She rolled her eyes and pressed her hand to her belly when it rumbled loudly. "Sorry. Didn't have time to eat my lunch."

"Guess we'd better do something about that." He took her arm. "Can't have your stomach growling when we're around live microphones again. People'll think a thunderstorm is brewing and skedaddle."

"Such a way with words you have, Galen Jones."

"That's Galen *Fortune* Jones, ma'am. As it happens, I haven't had any lunch yet, either. I got hung up at my place doing laundry." He made a face.

"Laundry happens to the best of us," she assured drily. Then grimaced. "Except Roselyn St. James. She probably has singing birds and talking chipmunks who take care of those menial tasks."

He smiled. "Who knew there was a redhead's temper lurking inside the redhead?"

"Trust me. Every blonde and brunette who's ever known her feels the same way."

"What's *Tomorrow's Loves*, anyway?"

"A daytime soap opera. She played Bianca Blaisdell." Her lips twisted. "The town tramp."

"Typecasting?"

"A nice thought. Roselyn's the center of her own world, but I suppose I can't really accuse her of being trampy."

They reached the buckboard and she took the veil off his shoulder and left it and her mic on the seat for the next show.

"What are you going to do if she doesn't give up on catching up?"

"She will." Aurora led the way back to the trailer. She didn't always change out of her costume between shows, but if they left the backstage area, she had to.

She changed as usual behind the screen and tsked over the fraying stitching near the zipper. They had a wardrobe department that took care of the costumes, making sure they were cleaned, etcetera, but Aurora could probably save time by taking her own needle and thread to it herself. For now, though, she found a pair of tiny scissors and clipped off the loose threads as best she could. Then she left the dress hanging on its padded hanger and went back outside where Galen was sitting on top of the picnic table, his boots propped on the bench.

He set his black hat back an inch when she appeared and smiled. "What's your fancy?"

For the briefest of moments, she considered saying "you." But given his reaction to her simple peck on his cheek the night before, she told herself to get over it and quickly. "Whatever is fast," she said instead. "But maybe not the Foaming Barrel."

"Afraid Roselyn's still lurking around?"

"No. But I already bought a hot dog there once today and if I go back for another, they're going to think I have the taste buds of an eight-year-old."

"A sandwich over at the saloon?"

She nodded. "That'll do. Maybe we'll be able to catch a bit of the show. Serena," she prompted when he gave her a blank look.

He pushed off the table. "I'll leave the dancing girls to Frank." Dressed in their everyday clothing, they were free to walk among the public areas, which allowed a considerable shortcut over to the saloon and they were able to find an empty table in the upstairs balcony that overlooked the stage.

She sat there to save the spot while Galen stood in the short line to give their orders, which would be delivered to their table when it was ready. He was back in a matter of minutes and set the number he'd been given at the edge of the table, then pushed the folded ten-dollar bill she'd laid out in preparation back toward her. "No wife of mine is paying for supper."

She left the ten on the table. "This is lunch."

"Splittin' hairs." He dropped his hat on the table and leaned his chair back on two legs. "Has it really been two years?"

She wanted to drop through the floor. It would be a nasty accident, falling through a lot of wood and aged brass, and surely successful at distracting him from the embarrassing question for which she had only herself to blame.

However, the floor beneath her was solid as could be, capable of handling a customer load three times as large as what was present.

"You *had* to notice that."

He smiled slightly. "It was a comment worth noticing."

"Not really." She toyed with the plastic order number, which was fashioned in the shape of a sheriff's star. "Horseback Hollow's not chock-full of eligible bachelors interested in the girl next door." She smiled. "Particularly considering the way your own family gets married all at once."

He let his chair come back down on all fours. "That was a busy day."

"Marrying off four of your siblings in one single ceremony? I'll bet it was."

"I'm surprised you weren't there," he mused. "Think I remember seeing your parents."

"Oh, yeah." She nodded. "Mama talked about it for weeks. The dresses. The food. I think she is afraid she's never going to have another wedding in *our* family." Particularly since Aurora had never found another soul interested in proposing after Anthony.

"She ought to come and watch you do it four times a day," Galen was saying drily. "That oughta cure her. So what were you doing that day?"

"I was over in Lubbock taking care of some ranch business for Daddy." She didn't want to admit that she'd preferred being useful anywhere else over being a wallflower at such a joyful occasion. "And I saw Delaney in the general store a few weeks ago. She's engaged now, too?"

"To Cisco Mendoza."

"Of the Mendozas who opened the Hollows Cantina?" Marcos and Wendy Fortune Mendoza had established the upscale Mexican restaurant the year before.

"He and his brother Matteo are cousins of some sort to Marcos. Julia—Liam's wife—is assistant manager there. She told me once, but can't say I paid much attention. Wendy, though, is *my* cousin."

Aurora was genuinely surprised. "Good grief. You have cousins *everywhere*, don't you?"

He smiled wryly. "Ever heard of FortuneSouth?"

"Telecommunications or something, aren't they?"

He nodded. "My mom's oldest brother, John Michael Fortune, founded it. He's Wendy's father." He toyed with the plastic number. "Everywhere we turn, there's a Fortune."

She studied him for a moment. "It's not just more people around the Sunday dinner table, is it?"

She wasn't sure at first he'd answer. But then he shook his head. "It's an adjustment." His lips twisted a little. "A big one. Particularly for my old man."

And of all Deke Jones's sons, Galen was most like him. She'd heard it time and time again. From Jeanne Marie. From Mark. "Families aren't always what we expect," she murmured.

He smiled wryly. "No. They're not."

She propped her chin on her hand, absently watching the fortune-teller who worked the entire park make her way among the tables on the main floor, offering up entertainment before the saloon girls started their show. "I had my doubts when the Mendozas opened the Cantina. I mean, we're Horseback Hollow. What did we need with such a fancy restaurant? But they said the place would draw business from all around, and they were right."

"Evidently they had plenty of experience from the restaurant Marcos ran in Red Rock. *Red.* My mom brought back some tamales from the place after one of her visits there. Better than any I've ever had, even at the Cantina."

Mention of Red Rock made Aurora think again of Anthony. Which made her think about Roselyn, which made her mood want to swing sideways all over again. "What about you?" She sat up again. "When was *your* last date?"

He raised a brow. "Pardon?"

"Well," she gave him a quick, cross-eyed look, "you know my dirty secret. Least you can do is even things up."

"Couple months ago, I guess."

"Naturally," she drawled, though she was a little relieved that it hadn't been just a few days ago or something. Not that she could imagine when he'd have time to be out dating considering how busy he was these days. But she also didn't want to know she was fantasizing about a kiss—a real kiss—from him when he was out kissing someone else. It just made her feel that much worse. "Anything serious?" She was a little proud of her flawlessly casual tone.

He snorted. "Rusty and Lila's fictional hitchin' is as serious as I get. I'm happy to leave the weddin' and beddin' to my brothers and sisters." He gave her a devilish grin. "I'll just stick to the beddin'."

Something else she didn't want to think about.

She looked back down again at the fortune-teller. The woman was reading a little girl's palm. "You'd think after ten years I wouldn't let Roselyn still get to me."

"Everybody's got their Kryptonite."

She glanced at him again. "And do you have something that renders you helpless?"

He shrugged. "Thinking about anything bad happening to my family." His gaze flickered beyond her. "Hallelujah. Lunch is here."

Aurora sat back while the server—dressed in a slightly less sassy costume than those the dancers wore—delivered their tray of sandwiches and soft drinks, collected the sheriff's star number and left again.

On cue, her stomach rumbled again and she eagerly unwrapped her BLT. "Yum," she breathed. "Now I really owe you. Wings and beer last night. My favorite sandwich today."

"Not to mention Rusty." His lips curved. "Roselyn."

"Yes, yes, yes. I owe you for it all." She took a sip of her orange drink, watching him over the top of her cup. "I told you I would help you out at your spread." She waited a beat. "Maybe you'd rather me do that dreaded laundry."

He chuckled. "Better you than ever letting my ma see the way it's always piled up these days. You should see my kitchen counters. They're even worse than the laundry room." He sketched a toast with his double-decker hamburger. "Eat up, kiddo. Time's a-wasting."

Sure enough, when she checked her watch locket, the time was passing more quickly than she'd thought.

She attributed it to the company.

She was halfway through her sandwich when the fortune-teller stopped at their table. She was an older woman with a bandanna tied around her head, and the gold coins hanging from her skirt belt jingled musically. "I remember you," she addressed Galen, and slid a glance toward Aurora. "This the one?"

Galen looked chagrined. "When the park opened, she told me I'd get married soon to a woman in white," he told Aurora before looking back at the fortune-teller. "Maybe you haven't noticed, but lately I've been doing it four times a day in *Wild West Wedding*. So I guess your prediction was sort of correct."

"Hmm." The woman looked amused. "We'll see." She focused on Aurora again. "Would you like your fortune told, my dear?"

Aurora chuckled. "I'll pass, thanks. The real guests of Cowboy Country deserve your attention much more than I do."

The woman smiled and set her hand on Aurora's shoulder. "Just remember, dear. Dreams are like prayers. They're usually answered in ways we never expect." Her eyes seemed to twinkle a little before she moved on to the next table, her peasant skirt swaying around her legs.

"Well, that was cryptic," Aurora said, shaking off the strange frisson that slipped over her. "What'd she do? Read your palm or crystal ball or what?"

"Palm." He held up his long-fingered hand, square palm toward her. "All those lines?" He traced them with his other hand. "Those're you." He grinned. "Or should I say Lila?"

On the stage below them, a skinny man garbed in a red-and-white-striped shirt and black vest sat down at the piano and began banging out old-time tunes, warming up the crowd for the show to come. "Have you seen the saloon show yet?"

He nodded. "I'm supposed to watch all of the shows. I finally caught the *Sunday Go to Meeting* deal last Sunday before dinner over out my folks' place. That was the last one left. And *Outlaw Shootout*, which isn't being performed right now, anyway."

"Right." She nodded slowly. "What sort of 'authentic' grade is Cowboy Country getting these days?"

He polished off the last of his hamburger in a huge

bite. "A solid B," he said after he'd swallowed. He wiped his hands and mouth with the napkin.

"That's it? I think I'm feeling indignant on behalf of all of Cowboy Country."

"Okay." His eyes crinkled. "B-plus. But only because the Trading Post and some of the ride attendants still have some work to go."

She laughed softly. "I might be hiding a redhead's temper, but you're hiding the heart of a softy, Galen."

"Don't let it get out. Would ruin my image."

She sketched a cross on her chest. "Your secret is safe with me."

"Finish that up." He nodded toward the last of her sandwich. "So they can still turn the table before the dancing starts."

She nodded and quickly devoured the rest of the delectable sandwich. "Nothing like bacon and mayonnaise coming together with tomatoes and lettuce on thick country toast," she said when she was finished. She crumpled her wrapper and napkin and took her drink with her as they left.

"Last time I went on that date, she ate a half a lettuce salad and moaned about gaining weight from the dribble of salad dressing she had." His fingers were light against her back, but still felt hot through her T-shirt. "Nice to see someone actually enjoy her food."

"Well, I wish some of it would stick to my ribs," she admitted. "I know nobody wants to hear it, but I think it's just as hard to gain a few pounds when you're trying as it is to lose them."

"You're fine just the way you are."

"I have the figure of a ten-year old boy," she dismissed, skipping down the wooden stairs to the main floor. "Probably why most guys mistake me for one of them."

He suddenly took the step in front of her, his arm barring her progress. "No guy worth his salt mistakes you for one of his own kind," he said evenly. "Just because you don't have that overblown look your old college roomie sports doesn't mean we're blind. So stop talking that way, would you?"

She realized her mouth was gaping like a fish out of water.

But he said no more. Just lowered his arm again and finished descending the stairs, where he pushed open the door and waited for her to pass through ahead of him.

She heard the door again after he'd joined her on the boarded sidewalk and glanced back.

The fortune-teller drifted out the door, her gold coins reflecting the sunshine so brilliantly that Aurora squinted against them. Then she turned and headed the opposite direction.

"Everything okay?"

Aurora nodded. "She's a little odd, isn't she? The fortune-teller?" She waved toward the departing woman. "I've met so many people who work here, but I just realized that I don't even know her name."

"She's a street performer," Galen dismissed. "I doubt she's supposed to be giving out her name to the guests. She's just supposed to keep 'em engaged. Speaking of which," he swept his arm ahead of him. "Ready to get hitched again?"

She held out an imaginary skirt and gave a quick curtsy. "If you'd be so kind."

The next afternoon, Aurora stood in the back door of Galen's house and tried not to gape. "You weren't exaggerating about your chores," she greeted.

He was shirtless and his bronzed shoulders bore a gleam of sweat. "Aurora?"

"In the flesh. Your doorbell doesn't work."

"I know."

"That's why I came 'round back." She pushed the casserole dish containing a fresh-baked batch of cinnamon rolls into his hands. "I'm here to get us back on even footing since I'm in your debt for two meals now. What have you been out doing already?"

"Digging postholes."

"That'd do it." A more backbreaking job, she couldn't think of. Not when a person was doing it with a plain old post-hole digger, which she suspected was Galen's way. "Set those in the oven," she told him. "You don't have to turn it on or anything, but they'll stay a bit warm in there. And—" she mentally rolled up her sleeves as she studied the countertops that she suspected were littered with every single dish, glass and pot he probably owned "—I will get to work on this mess."

"I've told you more'n once that you don't owe me anything."

"I know." She stepped past him, focusing harder on the state of his kitchen so she would be less aware of *him*. She'd waited until noon to come over to his place strictly because she'd half hoped she wouldn't find him home.

She could have left the rolls and bolted.

So much for that.

"But now I've seen all this," she said truthfully, "I'll never sleep at night again. No wonder you didn't want Jeanne Marie seeing this. She'd box your ears for sure." She automatically opened the cupboard beneath his sink, and sure enough, found an industrial-sized bottle of dishwashing soap and a brand new scrubby sponge still in its wrapper. Despite living so close, she'd never been inside his house before. But such habits were pretty universal, she guessed. That's where the soap was in her own folks' kitchen. "You need an electric dishwasher."

His kitchen was small and looked almost straight out of the Old West. There was even an ancient wood stove in one corner and an old rotary-dial phone on the wall, and he had the same kind of small white refrigerator that her grandmother had had, with the silver handle that controlled the latch.

Fortunately, she'd also noticed the perfectly modern refrigerator/freezer combo in his mudroom next to the washer and dryer when she'd come in.

"Aurora—"

"Go on." She dismissed him with a flick of her hand. "If you've got posts to dig, go dig."

"I'm done."

"Then have a cinnamon roll," she said easily. "And don't worry. Mama made 'em. I just defrosted them from the freezer and baked them, so you're safe from food poisoning. Because heaven knows I did *not* inherit her skill at the stove."

She heard the scrape of a chair as she ran water over the piled-high sink. She was going to have to empty the thing before she could put in the drain plug. She dared a quick glance over her shoulder to see he'd sat down at the old-fashioned linoleum table and was plucking a warm roll out of the dish with his bare fingers.

"They smell good," he said.

She hid her smile and looked back at the sink. She'd never met a single soul who didn't have an appreciation for her mother's baking skills.

She started stacking the dishes on the counter. "I think you need a wife for real, Galen."

He snorted. "What for?"

"To take care of this house for you." Now that she could see the bottom of the sink, she plugged it up, squirted soap under the running hot water and moved the dishes again back into the sink.

"That's awful old-fashioned sounding, coming from you."

She lifted her shoulder, tearing the wrapper off the sponge. "Some women adore keeping house for their man. My mama does, that's for sure."

"Your mama can work cattle right alongside your dad, too. I've seen her do it."

"As can Jeanne Marie. If you're opposed to wives, then at least hire yourself a housekeeper or something." She held up a bowl with some unidentifiable substance clinging to the bottom. "And learn to rinse your dishes, for goodness' sake."

"I'm a guy," he said around a mouthful of roll. "We don't rinse."

She gave him a look.

"Okay. *I* don't rinse." He licked icing off his thumb. "Who has the time? I'm busy marrying you all the live-long day. Does that sound like a guy opposed to wives?"

She laughed softly, turning back again to watch the soapsuds mound up in the sink. When they were sufficiently developed, she filled the other side of the sink with clean water, then turned it off and plunged the sponge into the suds. He had an open window over the sink that looked out at his barn a few hundred yards off. It looked freshly painted.

In fact, if you were outside Galen's house, it was clear that he didn't stint at all on the care, feeding and general upkeep of anything.

It was only inside that things seemed to have been hit with a tornado.

"Why don't you ranch with your dad?"

"I do. I just wanted something to call my own, too. You gonna get all horrified if I eat all of these things in one sitting?"

She looked over her shoulder at him and grinned. "I know. They're good, aren't they?"

"Slap-your-mama good," he murmured, lifting another roll out of the pan. "Though that's a saying I never quite understood. Slappin' my mama wouldn't have earned me anything but a tanned hide and an eternity in purgatory when my dad plowed me into the ground."

"That I can see." She attacked the stuck-on bowl again with the abrasive side of the sponge and finally managed to get it clean. She let it slide into the hot rinse water and started on the next. "Deke always struck me as a scary sort of father."

"Nah." He waited a beat. "Helped to stay on his good side, though."

She smiled. "I remember him hauling you and Mark home to our house once when you two were in high school. He seemed terrifying then. You'd been out joy-riding in your dad's old pickup."

He chuckled. "To my shame, a too-frequent occurrence. First time we did it, we were still in junior high. Twelve, thirteen years old, maybe."

"Hooligans."

"We were called worse. Now I think about it, it's a wonder he let me survive high school at all. Said I was making him old before his time. Didn't matter, of course, that I'd been driving tractors since I was half that age. Everybody around here learns how to drive when we're kids."

She smiled faintly. "I'd still rather be on our old John Deere than sitting in traffic in Lubbock."

"That's the truth," he agreed with feeling. "Dad still

has that truck, too. Works on it all the time. When I was a kid, it was just old. Now it's a *classic.*" He joined her at the sink and pulled a towel out of a side drawer.

"Is that clean?"

"Smart-ass." He shook it out. "From Christmas last year. Got a whole set of 'em from Ma."

"Probably hinting," Aurora said drily. She could feel her face starting to perspire and hoped that, if he noticed, he'd attribute it to the hot water she was submerged in up to her elbows. "It's June. Have you even used them yet?"

He immediately whirled the towel into a twist that she remembered only too well from her brother.

"Don't you snap me with that towel, Galen Jones."

His grin flashed. "I could put you over my knee instead. Something's gotta stop that smart mouth of yours."

She gave him a deadpan look and flicked a few soap suds his direction. They landed on the center of his bare chest and slowly slid downward.

The sight was more mouthwatering than thirty years of her mama's cinnamon rolls.

She swallowed hard and moistened her dry lips, knowing that she ought to look away, but somehow not being able to make herself do it.

The towel bunched in his hand. "Aurora—" His deep voice sounded even lower.

"Hey, hey! There you are!" A high female voice accosted them from outside the opened window, making them both jump. They looked out to see Roselyn standing there. "Don't you answer a simple doorbell?"

"Doorbell doesn't work," Galen and Aurora both said at the same time.

Roselyn laughed gaily. "Aren't you two cute as can

be?" She propped her hands on her hips and stared up at them through the window. "So are you going to let me in, or make me stand out here among the cattle?"

Chapter Seven

The cattle were nowhere near the house, of course, since his herd was grazing along with his pop's in their summer pasture several miles away, getting nice and fat for sale in the fall.

"What the hell's she doing here?" he asked softly through the smile on his face.

"How should I know?" Aurora answered similarly. "She's a nut job?"

Roselyn was picking her way across the green grass as if it were a foreign substance to her high-heeled shoes. Despite the basketball bump under her clinging bright blue T-shirt, she was dressed as if she were expecting pictures to be taken. Her black hair was loose today, reaching all the way down her back, and her snowy-white jeans were stuck to her legs like they'd been painted on.

Aurora leaned closer to the window and Galen had an uncomfortable jolt, wondering whether she was looking out to see if Roselyn was accompanied by the husband.

Aka Aurora's *ex*-boyfriend.

But when she spoke, all she asked was, "What are you doing here, Roselyn?"

"I couldn't find a phone listing for you, so I had to come in person."

Galen took a step back, realizing he was comparing the glossiness of Aurora's nut-job roommate to Aurora's easy—and preferable to him—look of fraying jeans shorts and a cotton plaid shirt with the sleeves pulled off.

And the way she was leaning against the sink, stretching forward a little to reach the window…

Well.

He looked away and decided he needed a shirt of his own. One with long shirttails hanging out to disguise the fact that he'd gone harder than a rock. "I'll be back," he muttered and bolted like a kid caught doing something he shouldn't. Like getting turned on by an old friend's kid sister.

"Coward," Aurora's whisper followed him.

"Damn straight," he returned, but not for the reason she obviously figured.

A woman more unaware of her own appeal, he'd never met.

He took the stairs two at a time, stopping off long enough to grab a towel from the hall bathroom to swipe over his chest before yanking on a clean shirt from the pile of laundry he'd yet to put away. He started to leave the room, but the unmade bed stopped him.

Growling under his breath, he flipped the quilt up over the mattress. It wasn't neat by any stretch, but at least it was a small improvement. Aurora already figured he lived like an animal.

He stopped dead in his tracks, narrowing his eyes on

the bed. Thinking about her and his bed in one thought process was more than a little disturbing.

He shook it off and headed back downstairs. Aurora'd already told Roselyn they were married for real. He was a little concerned that if he stayed away for too long, they'd have six kids together by the time he got back downstairs.

Roselyn was in the kitchen when he got there, leaning back against the counter with one spiky heel crossed over the other, and her eyes followed him the second she noticed him. "I was just telling Aurora about our home in California."

He couldn't have cared less about it, but he managed a vaguely interested grunt. "How'd you find this place?"

"It was easy enough." She languidly smoothed her hair over her shoulder, running her hand down the shining length of it. "Even Anthony recognized the Fortune name. So I asked around town where Galen Fortune Jones and his wife lived." She sent Aurora what seemed to be a calculating look. "Strange, though, that not too many folks thought he *had* a wife."

The expression in Aurora's blue eyes reminded him of a cornered kitten.

"We eloped a few weeks ago," he said abruptly. "News is still working its way around town."

"Well." Roselyn's sudden smile was blinding white and he felt a little surprised that the teeth weren't sharpened into points. "That explains it, then."

Aurora, on the other hand, was looking at him as though he was the one to have suddenly sprouted horns.

"So we're both brides who eloped," Roselyn said, looking back at Aurora. "Isn't that funny?"

Aurora nodded, her lips stretched in a humorless smile. "Funny," she parroted.

Roselyn gestured at the kitchen's disarray. "Obviously,

you're still in the process of moving in your stuff, Aurora. I remember the mess Anthony and I had when we got our first place. At least he took time to get a ring, though." She waved her hand. "Of course, that first one was replaced as soon as we had the money."

"Of course."

Galen wondered if Aurora even realized that she was holding a plate, dripping water on her pink-tipped toes showing through her casual flip-flops.

"Aurora's ring's still being sized," he lied and went over to her, lifting the plate out of her hand to swipe the dish towel over it. "Where are your kids today, Roselyn?" He figured that was a safer change of topic.

"They're having their naps with their daddy." Roselyn went from smoothing her hair over her boobs to smoothing her hand over her belly. "Anthony loves a little time to himself with them. I'm glad to say, though, that this one—" she tapped her belly "—is a single. A boy. Are you two going to have kids?" She laughed lightly. "Aurora, you're the same age as me. You're going to want to get a start on things. We're not getting any younger, after all."

"We haven't really talked about it," Aurora said faintly. "Um...Galen, could I have a moment? You don't mind, do you, Roselyn? You should probably sit, too. Have a, uh, have a cinnamon roll." She quickly set the newly washed and dried plate on the table next to the rolls that Galen hadn't quite yet decimated.

"Oh, Aurora," Roselyn chided. "I haven't eaten bread in years." But she did take one of the chairs at the table and crossed her legs, bouncing her high-heeled shoe that was white on the outside but had a dark red sole. He was pretty sure he'd heard his sisters talking about shoes like that, and that they were expensive as hell.

Guess they probably went with that fancy ring on Roselyn's finger.

Aurora grabbed his hand and pulled him out of the kitchen and well out of their intruder's earshot, into his den at the opposite side of the house.

He closed the door for good measure and as soon as she did, she rounded on him.

"Why on earth did you tell her that we'd eloped?"

"Should I have made up a church wedding with half the town present at our imaginary ceremony?"

"No." She thrust her fingers through her red hair and actually pulled on it. "I need to just tell her the truth. This lying business is getting out of hand."

"What does it matter?" he reminded. "You said yourself that she's here for a day or two and will be gone again for good. I think it bugs the hell out of her worrying that you're *not* married—"

"What?" She looked startled. "Why would she worry about that?"

"I don't know. Maybe she's making sure you're all tied up before she lets her husband within twenty feet of you."

Aurora shook her head. "That's ridiculous."

"And yet she keeps pursuing it. Are you saying it's because the two of you were such good friends?"

"Hardly." Aurora pressed her lips together. "I would have switched roommates, except I was afraid at the time that I would get stuck with someone worse. And, much as I don't want to admit it, in the beginning, being roommates with her wasn't awful. I didn't know a soul, and everyone wanted to know her. We went to a lot of functions."

"Parties?"

She gave a reluctant smile. "Well, yes, there were parties, too."

"That how you met Anthony?" He had a hard time saying the name without wanting to sneer. "At a party?"

"A fraternity party. Yes."

"Did you love him?"

Her eyes shied away from his. "It was a long time ago."

"Aurora."

She huffed. "I was engaged to him," she admitted flatly. "For all of three months. I thought he was the love of my life. Then he eloped with *her*."

He went still, not hearing much beyond the "engaged" part. "You only said before he was your boyfriend."

"Yes, well, what does it matter what I called him? He tossed me aside like a used tissue for Roselyn."

"I never heard you were engaged." Ten years before, he'd been working two jobs in addition to cowboying for his dad, trying to earn enough for a down payment on some acreage of his own. He'd been in Horseback Hollow all right, but he'd been damn busy, too, so he supposed it wasn't unlikely that he'd missed that nugget of local news.

"I don't imagine my parents had much time to brag about it. Mark killed himself a few months later."

He started. "He didn't *kill* himself. It was an accident."

She raised her brows. "Really? Mark, who'd been holding his liquor since long before he was legally of age to have any? Who'd been driving one vehicle or another since he was probably ten years old? He just *accidentally* drove his truck head-on into a tree? Don't kid yourself, Galen." Her voice was thin. "Instead of telling our daddy that he hated everything to do with ranch life—that he didn't *want* to inherit everything that Dad had ever worked for his whole life—he took the only way out of it that he thought he could. He never got a chance to go to college. He didn't know anything else. You were his friend. How could you not know that?"

"I was his friend," he agreed flatly. "And I'm telling you, he didn't do it deliberately. The guy I knew was too self-involved to hurt himself like that. He had his chances, too. He just didn't take them." Just because they'd been friends since childhood didn't mean he'd been blind to Mark's faults. But once the guy was gone, Galen preferred remembering the good over the bad. "Is that what your parents think, too?"

"They think the sun rose and set on him. The only thing they regretted was not being able to pay for him to go to college." She pressed her lips together. Then sighed. "What are we going to do about Roselyn?" She jerked her head toward the hallway leading to the kitchen.

"Toss her a celery stick and send her on her way?" Sooner or later, he'd straighten her out about her brother, but for now, Roselyn's presence was a ticking bomb. So he lifted Aurora's chin with his finger. "Invite her to dinner," he suggested calmly. "Get it over with. Two hours of playing newlyweds for her in exchange for getting her out of your hair forever."

"Why would you want to do that?"

"Because I like your hair." He gave her an encouraging smile. "Besides, she strikes me as a bully. If you invite her, she might back down. Come up with a half dozen excuses why she—" *and your ex-fiancé* "—can't make it, after all." In fact, he liked that possibility best of all.

"And if she doesn't?"

"Then she doesn't."

"But it's not going to be just her," Aurora muttered. "She'll have her husband and the kids."

He watched her face carefully. "Is that a problem?"

She lifted her chin a little. "No."

He almost asked if she was sure. But decided he wasn't sure he wanted to know that, either. Not when it was going to take some time to digest the fact that she'd been involved enough with the guy to be engaged to him.

The love of her life.

It made him want to punch something.

"So it's settled," he said evenly instead.

She pressed her lips together and nodded. Then she stepped away from him, squaring her shoulders as though she was preparing to face a firing squad.

That alone was enough to make him tell Roselyn whatever lies were necessary to send her quickly on her way even if it did mean having to meet Aurora's ex.

"Sorry about that," Aurora said when they returned to the kitchen.

"I remember what being a newlywed was like." Roselyn stroked her belly meaningfully. "Of course, Anthony still likes to act as if we are, too."

Galen managed not to grimace. He leaned against the cluttered counter while Aurora took the chair opposite Roselyn at the table.

"How did his interview go with Moore Entertainment?" Aurora asked politely.

"Beautifully." Roselyn's hand started straying toward the redolent cinnamon rolls sitting so near to her elbow, but veered away to rub against the metal edge of the table instead. "In fact, they've asked him to stay here for another couple days to meet with Mr. Moore himself. He'll be in town soon to see his daughter, Caitlyn.

"I hear she's almost engaged," she offered the news like someone doling out treats. "To Brodie Hayes. He's practically *royalty*. His mother is Lady Josephine Chesterfield. I saw her on television at William and Kate's wedding. Anthony tells me that they're all pretty much living here in Horseback Hollow, which is just unfathomable to me. Her daughter, Lady Amelia, started it off, no doubt, what with all that scandal last year when she was engaged to that duke or whatever he was."

"Amelia was never engaged to Lord Banning," Galen corrected. "The only reason there was a scandal was because the tabloids cooked one up." He could easily envision Roselyn courting those sorts of stories about herself, whereas Amelia had been desperate to avoid them.

"Your hubby certainly stays up on the local gossip," Roselyn told Aurora.

"I just stay up on the family news," Galen drawled. "Amelia and Brodie? They're my cousins. Lady Josie is my auntie," he added, just to see her reaction.

Which was pretty priceless. He even saw Aurora bite back a smile at Roselyn's slack expression.

"You don't actually *call* her that, do you?"

"I call her Josephine. She's my mother's sister." Immaterial to him at that moment that none of them had known that fact until recently.

"Look at you, Aurora." Roselyn recovered quickly. "Rubbing elbows with famous people after all."

"Strange how life turns out, isn't it?" Aurora's voice was smooth, but he still heard the irony underneath. "I'm surprised you would even consider living somewhere other than California. Or does Moore Entertainment have an operation there that I'm not remembering?"

Roselyn's lashes drooped as she studied her nails. "We're tired of California, actually. But Moore's headquarters is in Chicago. So—" she lifted her shoulder "—hopefully. Did you ever get back to school to get a degree?"

Aurora shook her head. "And you didn't need to, I guess, what with your stint as Bianca Blaisdell."

Roselyn's lips curved. She touched the base of her throat. "Bianca did rather put me on the map. It would have been such a waste if you'd gone on that audition instead of me."

Galen studied Aurora, wondering what other tidbits she was harboring in her pretty red head that she hadn't bothered to share with him. "Why's that?" he asked Roselyn.

"They were looking for a type." She lifted her shoulder. "My type."

Bitch? He wanted to ask, but didn't.

"They wanted a dark-haired siren, not a ginger-haired ingénue," Aurora said. "At least that's what Bianca turned into once you joined the cast of *Tomorrow's Loves.* Probably hard for you to give up the role."

"Well, they couldn't possibly replace me, of course. Bianca was too popular of a character to recast. My agent hears from the producers every couple months."

"Wanting you back?"

Roselyn just smiled and rubbed her belly. "I have more important things to focus on."

"When is the baby due?"

"End of September."

When his sister Stacey had been pregnant with Piper, she'd been nowhere near as big as Roselyn looked. He considered saying so, but figured the woman would take her offense out on Aurora. "Hate to break up your reunion," he lied, "but Aurora and I are expected somewhere in a little bit."

"We are? Oh, right." Aurora nodded. "We are." She rose from the table and pushed in her chair.

Roselyn could do nothing else but stand, as well. "Give me your cell phone number, Aurora, so we can firm up details for dinner before we leave town."

"I don't have a cell phone."

Roselyn whistled soundlessly. "That's taking the small-town life a little far, isn't it?"

"Not when anyone I'm interested in talking to is within shouting distance."

Roselyn hesitated, then laughed, as if she'd just gotten the joke. "Here." She snatched up the pencil hanging from the notepad attached to the side of his wall phone, and quickly wrote out her phone number. She tore off the page and set it on the table, then looked at Galen, expectantly.

Wishing there was some way around it, he told her the number of the house line, which she quickly jotted on the next sheet. "We'll plan on tomorrow evening."

"We've got performances tomorrow evening," Aurora said, looking so sincerely regretful he was a little startled. "All week, actually. I guess we'll have to give it a miss this time. But if you're ever in the area—"

"I'm not giving up that easily, Aurora McEl—" Roselyn broke off. "Sorry. Unlike me, I imagine you've taken Galen's name, traditional little soul that you are. We'll just get together after your last show."

"Won't that be a bit late for your kids?"

"We'll arrange a sitter service," Roselyn assured Aurora blithely. "I'm sure Vicker's Corners has *some* sort of agency we can use."

Galen was pretty sure that Vicker's Corners did not. And even though he could have named a half dozen people more than capable of watching her twins for a few hours, helping her out with child care wasn't on his short list of things to do. So he tucked his tongue behind his teeth and stayed quiet.

"We can meet at the Hollows Cantina," Roselyn continued. "On us, of course. Anthony can expense it and he's been saying he wanted to try the restaurant there, since the owners used to have something to do with some mildly famous restaurant in his hometown." She folded the note in half and tucked it inside her bra, then caught Aurora's shoulders in her hands and brushed her cheek quickly against hers. "I'm *so* glad I caught you two here," she added as she let go again and clicked her way to the back door again. "I'd have been brokenhearted if we didn't have another chance to catch up." With a wave, she sailed out the door.

Aurora's lips twisted. "Heaven forbid that Roselyn be *brokenhearted*," she said under her breath.

"That'll teach you to bring me cinnamon rolls." With the annoying woman gone, he scooped out another sticky confection with his fingers. "She'd have never caught us here together if you hadn't. She might have gone on her merry way, never to darken your door again."

"Proof that no good deed goes unpunished." Shaking her head, Aurora returned to the sink, where the soap suds had fizzled.

Galen studied her slender back as she turned on the hot water again. "Anything else she steal from you that I should know about before tomorrow night?"

She added more soap. "She never stole anything that turned out to matter."

He was glad to hear the words, though he wasn't entirely convinced she meant them. Not about the feckless idiot who'd chosen Roselyn, anyway. The idiot whose name Aurora wouldn't even voice. "What about that audition thing?"

She tucked the soap back under the sink and straightened to plunge the sponge back into the water. "I am sure it turned out exactly the way it was supposed to."

"Why didn't you go?"

She hesitated. "Because I didn't get the message that they'd called for me until after she'd already gone in my place. We, um…" She sighed. "We had a pin board on the back of our dorm room door where we put each other's messages. And that particular one had fallen off."

"Convenient."

Her only response to his sarcasm was to rotate her shoulders. "Doesn't matter. They may have wanted me to audition, but they cast *her*. She obviously wowed them."

"You might have wowed them, too, if you'd have had the chance. How'd they pick you out to ask you to audition in the first place?"

"Somebody with the show saw a student production I was in."

"Shakespeare or something, I suppose."

"Not even. It was a two-act written by an upperclassman. Last I heard, he ended up being an insurance salesman. If you go back and catch up on what my classmates are doing now, there are only a handful of people who made it in the arts. Roselyn's the most commercially famous."

"Because she did a daytime soap."

"Don't pooh-pooh it. While her character was tramping her way through scenes, the show had better daytime ratings than some prime-time shows. In a matter of just a few years, she became one of the highest-paid actresses in daytime."

"Is that why you wanted to study acting? You wanted to get rich and famous?"

"I studied theater because I was interested in all aspects of it. Playwriting, acting, production. Mostly I just wanted to act. Be someone other than me for a while."

"Only dream I ever had was being a rancher."

"Which makes you luckier than most." She finally gave up her pretense of washing dishes and turned to face him again. "How many people in this world never get to do what they've always dreamed of doing? More than those who do, I'm sure."

"Mark thought ranching was settling."

Her eyes darkened. "I know. But he never seemed to know what else he could do that would feel differently."

"Do *you* think it's settling?"

"I had a choice. I could have taken out more student loans and gone to a school closer to home. Could have joined a community theater group in Lubbock, or even started one up in Vicker's Corners. I'd have still been here to support my parents. But after he died, I couldn't seem to put one foot in that world and keep the other at home. In my mind, it was one way or no way. Probably the same mind-set Mark had, only he went the way of *no*."

"I'm telling you, he didn't do it deliberately, Aurora."

She looked away, but not quickly enough to hide the sudden sheen in her eyes. "If I could believe that, maybe I wouldn't still be so angry with him."

He exhaled and went over to her, pulling her against him. Her head tucked neatly under his chin and he felt her arms slowly circle around his waist. "It was an accident, Aurora. That's all."

She sniffled. "It's been ten years. I know I'm supposed to be able to let it go."

He rubbed her back, swallowing his own feelings about her brother. They'd been thick as thieves throughout their adolescence. Mark could have had so much more in his life. But he'd already started throwing away his opportunities long before he'd chosen to drink and drive that night. "I should have paid more attention to you after his accident."

She pulled back at that, looking up at him with genuine surprise. "Why?"

He would probably kick himself later.

But right now?

He lowered his head and slowly brushed his lips against hers.

Chapter Eight

The sound of Aurora's blood rushed in her ears like a freight train.

She'd barely adjusted to the fact that Galen was *kissing* her when he was already lifting his head again.

"That's why," he said gruffly. "I should've paid more notice to what you were going through. You were a friend."

She swallowed and pulled her arms away from him, and gripped the edge of the countertop behind her back instead.

There was that word again. *Friend.*

"You helped out," she reminded. "Your whole family did. Jeanne Marie brought food and sat with Mama plenty of times. You and Deke and the boys helped Daddy. Most of the town pitched in one way or another. Just like they always do when there is a need. Just like you've helped out playing Rusty." And now he was playing her real-life husband for Roselyn St. James's benefit. "And...and everything." She felt like an insect on a pin that he was studying and slid out from between him and the counter to retrieve the casserole dish from the table.

"No amount of these things—" she held up the pan in which only a single roll remained "—can ever make up for everything you've been doing." She set it on the counter and walked over to the wall phone, lifting the receiver off the hook, and began punching out the numbers that Roselyn had written.

"What are you doing?"

"Calling to tell her the truth. And that there's no reason—" She broke off when he plucked the receiver out of her grasp and dropped it back on the hook. "Galen, lying like this isn't right."

"Consider it our own student production."

She looked up at him, studying the line of his jaw, its sharp angle blurred slightly by a haze of razor stubble. "I don't understand you sometimes."

"Not sure I understand me, either." The corner of his mouth kicked up, though he didn't look the least amused. "But we'll get a dinner at the Hollows Cantina out of it. How bad can that be?"

Aurora smiled weakly. She hoped they wouldn't find out.

"Does this look all right?" Feeling stupidly nervous, Aurora stepped out from behind the changing screen the next evening following their last show, and held out the sides of her dress as she looked at Galen.

He'd changed, too, out of his Rusty shirt into a black dress shirt that he'd tucked into dark blue jeans. "Dress is fine."

High praise. She tried not to feel deflated. "I made a

dash over to Lubbock yesterday afternoon after I left your place." Which had been soon after "the kiss."

He'd escaped even before she had, claiming he still had more chores to take care of. She'd finished cleaning up his kitchen in record time, half afraid he'd return before she'd left, and half afraid he wouldn't. When at least that one room was restored to order and he still hadn't, she'd called herself lucky and left, too.

The trip to Lubbock had been as much to distract herself from thinking about what he'd said, and done, as it had been to buy a dress she'd really had no business buying when she had a handful of perfectly serviceable dresses she could wear to the Hollows Cantina.

Retail therapy was supposed to be good for what ailed a person. It still hadn't helped her forget that he'd kissed her.

Now, she self-consciously smoothed down the sides of the clinging blue fabric that gathered together slightly over her left hip, giving the appearance of curves that she didn't otherwise possess. "I would have just gone to the dress shop I usually go to in Vicker's Corners, but was afraid I'd run into she-who-must-not-be-named." She knew she was babbling nervously, but couldn't help it.

They were alone in the trailer. Everyone else had beat a quick exit as they usually did after the last show of the day. She stepped around Galen to look in the larger mirror that was situated above the bank of drawers. "I'd rather wear boots than these pumps, but I knew even my good Castletons wouldn't look right with this dress." Except for the bobby pins in her hair, everything she wore from the skin out was brand-spanking-new. She tugged at the surplice neckline that, again with the aid of subtly gathered fabric, gave her chest more oomph than either nature or the new one-piece body briefer had actually endowed. "Even though the Castletons cost more," she added with a nervous giggle.

"These are Castletons," he muttered and she glanced at the well-shined black cowboy boots beneath the hem of his jeans. "I bought 'em because they were a good investment. Built to last."

She smiled a little. "I doubt you've ever bought anything because it was a fashion statement."

His lips twisted. He reached into his pocket and pulled out a small box. "'Cept this, I suppose."

Dismay warred with a discomfiting sense of longing as she stared at his reflection in the mirror. The box was square. Black. Some insane part of her mind wondered if girls were born with a genetic ability to recognize a ring box when they saw one.

The saner part of her mind still warily made her ask, "What's that?"

"You can't be a bride without a ring. But I'm not going down on a knee here." He pushed the box into her hand.

She immediately tried to give it back. "What you told Roselyn yesterday about the ring being sized was fine. We don't need this."

"It's just some costume thing."

It doesn't matter! She wanted to let the thought loose, but didn't. Costume jewelry or not, she had a strong distaste for putting on a ring from him that meant nothing. She pulled the top off the small box and looked at the shining, oversize stone set in some whitish metal.

"Considering I found it in the drugstore, I hope it doesn't make your finger turn green after wearing it an hour."

She lifted out the ring and pushed it on the ring finger of her right hand. It was a little loose, the large diamond-like stone listing slightly to the side. "Looks like something Roselyn would choose."

"So does that dress."

Aurora sighed and looked at her reflection again. He was right, naturally. The sophisticated cut of the dress wasn't at all her usual taste. Nor was the way she'd twisted her hair into a thick bun at the nape of her neck.

"And the ring's on the wrong hand."

"I'll move it when I need to." She had absolutely no enthusiasm inside her for what they were about to do. "We could be rude and stand them up."

He set his black cowboy hat on his head and pushed open the trailer door. "Is it Roselyn you're afraid of seeing, or her husband?"

Her mouth opened. Closed. "I'm not afraid of either," she finally said.

He touched the small of her back and nudged slightly. "Then there's no reason to stand 'em up."

"Except for Roselyn being a nosebleed," she reminded. She stepped out of the trailer, careful in her high heels. She wasn't inept in them. She had simply never had a pair quite so high before. Five extra inches brought her up so far she could nearly look him in the eye.

For some reason, it felt oddly empowering. She'd heard of power suits. Maybe there was such a thing as power heels.

She shook off the whimsical thought in favor of not tripping over her own feet.

"It was a good audience tonight," she said once they left the backstage area behind to cut across the park. "Particularly for a Monday." Better to talk about work. Keep her mind off personal.

As if that were even possible.

"Hear anything about a real replacement for Joey?"

She shot him a quick look. "No. You?"

He shook his head. "I'll call on the casting department tomorrow. Try to light a fire under Diane."

"I'm sure she'd like that," she muttered, remembering the way the other woman's eyes had chowed down on Galen that first day. Though she had to admit that he didn't look any too pleased at the prospect.

Instead, he changed the subject altogether. "Hear anything from your parents? They get off on their cruise yesterday okay?"

"Yes. When I got back from Lubbock, there was a message on the machine from them. They sounded giddy as kids. Mama couldn't believe there was a phone inside their stateroom."

"Why *don't* you have a cell phone?"

"What? Oh." She was having the hardest time keeping her thoughts in line when all they wanted to do was stray into fantasyland where she and Galen were on a real date that had nothing whatsoever to do with Roselyn St. James. "It's just another expense." They passed by the line for the Gulch Holler Rapids and could hear squeals of delight from the riders splashing down nearby. "Who needs that headache?"

"You do, driving that old truck of your dad's back and forth to Lubbock every time you turn around."

She stopped in her tracks and stared at him. "I don't go to Lubbock every time I turn around. And even if I did, why on earth does that bother you now?"

"It's a matter of safety." He sounded gruff. He moved her aside so she didn't get run over by a group of teenagers racing to their next attraction. "I'd say the same thing to my sisters."

She started walking again. Nervousness had plummeted to resignation. "Never seemed to be much point having a cell phone here in Horseback Hollow." Sisters. That was even worse than being placed by him in the friend category.

It was okay for friendship to turn to romance.

Not so with sisters.

"The landline has always been good enough for my folks. Guess it's been good enough for me."

"Ever think about living somewhere else?"

"Meaning at the ripe old age of thirty, I should?" Didn't matter that she'd thought it more than once herself. She didn't necessarily need him pointing it out, too.

"I wasn't implying anything."

"With all my newfound wealth playing Lila the Wild West Bride, I could buy up a McMansion in Vicker's Corners," she added tartly.

"It was just a question!"

She sighed noisily. "I'm sorry. I'm a little tense, I guess. Portraying Rusty and Lila is one thing. Playacting newlyweds in our own skin is obviously another matter." She forced a chuckle. "As if anyone would ever believe you and I—" She couldn't make the rest of the words come and was glad the sun was starting to go down. Hopefully that meant he couldn't see the way her face was hotter than Hades.

"You studied acting, at least."

"*Now* you regret not letting me fess up?"

"I'm not regretting anything."

She wasn't so sure. But she said nothing more as they continued making their way through the park and back to the employee area again.

Since they'd known they were going to the Hollows Cantina after their last performance, Galen had picked her up on his way into Cowboy Country for the day so that they wouldn't have two vehicles to deal with, and she automatically headed toward his truck when they reached the parking lot.

She didn't even notice Frank Richter sitting on the hood of his car until they were passing him.

"Lookee, lookee at Rory." He slid to the ground in their path and ran his eyes up and down her. "All dolled up." He whistled through his teeth. "Fancy and sweet."

Aurora grimaced. "Save it for your saloon girl. She's more likely to appreciate it." She stepped around him. Galen's truck was only a few yards away.

"There's a lot I could do that you'd appreciate, if you'd let yourself," he said after her.

She ignored him.

Galen didn't. "Lay off, Richter." His voice was flat. "The lady is with me."

Aurora looked back in time to see Frank lift his hands peaceably.

"Sorry, man," he said. "Didn't know."

"Now you do." Galen's long stride caught up to her. He unlocked the passenger door and waited until she'd climbed inside before closing it and going around to the driver's side.

"I told you not to take anything Frank says seriously," she said when he got behind the wheel.

"And you need to get your head out of the sand if you think he doesn't mean what he says."

She studiously fastened her seat belt. "Brotherly advice?"

"Common-sense advice." He drove out of the parking lot.

They arrived at the cantina all too soon. Even on a Monday evening, the place was busy. The tables up on the second story's open-air terrace were all occupied.

"Maybe we won't be able to get in," Aurora said hopefully as they walked through the front door.

As soon as they did, though, Galen's sister-in-law Julia waved them into the dining room.

"I've got one of the best tables in the house waiting for you," she said as she led them to a two-top near the wide wood and iron staircase that was a focal point in the center of the room.

"We're meeting another couple," Aurora told her quickly.

"I know." Julia smiled at her. She was a few years younger than Aurora. But even though they hadn't been classmates, Aurora had still known her from school and from Julia's family's grocery store, the Superette, where the other woman had worked before the Cantina opened. "I can't believe you know Roselyn St. James!" Her eyes sparkled. "*Tomorrow's Loves* used to be a secret addiction of mine." She pointed at Galen. "Do *not* share that fact with Liam. He'll never let me live it down." She looked back at Aurora. "Ms. St. James called yesterday to make reservations. I didn't take the call, but I heard that she made that call herself. Wouldn't you think an actress like that would have 'people' for that sort of thing? Anyway, I *did* take the call she made just a little while ago that she and her husband weren't going to be able to make it after all, but—" She broke off when Aurora let out a delighted shriek.

"She canceled." Practically bouncing, Aurora looked at Galen. "She canceled, she canceled, she canceled!" She very nearly threw her arms around his shoulders, she was so relieved. Only the dawning realization that she was making a scene in the middle of the Hollows Cantina dining room where nearly every table was occupied made her control herself.

He had a half smile on his face. "All that worry over nothing."

Julia pulled out one of the chairs at the table. "Anyway, in her message, she apologized for the short notice but she has a sick child, said to enjoy your evening together, dinner was still on them and she'd be in touch."

"The evening is definitely looking up," Aurora said, looking at Galen. "Should we stay? Or just consider ourselves lucky and call it a night?"

In answer, he pulled out the second chair at the table.

Entirely containing her delight was simply not going to happen, so she let it find its escape in the smile she figured was stretching toothily across her whole face. She sat down in the chair and took the thickly bound menu that Julia handed her. "Thanks."

"My pleasure." Julia handed the second menu to Galen when he was seated, as well. "So, aside from learning our own Aurora McElroy has brushed elbows with the Famous, *this* is how I learn the two of you are together?"

Aurora's delight skittered sideways and crashed into the staircase two feet behind Julia. She eyed the other woman with dread. "What did she tell you?"

Julia widened her eyes humorously and gave Galen a look. "You guys didn't stop off at the Two Moon for a few drinks before you got here, did you? Ms. St. James apologized for the short notice, wanted you to enjoy—"

"Aurora means besides that," Galen interrupted.

Julia looked from Galen to Aurora and back again, as if she were trying to read between narrow lines. "She and her husband were meeting another couple." She lifted her palms toward them. "You."

"That's it?"

"What else should there be?" Julia asked suspiciously. "What's going on?"

"Nothing," Aurora assured quickly. "And we, uh, we're not *together.* We're just—"

"—friends," Galen inserted. "Roselyn was at Cowboy Country the other day and ran into Aurora."

"We were college roommates," Aurora added. "Haven't seen each other in years."

"So they wanted to catch up," Galen finished.

Julia's attention was bouncing back and forth between them. "Interesting." She drew out the word. Then she looked at Aurora again. "Judging by your reaction that you were stood up, I guess you're not overly disappointed."

Aurora smiled wryly. "Probably be good if we never mention that again."

Julia leaned toward her, lowering her voice conspiratorially. "Too bad you had thirty-some people here witnessing it." She straightened once again. "I have strict instructions, along with a valid credit card number, to make sure you thoroughly enjoy your evening. So, can I start you off with drinks?"

"Beer," Galen and Aurora said in unison.

Galen grinned faintly. "Anything Belgian," he elaborated.

"I have just the thing," Julia said with a grin, and left the table. Unlike all of the servers who were dressed in pristine white shirts with black aprons tied around their hips, Julia wore a slim-fitting gray slack suit that fit her tall figure perfectly.

"And then there were two." Galen's voice drew her attention back.

"Yes." She made a production out of straightening the edges of her heavy silver flatware where it sat atop a chili-red cloth napkin. "Talk about escaping from the frying pan."

"Doesn't that saying usually end with someone going into the fire?"

"Hmm." Thanks to Roselyn's cancellation, Aurora and Galen had landed in their own fantasyland. Only it wasn't a fantasy, because the two of them would never have been out together like this for real. Not as anything other than "friends," at any rate.

"That's an ominous sounding *hmm*."

She finally looked up at him. "Sorry." She shook off her internal director. "I think I'm feeling guilty to be having dinner at their expense."

A waitress whom Aurora didn't know arrived at the table with two short-stemmed glasses, filled with golden beer topped by a thick, creamy head. "Welcome to the Hollows Cantina. I'm Faith," she introduced. "I'll be serving you tonight. Can I bring you a chef's sampler to start?"

Galen's gaze caught Aurora's. "Absolutely."

"I'll get that started for you." Beaming, Faith left the table.

"No," Galen said after their server was gone. "I'm not feeling guilty at all. It's the least she owes you for commandeering your audition way back when. So tonight, it's time to feast." He picked up one of the glasses. "Enjoy."

She felt a smile tug at her lips. She lifted her glass as well, and tapped it softly against his. "Enjoy." The beer tasted heady. Much more so than the usual domestic brands served up at the Two Moon. "Never knew you were such a connoisseur." She sipped again. "Wow. This is just...wow."

He smiled. "Exactly. But knowing that a beer imported from Belgium tastes better than the glug they serve over at the Two Moon doesn't make me a connoisseur. It's also stronger than that stuff over there, so keep that in mind."

"You don't have to worry about me drinking three of them," she assured. One was going to be ample.

She just needed to remember to keep her feet firmly on friend-slash-sister turf so she didn't end up embarrassing them both again.

Julia gave them a benevolent smile as she walked by with another party, heading toward the staircase. It was clear that *she* didn't buy into Aurora and Galen's platonic claims.

"Funny how Julia and Liam ended up together," Aurora murmured, watching his sister-in-law ascend to the second floor. "I don't remember her ever giving him the time of day back in school."

"She didn't. He had plenty of ego and plenty of girls. She was probably smart, not wanting to be one of the crowd."

"He couldn't have had as many girlfriends as Jude," Aurora countered. "Seemed like he changed girlfriends like they were flavors of the day."

"That was Jude," he agreed wryly. "Once he met Gabriella, though? Put a fork in him. That boy was done."

She smiled and toyed with the base of her glass. It was shaped similarly to a brandy snifter, except the glass above the round bottom was taller and curved in close to the top, then out again at the rim. She'd never thought of beer glasses as being pretty, but this one was. "You had your fair share of girlfriends, too." Not as many as Mark, perhaps, but Aurora certainly hadn't been the lone female crushing on Galen Jones.

"I s'pose. Never wanted to marry any of 'em." As if he'd lost interest in the conversational thread, he flipped open the menu.

"Find the most expensive thing you can," she suggested darkly.

His white teeth flashed in a quick grin. "Too bad my tastes aren't exactly fancy."

She swallowed another sip, savoring the rich flavor. "Nothing wrong with being a meat-and-potatoes kind of man." So sayeth the meat-and-potatoes kind of woman.

"Good thing." He closed the menu again. "Horseback Hollow wouldn't exist otherwise. What are you going to have?"

Galen Fortune Jones on a plate?

She quickly set down the beer. It was obviously dangerous stuff. After only a few sips, she found it hard to focus on the print when she opened her menu.

She probably should have eaten something that day.

But nerves had made the idea of food wholly unpalatable.

"I don't know." She closed the menu again. She gestured toward their glasses. "You chose excellently once. So whatever you're having, they can make it two."

He leaned a little closer, which at their small table, meant he was *much* closer. His eyes crinkled. "You're already buzzed, aren't you." It wasn't a question.

She moistened her lips, angling her chin. "I don't know what you mean."

He laughed softly and beneath the table his knee brushed hers.

Accidentally, she felt certain.

But he left it there, even after Faith returned with their appetizer.

The server set the oblong plate in the center of the small table, and provided them each with empty smaller versions. "Roasted shiitake and portobello mushroom mini quesadillas," she described, waving her hand over each item on the platter. "With a serrano chili sauce. Jalapeño-cheese fritters. And of course, crab Veracruz.

Would you like to take more time with your entrée selection?"

Aurora stared at the display of food. Her mouth was already watering. "Who'll need an entrée after all this?"

Faith smiled. "I'll bring you extra chili sauce. Everyone always wants extra." She headed off again.

"I'm sure somewhere in the world, this is sinful." She took Galen's plate without asking and filled it. "But I think I just don't care." She handed it back to him, then took a few of the tiny quesadillas for herself, managing not to shovel one into her mouth too quickly. She thought her eyes might roll back in her head from the bliss that immediately exploded on her taste buds. "Heavenly," she breathed, only to realize a moment later that he hadn't touched his own plate, but was staring fixedly at her. "Do I have food on my face or something?" She grabbed the napkin from her lap, starting to lift it.

"No."

"Then what?"

He shook his head a little. "Nothing. I figured your smile was as dangerous as it got. But I guess I was wrong."

She wasn't sure at all what to make of that. Except that there was something in his eyes that wasn't at all friend-slash-brotherly. And fantasyland suddenly didn't seem such a far-off fantasy, after all.

She moistened her lips and leaned forward a little. Considering the closeness of the table, was it any wonder that her ankle accidentally brushed against his leg? "We're supposed to enjoy, right?" She picked up her glass again and tilted it slightly toward him. "So…enjoy."

His eyes seemed focused on her mouth. His jaw shifted to one side. Then centered again, and his gaze met hers. "This could get complicated."

Later, she could blame it on an empty stomach and the wallop of a strong beer. "Or it could be very—" she lowered her voice a little more "—*very* simple."

Chapter Nine

Simple?

Galen nearly choked.

There was nothing simple about his body sitting smack-damn-dab in the middle of a crowded restaurant when the rest of his spirit was already five miles down the road with Aurora, knocking pictures off his bedroom wall.

He dropped his hand down beneath the table and wrapped it around her bare ankle before she slid it any higher toward his knee.

Her blue eyes widened.

He rubbed his thumb deliberately over her smooth skin. "You sure you want to play this game?"

Color rose in her cheeks, but she didn't look away.

She also didn't immediately assure him that she did, which was an answer in itself.

And unless she was sure, damn sure, he wasn't going to seduce her into it.

Because she *was* a friend.

He released her ankle and picked up his fork, jabbing it into one of the quesadillas that he had no interest in whatsoever since he hated mushrooms. But choking it down might keep his mind safely occupied with something other than peeling Aurora out of that ungodly sexy dress she'd obviously bought to impress Roselyn.

Or her husband.

Faith returned with the extra sauce and an expectant look. "Have you two had a chance to decide what you'd like?"

He knew what he'd like.

She just was on a menu he wasn't sure he could afford.

"Rib eye and enchiladas." He didn't need to look at Aurora to know that she was looking anywhere other than at him. "She'll have the same." It was her own damn fault if she didn't like the choice.

"Excellent." Faith glanced over the table with practiced ease. "Another Duvel?"

He hadn't finished the first. But he nodded, anyway.

He didn't believe that sleeping with Aurora would be very, very simple.

But he did believe he was in for a very, very long night wishing otherwise.

"There you are." Two hours later, Faith handed Aurora a small brown bag with a woven handle. "Mango-infused crème brûlée to go."

"Thank you." They hadn't ordered it. But Julia had insisted on sending them home with dessert. And even though she'd assured Galen that it wasn't necessary because she could add it to Roselyn's tab, he'd insisted on leaving the tip for Faith.

As for Aurora?

She was fairly certain she would never drink another drop of alcohol if she was going to be around Galen.

Neither her nerves nor her pride would be able to take it.

She even wished they hadn't been so practical about using only one vehicle. Because it meant that Galen had to drive her home.

And even though she'd been wearing her big-girl panties for some time now, when they got there, he still insisted on walking her up the hill to the front door. And then, even though it was closer to midnight than eleven, she felt compelled to ask if he wanted to come in for some coffee.

At least that had been the protocol the last time she'd had a "real" date.

She pushed open the front door. "And before you turn me down again, coffee isn't a euphemism for anything else."

"I didn't think it was. Why isn't your front door locked?"

She flipped on a light, giving him a look. "This is Horseback Hollow. Nobody locks their doors."

"Pretty sure that some do." He followed her into the kitchen where she pushed the crème brûlée, bag and all, into the refrigerator. "Particularly now that strangers are coming from all over to visit Cowboy Country. Get that dessert back out of the fridge."

She was stuffed to her gills from dinner. Hadn't been able to eat even half of her delicious steak, much less the spinach-and-crab enchiladas that had been loaded with everything nature had never intended. "If you're still hungry, why didn't you eat it at the restaurant?"

"Because they were trying to get the place closed. In case you haven't noticed, it's late."

"And morning's going to come as early as it always does with all of its attendant duties." But she pulled the bag back out, removed the ceramic dish that Julia had said they could return later, and set the dessert on the table, which was easily as outdated as the one he had in his own kitchen. "Knock yourself out." She set a spoon on the table, too. "If you want coffee, fix it yourself. I'm going to bed."

He sat down and tapped the back of the spoon on the crispy veil of burned sugar topping the rich custard. "Sure you don't want some?"

She started to leave the kitchen. "My mood for dessert has mercifully passed."

"For the record—" his deep voice followed her "—I didn't turn you down."

Everything inside her went alert. She turned on her heel and returned to the table. "Yes, you did."

"No." He angled sideways in the chair to face her. "I asked if you were sure you knew what you were doing."

Her mouth went dry.

"And you gave me the same panicked look then that you've got on your face now." He picked up the spoon again and cracked through the dessert's topping. "That is not *me* turning you down."

"I'm not panicked." She pushed the words out.

He swallowed a spoonful and raised a disbelieving eyebrow. "Really? You want to play footsie under the table now when you've had a decent meal to sop up your few sips of beer?"

She frowned at him. "Are you trying to pick a fight?"

He set the spoon down again. "Give me your foot."

"I beg your pardon?"

He hooked one arm over the back of the seat, his legs

sprawling, and tapped the edge of the seat. "Right here. High-heeled shoe and all."

He wasn't just trying to pick a fight.

He was trying to scare her off. And good.

But he was right. She'd had a decent meal to sop up her few heady sips of beer. So she was thinking very clearly this time, despite the fact that she was usually sound asleep long before that hour of the night because she'd have to get up in a few hours and tend to things around her daddy's ranch.

And she decided then and there that she wasn't going to be that accommodating.

She knew what she wanted. Galen.

If he didn't want her in return, he could darn well say so once and for all.

So she lifted her foot and placed the toe of her frivolously purchased pumps on the edge of the seat, right there between his thighs. She stared him down, challenging. "This what you had in mind?"

He put his hand around her ankle again. His fingers were long enough to circle all the way around, and his thumb rubbed over her ankle bone.

She inhaled sharply, and the sound seemed loud in the silent house.

"You need me to answer that?" His hand drifted up the back of her calf, creeping toward her sharply bent knee.

Heat streaked through her but she remained put, even though her legs were turning to mush.

"I guess not," he murmured. His other hand nudged the hem of her dress farther up her thigh. It relieved the deep blue fabric of being stretched beyond its capacity, but only added to the wealth of tension building inside her. Particularly when he pressed his mouth against her knee, watching her through his dark lashes.

She couldn't stop the shiver that worked down her spine when his hand cupped the back of her knee, and kept going, moving slower than ever against the back of her thigh.

"You don't have freckles."

"You can't tell that by touch." Her voice was faint. "I have them."

"On your nose." His hand slid another inch. Then two. "Anywhere else?"

If he kept going the way he was, he'd find out. That fact was obvious to them both.

She swallowed again. The only man she'd ever slept with had been Anthony, and that had been so long ago now, she'd wondered if she was destined to dry up and eventually blow away like a pile of dust. "A few." She clamped her teeth together as his fingers grazed the smooth edge of the undergarment the salesgirl had promised wouldn't show through the clinging dress like regular panties and bra would.

He followed the high-cut leg of the slick fabric over her hip.

"Where?"

She swallowed again. Freckles. He was talking about freckles. "Right about where your—" she sucked in a sharp breath "—fingers are."

"Hmm." He pushed her dress even higher over her thigh. "Interesting."

Was it? She didn't think so, but then again, she couldn't think straight, because he was kissing her thigh now. Of their own accord, her hands found his head and her fingers threaded through the thick dark strands. The fake diamond that she'd never moved from her right hand, or removed at all for that matter, winked in the overhead light. "Galen?"

He made a sound. She guessed a response.

"Do—" she hauled in a breath of bravery "—do you want to go to my room?"

"Eventually." His hand drifted over her rear. "Sort of enjoying this at the moment."

Heaven help her, so was she.

Her head fell back and she stared blindly at the white-painted tin ceiling. Lila had never swooned so much over Rusty.

His other hand slid up the back side of her unbent leg, moving beneath the dress. "That day at Cowboy Country," he murmured, "after I did that first show with you. You put on a dress. You remember?"

She made a sound. As much of a response as *she* was capable.

"And those Castletons you love."

"Blue stitching," she breathed, trembling as much from the deep timbre of his voice as she was from his touch. "Christmas present from my folks." She sucked in more air when his hands roved over her rear. "Few years ago," she finished.

"I'd never seen anything prettier." He tugged at her dress now, pulling the hem up to her waist. "Take this thing off."

She mindlessly pulled the stretchy fabric over her head, never more grateful for the absence of zippers and buttons in her life, and dropped it on the floor.

When he was silent, she made herself look at him.

The fear that he would still change his mind, still reject her, floated away like dandelion fluff in a breeze.

Because his expression was…reverent. And the hands that reached for her again weren't entirely steady.

She trembled and moistened her dry lips, slowly lowering her foot back to the floor. Instinct had her reaching for the pins containing her hair. She pulled them out and they dropped, too, with soft pings on the floor until she felt the bun unravel and her hair hung down her back. "Anything else?" she whispered, knowing that she'd do nearly anything he asked as long as he kept looking at her the way he was.

But he didn't answer.

His hands circled her waist and he rose, standing so close to her she could feel his belt buckle pressing into her belly. Then his palms roved up the sides of her body briefer, where the smooth satin gave way to equally smooth translucent black mesh. He reached her arms and slid his fingers beneath the narrow straps, tugging them off her shoulders, pulling down, down, until the satin cups dragged below her breasts. And even then, he kept pulling, peeling the undergarment down her hips, then her thighs, until it finally fell to her ankles, caught on her high-heeled pumps.

She quivered, her skin feeling hot and too tight as his fingers slid between hers, balancing her as she stepped out of the puddle of satin and mesh.

"Beautiful," he murmured, kissing her bare shoulder as he released her hands. They found their way immediately to the buttons on his shirt, quickly dispatching them as the evil that they were, until she could shove the fabric aside and greedily reach the warm flesh beneath.

"Soft," she whispered, when her palms finally discovered what the swirls of dark hair felt like.

"That's not a problem right now," he muttered on a rough laugh. His arms swept around her back, pulling her tight against him, until it wasn't only his belt buckle pressing against her.

She trembled wildly, still managing to pull his shirttails out of his jeans and out of the way until her breasts were flattened against his chest. "Galen—"

His mouth covered hers, swallowing whatever words she didn't know she was going to say anyway. She twined her arms around his shoulders and kissed him back with everything that had been building inside her for the past few weeks.

For the past few decades.

And she cried out when he suddenly jerked back, swearing a blue streak, which wasn't at all Galen's way.

He stepped around her, his hands on his hips, his wide shoulders bowing. "I don't have any protection with me," he said.

If her head hadn't already been swimming from *him*, relief would have done it. "I'm on the pill." Then when his gaze swung around to hers, she flushed. "It, uh, just because it regulates my…my period. You know. Not, um, not because I do this—" She clamped her lips shut, because she was blabbering and he'd started smiling a little.

"I'm glad." He took her head and pulled her toward him. "About the pill. And about the reason. And now I know where they are. The other freckles." His callused hand slid boldly over her hip, covering the pale dots that she'd groaned over her entire life. Until that moment. "Kick off your shoes."

Desire was a writhing thing inside her, sending tendrils from the center of her being through every finger, every toe. Standing there naked as the day she was born, the only armor she had against the emotion churning inside her were the remaining lethally high heels. They helped remind her that, to him, this was a game.

A highly charged, lose-your-mind contest of who would blink first.

And for some reason she was afraid that taking off

her shoes—toeing off that last bit of black leather and stilt-high stilettos that kept her from being entirely, utterly bare—meant she was blinking, fast and furiously.

She wasn't ready to bare her heart.

She wasn't ready to feel that vulnerable. That needy.

Didn't matter that she feared she already *was*.

Keeping the shoes on at least let her pretend otherwise. So instead of kicking them off, she stared into his eyes. "Take off your jeans."

It didn't seem logical that eyes so dark a brown as his could look like they were lit by a flame, yet that's how it seemed when the corners of his lips crooked up and with one hand, he unfastened his leather belt and popped open the button at the top of his fly.

Her blood, pooling low in her midriff, rushed throughout her limbs, heating the surface of her skin while the rasp of his zipper sounded loudly in the room. He sat down again only briefly, to pull off his boots and let them drop onto the floor even more loudly. Socks followed, and then he stood again and pushed off his jeans and the dark gray boxer briefs he wore beneath.

She almost wished then that she hadn't been such a stickler about her shoes, because she felt like the world tipped a little on its axis, and she actually had to reach out and steady herself with a hand on the table behind her. She was a rancher's daughter, for crying out loud. She'd even had a lover, albeit briefly before he'd thrown her over for her roommate.

What was it, then, about *this* man, that so completely undid her?

He raised a sardonic eyebrow when all she did was stand there, transfixed. "Satisfied?"

"Um." She swallowed.

He smiled faintly. Indulgently. "I'm not." He closed his

hands over her hips and pulled her against him and absorbed her gasp in his kiss. "Keep your shoes on, then," he murmured when his lips finally slid away. "Maybe next time, I'll keep my boots on."

Next time? The thought was headier than any alcohol could have ever been.

His lips brushed over her jaw. The side of her neck and his palm found her breast. "You still have the same bedroom?"

Of course. She hadn't visited the house he now lived in until the previous day, but he'd often been at hers. Always with her brother. She even had the same full-size bed, though the movie posters and girlish furnishings had mercifully fallen by the wayside in favor of more adult tastes. "Yes."

He immediately took her hand and pulled her up the narrow staircase that led from the kitchen to the second floor. Even though it was dark up there, he didn't need a light, turning accurately on the landing toward the two bedrooms at one end, opposite of where her parents' room was situated.

She had a vague thought about the clothing they'd left strewn about on the kitchen floor, but that thought fled the second they entered her bedroom and he pressed her against the wall just inside the door. "Where were we? That's right." His hands found her breasts, his thumbs circling the rigid peaks in a maddening way. "Here."

She thrust her fingers through his hair, pulling his mouth to hers. *"Here."*

She could feel the curve of a smile on his lips as they pressed against hers. "Whatever the lady wants."

She finally pulled her foot from her shoe and ran it up the back of his calf. "She wants you."

He went still for a moment. "Are you sure about that?"

She tasted his throat and wanted to hum from pleasure. "Very. Very sure."

He groaned a little, opening his mouth hungrily over hers. His hands burned down her thighs and he lifted her right out of her other shoe, pivoting smoothly to press her down on the bed. The ancient mattress sank and the even older bedsprings squawked. He laughed softly. "I'm glad your parents are gone and the nearest neighbors are two miles away."

She pressed her forehead into the crook between his neck and shoulder, loving the heat and scent of him almost as much as the weight of him on top of her. She blindly swiped her hand against the pillows crowding them, knocking them out of the way, and not caring when she heard something fall off her nightstand. "Stop talking."

"Yes, ma'am." His hand slid between her thighs finding her wet center, and she groaned, grabbing handfuls of bedding to keep from launching into space. "That better?"

She arched against him, shuddering, and his mouth latched onto her nipple, scraping it lightly with his teeth. She gasped and reached between them, guiding him home. "That better?"

His answer was a harsh breath as he sank into her, and she cried out his name. And then there were no more challenges. No more blink-first moments.

There was only him, filling every fiber of her being as he drove them headlong into perfection.

She woke to the smell of coffee, and for a minute, confusion reigned.

But the second she rolled over, realizing she was naked

and the bedding was barely hanging on to the mattress, it all came back.

She hadn't been dreaming again about making love with Galen.

Making love with him this time had been exquisitely real.

She clutched the sheet to her chest and sat up, wincing a little.

"Sore?"

She flushed and looked at Galen, who'd appeared in the doorway. He wore only his jeans and was carrying two coffee mugs. Ordinarily, coffee was her first priority of each day.

The way he looked, though, made her rethink that practice. If she saw him like that every day for the rest of her life, she would never tire of the view.

Which was a thought she knew she shouldn't be having.

She pushed her hair out of her face. There was usually a windup alarm clock on her nightstand, along with a few books from the Vicker's Corners Public Library and a box of tissues. But everything had been knocked off the stand and she flushed harder, remembering just how that had occurred. "What time is it?" The sun was shining brighter around the edges of her window curtains than it should have been.

"Almost nine."

"Nine!" Horrified, she scrambled off the bed, dragging the sheet with her just as she'd seen countless times in movies and television shows.

Reality, though, had her promptly tripping right over her tangled feet, and she landed on her face on the mattress with an ignominious bounce.

"What are you trying to do?" Galen's voice was mild. His eyes though, were laughing.

"Retain some dignity," she muttered, yanking the sheet back over her bare rear end.

His amusement reached his lips and he strolled into the room. He set the coffee mugs on the nightstand and when he sat, the springs squeaked again and the mattress dipped under his weight. Helped along with gravity, when he tugged on the sheet, she rolled with it toward him. "I liked that view," he murmured, pushing the white cotton sheet aside to run his hand over her bare thigh where he'd discovered one of her patches of freckles.

Before they'd finally been done for the night, he'd even turned on a light and to her blushing, panting delight, thoroughly examined all of them. More than once.

Even now, his fingers dipped between her thighs, grazing her hypersensitive flesh. "I like the touch even more," he murmured.

She exhaled shakily. "Me, too."

Galen leaned down on his other arm. There was a tender squeezing inside his chest he wasn't accustomed to. Making love with Aurora was a feast for every sense he possessed. "Not too sore?"

She turned her head against the mattress and her eyes, bluer than the Texas sky, met his. "No."

He studied her intently, looking for her tells. There was only one this time, though, and it was the brightening of the freckles sprinkled across her nose. "Liar."

"You keep doing what you're doing—" her words were throaty "—and I'll quickly forget."

Sounded good to him, and he slid his fingers through her slick moisture, loving the way her pupils dilated and her lips parted.

"Your face is so expressive," he murmured, leaning

down a little more, but never taking away his intimate touch. "You smile and it shows in your whole body." He delved deeper, discovering that if he pressed here, she whimpered softly, and if he stroked there, she shuddered sweetly. "And when I do this—" he circled the tiny knot of nerves and watched her eyes flutter "—I can feel it in your whole body."

"Galen—"

He shushed her softly. "Just this. Let me do just this."

Her lips parted and her legs moved restlessly, but he simply dropped his thigh over the back of hers, holding her still. "You are so beautiful," he murmured, pressing his whole palm against her, rocking her gently, knowing just that moment when she tipped over the edge because color bloomed over her entire body and her hands fisted around the sheet and she moaned his name as she convulsed against his fingers.

She closed her eyes, sighing deeply, before turning on her side and reaching for him.

And even though it would be the easiest thing in the world for him to pull off his jeans again and drown in her sweetness, he didn't.

He caught her hand in his and kissed her knuckles instead. "You're sore," he reminded softly.

"But—"

"And we've got chores to do." He lightly smacked her flank. "So stop lazing around, woman."

Before he fell to temptation despite his better intentions, he pushed off the bed and grabbed one of the coffee mugs. "Drink up." He handed it to her. "We'll take care of things here, then head to my place. Two able bodies are better than one, and if we're fast, we'll manage to get the necessities taken care of before we have to get to Cowboy Country."

She sat up, looking like a red-haired Aphrodite rising from a sea of white sheets. "And after that?"

He smiled slowly, and because he possessed only so much resistance, he bent over her and brushed his lips slowly against hers. "My bed's a king," he murmured when he straightened again. "And it doesn't squeak."

Chapter Ten

"Hey." Galen stood on the outside of the changing screen. "You going to be done soon?" The last show of the day was done and he and Aurora were alone in the wardrobe trailer, because everyone else had already left. Aurora, though, was being uncommonly slow.

So much so, that he wondered if he was alone in wanting to get her…alone.

They hadn't talked about what had happened between them during the past twelve hours. Not that he was anxious to. But it seemed as if that's what women always wanted to do. Talk.

That morning, though, after she'd pulled on old jeans, boots and a T-shirt, she hadn't seemed inclined to talk about anything other than the chores they'd dashed through at her place, then his, just to get to Cowboy Country in time for the noon show.

"You all right back there?"

From the other side of the screen, he heard her huff.

"I need help." She poked her head around the side. Seeing nobody but him, the rest of her followed. She lifted her left arm to show that the side of the dress was partly opened, revealing a slice of creamy skin. "The zipper's stuck."

She had a quartet of pale freckles on the underside of her sleekly muscled arm. If he kissed her there again, she'd giggle, because she was ticklish. If he kissed her where the dress was parted, she'd make that sighing sound she made, and they'd end up being even later getting home.

Safer to stick to the freckles than the side of her breast that was partially visible. "There's a zipper?"

"Obviously." She tugged at the fabric where it was parted. "Right here. I've been meaning to get it fixed, but—"

He leaned closer to see. The zipper. The freckles. The soft, smooth skin. Personally, he knew which was the *least* interesting. "But…?"

She lowered her arm a bit. "Someone keeps distracting me."

"Is that a complaint?" He trailed his fingertip over the pale freckles and she shivered, yanking her arm down.

"Don't tickle!"

"Don't be so tempting." He pushed up her arm again and managed to catch the zipper pull between his thumb and forefinger. It wasn't just nearly invisible, but minuscule as well, and try or not try, his knuckles pressed against her breast. "And I think—" he attempted moving the zipper pull both up and down and failed "—you're stuck."

She smiled wryly. "Well, I already knew that."

"I thought this dress fastened up the back. You know,

with these laces." He tugged on the silky cords that criss-crossed down her spine.

She peered around her arm at him again. "Disappointed?"

He laughed softly. "Doesn't matter to me what you're wearing. It's the same you underneath whether you're wearing beads and lace or T-shirt and jeans." And if he slipped his hand through the gap where the zipper was partially undone, he could fill his hand with *her.*

But just because the trailer was empty at the moment, didn't mean it would stay that way.

So he tugged again at the zipper, and again, it didn't budge. "Thing's not moving. Can you rub some bar soap on it or something? That's what my mom always does with stuck zippers."

"That's a thought." She lowered her arm. "I'm just going to have to wear it home, I guess. Figure a way to get out of the thing so I can fix it before tomorrow." She slipped behind the screen for a moment and came out again with a bundle of clothing in her arms. The old-fashioned boots of her costume had been replaced by her flip-flops. "I can't cut through the park wearing the dress."

"So we'll walk around the long way." He angled his head, eyeing her, then grabbed his Rusty shirt off the hanger. "Put this on, though."

Her eyebrows lifted. "Nobody can see the zipper underneath my arm." But she took the shirt anyway and pulled it over her shoulders. The sleeves hung past her hands and the shirttail nearly reached her knee. She gestured at the wall mirror. "I look ridiculous."

"I was thinking you looked damn cute."

She ducked her head quickly and reached for the door,

but he still saw the shaky smile she tried to hide as he followed her down the metal steps.

They took the circuitous backstage route around the park to the employee lot and as soon as he opened his truck door for her, she pulled off the oversize shirt before climbing inside. "Too hot outside still for this dress and your shirt."

"It has been hot." He closed the door and went around to the driver's side. "Bet Hollow Springs is getting plenty of use these days." The swimming hole was Horseback Hollow's hidden gem.

"Imagine so." She rolled down her window as they drove out of the lot. "I remember you and Mark used to go there a lot."

"Everyone in our high school class went there a lot." The swimming hole was backdropped by red rock cliffs and a waterfall. Mostly accessible on horseback, it had always been a natural draw for Horseback Hollow residents. "I still hope it manages to stay under the radar with all the tourists coming to visit Cowboy Country."

"You said that a lot when you were arguing against it opening."

"Wasn't arguing. I was just stating an opinion."

She lifted her hand peaceably. "Okay."

"Would *you* want a bunch of strangers tramping up there, polluting things with their monster coolers, trash and noise?"

She sent him a sideways look. "I am *sure* you guys didn't go up there with sketch pads to draw the local flora and fauna. You took beer. And snacks."

"Not always beer," he defended.

"Maybe not. But how is it any different between what you guys used to do up there and what somebody from…

Skokie...might do up there now? If they even found their way there, that is?"

"Just is."

She shook her head, chuckling. "Whatever you say." She hung her hand out the window, turning it against the wind as he picked up speed. "When's the last time you went out there?"

"Not since last summer. You?"

"Years." She was silent for a moment. "Not since before Mark died."

"Because the cemetery's out that way?"

Aurora should have expected the question. She wasn't sure why she hadn't, except that when she was with Galen, she didn't think much about anything but Galen. "Because I'm not particularly keen on swimming," she lied.

"I remember otherwise."

She shot him a look.

"You think I don't remember the way sometimes you tagged along with Mark?"

"Only because Mama made him take me."

"You were like a skinny little redheaded fish. Couldn't get you out of the water once you were in. And then when you finally did get out, 'cause it was time to go home, you pouted."

"I did not."

He lifted his hand as though he was swearing an oath. "Truth."

She couldn't help but smile a little. "Fine." She looked out the window again, enjoying the feel of the air blowing over her. "I used to like swimming out there." Primarily because, back then, she'd wanted to do anything her big brother had been doing. And as she got a little older, because there was always the likelihood that Galen would be around. "I had a terrible crush."

"Pardon?"

She flushed, realizing she'd spoken the words aloud. What was *wrong* with her? "Nothing."

But he was eyeing her, his strong wrist hanging over the top of the steering wheel and his long middle finger tapping the dash on the other side. "You had a crush on…who?"

Mortified, she stared down her nose at him. For all the good it did. "Nobody."

He smiled faintly. "We should ride out there on Sunday."

"To Hollow Springs?" She fiddled with one of the wood-like buttons on the front of his Rusty shirt that she held folded on her lap. "Sounds nice."

He reached across the console between their seats and dragged his finger through the partially opened zipper under her arm.

She shivered and clamped her arm down. "Don't *tickle me*!"

His grin flashed. "I know one thing. You're gonna look a mite different in a swimsuit these days than you did back then."

So would he.

He'd been unreasonably handsome as a teenager. But now he was a man. A ruggedly handsome, broad-shouldered, hardworking, ranching man.

"I'm not even sure I have a swimsuit anymore." She suddenly lifted her finger to point at him. "And I am *not* skinny-dipping."

"Ever?"

"There'll be a couple dozen people there on a hot Sunday afternoon. Neither one of us will be skinny-dipping.

Unless you fancy getting picked up by the sheriff's department for public indecency."

His grin flashed again. "Can't blame a guy for his fantasies."

She turned her face to the wind, wishing it were cooler so there was some chance of it dousing the heat in her cheeks. "Being publicly indecent?"

He laughed softly. "Chicken."

She bit back her own smile. "Yup." They'd reached the highway, but instead of slowing as they neared her turnoff, his speed stayed steady.

Which had her wanting to smile all over again because they were obviously going to *his*.

He hadn't done a single thing differently during their performances that day. Rusty's passionate clinch with Lila still hadn't involved locking lips. Which, considering everything, had left her doubting that he'd really meant what he'd said that morning about his king-size bed.

Soon he was slowing, though, and turned up the graded road to his place. He parked around the rear as usual, and not until they were heading up the back porch did she stop to think that she was still stuck inside Lila's wedding dress. If the bar-of-soap trick didn't work, she wasn't sure how she was going to get out of the thing, short of scissors. "I don't suppose you have a needle and thread." She held out the sides of her dress. "In case I have to have you cut me out of this thing."

He pushed open the back door and reached inside to flip on the mudroom light. "I've got a sewing kit around somewhere. Ma's doing." He turned back to her and suddenly swept her off her feet.

She gaped. "What are you doing?"

"Why, Lila," he drawled, "what d'you think I'm doing?"

She giggled as he carried her over the threshold. "Oh, *Rusty*. You're my hero."

He chuckled and plopped her on top of the white washing machine sitting next to the big refrigerator. He opened a storage cupboard next to that, pulled out a paper-wrapped bar of soap and turned back to her. "Let's get that dress off you."

She obediently lifted her arm. "Sweet-talker."

He ran the edge of the bar over the zipper, above and below the pull, and even managed to work it down the inside of her zipper, though she had to completely pull her arms out of the lace shoulder band for him to manage it.

"What's this?" The second he touched the gold chain hanging between her breasts, she remembered that she'd also strung his drugstore ring on it that afternoon before their first show.

"Lila wouldn't wear a ring like that," she managed blithely. She had one arm crossed over her bare breasts, which was kind of silly, she supposed, now that he'd already seen, touched and tasted nearly every inch of her. "But I figured I'd be inviting the Roselyn-devil back if I didn't keep it handy." It was a blatant lie. But how else could she explain her unwillingness to toss the ring aside when she hadn't wanted to take it in the first place?

"Superstitious?" He smiled slightly as nudged her arm higher, and away from her breasts as he tested the zipper before going to work again with the soap. "She doesn't have any reason to come back."

"One hopes." She would have felt foolish sitting there with her dress pulled down below her breasts, but stuck in place over her rib cage, if it weren't for the way his heated eyes kept straying away from the task at hand. Instead, she was only increasingly impatient for him to finish the job. She was awash with need, practically squirming where she sat on top of the washing machine. “Hurry up.”

“What do you want me to do?” He lifted a brow, though his innocent look didn’t fool her for a second. He knew exactly the torment he was causing, and was enjoying it. “Tear it?”

“Tempting.” She managed to push the soap out of his hand and pulled his palm to her bare, tight breasts. The flare of surprise on his face was worth the boldness, and she looped her hand behind his neck, pulling his head to hers. “Just kiss me already.”

He stepped closer and brushed his mouth over hers. “You’re suddenly getting very demanding.”

She could feel his smile against her lips. “You have no idea.” She reached down his spine and gathered the fabric of his T-shirt in her fingers and pulled upward.

He laughed softly and let her yank the thing up and off his head. “Keep this up and you’re not gonna get out of that dress and we’re not gonna get outta the laundry room.”

She didn’t care. She was ravenous for him. “You never kiss me onstage.” She pulled his head back to hers and ran her lips along his jaw. He needed a shave, and the rough razor stubble tickled her lips. “Why?”

“’Cause I’m not an actor.” He caught her face between his hands. His dark gaze was anchored on her lips. “I’m not Rusty kissing Lila. I’m Galen kissing Aurora. And I don’t want an audience of hundreds at Cowboy Country for that.”

Something sweet squeezed inside her, even more enticing than the desire flooding her. “We don’t have an audience now,” she whispered.

“No.” He brought his lips to hers. Rubbing. Nibbling. Teasing, until she was nearly whimpering for more.

And then finally, oh, finally, he tired of toying and kissed her in earnest, and when he pulled back the next time, they were both breathless and her hands trembled as she fumbled with his belt.

"That's not the zipper we were supposed to get down."

She took almost indecent pleasure in the sound of his belt slithering out of his belt loops when she pulled on it. "Are you objecting?"

In answer, he pushed his hands through her hair, pulling it out of the ponytail holder and letting it fall around her shoulders. She knew men were visual creatures, and there was something electrifying about knowing Galen looked at her and liked—*liked*—what he saw.

Then his mouth was on hers again while his hands delved beneath her dress, divesting her of her panties while she hastily shoved his jeans aside, and she cried out when he thrillingly claimed her, right then and there in his laundry room.

With his boots on.

The rest of the week passed in a similar vein, leaving Aurora in a constant haze of delight. Fortunately, the soap bar had successfully done its job on the zipper that first night after she and Galen had finally stumbled, exhausted, from the laundry room. She'd gotten out of the dress and mended the fraying satin alongside the zipper using the thread and needle from the sewing kit he'd unearthed from a drawer.

Between the two of them, in the mornings they managed to take care of their more critical ranch chores, then perform four shows a day at Cowboy Country with Galen making his "authenticity consultant" rounds between each, and fall into Galen's king-size bed at night in a greedy tangle of arms and legs.

By the time Sunday rolled around and they were able to sleep until seven—a nearly unheard-of hour—Aurora knew she'd never been happier in her life.

She just hoped that this time, her happiness didn't have an expiration date.

"Come on, missy." Galen sauntered through the back door of his kitchen where she'd been cleaning up after the eggs and biscuits she'd fixed for breakfast, and plopped the straw cowboy hat he was carrying on her head. "Horses are saddled and day's already wasting."

She thumbed back the hat, grinning at him. Not surprisingly, Galen was holding true to his suggestion earlier that week that they go to Hollow Springs. "You shouldn't have showered with me after we finished the chores if you were worried about wasting time." She draped the damp dish towel over the side of the sink and handed him the plastic-wrapped sandwiches she'd made to take with them, along with an oversize thermos of lemonade.

"All a matter of priorities." He led the way out the back door and they walked across to the pen where he'd saddled up two quarter horses while she'd been cleaning up from breakfast. He tucked the sandwiches in one saddlebag and the thermos in the other. Then he handed her the reins for the pretty bay. "You can take Esther here. She's better behaved than Pepper." He patted the rump of the buckskin crowding next to him, nudging the pushy gelding away. "You need help getting up?"

"Esther." Aurora tsked. "Such an unromantic name for such a pretty girl." She ran her hand down the horse's glossy red coat. "And I've been getting myself on and off horses my whole life." To prove it, she tucked the toe of her tennis shoe in the stirrup and nimbly pushed herself up into the saddle.

He automatically checked the stirrup length, adjusting

them up a few notches. "What *should* I have named her? Juliet?" He tucked her toe back in the stirrup. "Better?"

She stood up, testing. Riding in flat-soled shoes was never a good idea, even for an experienced rider, but they were heading to Hollow Springs. She was wearing an ancient swimsuit under her cutoffs, and T-shirt and boots would have just been too hot.

Even Galen was wearing tennis shoes, along with cargo shorts that hung off his hips in a very distracting way. The only thing he hadn't eschewed was his cowboy hat, though today it was a tan Resistol rather than his usual black Stetson. He took Pepper's reins and led him on foot out of the pen, waiting until Aurora and Esther came through before pushing the pen gate shut. Then he easily swung into the saddle and Aurora had to stifle a purely female sigh of appreciation.

It was something to realize she'd had to get to the age of thirty before she could fully appreciate the beauty of a man on a horse.

Or maybe it was just *this* man.

Out of habit, she started to reach for her watch locket and the ring that still hung beside it, but she'd left it on the nightstand in his bedroom. The watch was old. Not the least bit waterproof, and after they spent at least an hour on horseback just to get to the springs, she fully intended on getting wet.

Galen took the lead, heading away from the highway and across his land, which stretched out flat and open beyond the barn. Eventually, they'd cross onto his folks' property, then hers, and after that, they'd follow one of the county riding trails meandering around Horseback Hollow until they reached the springs.

If the horses were poky, it would be a few hours before they got there. If they weren't, they'd make it in half the time.

Either way, she was happy with the creak of saddle leather, the warmth of horseflesh and the smell of summer grass in the air. Mostly, she was happy watching the easy way Galen sat his horse.

He'd said the only thing he'd ever wanted to be was a rancher. And even though he was only plodding across the land on a pleasure ride, she still could see how natural that choice was. For Galen, horses and cattle and all that went with them were exactly who he was.

She squeezed her knees slightly and Esther picked up the pace until she drew even with him and Pepper. "Race?"

His teeth flashed. "You've never ridden Esther. You don't know what she's capable of."

"She's one of your ranch horses," she returned. "I'm pretty sure I have an idea." Without waiting for him to agree, she lightly pressed her heels and she felt Esther's immediate reaction as her muscles gathered together before she launched forward.

Exhilarated, Aurora sank down in the saddle, clamping one hand on top of her head to keep the hat from blowing off, and laughed as she flew across the countryside on the back of the beautiful horse.

The sight of Aurora's red hair flying out behind her as she leaned low over Esther's back nearly took Galen's breath away.

Like everything else she did, Aurora threw herself into it, body and soul.

Pepper was prancing around, anxious as hell to chase after them. He was ten years younger than Esther and full of eager pride. "All right, pal," Galen murmured, and let the horse do what nature intended.

It took only a few minutes, and they were drawing even with Aurora, who sent him that whole-body smile that never failed to make him feel good inside.

And then they just rode.

It was late in the afternoon by the time they finally reversed the trip and started back after spending hours lazing around the swimming hole.

Predictably, the place had been packed, mostly with teenagers who reminded them both of days long past. Aurora could have passed for one of them, as she'd flitted in and out of the water in a faded green one-piece that showed off her slender, fit figure.

Galen had spent less time in the water than she had, more content to sprawl on the bank and watch the young bucks try to flirt with her even more than they were flirting with the girls their own age.

They'd climbed the red rocks above the waterfall, though she'd drawn the line at jumping down into the swimming hole below like some of the more foolhardy kids were doing. Like he and Mark used to do. They devoured the roast beef sandwiches she'd made, guzzled the gallon of lemonade and felt their skin get red from the sun.

All in all, it was one of the most perfect days Galen could ever remember having.

As they rode back, Aurora seemed content to rock along in her saddle as the horses picked their way across the rough dirt trail. When they got to one fork in particular, though, she pulled up on the reins.

Pepper stopped, too, and Galen folded his wrists over his pommel and eyed Aurora.

The right fork took them toward their spreads.

The left would take them toward the back side of the

cemetery, which was accessible by car from the highway on the other side.

Her nose was pink from too much sun and her hair was a mess of tangles hanging loose around her shoulders. And the way she was looking left made him hurt inside.

"When's the last time you went there?"

She finally looked back at him. "His funeral." Her lips twisted at the surprise he couldn't hide. "I know. Horrible of me."

He shook his head. "Wasn't thinking that at all." He waited a beat. "You want to go there now?"

She hesitated. "I don't know." She chewed her lip. Then her eyes met his. "How can you be sure?"

He didn't have to ask what she meant. "Your brother wasn't suicidal, Aurora. It was an accident. A terrible, rotten accident that would never have happened if Mark had had the sense not to get behind the wheel."

She plucked the stitching on her pommel. "I went off to college. He didn't."

He knew where she was going, and felt a knot in his chest. "He was accepted to A&M same as I was."

"And he didn't go because of the money."

He silently apologized to the friend he'd once had. But Mark was gone. And Aurora was very much here. "He got a better scholarship than I did."

Her eyes widened. "What?"

"He didn't take it because he didn't *want* to go," he said evenly. "He'd only applied in the first place to make your parents happy. I was there when he opened the letter. We were eighteen years old. He made me promise never to tell anyone what he turned down." Mark had even burned the scholarship letter to make certain it wasn't seen by anyone.

Her eyes reddened. "Did my parents know?"

"He obviously never told them, or you wouldn't be thinking what you've been thinking all this time." He sighed. "After he died, there was never a right time to. They were devastated enough without learning that he could have gone to school like they'd wanted." He willed her not to look away from him. "When you went off to UCLA, you weren't stealing an opportunity from him, Aurora. You didn't take anything from him by going off to live your own life."

She blinked hard and a tear slid down her cheek. "College was a dream of mine. Why would he turn down that opportunity for himself?"

"There never was any explaining your brother," he murmured. "I should have told you before now."

She sniffed, finally looking away and swiping a hand over her cheek. "So why didn't you?"

"Because I wasn't sure breaking an old promise to him wasn't just going to cause more hurt." He'd also been busy lately working on not falling for the man's little sister. A woman who, for as long as he could remember, had yearned for something other than the kind of life that was in Galen's DNA.

She absorbed that. "Knowing he had a chance like that and—" She broke off and shook her head. "It would have broken my parents' hearts even more." She laid a loose rein against the left side of Esther's neck and the horse obediently headed toward the right fork, and away from the cemetery.

Galen stifled a sigh. Just because he figured she needed to visit her brother's grave if only to finally vent her anger or confusion or sadness didn't mean it was the right thing for her. Only she could decide that for herself.

So he nudged Pepper along after her and they rode back to his place in silence. When they reached the barn, she slid off Esther's back and replaced the bridle with a halter before unsaddling her. He knew offering to do it for her wouldn't be welcomed, so he focused on doing the same with Pepper. When she pulled the saddle clear, though, he silently took it from her, carrying both into the tack room, hanging everything over the racks there before wiping a cloth over the saddles. Then he grabbed the bucket of grooming tools and rejoined her outside the barn at the wash rack, where she was already hosing the sweat from Esther's coat. When she was finished, she handed him the hose and used the scraper from the bucket to remove the water.

"You're a love, aren't you," she murmured as she sluiced water from the horse's back. Esther looked blissful.

Pepper, not so much. He wasn't quite the fan of water that Esther was, though he had calmed down some about it since Galen had bought him at auction a few years back. He could have made shorter work of hosing him down, but there didn't seem to be much rush, and it was uncommonly peaceful working alongside each other.

Eventually they finished, though, and he turned them out to pasture with his three other ranch horses. "Thinking about hiring one of Quinn's nephews to help out around here."

They were hanging with their arms over the wood rails overlooking the pasture, and she lifted her eyebrows. "Jess's oldest?"

He nodded. Quinn's sister had a passel of kids. All boys except for a baby girl born about the same time as Quinn and Amelia's Clementine Rose. "Jason can use the money and I can use the help."

She'd rested her chin on her folded arms and she turned her cheek to look at him. "How old is he?"

"Sixteen. Just got his driver's license, and Quinn says Jess is tearing her hair out over it. He's got more energy than she knows what to do with." Unlike Quinn, Jess and her husband, Mac, were high school teachers. "I thought he could burn some of it off learning how to throw hay bales instead of baseballs."

She smiled slightly. "Sounds like—" She broke off at the toot of a car horn that made them both jerk around to look back toward the house, where a gleaming black SUV had pulled up next to his dusty pickup truck. "Well, crud on a cracker," she muttered.

Galen sighed, watching the dark-haired Roselyn St. James climb out of the SUV and wave her hand at them. "My thoughts exactly."

Chapter Eleven

Aurora watched Roselyn open the rear door of the SUV, and a moment later, her two dark-haired children were on the ground, short legs pumping as they immediately made a break for it. "What could she possibly be doing here now?"

"Don't know, but I want those kids staying in sight." He set off to intercept them before they even thought about getting too close to the barn, which Aurora knew wasn't the least bit childproof.

Sighing, she pushed her hands in her front pockets and headed toward Roselyn. At least she hadn't appeared with Anthony in tow. From the corner of her eye, she saw Galen grab the twins by their hands and redirect them back toward their mother and safer regions again, and something inside her squeezed at the sight.

Then Roselyn reached her with her typical kiss-kiss hello. "I've been calling you all afternoon," she said brightly.

"We were out." She found her gaze straying to Galen again. If he ever *did* become a father—

Her wayward thought screeched to a halt.

He'd made it more than plain that he wasn't one for weddin' and beddin', so there was no point in fantasizing about things that weren't.

She looked back at Roselyn. "Why were you calling?"

"To chat, of course."

Aurora rubbed her nose that, after the copious amounts of sun she'd had that day, was likely to be peeling before long. "Roselyn, what is going on?" She was tired of pretense. "You didn't indulge in idle chatting when we were nineteen years old. Why are you pretending now that we're long-lost best friends when you know nothing could be further from the truth?"

The other woman looked wounded. So sincerely wounded that Aurora's conscience nipped at her heels.

Then she remembered that Roselyn was an actress. A decent one at that, and Aurora mentally kicked the nipper to the curb.

"That was a long time ago," Roselyn said after a moment. "You've obviously moved on. Eloping and all." She waved her fingers toward Galen and the twins. They'd stopped off because one of the tots had squatted down to pluck the yellow heads off the dandelions growing through the grass. "Haven't you?"

Aurora nearly chewed off the tip of her tongue. But she nodded. "I figured you would have left town by now," she added. Wished, more like, but despite everything, she couldn't bring herself to be so brutally honest. Particularly when she was lying about being married to Galen in the first place.

Roselyn brushed at her arm, left bare by the bright

red minidress she wore. "Mr. Moore just got to town. He hasn't had a chance to meet with Anthony yet."

"In other words, you've been stuck in Vicker's Corners for more than a week now?"

"Anthony's had a lot of meetings." Roselyn's lips twisted a little. "There's nothing to *do* here! How do you stand it?"

Aurora's gaze strayed to Galen again. He was crouching down, helping the other twin find her share of dandelions as well, letting her drop them into his upturned cowboy hat. "I stand it just fine," she murmured.

"But you wanted so much more out of life," Roselyn said. "I might not remember everything, but I remember that. You wanted to act." Her lips twisted. "I wanted to be a star." She was watching her children, also. "Men turn everything upside down."

Aurora couldn't really disagree. "I'm sure most men would say that about women."

"How democratic of you." She was silent for a moment. "Anthony's having an affair."

Aurora blinked at the bald pronouncement. "Roselyn." She opened her mouth again, but nothing came. For the first time, she noticed the tight lines around the other woman's eyes. Lines that no amount of acting could produce. "I…I'm so sorry."

"I don't know why." Roselyn hadn't turned her eyes away from her twins. "He had an affair with me while he was with *you*. You hated me for it." She lifted her shoulder. "I never thought the shoe would be on the other foot." She tugged at the side of her dress. "But then I never thought I'd be a whale all over again. All I'm doing is getting fatter and aging and you—" She swept her hand out. "You don't look any different at all."

"My mirror wouldn't agree. And you're not a whale,"

Aurora chided. "You're pregnant." She didn't know what to make of this woman. Or the compassion swamping her.

She brushed her hands down the sides of her shorts. She was dusty from the ride and felt positively crinkly. Which was nothing compared to being betrayed by the man whom you should be able to trust most in the world.

She looked Galen's way again.

He was sitting right down on the grass now with one of the twins on his lap while the other one rained dandelions on top of his head. Then he looked her way, a ruefully indulgent look on his face.

And she knew in that moment that whatever did or didn't happen between them, she was still going to love him forever.

She folded her arm around Roselyn's rigidly held shoulders. "Come inside," she said quietly. "Sit down. Toni and Tiffani will be fine with Galen for a while."

Roselyn didn't protest. But she did lean awkwardly over and pull off her high wedge-heeled sandals. "My ankles keep swelling," she said thickly.

Aurora sighed a little. "Then why wear shoes like that, Ros?"

"Because Anthony likes them." She was holding them by the leather straps and suddenly tossed them on the ground and walked with Aurora barefoot across the grass to the porch.

Inside the kitchen, she sat wearily on one of the chairs at the table and Aurora pushed a second one close. "Put up your feet." Then she filled two glasses with ice and the sun tea that she'd left in the window that morning. She added a slice of lemon to each and set one in front of Roselyn. "It's not decaf," she warned. "So if you want something else, say so."

Roselyn shook her head and sipped at the tea.

"Now." Aurora sat down opposite her. "How do you know he's having an affair?"

"Because he hasn't touched me since—" She gestured at her swollen belly.

Aurora circled her hand around the glass. She obviously had no personal experience in marital matters. "Did you ask him? Catch him?"

"He's smarter than that," Roselyn dismissed, sounding more like her usual self. "And no, I didn't ask him. What's the point when the truth is so obvious?" She didn't look at Aurora. "I thought it was with you."

Aurora sat up straight. *"Me!"*

"In the last six months, he's made three trips to Texas without me. He's *claimed* it's because he's looking for a job. Which is pretty hard to believe, considering he never liked anything about Texas." Her dark eyes flickered up to pin Aurora. "Except you."

"Roselyn, I haven't seen Anthony since we were in college."

"So I insisted on coming with him this time." Roselyn went on as if Aurora hadn't spoken. "I decided I was going to see for myself. It was easy enough to find you since Anthony's kept track all these years." She ignored the start Aurora gave. "Only once I tracked you down at Cowboy Country, I learn you're wallowing in newlywed bliss. There's no way you'd have changed so much that *you'd* be having an affair with one person and marrying another."

Aurora supposed there was some sort of compliment in there. And given Roselyn's suspicion, she gave up the thought of coming clean about her and Galen. Heaven only knew what the other woman would think if she learned there was no "newlywed" involved at all. And despite Roselyn's behavior in the past, Aurora had no desire to upset a pregnant woman.

"Maybe he really *is* looking for a job," she suggested, instead. "Isn't that what the interview with Moore Entertainment is all about?"

Roselyn's lips compressed. She nodded, almost unwillingly, it seemed.

"Have you *talked* to him about it?"

"About the fact that he's obviously sleeping with someone other than me?" She made another face. "Clearly you don't understand how humiliating this is."

Aurora held her tongue on that score. "You were wrong about me," she said. "Maybe you're wrong about him. He hasn't, uh, hasn't left you. Has he?"

"Of course not." Roselyn looked even more insulted. "He might not want *me* anymore, but he certainly wants our children."

"Is this the real reason you canceled out on dinner the other night? Because you'd decided I wasn't a…a threat?" The very thought of it would have been laughable if it weren't so sad.

Roselyn didn't answer. Possibly because the phone on the wall took that exact moment to ring shrilly.

Aurora stared stupidly at it.

"Aren't you going to answer?"

She smiled weakly and plucked the phone off the hook. "Hello?"

There was a brief pause. Then a woman's voice. "This is Galen's mother. Is he around?"

She felt her cheeks heat as if she'd been caught with her hand in the cookie jar. "Hi, Jeanne Marie," she greeted. "It's Aurora." Only Roselyn's presence edited off the McElroy that she very nearly added. "Galen's outside at the moment. I can get him for you, though, if you want to hold on a second."

"Aurora!" There was no mistaking the woman's surprise though she didn't come right out and ask *what* she was doing answering her son's telephone. "No, don't interrupt him. Just let him know I called."

"I will."

"Thank you, dear." Jeanne Marie's voice was warm. And then the line went dead and Aurora hung up the phone.

"Galen's mom," she told Roselyn, feeling hideously awkward.

"In-laws." Roselyn's voice clearly said she was not a fan of them. She put her feet on the floor and pushed herself off her chair. In just the week since that first kiss-kiss at Cowboy Country, her belly seemed to have gotten more prominent. Holding a hand to the small of her back, she went to the window over the sink and looked out.

Then she turned around. "I should go. Anthony thinks I've taken the twins back to see the piglets at Cowboy Country's petting zoo. If they're not chattering about it when they see him, he'll know I didn't."

"Just ask him, Roselyn."

The suggestion only earned her a pitying look. "Because he's likely to tell me the truth? You really are naive, aren't you?" She went to the phone and quickly wrote out a number on the pad there. "That's my agent's personal number in New York," she said, not looking at Aurora. "She's a shark and she's good. You decide you want more than this place, call her. Stage work. Soaps. Commercials. Whatever you're after, she'll get you there. Tell her I sent you." Then she took a final sip of her tea and walked toward the mudroom.

Aurora followed her out, feeling wholly bemused and

more than a little helpless. "You're still staying at the B and B in Vicker's Corners?"

Roselyn nodded and headed down the steps. "Godforsaken little place that it is, it's still better than anything else around this area. At least until that hotel finally gets built at Cowboy Country. Toni. Tiffi." Roselyn called her toddlers, who were lying on their backs looking up at the clouds with Galen almost exactly the way Aurora could remember doing with Mark when she was little. "Time to go," Roselyn said as she picked up her shoes.

Galen rolled to his feet and the little girls did, too. He dumped several dandelion heads out of his hat and put it back on his head before walking with the twins over to Roselyn and Aurora.

She could see the questions in his eyes that she also knew he wouldn't voice until Roselyn was gone. "Your mom just called."

Consternation joined the questions.

"Come on." Roselyn held out her hands for her daughters. "Let's go see the piglets."

The prospect clearly excited them more than dandelions. They nearly fell over their feet running toward the SUV, bypassing their mama's hands altogether.

Aurora followed, lifting the twins up into the back seat so Roselyn wouldn't have to. "Roselyn." She couldn't believe what she was inviting. "Stay in touch, okay? Let me know how you're doing."

Roselyn climbed awkwardly behind the wheel and tossed her shoes onto the passenger seat. "You're too nice for your own good, Aurora. Someday that'll be your downfall."

"I'd like to think it would be the opposite." She stepped back from the vehicle when Roselyn started the engine, and returned the twins' enthusiastic waves as she drove off.

Galen tucked one of the dandelions behind her ear. "So what was that all about?"

Aurora told him about Roselyn's suspicions. "I never thought I'd feel sorry for her, but—" She broke off and shook her head, looking up at him. "I was going to tell her the truth about us, but I didn't want to upset her any more than she already was."

"Ever occur to you that she and her husband probably deserve each other?"

Aurora hugged her arms around her waist, trying not to wonder what she'd need to do to deserve Galen.

For real.

"I think she's really in love with him." Then she didn't want to talk about Roselyn and Anthony any longer. "Sorry I answered your phone. It was just ringing, and it would have looked odd for me not to."

He shrugged. "Not a big deal." He hooked his fingers through her empty belt loops and tugged her close. "Like her or not, Roselyn's got some cute little girls."

"Mmm-hmm. They certainly appeared to be quick fans of yours." Which made them smart three-year-olds in her book. She flicked a yellow dandelion petal off his shoulder, then slid her arms around his waist, glad that he didn't know what a mess of gelatin she'd turned to on the inside. "Don't you ever think about having any of your own?"

"Nope." He lowered his head and nipped at her bottom lip. "Wanna get nekkid?"

His immediate dismissal of the notion of children wasn't a shock. More a confirmation of what she'd already told herself. She made herself find a smile, though. "There is a *world* of difference between being naked and being nekkid."

"I know." His smile was lazy. "Naked is just being unclothed. Nekkid is being unclothed and up to mischief." He waited a beat. "So?"

He wasn't going to suddenly fall in love with her and start spouting hearts and roses and proposals. She knew that. But that didn't mean she wasn't going to grab every moment with him that she could.

It was going to have to last her for a long time once it ended.

So she stretched up and brushed her lips quickly over his. Then she went back down on her heels and pulled away from him. "Call your mama," she said, heading toward the house. She looked at him over her shoulder, giving him her best imitation of a come-hither smile. "Then come find me. I'll be *nekkid* in the shower."

Galen watched her saunter up his porch steps, her slender hips swaying.

Only once she was out of sight did he shake off the effect she had on him and follow. He stopped in the kitchen long enough to call his mother.

Not surprisingly, she didn't mince words. "What's going on between you and Aurora McElroy?"

Over his head, he could hear the sound of water in the pipes and imagined Aurora stripping off, stepping beneath the shower spray. Didn't matter that they'd already shared one shower that morning. His body was raring to repeat the experience.

"Nothing's going on," he lied. Last thing he needed was Jeanne Marie making more out of the situation than there was. "What with me spending extra time at Cowboy Country helping out with that show of hers, she's helping out with a few things over here. What were you calling about in the first place?"

Judging by the "hmm" she gave, his mother wasn't going to be that easily convinced. "Just to tell you that we're having a late supper tonight. Delaney and Cisco are back from Red Rock and they brought tamales from *Red*. I'll expect you in an hour."

Aurora and tamales. There were definitely worse ways to cap off a day. He absently noticed the long-distance phone number written on the pad beside the phone. "Not sure I can make it that fast."

"Yes, you can." His mother's voice was excessively dry. "Bring Aurora with you."

"She's just a friend, Ma."

"A friend who answers your phone? You know, I've heard she has been spending her nights at your place."

He exhaled, mentally cursing the Horseback Hollow grapevine that seemed to operate all on its own accord. "If you've already made up your mind about something, why're you asking me?"

"She's a nice girl, Galen. Don't be careless."

His ears burned as if he were ten and caught looking at a girlie magazine. "I'm never careless," he reminded.

"Not with most things. But a girl's heart is not most things."

Interesting that she didn't have much to say about *his* heart. But before he could point that out—as if he ever would—she'd said, "I'll expect you in an hour," and hung up.

He dropped the phone back on the cradle, stifling an oath. Then he went upstairs to his hall bathroom and hooked his fingers around the shower curtain. "Anyone else call besides my mom? There's a number on the message pad."

"It's for Roselyn's agent." She tipped her head back into the water spray, her eyes closed as she rinsed away the shampoo. "In case I want more than Horseback Hollow." Her lips held a wry curve. "Never would have expected that of her."

Something inside him went still. "You going to use the number?"

She let out a soft snort and shifted her head out of the water. "Everything all right with your mom?"

Her hair streamed like red lava around her shoulders and soap suds were sliding down her hips and thighs. He overlooked the fact that she hadn't actually answered about the agent. "How do you feel about tamales?"

"Tamales?"

"No euphemism." He yanked off his shirt. "My sister and Cisco brought some back from his cousin's place in Red Rock. My mom's expecting us both." He kicked off the rest of his clothes and stepped under the water with her.

The close confines of the shower stall meant they *had* to stand close. By necessity of the heat inside him that he was beginning to think only Aurora could soothe, he brought them even closer.

She caught her breath. "Both? You, uh, you want me to go with you?"

"You want to be the one to tell Jeanne Marie Fortune Jones no?" He turned his back to the spray so the fine work his hands did taking over the soapsudsing business didn't get washed away before he drove Aurora as crazy as he was feeling.

"No," she said faintly.

"Me, either. Gonna have to convince her nothing's going on, though. Or she'll be tracking down your mama in Alaska to make up a guest list for our wedding."

"Ha-ha." Her voice was even fainter and he let the soap fall to the shower floor between their feet.

And then there was no room left at all for thinking about anyone else but Aurora.

"Did you hear?"

Aurora finished fastening her hairpiece in place and looked around the screen at Frank. It was Monday. The start of another six days of performances. "Hear what?"

"I got the Branson gig." He stroked his mustache as he glued it in place. "They're starting an entirely new production there. Rehearsals begin in two weeks."

"Congratulations." She couldn't say that she was going to miss him terribly. Unless he was in his role, he was a pain in the neck. But when he *was* in his role, he'd done a good job. "You'll be hard to replace."

"Harder than Joey," he agreed absently. "Couldn't have pulled in just any old cowboy off the street to play my part."

Galen wasn't just any old cowboy. But she wasn't going to debate the point with Frank Richter. She ducked back behind the screen and stared at herself in the narrow slice of mirror. Even with the makeup she'd applied, her sunburned nose still showed through.

"They've still got parts to fill," Frank went on. "At least three female. You ought to give it a shot."

She frowned and looked back around at him. "In Branson?"

"Yeah." He was staring at himself in the mirror as he did his familiar series of facial exercises. "Moore Dinner Theatre. Helluva lot better there than Horseback Hollow. Show's a full hour, for one thing. Not this ten-minute farce business. And even though you don't fill out a saloon girl's costume, I heard you can at least dance."

She made a face and pulled her head back behind the screen, making her feel rather like a turtle, poking her head in and out of her shell. She ran her hands down the sides of her corset wedding dress. Considering the past week, Galen seemed perfectly happy with her slight figure. "I'm not interested in going to Branson."

"Why not?"

She eyed herself in the mirror. "Because my life is here." And for the first time in her life, she was entirely glad for that.

For one simple reason. Galen was here.

When they'd arrived at Cowboy Country a short while ago, he'd headed yet again to the casting department to see what was going on about replacing Joey. He hadn't yet made it to the wardrobe trailer to change.

She wasn't worried, though, that he wouldn't make it in time for the show. It took Galen only minutes to prepare.

"You're wasting yourself here," Frank said. "Seriously, Rory."

She made a face at her reflection. *"Aurora,"* she corrected, even though she knew it would fall on deaf ears. "I'm not interested in Branson," she said again and wondered what he'd say if he knew she had the personal number for Roselyn St. James's agent. She'd put it in her wallet, more for posterity's sake than because she ever intended to use it.

"If you say so." Frank sounded doubting. She could hear him moving around and the sound of the trailer door opening. "See you at the buckboard."

When he left, the trailer was silent. She lifted the gold chain from the front of her dress and studied the drugstore ring that nestled against her grandmother's watch. "You're in over your head, Aurora," she told her reflection. The woman looking back at her didn't appear particularly shocked by the news flash. "Just go with the moment, right? Live for the now? Don't worry about tomorrow?"

Or next week. Or next year. Or the rest of your life.

"You—" she pointed at her reflection "—are no help at all."

And you—the reflection pointed back—are losing your marbles if you think sleeping with him means anything more than just that.

Aurora ignored her and left the trailer, heading toward the buckboard to double-check that her veil and microphone headset were there.

She'd only made it halfway, though, when she spotted Galen, walking toward her with Caitlyn Moore and a group of a half dozen others. Suits. Because they definitely didn't look local, even though most of them were wearing jeans.

Nobody wore jeans as well as Galen.

She smiled and sketched a wave, not wanting to interrupt him when it looked as though he was wearing his "authenticity consultant" hat. And even though he dipped his black Stetson toward her in acknowledgment, he didn't smile back.

Unease wafted over her as the group neared. Because of the country music playing over the park sound system, she couldn't make out much of their conversation. Just a few words here and there. The kind of words she assumed jean-wearing "suits" tossed about during business meetings.

A few more feet and the group came level with her. Caitlyn sent her an unusually bright smile and Aurora realized the distinguished-looking man next to her was probably her father, Alden Moore, finally back in town to visit her.

Galen walked by her, close enough to touch if she

reached out her hand. And she very nearly did, except it had also dawned on her that Alden Moore wasn't just visiting his daughter.

According to Roselyn, he was also having a meeting with her two-timing husband.

And suddenly, there he was.

Anthony. Wearing a perfectly tailored gray suit and tie and looking straight at her with a smile on his handsome face that was too familiar after all this time. "Aurora!"

She'd been afraid of what she'd feel seeing him again. Loss. Pain. Anger over what he'd done to her. What Roselyn thought he was doing now.

Strangely, she realized she didn't feel much of anything, except extremely self-conscious when he broke off from his group and crossed toward her, his hands stretched out.

"Aurora," he said again when he reached her, and pulled her in for a tight hug she neither expected nor wanted. "My God, look at you. You haven't changed at all except to grow lovelier."

She pushed at his arms, feeling her face turn red, because not only Galen was watching, but the rest of them were, as well. "Hello, Anthony." She dared a quick look past him, but the brim of Galen's hat was pulled too low for her to see his eyes. "Roselyn mentioned you were meeting with Moore Entertainment." She'd mentioned a lot more than that, of course, but Aurora had no desire to open up a can of worms that belonged between him and his wife.

"Yeah." His smile was as blindingly white as Roselyn's. "I think we have a lot to offer each other."

He was slightly taller than Galen, with none of the muscular brawn. And there'd been a time when she'd thought she'd spend her life looking into his striking blue eyes.

But he'd *never* made her feel the way Galen did.

And the realization was more than a little freeing.

"I'm sure you do." She glanced at Galen again. "Thanks, by the way, for dinner last week. Galen and I were sorry you and Roselyn couldn't make it, but we… enjoyed ourselves."

"Ros said Toni was getting a fever. She didn't want to leave her with anyone. She was fine the next morning, though."

He obviously figured that was news to her, which probably meant that Roselyn hadn't told him about her visit the previous day. "That's good." She'd wrapped her hand around her locket and the cheap ring without even realizing it. "I don't want to keep you from your business."

"You're right. Mr. Moore's doing well these days, but I don't think Caitlyn wants him on his feet for too long." He leaned down and brushed a kiss over her cheek. "We'll talk later."

She managed a noncommittal smile, though she wasn't foolish enough to respond.

He returned to his group and they continued walking down the backstage area. When they reached the far gate, though, she saw Galen shake Alden Moore's hand, then turn back toward her.

She shivered a little, despite the sun almost directly overhead, and felt the sharp edges of the costume ring against the inside of her fist.

"I ran into them all when I stopped by the casting department," he said when he reached her. "Mr. Moore wanted a personal report on how I thought things were coming around here." He yanked open the trailer door and went inside.

Aurora gnawed her lip and followed. "Are you all right?"

He flipped his black cowboy hat onto a high shelf and yanked his T-shirt over his head. "Are you?"

She stared at the play of muscles in his tanned back. She knew it was suntan, because she'd seen up close and personal just where that tan ended.

If there hadn't been a tightness in his voice, she'd reach out now and stroke her hand up his spine and over all that beautiful muscle.

But there *was* a tightness in his voice.

"Why wouldn't I be all right?"

"I don't know." He yanked on Rusty's shirt and slammed the white cowboy hat on his head. "You just saw the love of your life again."

His vehemence had her blinking. "He's not—"

"He didn't know who I was until Caitlyn, in her infinite good manners, started introducing everyone."

Unease settled perilously close to dread. "He didn't—"

"—mention that you and I were *newlyweds*?" He air-quoted the word. "Fortunately, he managed to avoid saying it outright. But he damn sure left everyone with the impression that we were together."

She let go of the locket. And the ring. "I'm sorry."

"Caitlyn, no doubt, will mention the news to Brodie." His voice was flat as he finished buttoning the shirt and flipped up the collar to pull on the string tie. "It's only a matter of time before it gets to my parents."

"And that has you all riled. That your parents might think we're...together." After they'd spent two hours with them the evening before over tamales, while Galen had gone out of his way to treat her no differently than he'd treated his sister Delaney.

"I'm not riled."

"Well, you're *something*!"

"Casting still doesn't have a freaking replacement for Joey." He jerked the tie into a knot. "I'm stuck in this godfor—" He broke off when the trailer door opened and Cammie and two other girls entered, giggling over something.

Aurora smiled tightly and stepped aside so they could get through.

"If you've hated playing Rusty so much," she said carefully, "why haven't you stopped?"

He didn't answer. Just shoved open the trailer door again. "Show's gonna start in a few minutes."

She almost didn't care. Only a semblance of professional pride made her leave the trailer ahead of him. "Galen, I'll explain what happened. There's no reason for your family to believe we're...involved."

Particularly when he was making it abundantly clear that they were not. No matter what had happened between them over the past week.

"And the love of your life?" His lips were thin. "He got the job, by the way. But it isn't in Chicago."

Her stomach started to fall away.

"It's right here in Horseback Hollow." He threw out his arm. "Hell, it's right over there beyond some hedges and a fence. He's gonna be working on the Cowboy Condo project."

She stared. "I didn't know the hotel project was back on track."

"That's all you've got to say?"

She spread her hands, helplessly. "What do you *want* me to say? Do you think I *knew* anything about this?

Maybe you're like Roselyn and think *I'm* the one he's messing around with!"

A sharp whistle drew her attention toward the buckboard, where Frank was waving at her impatiently, and Aurora realized the announcer was giving their cue over the loudspeaker. She could see Galen realized it, too.

"I don't want you to say anything," he said flatly and turned toward where Cabot was waiting with the horses.

Stymied for a solution to anything, least of all a Galen she couldn't figure out, she picked up her skirts and ran to the buckboard. She clambered up beside Frank and hastily donned her mic and barely got her veil on before Blackie shot out from the gate.

When she looked back to see Galen, though, and share the same thumbs-up they shared before every show, he wasn't looking her way at all.

Chapter Twelve

Later, though Aurora wasn't sure how, they got through all four shows without some fresh disaster falling on her shoulders.

But when it came to climbing in Galen's truck to go home, she nearly balked.

Did she just tell him outright to drop her off at her own place?

Did she wait to see if he automatically took her to his the way he'd been doing for days now?

She did neither.

She just climbed up in the seat beside him and stared out the window, not saying anything.

They drove past the hotel construction site that, for the past few months at least, had been surrounded by chain link while the unfinished framing itself sat abandoned to everything but the weeds sprouting up around it.

She closed her eyes against the sight.

And when she felt the truck bounce over a cattle guard several minutes later, she had one answer at least.

Because Galen was driving up to her place.

He stopped at the base of the hill, but didn't put the truck in Park. Didn't turn it off. Just hit the brakes and eventually the tires stopped crunching over the graveled drive as they rolled to a stop. "You need a ride to Cowboy Country tomorrow?"

She breathed slowly through the hollowness that yawned open inside her.

Because there was her other answer.

"I've got the truck." Feeling older than she should, she pushed open the door and slid out. "Thanks for the ride." The words sounded choked, but there was nothing she could do about that, except slam the door shut and hurry up the hill to her front door.

Once she got behind the privacy of that, she could fall apart.

She walked blindly because of the tears glazing her eyes, but since she'd been walking up and down the same hill her whole life, it didn't much matter. And between every step, she expected to hear the sound of him driving away.

He waited, though, until she reached the front door and fumbled with the damn fool key, because he'd insisted she start locking it, so she had.

She finally managed to unlock it, though, and stumbled inside, slamming the door shut behind her so she didn't have to hear him drive away, too.

"Should have paid more attention to the woman in the mirror," she said thickly.

Then she sat down on the floor and cried.

The next afternoon, Galen stared at the blonde coming out of the wardrobe trailer wearing Aurora's wedding gown.

He'd deliberately gone by to pick up his Rusty gear earlier, just so he wouldn't run into her any sooner than he had to.

But now there was another woman wearing her costume?

He looked at Cabot. "Who the hell is *that*?"

Cabot shrugged. "Sophie somebody-or-other."

He ground his molars together. "She's wearing Aurora's costume."

Cabot gave him a strange look. "Looks like. Maybe she called in sick or something."

"And this *Sophie* just magically appears?"

"She's Aurora's understudy. Think she usually dances in the saloon show."

He felt like something had shaken loose in his brains. "Aurora has an understudy? Why didn't Joey have one?"

"Rusty's a bit part in comparison to hers. Same as mine," Cabot said. "You gonna be all right?"

No, he wasn't going to be all right. The only reason he was doing this infernal show was for Aurora's benefit.

And now she wasn't even there?

The theme music was already playing and Cabot was swinging up into his saddle. "We're gonna miss our cue if you don't get a move on."

Galen swore under his breath and mounted Blaze.

The next ten minutes, give or take, were some of the worst Galen had ever experienced. He plowed through it with grim determination, pledging Rusty's troth to an unfamiliar Lila who didn't smell like flowers or smile with her whole body.

And the second he got backstage after that particular misery, he strode off for his pickup truck in the parking lot. But when he got to her place, her ranch truck was gone. The front and back doors to the house both locked up tight and leaving him wanting to tear the damn things off their hinges.

He should never have agreed to play Rusty in the first place. It had only ended in a snowball of complications.

Feeling fouler than he could ever remember feeling, he returned to Cowboy Country and went straight to the casting department.

For three weeks he'd been visiting Diane's office. For three weeks he'd ignored her blatant come-ons while she'd insisted she couldn't find someone to play Rusty.

A "bit" part.

"Get somebody else," he said the second he entered her office. He stared her down. "By the end of the week, or else you're gonna be explaining to Caitlyn Moore and her daddy why you've been sitting on your thumbs about it all this time."

"Now where's the fun in that?"

"I mean it, Diane." He planted his palms flat on her desk and was glad that, for once, there weren't any hopeful applicants sitting in the chairs in front of her desk. "All those suggestive comments of yours that I've been ignoring? Some might consider 'em harassment. And I'm pretty sure Moore Entertainment isn't going to want *that* embarrassment hitting them on top of everything else they've dealt with. Do you?"

She pressed her lips together, then she just looked bored. "*Outlaw Shootout* can replace *Wedding* in a heartbeat. Something I reminded your girlfriend of just this morning."

His nerve endings sharpened. He straightened, pulling his hands off her desk so he didn't succumb to the temptation to wrap them around her neck. "Aurora was here this morning?"

"When she came in positively begging me to find a

new Rusty." She propped her chin on her hand. "Trouble in paradise?"

"Get a replacement," he said through his teeth. "Or put this Joey guy back on a horse whether he's wearing a cast on his leg or not. And if I hear one word about *Outlaw Shootout* replacing *Wedding*, I'm still gonna add your name to the top of my next report to Caitlyn." There were other people than just Aurora who were depending on the show. "Are we clear?"

She rolled her eyes. "Fine. I don't know why you're getting so upset. Like I told Aurora, Sophie Maxwell can play Lila perfectly well while she's in Branson—"

He slapped his hands on her desk again so fast she actually rolled back in her chair. *"What?"*

"She's in Branson." Startled or not, Diane recovered quickly. She picked up her pen and tapped the end of it on her desk between his hands. "Flew her out on a charter a few hours ago so she could meet with the producer there for the new show the dinner theater is opening."

He snatched the pen out of her hand when she ran it up the inside of his wrist, and tossed it down in disgust. "She's auditioning."

"More like discussing rehearsal schedules. It's a foregone conclusion that she'll get the lead. The director wants her and he usually gets what he wants." She waited a beat. "Still anxious to save the day where the rest of your cast mates are concerned?"

He turned on his heel and walked out of the office.

At the best of times, being around the woman made him feel like he needed to be doused in disinfectant afterward. Now was no different even though she'd unintentionally answered the question of Aurora's whereabouts.

And confirmed what Galen had known all along.

That she wanted a life beyond Horseback Hollow.

Beyond him.

He was still wearing his Rusty costume, but he flouted the rules and walked straight through the public areas, intent on getting across to the wardrobe trailer the fastest way possible.

He was so intent on his goal, he nearly ran right over his little sister Delaney where she was standing in the middle of Main Street having her palm read by the same fortune-teller who'd read his.

Delaney laughed when he bumped into her and caught his sleeves to steady herself. "Cowboy Country is a small world. Where are you off to in such a rush?"

He glared at the fortune-teller, who just smiled slightly and moved off, her belt jingling.

"Galen?" Delaney cocked her blond head. "You all right?"

"What are you doing here?"

Her eyebrows rose a little. "Cisco's meeting with Caitlyn's father about the hotel project."

At one point, before the project had been mothballed, Cisco had been on the development team. Though he hadn't admitted it at first, which was one of the reasons why Galen still had some reservations about the guy being good enough for Delaney. She might have forgiven him for nearly breaking her heart along the way, but Galen hadn't.

Which meant there were now two men on the project he had a problem with.

"I thought Cisco quit Cowboy Country." That's what the guy had claimed when he'd been trying to win back Delaney's trust. "Guess that was a lie, too."

"Oh, Galen," Delaney tsked. "Relax. Cisco isn't working for Cowboy Country. All he's doing is explaining the original plan he had for the project. The one that never got submitted in the first place but should have. For heaven's sake, you know all he could talk about the other night over tamales was his work with the Fortune Foundation. So what's got your tail in a twist?"

He grimaced. "Nothing." He realized he was watching the fortune-teller, who'd stopped to talk with a pregnant woman holding a little boy by the hand, and looked away. "Nothing," he repeated more firmly. "So you're just hanging around waiting for Cisco?"

"I thought I'd finally take in your and Aurora's show while I'm waiting." She glanced at the old-fashioned clock hanging on a pillar outside the Main Street Post Office, which—aside from the displays of collector's stamps that a person could purchase—operated as an honest-to-goodness post office. "Doesn't it start at two?"

His mood darkened even more. "Yes. But Aurora's not here."

Her brows pulled together. "Why not?"

"Because she's in Branson. Learning about her fancy new part she'll be playing there."

Delaney's eyes widened. "But I thought you two were—"

"What?"

She made a face. "Dial down, Galen. Good grief. You didn't really think any of us were fooled by that act the other night, did you?" She lowered her voice in what he assumed was supposed to be an imitation of his. "Just helping each other out. Like neighbors do." She gave him a deadpan stare. "Neighbors who are *crazy* about each other, maybe."

"There's nothing serious between us." He eyed the clock, but in his mind, he was seeing the way Anthony-the-ass had grabbed Aurora.

And she'd let him.

"Right. And there was nothing serious between Cisco and me." She waved her left hand, which sported an engagement ring. "Why can't you just admit you're not as committed to the big bad bachelor club as you always claimed?"

He exhaled impatiently. "What good would that do, Delaney? Aurora's always wanted more than Horseback Hollow. And now, after too many years of waiting, she's finally out there getting it."

"I don't know, Galen. The other night I thought she looked like a person who wanted nothing more than *you*."

He shook his head.

She looked impatient. "How do you know?"

"Because she would have said!"

"Did *you*?"

He glared down at her. What was it about little sisters that left you either wanting to protect them from every scrape and bruise or lock 'em in the basement to keep them from bugging the crap out of you? "There's nothing to say."

She exhaled noisily. "Right. Color me corrected, then." She waved her hand dismissively. "Carry on with your enduring bachelor nonsense, then. I'm sure you and the twenty cats you'll have some day will be very happy together." Her annoyed expression dissolved, though, when she spotted Cisco heading toward them.

Galen's mood, however, found a fresh sinkhole of brand new depths, because Aurora's ex-fiancé was walking alongside Cisco. "Perfect," he muttered.

"Don't you go running away," Delaney said from the corner of her mouth. "You're gonna stay and be polite to Cisco. Someday, he's going to be the father of my babies."

He shot her a look.

"Oh, for…I said *some*day." She tilted up her cheek for

Cisco's kiss when he reached them. "You were quicker than I expected."

"Yeah." Cisco nodded at Galen. "Galen. Good to see you." He gestured with his hand toward Anthony. "This is Anthony Tyson. He's—"

"We've met," Galen cut him off. "How's your wife?"

Anthony's eyes narrowed slightly. "Fine," he said cautiously. "And *your* wife?"

Both Delaney's and Cisco's heads swiveled around to Galen at that.

Crud. Crud on a huge freaking cracker.

"Wife?" Delaney asked carefully.

"She's not my wife," he gritted. "And if she were, I damn sure wouldn't be cheating on her."

Anthony stiffened. "That was a long time ago. Aurora and I were just kids, practically. I never meant to hurt her."

"I'm talking about Roselyn."

Anthony waited a beat. "Excuse me? You want to run that past again? Because it sounds like you're accusing me of cheating on Roselyn."

Delaney and Cisco were both watching with something akin to morbid fascination.

"I'm not accusing you of anything. Just repeating what your own wife believes."

Anthony's head snapped back. If Galen weren't inclined to loathe the guy on general principal, he would have given him props for looking genuinely shocked.

"Um, Galen?" Delaney tugged at his sleeve. "Maybe this isn't something for—"

He shrugged her off. "She thought it was Aurora, you know. Maybe figuring things had gone full circle or something."

"The first time I've seen Aurora in ten years was yesterday!"

"Galen—"

"Not now, Delaney." He didn't take his eyes off the other man. "And maybe I've wondered more 'n a little that she was still hung up over you, but Aurora's no cheat. She'll put everybody's needs before her own, and she damn sure deserves whatever shot she's taking, but she's…no…cheat."

"Galen!" Delaney yanked harder on his arm.

"Dammit, Del," he barked. *"What?"*

Cisco suddenly pushed Delaney behind him. "Back off, Galen," he said tightly. "You don't talk to Delaney like that. Not when I'm around."

"Hold on to your chaps, folks," the announcer boomed over the loudspeaker, *"'cause there's a hog-tying good time happening in just a few minutes down on Main Street with Wild West Wedding!"*

The cue for their show.

He wanted to swear.

Instead, he eyed Cisco, who for the first time had just earned some honest respect in Galen's eyes. "You're right." He looked past him to his baby sister. "Sorry."

She just watched him with concern. "It's okay," she said faintly.

The theme music for *Wedding* had started and Galen knew he had about three minutes to haul his butt backstage or Lila wouldn't have a Rusty to rescue her at all. "I gotta go—"

"Then go!" Delaney shooed him with her hands.

He set off toward the corner side street, grateful that he was at least closest to the gate Rusty and Sal the Sheriff used.

"She's wrong." Anthony's voice carried after him even over the loud music. "Roselyn's wrong."

Galen didn't slow, though he looked over his shoulder. "Don't tell me. Tell *her*."

Then he dismissed the man from his mind and broke into a run, careering around the corner just as the gate ahead of him started to open and the first of Frank's goons pranced out on an excited horse.

He ran flat out and nearly vaulted onto Blaze's back just inside the gate. He took the reins that Cabot handed him.

And then they were chasing down Main Street all over again.

After the wrong Lila.

Chapter Thirteen

"Thanks, Laurel." Aurora descended the steps of the small charter jet that had been piloted by Laurel Redmond Fortune.

The tall, blue-eyed blonde smiled. "Was the flight as bad as you expected?"

Aurora smiled ruefully and shook her head. "I didn't expect it to be *bad*. I've just never been on a small jet like this before." She stepped onto the pavement where the sleek airplane was parked near the hangar housing the flight school and charter service Laurel ran with her husband, Sawyer Fortune. "I still can't believe we made it to Branson and back in a single day." It was too late for the six o'clock show, but if she wanted, she had ample time to make it to Cowboy Country for the last performance of *Wedding* for the day.

If she wanted. Playing Lila was one thing. Seeing Galen after the way they'd left things the day before was another.

Having left without giving him any warning about her understudy, Sophie, wasn't going to help any, either.

"The advantages of a charter service," Laurel was saying as they headed toward the hangar. She unzipped the front of her khaki-colored jumpsuit, revealing a plain white tank top, and tugged her arms right out of the jump-suit sleeves, leaving the top of it hanging down from the elastic-cinched waist. "Even with the breeze, it's still hot. Those clouds up there are like a blanket, holding the heat in. One of the things I miss since we moved to Horse-back Hollow from Red Rock is easy access to a swim-ming pool," she said ruefully.

"You need a few hours at Hollow Springs."

"Someone was mentioning that place the other day. Who was it? Oh. Jensen Fortune Chesterfield. He's been up there with his girlfriend, Amber."

Jensen. Brother of Amelia. Making him a cousin of Galen's as well as Laurel's husband, Sawyer, though she'd be hard-pressed to figure out the exact branches of that particular family tree. "Lot of Fortunes around," she mur-mured, then flushed at the amused look she earned from Laurel.

"They do seem to have come out of the woodwork," she agreed. She pulled open a metal door and a rush of cool air-conditioned air blew out over them. "Hey, Mat-teo," she greeted as one of her pilots also came out the door. "Heading home?"

The handsome man grinned, though his long pace didn't slow. "Picking up Rachel at the office and head-ing out for a picnic at Hollow Springs," he said over his shoulder.

Laurel laughed, giving Aurora a wry look. "I *am* going to have to get Sawyer out there, obviously. So are you really going to be working at that dinner theater in Branson?"

Aurora lifted her shoulder. "I don't know." When she'd seen Diane that morning, the casting agent had insisted Aurora "hop over for a look-see." She'd booked the charter flight without giving Aurora the chance to protest.

At least going to Branson, Missouri, had given her some breathing room before she'd need to face Galen again. But just because she'd met with the producer and director for the new production they were mounting at the popular dinner theater didn't mean she'd be offered anything. She'd actually spent more time on the plane with Laurel going and coming than she had in the popular vacation destination.

"Pretty flattering to be considered, I imagine."

Aurora nodded. "This is embarrassing, but should I be tipping you or something?"

Laurel laughed and shook her head. "We have a contract with Moore Entertainment." Her eyes danced. "All *you* need to do is pass on the word that you were very satisfied with the service we provided."

"That I can do." It had been a day trip only, so she had no luggage or anything. Just her purse and her meager portfolio. "Thanks again," she said before heading over to her truck, which she'd left in the small parking lot next to the hangar.

It was stifling hot inside and she rolled down the windows, her thoughts returning to Hollow Springs with Galen.

Sighing, she drove away from the small airfield. Past the cemetery. The hotel construction site. The parking lot lights for Cowboy Country were visible when she suddenly turned around on the highway and drove back to the cemetery.

She parked in the small parking lot, and even though it had been a decade, she easily found her brother's marker located on a gentle grassy ridge, and stared at the inscription. *Beloved Son.*

Her eyes burned and she knelt down in the grass, swiping her hand over the granite, brushing away the dust and a sweet gum leaf that was clinging to the surface.

"What do you think, Mark?" Her voice sounded loud in the silence. "Branson? Call Roselyn's agent? Give performing a real shot?" She flicked away another leaf, then turned around and lay down beside the marker, staring up the sky. "You broke their hearts," she whispered. Her chest ached. "You broke mine."

She sniffed and watched the clouds Laurel had complained about drift overhead. "If you were here, I'd kick your butt." She sniffed again, her vision blurring. "If you were here."

She closed her eyes, throwing her arm over them. In her mind, she could hear her brother's laughter. *You could try*, he would have said.

She inhaled a raw breath. "If you were here…" She lowered her arm and stared at the sky. The clouds. "I'd tell you I miss you."

A welcome breeze drifted over her, bringing another sweet-gum leaf from the trees that dotted the small cemetery. She caught it, midair, twirling the deep green leaf by the tiny stem. "Remember how you used to throw sweet-gum seed pods at me? I think Daddy even grounded you once for it."

And you never got caught even when you put a pile of them in my bed.

She smiled faintly through her tears. "You'd like Horseback Hollow these days. Particularly Cowboy Country. All those pretty saloon girls." The tiny stem felt uneven as she rolled it between her thumb and finger. "Cammie would never give Frank Richter a second glance if she saw you first." Tall. Auburn-haired with a devilish smile and a sense of humor to match.

The image in her head wavered like a flag blowing in the wind.

She exhaled deeply and stared at the leaf. When she lifted her hand and released the tiny stem, the vaguely star-shaped leaf caught the breeze just long enough to land on the granite marker.

"If you were here," she said, sighing, "I'd tell you I love you."

Then she just lay there on grass that was cooler than the air around them, watching the clouds slowly drift in the sky. And when she pulled on the gold chain and checked the time on her grandmother's watch locket hanging beside the drugstore ring, and saw that it was now too late to make it to the last show of the night, she finally rolled onto her knees again.

The sweet-gum leaf was still sitting on her brother's marker. She smiled a little and left it there.

Then she got back in her daddy's truck and drove home.

The next morning, Aurora knew the moment that Galen entered the wardrobe trailer even though she was behind the changing screen.

There was an unmistakable shift in the air.

And she was glad for the meager protection the screen provided as she carefully pulled up the zipper on her dress because there was a new batch of fraying threads after Sophie's use of the costume the day before.

"Frank." She heard his deep voice greet their cast mate.

"Galen."

She pressed her lips together a moment, almost but not quite able to be amused at the brief male exchange.

She heard the slide of drawers. The shuffle of hangers. All too vividly imagined Galen's bare chest before he pulled on Rusty's shirt. His thick dark brown hair before he replaced his own black Stetson with Rusty's white one.

She didn't even realize she was holding her breath until she heard the trailer door open and close again, signaling his exit.

She blew out a low breath. Checked the zipper under her arm one more time, and the buttons on her old-fashioned boots. She already had on the hairpiece of ringlets and was as ready for the first show of the day as she could be.

Which meant hanging out behind the changing screen was the same thing as hiding.

She slipped from behind the screen, then felt the world's axis seem to tilt a little.

Because it wasn't Frank standing in front of the big mirror, gelling up his eyebrows and admiring his reflection.

It was Galen, leaning back against the bank of drawers, his arms crossed over his wide chest.

"Hi," she said on a puff of air.

"Wondered how long you were going to hide back there."

She flushed. "I wasn't hiding."

His lips twisted. "I knew you were here. I parked right next to your truck in the parking lot."

"Oh." In the lexicon of brilliant responses, that had to be right up near the top.

"Congratulations." He shifted, unfolding his arms to cup his big palms over the edge of the drawers on either side of him. The position made his wide shoulders seem even wider. "Hear you and Frank are heading off to Branson."

Her mouth felt unaccountably dry. "That's a little premature. Frank's going. I'd need to be offered a part first."

His eyes were unreadable. "Have it on good authority that's a foregone conclusion."

She swiped her hands down the sides of her dress, fussing a little with the way the lace was lying. "Says who?"

"Diane in casting."

"Oh." There was that brilliant response again.

He was silent for a moment. From outside the trailer, she could hear the muffled sounds of voices and the clip-clop of horse hooves. "She found a new Rusty."

She actually felt a little faint. "What? Just like that?"

His lips twisted. "Just like that." He shifted slightly. "And I think Caitlyn's got no reason to worry anymore about Cowboy Country's authenticity."

"Finally earned an A?"

"I can hang up Rusty and my clipboard after today."

"You must be relieved."

He nodded once, his expression unsmiling. "So, you gonna go to Branson?"

She chewed the inside of her cheek. "I…I'd need to talk with my parents first."

"They'll be back in a few days."

She nodded jerkily and started to nervously pull out her watch locket, but narrowly remembered not to. Instead, she imagined the feel of the silly drugstore ring burning against her breast. "I have to pick them up from the airport in Lubbock Friday night. After the last show."

"And? Are you gonna go?" he asked again.

"Do—" She broke off and swallowed the knot in her throat. "Do you think I should?"

His jaw shifted to one side, then slowly centered. "That's not something for me to say."

Her chest hollowed out. "That's answer enough," she managed huskily.

He looked pained. "Aurora—"

She lifted her hand. "It's okay, Galen. We are who we are and nothing can change that." He loved being a rancher more than anything else.

It was only her lot in life to realize she loved him more than anything else.

She couldn't look at him and swiped her hands down her skirt again. "I'd better make sure my mic and veil are in the buckboard. It's almost time to start."

He nodded silently.

It took everything she possessed to move past him to the door. To circle the knob with her sweaty palm and actually get the thing open without fumbling with it.

He followed her outside, but headed over to the picnic table where Serena was standing, stretching out over her foot propped on the top of the table.

His pretty first-kiss girl gave him a wide smile.

Aurora looked away and headed to the buckboard. The mic and veil were just an excuse. The production crew would already have ensured everything was where it belonged, regardless of *who* last wore Lila's costume.

Frank was already sitting on the buckboard bench and he knocked his shoulder against hers when she climbed up next to him. "Branson, here we come." He angled his head toward hers. "Got some good times ahead for us, Rory."

She couldn't even summon enough interest for her usual annoyance. "Why does everyone assume I want to go?"

"Because why *wouldn't* you?"

Why indeed?

Only exercising more self-control than she knew she possessed kept her from looking back at Galen.

"How long have you wanted to be a performer, Frank?" Because that's what they were. There was no serious acting going on here. Just good old entertainment for a crowd.

"Ever since I can remember." He toyed with the white roses on the band of her veil. "I like the applause," he murmured, then gave her a leering smile. "And the girls."

Her lips stretched. "You remind me a little of my brother."

He gave a wounded laugh and slid his arm around her shoulders, leaning his face close to hers. "That is *not* what I like hearing."

She rolled her eyes and lifted his arm off her. "How's Cammie taking the news of your leaving?"

"Devastated, of course." He twirled his handlebar mustache.

"In other words, she's already moving on," Aurora translated.

"Some kid with a Mohawk who works on the Twin Rattlers line."

She actually found a chuckle from somewhere at that. "Glad you're not suffering a broken heart."

He smiled wryly. "What about you? Performing in your blood, too?"

She heard the phrase "hog-tying" over the loudspeaker, and pulled on her mic piece. "I used to think it was." She fit on the tight veil. "It's fun, but—" She broke off and shrugged. Now it was just a poor substitute for everything that really mattered.

And for once, when Frank dropped his arm around her shoulder and squeezed, she let him.

Because in the end, he was harmless. It took a man like Galen to make a true impact.

An impact she was going to carry for the rest of her days whether she went to Branson or not.

"We'll give 'em a helluva show," Frank said in her ear.

"Sure thing, Frank." She smiled. "Why not?"

Watching from behind them, Galen's hands tightened on Blaze's reins at the sight of Frank and Aurora's heads so close together. Tightened so much so, the horse started backing up.

He immediately released, and the horse stopped and bobbed his head a few times. "Sorry, pal."

"Here." Cabot handed him the prop deed and for what felt like the millionth time, Galen tucked it inside his shirt while the theme music started playing.

Ahead of him he watched Aurora tip her head back in those few seconds before the buckboard would hurtle past the gate, and waited with a knot inside his chest where his heart was supposed to be for her to glance back at him.

She didn't.

And a moment later, her passionate voice carried through the park. "My daddy will roll over in his grave if the railroad comes through our land!"

Beside him, Cabot and the others were heading through their gate. It was a good thing Blaze knew his part well, too, because if it weren't for the horse, Galen would have been left behind.

He got through the next ten minutes by rote. Couldn't have remembered a single thing he did or said until he rode, hell-bent for leather, up Main Street toward the stage and Aurora, whom he could see struggling mightily against Frank's grip. He heard the *crack!* of Frank's pistol and Harlan's Preacher Man's nervous words. "Take Lila to be your wife."

"I do," Frank yelled, pulling Aurora closer than the script had ever called for. She bent almost backward trying to get away, her long red curls nearly sweeping the floor of the stage as Galen jumped from Blaze's back to storm up the stage and tear her away.

"She'll never be yours, Frank. Not ever!" He clean forgot about the deed inside his shirt that he was supposed to wave at the man. Forgot everything except the fact that Aurora was going to go off to Branson with the other man. And if she didn't go to Branson, she'd be going somewhere else. Somewhere else without *him*.

Sal the Sheriff suddenly charged up the stage, ably covering Galen's gaffe as he dramatically announced that Rusty held the deed to the contested ranch; he'd seen it with his own eyes!

Galen was close enough to see the surprise in Frank's eyes, but he rolled with the situation and pulled Aurora back to his side with a proprietary leer, lifting her right off her feet. Her legs swung around, kicking in the air. "Wife or not, Lila's mine," he vowed and turned the fake pistol on Galen. "*I'll* be the one kissing her," he goaded with a truthfulness that had Galen seeing red.

Aurora had always dismissed the man, but Galen knew better. Knew that Frank wanted her. And once he got her away from Galen, maybe he'd even get her.

"That's right, cowboy," Frank was continuing. "*I'll* be the one—"

Galen's fist plowed into Frank's chin, and the other man's head snapped back, his eyes rolling.

Aurora yelped as Frank started to fall backward off the stage, taking her with him, until Galen managed to grab her from behind, hauling her back from midair by her wedding dress, which let out an audible rip while the audience stomped their feet and cheered.

Sal the Sheriff and his deputies were scrambling around, trying to cover the fact that Frank wasn't acting as he groggily landed in the center of the in-ground airbag well-disguised below the pile of horse poop.

Aurora's eyes stared into Galen's, looking shocked.

Suddenly, you could have heard a pin drop.

"I didn't think you'd catch me," she whispered.

"I'll always catch you." He didn't care that there were at least a hundred people below the stage hanging on every word. Didn't care about a damn thing but Aurora. "I don't want to lose you."

She blinked hard against the tears turning her blue eyes to sapphire and pressed her hands hard against her breast. *"Why?"*

He'd split his knuckles when he'd punched Frank, but that wasn't what made his hand shake as he gently touched her cheek. "Because I love you."

Her lips parted. Her eyes searched his. "You…do?"

"Stay with me. I know you deserve more. Want more. But—" His chest ached. "Stay," he finished hoarsely. "Marry me. And have little girls with red curls and little boys who'll make us old before our time."

"Stay," someone from the audience yelled out, and Aurora let out a watery chuckle.

She touched his cheek. His lips. Took his hand in hers and gently kissed his split knuckles. "I love you, too. More than I ever thought I could love anyone."

"He he he," Preacher Man laughed loudly, waving his Bible in an obvious attempt to get things back on track. "All this *love* going around, anyone wantin' to get hitched?"

Aurora swiped her hands over her cheeks as Galen's teeth flashed. He tucked his arm around her shoulders and turned her toward the mayor. "I do," he said loudly.

"And I do, too," Aurora agreed.

Harlan gaped for the audience, who laughed. "Well, then, I guess I pronounce you husband and—"

"Wife," Galen finished, and bowed Aurora deep over his arm. "I love you," he murmured, and in full view of God and Cowboy Country, he covered her mouth with his.

Epilogue

She wore white.

Her red hair danced down her spine in a swirl of curls while she clutched a bouquet of yellow daisies in her hand. And on her feet, below the dress that dragged a little in the grass because there'd barely been any time allowed for planning the wedding they held in his mama's backyard, she wore her favorite Castleton boots with the blue stitching.

Galen was certain there'd never existed a more perfect bride since she'd stepped right out of his dreams.

The mayor—though Galen supposed he might have had the authority to do so—did not marry them.

A real preacher did that. With a real Bible held in his hands while Aurora and Galen said their vows under a perfectly blue Texas sky, and he slid a ring—a real ring and not that drugstore one, which she still wore on a chain with her grandma's watch—on her wedding finger.

Fortunately, Jeanne Marie had had a lot of practice of late putting on weddings in her backyard, which came as a relief to Aurora's folks, who were back from their cruise barely a week and still dazed over finding their daughter engaged and anxious to marry their longtime neighbor. Jeanne Marie knew how to organize her family—even the newer members of it—and everyone had done their part.

So while the time for planning might've been short, the results were not.

White chairs were lined up in precise rows in front of his mama's prized flower beds. Delaney and Stacey had spent an entire hour tying ribbon bows around each of the chairs.

He still wasn't real sure why, though he had to admit the end effect was pretty enough. And Aurora had looked all misty-eyed over it, so in Galen's book that counted for a lot more.

Even Deke's ancient truck had been banished from view. In the spot where it usually sat, there were tables instead. Covered in white cloths and bearing food from not only Jeanne Marie's kitchen, but Pru McElroy's, and the Hollows Cantina. And the cake, made by Wendy Fortune Mendoza, was the centerpiece of it all. A towering thing that somehow managed to look as airy as Aurora's dress, with daisies sprinkled around to match the blooms that were woven into the hair hanging down Aurora's back.

Galen was looking forward to the time when he could get her alone and he'd slowly tug those flowers free. But that time was yet to come.

When he'd questioned the size of the cake just that morning, Jeanne Marie had assured him the thing had needed to be so large, since it was feeding half the town. Or so it seemed when a person started counting up all the

Fortunes, the Fortune Chesterfields, the Fortune Joneses, the Mendozas and every other iteration of Fortune that Galen could imagine.

There were guests who weren't related at all, of course. All of the cast and crew from *Wild West Wedding*. Even Frank Richter, who'd put off leaving for Branson for a day so he could be there. He still sported an ugly bruise on his jaw, which he could have rightfully held against Galen. But according to Aurora, he'd decided the bruise only added to his appeal with the ladies. There was also Roselyn St. James, who managed to cause a stir among anyone who recognized her from television. She and Anthony sat in chairs toward the back where they tried to keep their twins relatively contained.

It was a futile effort. But Toni and Tiffani weren't the only tots chasing around on short legs. They had plenty of company.

Galen didn't know what would happen between Aurora's ex-fiancé and his wife. Didn't much care, now that he knew the other man didn't leave even a lingering memory in Aurora's heart. Aurora, though, believed the couple would find their way.

But that was Aurora.

For now, he stood with his arms around her shoulders, holding her cradled in front of him where he could smell her hair and watch over this place and these people that he loved almost as much as he loved her.

Not surprisingly, it was his mother who corralled the wildly varied guests together when the toasts started. She dragged Deke up beside her. Galen figured his dad wasn't as reluctant as he liked to act, though.

Because, like everyone said, he and his eldest son were a lot alike.

"I want to thank y'all for coming," Jeanne Marie said,

holding up a plastic cup filled with the expensive champagne her brother James Marshall had insisted on contributing to the event. "There's never anything more joyous to bring family and friends together than two people committing themselves to each other." She smiled up at Deke, who'd closed his big hand over her shoulder. "Except maybe when those two people start bringing children into their lives," she added pointedly, earning a ripple of laughter.

"Particularly when you're not getting any younger," Liam inserted loudly, which earned him an elbow from Julia.

"You're not far behind him," she pointed out, which earned another ripple of laughter.

"Don't you worry," Galen returned. "I think Aurora and I will manage well enough despite my advancing decrepitude." He kissed Aurora's blushing cheek, because she'd already told him she was tossing her birth control pills out the window the moment they left on their honeymoon.

They weren't going far. Just an hour flight to Red Rock, where there was a resort hotel Amelia and Quinn recommended. They'd take a long weekend there. But then they'd come back. Aurora to her shows and the temporary Rusty until Joey returned, and Galen to the ranch.

"Anyway." Jeanne Marie corralled her kibitzing offspring. "To the newest member of our family—" she gestured with her cup "—Aurora. Thank you for making my firstborn happier than I've ever seen. If for no other reason at all, that's enough for us to love you."

Aurora smiled tremulously. "Thank you, Jeanne Marie."

"Now." Jeanne Marie cast an eye over the guests. "Unless anyone has something else they'd like to add, this food here's—"

"I, um, I have something to add." Sitting next to Delaney between Cisco and Matteo Mendoza, Rachel Robinson stood up from her chair, looking nervous. Even from where Galen and Aurora stood, they could see her squeeze Matteo's hand. Then he stood and closed his arm around her shoulders.

"We have something to add," he said encouragingly.

Aurora lifted her head. "We're gonna hear about another baby," she whispered to Galen.

"Probably." With everyone else's attention momentarily off them, he let his palm slide across her flat abdomen, imagining it swelling soon with *their* child. "Can we skip out now?"

She laughed softly, going up on her toes a little with that smile of hers. "There's food to be eaten and cake to be cut."

"And a wife to bed," he murmured, brushing his lips over hers. "Which is more important?"

She smiled against his lips. "A valid point."

"—anyway." He was vaguely aware of Rachel talking again. "I'm not sure if now's the right time or not, but there's already another Fortune in the family." She hesitated for a moment. *"Me."*

That got even Galen's and Aurora's attention.

They weren't the only ones looking at Rachel with surprise.

Matteo gently patted her shoulder. "You've come this far, Rachel, you can say the rest."

She nodded, then looked from Jeanne Marie to Lady Josephine, who was bouncing her granddaughter Clementine Rose on her knee, to James Marshall who was sitting next to her. "Do, uh, do any of you remember ever hearing about a cousin named Jerome? J-Jerome Fortune?"

"More Fortunes," Galen murmured, kissing Aurora's cheek again. As far as he was concerned, his brand-new bride was a lot more interesting. "*Now* can we go?"

She laughed softly, grabbed his hand, and while everyone was still gaping at Rachel and Matteo, they made a run for it.

* * * * *